The v...
shroudi...
ing war...

There was one light in all the world.

It came towards us, over the meadow, from the direction of Thorolf Skjalg's grave.

We all saw him. The warriors groaned. They wept. They yammered like dogs. Some shouted, "Thorolf! It's my Lord Thorolf come out to walk again."

He was a tall man, dressed in full armor, with shield and spear and sword at his belt. He glowed all over with blue fire. He was coming to us.

"It's the battle-fetter!" someone cried. "Run! We've got to run!" But no one ran. No one stood on his feet. A few tried to crawl, but most stayed in their places, watching the walker-again come nearer and nearer.

I could see Thorolf's eyes now. They were green-yellow, round and cold.

Then a hand fell on my shoulder. Erling said, "A psalm, Father! I don't ask you to fight, but sing me a psalm that I may fight—that one about the mountains falling into the sea and shaking!"

I found I still had the crucifix in my hand, gripped so tightly it was wet with my blood. I tried to moisten my lips. "Deus noster refugium . . ." I croaked. *God is our refuge and strength . . .*

I saw the demon cast his spear, and saw his mouth open in something like laughter. I saw him fend Erling's spear in return. I heard the whacking of blades on shield, and saw the dead man lean and whirl; and his leaps were head-high and his whirls faster than birds' wings.

I spoke my psalm again and again, gripping the crucifix as a drowning man clings to driftwood. . . .

Also by this author:

Wolf Time

THE YEAR OF THE
WARRIOR

LARS WALKER

THE YEAR OF THE WARRIOR

This is a work of fiction. All the characters and events portrayed in this book are fictional, and any resemblance to real people or incidents is purely coincidental.

Erling's Word copyright © 1997; *The Ghost of the God-Tree* copyright © 2000, by Lars Walker.

All rights reserved, including the right to reproduce this book or portions thereof in any form.

A Baen Book

Baen Publishing Enterprises
P.O. Box 1403
Riverdale, NY 10471

ISBN: 0-671-57861-8

Cover art by Gary Ruddell

First printing, March 2000

Distributed by Simon & Schuster
1230 Avenue of the Americas
New York, NY 10020

Typeset by Windhaven Press, Auburn, NH
Printed in the United States of America

contents

Erling's Word 1

The Ghost of the God-Tree 277

List of Main Characters
    & Pronunciations 559

Erling's Word

Book I of the
Saga of Erling Skjalgsson

To my Aunt Jean...
Frequently mistaken for an angel.

CHAPTER 1

Maeve screamed when they raped her. She screamed all the time they were raping her, and they raped her many times, for she was young and fair. I tried to run to my sister, straining the chain they'd bound me to, until some merciful soul laid the hammer of his axe against the base of my skull.

I was marching when I awoke, chained in a line with all the other Christian souls the Northmen had taken, men and women, the young and the strong and the hopeful. We hoped again the following day when a troop of bold young lads from Collooney came pounding over a hill and down upon us, swinging their axes and shouting their slogan, and they looked like the angels of God to me, beautiful as the love of children. But the Northerners met them with a tough shield wall and cast their spears and offered them axe and sword and thrusting spear, and those fair lads died, except for a few who were taken and bound with us. After that we saw no more resistance. The king was warring with the O'Neill that year, and much taken up with other things.

My head ached as if Satan had poked a toe in my eye, but I cared nothing for that. I had set my heart to praying. The abbot would have wondered at the fervor of my prayers. I pleaded—I begged God—I promised Him that I would be a monk and a priest if only He would deliver me and my sister. I prayed without ceasing; I made vows to all the saints I could think of. I watched the heavens and the earth for an answer, refusing to doubt.

The Northerners had their camp in a river mouth in Sligo Bay, and they loaded us into one of their ships—a fat *knarr* with an open hold amidships, where we huddled with the beasts they'd stolen, and ate much the same fodder. I gazed back to shore, squinting for my miracle, refusing to know that I was leaving Ireland. I had no words for what was happening, but surely we weren't being taken across the sea. God was too good to let that happen.

But when we rounded Inishmurray and Sligo Bay fell from sight and only the waves to port and strange shores to starboard, I knew that my miracle would not come. And so I knew there was no God, and the only thing left was to die.

We were chained starboard of the mast, balanced by the livestock to port. The Northerners had strung a rope down the center and warned us not to approach it. When one of them was making his way from the stern to the foredeck, I gathered up my length of chain and threw myself at him. I caught him unguarded and we struggled a moment before the other Northmen pulled us apart and kicked me bloody. Then one of them, a squat bruiser who'd lost part of his nose and spoke barbarous Irish, put his face down near mine and said, "We're going to Visby on Gotland to sell you. If you make us mad we won't kill you, lad, no—we'll sell you to the Arabs, who'll take you far off to Eastland and geld you so you'll be quiet and good."

So I limped back and sat in bilgewater, and Maeve

stretched to the end of her chain so that she could just touch my hand, and wept, and we sat like that until I slept.

Many are the years and uncounted the miles since the White Northerners took us from our home in Connaught. Where is Maeve now? With our ancestors, I suppose, long since, and glad of the rest. And I, against all hope, have stood before kings. I have seen a saint made and had for a friend the greatest hero since Cu Chulainn. I've seen high times and headlong deeds to outrun and leave in the dust all the dreams I dreamed, woolgathering in the monastery when I should have been construing my Latin.

But I call God's holy Mother to witness, I'd drown it all in the sea like a kitten if it would unmake one day of my youth and draw my sister's tears back into her sweet eyes again.

If ever a morning was gotten out of wedlock, that had surely been it. It had been raining the stones underground when I trudged into my father's yard to tell him that the abbot had driven me out of the cloister with a stick, shouting, "Son of six devils, you have the spleen of a tomcat and the brains of a chicken in the egg! You will never make a monk though Saint Columcille himself come down from heaven to box your ears!"

My father, of course, had no choice but to beat me about the head with curses, which I endured with Christian patience, and he was still at it when the Northmen swarmed down. They killed him, and my mother, for being too old to sell and my brother Diarmaid for no particular reason, but they took me and Maeve, and then she was screaming, "Aillil!" and the rest you know.

I dreamed I rode a snorting stallion over a pitched landscape.

High were the mountains, steep-sided, their peaks sharper than needles.

Deep were the canyons, cataract-cut, riven with yet deeper fissures and crevices that belched smoke, and sometimes I could glimpse the glow of Hell's fires at their bottoms.

But my steed spurned them all, leaping from peak to peak, clattering up and down rock faces, his hoofs striking sparks and making a noise like hammered steel. He was red as blood, my steed, with white ears and golden mane, tail and feet. On closer examination I discovered that he was attached to me where my privates should have been.

"Aillil, old son," I said to myself, "the abbot was right after all. He always said your organ would run away with you one day."

I tried to rein the horse in, but learned quickly I had no control over him.

"What do you want?" I cried, dizzy with fear.

Then I saw what he wanted.

There in the blue distance, poised on an outcrop like a goat, I caught a glimpse of a white hind. She was a glorious thing to look on, the fairest of God's creatures, whiter than ermine in January, with red antlers and black feet and eyes the color of a lake full of sapphires. The moment I saw her I wanted her, but as she bounded away I knew I could not have her.

"Such is not for us!" I cried. "That creature was not meant for farmers' sons! She's a proper quarry for Finn MacCumhail, or Bran son of Febal. Such as we can never catch her, and if we could what would we do with her?"

But my steed cared nothing for sense. On he plunged, and my heart rabbited back and forth between my collarbone and my belly as we leaped the heights and plunged headlong, but never came nearer our quarry.

And then we were across the mountains, and a

broad, emerald plain, richly rivered and wooded, spread before us. To enter that land we must needs ford a raging river, broader than Shannon, and on its near side stood a man fifteen feet tall, with skin black as a Welshman's heart and long, straight black hair down to his waist, and a great axe in his hands. His face, strangely, looked a bit like the abbot's.

"Pay the toll if you would cross!" he roared.

"And what is the toll?" asked I.

"Your head, cut off neat at the neck!" he cried, and I tried to turn about but my steed would not be curbed. I heard the great axe whistle in the air and twisted to avoid it. . . .

The next evening, while we lay up in a harbor in the Hebrides, somebody whispered to me, "The Northerners are talking about you." I looked up at a cluster of them on the foredeck who whispered and pointed at me. I tried to dwindle from sight, but they hopped down into the hold, grabbed me and held my arms and legs.

I bellowed and cursed them for heathen horse-eaters, but they paid no mind as they brought out a razor and shaved the crown of my skull.

"We're barbering you like the Christian priests," said the boy with the bad nose. "We marked your robe, and sometimes there are churchmen in Visby who'll ransom priests at a good price."

It's a marvel the cuts I got didn't mortify.

We sat in bilge and vomit and waste all the way, in storm and fair weather, and the sun beat down on us, and the rain soaked our uncovered heads, and the ship bucked like a spring heifer and I was always sick. We were Irish when we boarded that ship. We were beasts when they unloaded us in Gotland.

They marched us up the jetty and into the walled town, and they kept us in sheds, the men apart from the women (I never saw Maeve again).

I saw no Arabs in Visby (it turned out the Arab trade had dried up long since), nor any churchmen with ransom-silver. But from time to time the slave-monger would bring in some prosperous Northman, perhaps a tattooed Swede with bloused eastern breeches or a Dane with his hair combed down in a fringe in front. He'd point out three or four of us and we'd be unlocked and led out, to be poked and pinched and examined for spots, and our teeth counted. I'm sure I was no beauty—filthy and bruised, my head sunburned and scarred and my robe ragged and the color of every kind of dirt.

I forget how many days we'd been there when I was led out for the approval of some fat old bastard in a fur cap (worn purely for show—the weather was mild), and the son of a carthorse let his hand linger longer on my backside than I thought strictly necessary. I'd believed I had no fight left, but the next thing I knew my fingers were about his neck, and everybody was grabbing at me, and then I was down in the dirt, being savaged with a whip, and I screamed a curse at God, who had the almighty temerity not to exist when an honest man needed Him.

And then the whipping stopped, and I looked up at what seemed the tallest man I'd ever seen. His hair, old-man white like that of many Norse, glowed in a sort of halo around his head, tied with a gold ribbon about the temples. His beard, in contrast to his pale hair and skin, was a reddish brown. He wore a red shirt edged in gold, and a sword hung at his waist. He smiled at me, and I thought it was surely the Archangel Michael.

"I took you for a priest, but you look a little young," he said, in passable Irish.

"Just ordained," I lied.

He spoke to the slave merchant and the fat man, and they argued for a few minutes, pointing at me, the fat man clutching at his throat, and at last the tall man said something to one of his followers (there were about thirty) who brought out a purse and gave some silver coins to the merchant. The merchant weighed them in a little balance and gave part of them to Fat-ass, and I was unchained and taken away by the tall man and his bullyboys.

They brought me to a certain building, and the tall man said, "My name is Erling Skjalgsson. You've that robe and tonsure to thank that you've just brought the highest price I've ever paid for a thrall, not to mention being spared the flaying of your skin off you alive. I bought you because I need a priest.

"I will not lie to you—I mean to take you to my home, Sola in Norway, and your welcome is unsure. I am a Christian; my father is not. My last priest he killed, and I could not avenge him under the circumstances. I make no promise that things will go better for you.

"But this I do promise. My priest cannot be a thrall. If you wish to come with me, you will come as a free man. If you refuse, I'll sell you—but not back to the merchant, or the fat man."

What could I say to him? What would you have said? He wouldn't make the offer if he knew I was only a failed monk. I knew enough of the offices to be priest for his purposes. God wouldn't care—how could He, not existing as He did?

"I accept your offer with thanks," I said, kneeling.

"Very well," said Erling. "This will be our first stop. It's a bathhouse."

CHAPTER 11

I asked my Lord Erling, when they brought me before him in the clean priest's robe he'd gotten somewhere, if he would buy my sister as well. He didn't have to try, but he did. Maeve was gone. The merchant said he'd sold the girl, he forgot to whom.

We sailed out early the next morning. Erling walked beside me down to the harbor and pointed out his ship where she lay by the jetty.

"I know little of ships," I said, "but that looks to me a flying thing." Loath as I was to grant beauty to anything in these heathen lands, the vessel seemed to me graceful as a bird, slim and deadly.

"A flying thing indeed, Father Aillil," said Erling. "Her name is *Fishhawk*. She has twenty-eight rooms. That means it takes fifty-six men to row her. *Fishhawk*'s the fastest ship in Norway."

"Fifty-six oarsmen," said I. "You've a lot more than fifty-six men here." A great crowd of stout towheads were climbing the gangways, loading my lord's final purchases.

Erling laughed. "Over two hundred. They have to take it in shifts after all."

"But surely you could do with fewer than two hundred."

"The rest are for the sport."

"The sport?"

"Wait. You'll see soon enough."

I shed tears as we left Visby behind, casting off my last ties to Maeve.

Erling assigned one of the men, a freckled lad named Thorkel, not yet twenty, born in Dublin, to start me learning Norse. I found it easier than I might have thought, as it's similar to the damnable English tongue, of which I'd picked up a few scraps. My trouble was my stomach. Then and since I've been a bad sailor, and I spent the bulk of my time (and the bulk of my meals) at the rail. I lived for our nightly anchorages and encampments ashore. I had just jettisoned my breakfast one morning when Thorkel clapped me on the shoulder and bade me look across the water, where a ship was lowering its sail and unshipping its oars.

"Now for the sport!" he cried.

"What's this sport?"

"This stretch around the point of Jutland is the thickest hunting ground in the world for pirates. They see us; they take us for a merchant ship and close in to fight, as these Vikings are doing now."

"Is that why you don't carry a dragon head?"

"The very reason."

"What if they come with more than one ship?"

"Two ships we'll fight. More than two—there's no shame in running. But wait—can you see? Up by the Viking's prow?"

"There's a man up there—he's shouting something down to his captain."

"They've spotted our armed men. They see we're more than they can handle. They'll hoist sail in a moment and fly."

"But you can catch them, can't you?"

"We can catch anything."

Every man but I seemed to know his job. Some handled the rigging, following the mate's orders, letting out the lines and setting the stretcher boom to get the most of the wind. Others carried weapons up from stores, mostly bows and arrows and casting spears, for swords and axes and shields and thrusting spears the men had of their own. Others spread sand on the deck to soak up blood, and all looked to their own gear, whether helmet and chainmail brynje or leather cap and padded jerkin.

Erling came back to me, wearing a bright brynje and a gilded helmet with a nosepiece. He carried a plain axe and a yellow shield—round and light, about a yard wide in the Viking fashion—and a leather cap with an iron frame.

"You'd best have these, in case of mischance," he said.

A big warrior named Steinulf objected. "I like not this arming of thralls," he said.

"Father Aillil is my freedman," said Erling. "More than that he is God's priest, and a mighty warrior in the household of the Lord. He'll pray a prayer to take the wind out of that Viking's sail and turn the hearts of his men to piss. You can do that, can you not, Father Aillil? A proper Irish prayer full of proper Irish curses?"

I laughed as I took up the arms. "I'll curse those devils for you, my lord, and with a good will. I'll make their heavens bronze and their sea blood. I'll call the souls of their victims up to tear out their livers."

What followed was sweet to my heart. I forgot my seasickness; I forgot that I no longer believed in God. I stood up in the stern before the steersman and watched as the Viking, with its diamond-patterned sail puffing, fell steadily nearer in spite of its crew's efforts. Soon we could make out the worried faces of the warriors above the thwarts.

"O God of hosts," I cried. "O God who gave might to Samson and victory to David, who smote the power of the Amorites with Thy strong hand and laid them in the dust, both them and their women and their little ones, do Thou stand with us Thy warriors in this holy battle. May the heathen see the power of Thy strong right arm and be unmanned. May their hair stand on end, and turn white, and fly out; may their ears buzz, and flap, and gush with blood; may their eyes see visions of the devils who will soon be their tormenters, and go blind, and fall out upon their cheeks, and be pecked at by seagulls; may their tongues break out in sores, and swell, and stuff their mouths and choke them. May their hearts hiccup in their chests, and batter their ribs, and lodge in their throats; may their stomachs be filled with squirming piglets, and swell, and burst, so that they trip on their guts. May their kidneys and rumps let loose together, and the waste fill the ship, so they drown in it; may their hands blister and blacken and shrink into claws like an eagle's and turn against their own faces and throats. May their knees hammer one on the other so they hear it in Jerusalem, and so break their legs and crush their stones; and may their feet tread on nails, and thorns, and venomous serpents, and swell to such size and weight as to bear them down to the bottom of the sea. May their fathers curse their names, and their mothers slice off the breasts that suckled them for shame, and may their uncles and cousins cry, 'Oh, that the day had never dawned when such a coward and woman and slinking dog was born to our blood!' "

With these and many other sweet coaxings I called wrath down on our enemies, and as we drew ever closer our men began to whistle and shout, and the bowmen on either side loosed their arrows, but we warded ourselves with our shields and they did us no harm. And at last the Vikings gave it up and lowered sail again, clearing their decks for defense and massing their shields on the near rail.

And Erling shouted for the men to lower our own sail, and even as it was done the oarsmen slipped their oars out through the holes, and the boatswain started them a song, and they sang as they rowed, keeping time, and I sang too, although I did not know the words, and then we closed with her on our starboard side, and the starboard rowers shipped their oars, and their comrades were already shielding them at the rail, and the ships bumped and scraped, and our men threw grappling irons, and then the dance began.

Oh, it was fair to hear the clang of steel, and the shouts of the warriors. I trotted about and found spears and stones that had been cast into our ship, and I took them up and cast them back where they came from, singing all I could remember of an imprecatory psalm. It wasn't long before our men had broken the shield wall, and then we were over the rails and on them—Erling Skjalgsson, his helmet shining, the first, and I, my robe kilted up in my belt, not last.

And oh, I was ready to believe in God again, for here at length was the thing I had dreamed of, to face the Northerners man to man with arms in my hands, and give them back twice and threefold for all they had done to my father, and my mother, and my brother and poor little Maeve. If these weren't the very Vikings who'd done those things, they were close enough and just as wicked. I knew no fear. I knew no weariness. I hewed and I shouted and I fended with my shield, and something like a red mist rose before my eyes, and when it was gone my own comrades were holding my arms, keeping me back from a few wounded wretches who had yielded themselves. And all the rest of that pirate crew lay dead or dying, and Erling's men were dumping them overboard. And I fell on Thorkel's neck, weary of a sudden, and I wept, or laughed.

They found a chest of silver in the Viking's hold, along with bales of woolen cloth, and the spoil was divided that afternoon, and I got my share.

And Erling ordered a cask of ale broached, and he said to his men, "What think you of my priest now?"

And the crew (and Steinulf was loud among them) cheered me three times over, and said that their lord had found a very proper man of God indeed.

CHAPTER III

"Is my Lord Erling a king's son?" I asked Thorkel one afternoon when we'd rounded the Skaw and the oily North Sea was less vile than usual and I'd just been to the rail and so felt a little better. "I know there are many kings in Norway, as in Ireland."

"Best not to speak to Erling of kings," said Thorkel. "We've had a few high kings in Norway—Harald Finehair and Haakon the Good and Erik Bloodaxe, but they run to short lives. We've plenty of small kings, who rule whatever land they can stretch their swords over, and *jarls*, who are much the same as the small kings, except that a jarl's son can never be a king.

"Erling is a great-grandson of Horda-Kari, who laid all Hordaland under himself, but kept the title of *hersir*, not even bending to call himself jarl, although it's a higher title, for he and his race are proud that way.

"Horda-Kari had four sons—Thorleif the Wise was the first. Second was Ogmund, father of Thorolf Skjalg, Erling's father. Third was Thord, whose son Klypp the Hersir slew King Sigurd Sleva, son of Erik

Bloodaxe, for raping his wife, and the fourth is Olmod the Old, who still lives.

"Skjalg's estate is Sola, in Jaeder, the northmost stretch of Rogaland. Ogmund Karisson took it, and a piece of Jaeder, after its old lord picked the wrong side at the Battle of Hafrsfjord, where Harald Finehair became high king. Harald gave Sola to Ogmund and offered to make him a jarl, but he too turned the title down, for he saw how men kissed Harald's backside for it, and he said it made him want to puke. All this brought him great honor, for the Horders' power was now pushed into Rogaland, and Jaeder is some of the richest farmland in Norway. And our Jaederers are mostly pleased too, for Skjalg and Erling are the best of lords. Only this business of Christianity makes bother, and nowadays the old man hasn't a good word to say to Erling, though you can see he's pleased when men tell his son's deeds.

"We're following the coast of Agder now. Aft, to the east, is the Vik, where they pay tribute to the king of Denmark. Soon we'll pass Lindesness and the southmost point of the land. Then we swing north along Rogaland, and Jaeder. Sigurd, son of Erik Bjodaskalle, is hersir at Opprostad, south on the coast from us, and a worthy man, but his brothers Jostein, Thorkel and Aki are bitter towards Thorolf and Erling, thinking their inheritance whittled. They're descended from Viking-Kari, another Horder who got lands from Harald Finehair. Ogmund bested Kari in a boundary dispute, and they have long memories.

"Further north is Hordaland, then the Fjords and Sogn and More. Then comes the Trondelag, where Jarl Haakon lives, who is overlord of Norway. He's a strong heathen, and a great friend of Skjalg. Beyond that, the far north where only reindeer and bear and heathen Lapps dwell, but great profit can be made by hardy men."

"It must be hard to ward so long a coast."

"We have a means worked out by Haakon the Good years back. Haakon was the best king Norway ever had, and descended from Horda-Kari on his mother's side. There are balefires set up on hills along the entire coast, from Lindesness to Halogaland. If an enemy fleet is spotted, they light a balefire, and the wardens at the next fire see it and light their own, and on up the coast. At the same time the wardens send word to their lords, who send out war arrows to cry up a levy of men and ships."

"Suppose the wardens saw a simple pirate fleet and took it for an invasion?"

"That's a problem. Haakon set grave penalties for any who gave a false alarm. Which was his bane, as it turned out. He was caught unwarned with a small force, took an arrow wound and died."

"And what do you do about such pirates?"

"We have small fires of our own, easily told from the great fires such as we keep at Tjora and Tunge. We have to buy the wood, as there's no forest on Jaeder, but it's worth it. And of course a simple horn signal will raise a local defense."

"There's comfort in knowing that your folk live in fear of Vikings the same as we."

Thorkel spat and said, "Yes, we're becoming good Christian sheep, more every day."

"Are you all Christians?" I asked. "I see some of you wear ornaments like crosses, but they're oddly made."

"Those are Thor's hammers. Erling compels no one to take his faith, though he favors Christians."

"Are you a Christian?"

"Oh aye. I was baptized in Dublin. It matters little to me one way or the other, but nowadays it's prudent to be a Christian in the wide world."

Then he wanted to drill me on my Norse, and soon I was sick again.

It was raining the day we passed the wide, surf-pounded Sola Bay, rounded the point at Jaasund, acclaimed by seagulls, and sailed down the broad Hafrsfjord (where Harald Finehair made himself high king). But it's usually raining in Jaeder. In the course of these recollections I may from time to time neglect to tell you what the weather was like. When that happens, you may assume it was raining.

The warden at the landing at Somme trotted down the jetty to greet us, spear and shield in hand. I followed Erling down the slippery gangplank and felt rocky on solid earth again. But I knelt and kissed the jetty's stones and swore I'd never get on a boat again (which God took as a challenge).

"Hail, my Lord Erling," said the warden. "I've sent word to the steading for your mother."

"And where's my father?"

"He rode up to Kolness to knock some fishermen's heads together. Some dispute over berths. Here come your mother and the household."

Fishermen looked up from their nets, and their families stared out the doors of their cottages at us as we trooped up the jetty and past the boathouse to meet the household. Erling's mother, who led a wet procession of housefolk and thralls, wore an overdress of embroidered wool wrapped around her body under the arms, over a long, pleated underdress of linen. The overdress hung by cords fastened with a turtle-shell brooch above each breast. A red shawl was draped over her shoulders, and a white linen cloth covered her hair. She was a tall, handsome woman, and her son favored her. The two fair-haired young women who stood on either side of her favored her too, and I took them for Erling's sisters. They giggled and pointed at me, but I pretended to be too high-minded to notice.

I was more interested in a fourth woman there. She was small, and her uncovered hair was the color of honey, smooth and shining. Her face was oval, her nose fine and her blue eyes bright under arched brows. She had a face you'd want to reach out and stroke, just to know if it was as smooth as it looked, like a pearl.

"Greetings, my son," said the older woman after Erling had drunk the horn of ale she'd brought and she and the lasses had embraced him. "You'll want a meal after your journey. Come to the hall; the thralls are cooking now, and we can drink until they've done."

"How's father?"

"He complains of his stomach and his bones; he chases the thrall girls but only out of custom. Nothing has changed. Who is this man in women's clothing?"

"You've seen a priest before, Mother."

"I'd hoped never to see another. But he must be fed, I suppose, like honest men."

The women turned back the way they'd come, and Erling gave orders to an overseer for the unloading. Then we set out for the steading.

The little I could see of the land did not impress. It was flattish, with sandy fields of tough grass facing the fjord. But the land rose somewhat beyond the waste, and our path led upward and to the southwest, past the fields of Somme farm to Sola itself. There was hardly a tree in sight. Moss and heather grew among the stones, which lay everywhere, singly and in heaps, in the meadows above. A large area atop the highest hill was hemmed by a low stone fence, and a walled lane led through it to the steading of Sola. The fields within the fence sloped south and looked well manured, but were nothing you'd remark on in Ireland. A hog watched us, rubbing its chin on a fence stone.

"Who's the girl with the lamplight eyes?" I asked Thorkel.

"She's Halla Asmundsdatter, Erling's leman."

"A strange name for someone so plainly Irish. I think she's the loveliest woman I've ever seen."

"It's said she's the fairest woman in Norway, save

only Astrid Trygvesdatter, who is of course a king's child."

The steading was a loose rectangle of mostly turf or stone, turf-roofed buildings (some of them looking for all the world like little hillocks) around a central yard at the top of the hill. Largest of the buildings was the hall, wood-built, long and high, flanking the yard on the north. We entered through a side door near one end, then turned right through another door into the main hall. Two lines of wooden pillars marched down its length on either side of a long hearth. Low platforms ran along each wall outside the pillars, and on them benches and trestle tables had been set up. Helmets and shields and swords hung on the walls, and all the woodwork was carved with those squirmy beasts that writhe in pagans' brains, childish copies of the lovely Celtic knot with no art or balance to them. A peat fire burned in the hearth and the blue smoke hung about the rafters so that they could not be seen. Midway down either side a large chair with arms, big enough for two, was set on a dais between two pillars of great size, carved in the shapes of round-eyed, teeth-gnashing warriors.

"Sit in your places and the thralls will serve you," said Erling's mother. Erling went to a seat on the bench to the right of the north high seat and beckoned me to come up beside him.

Erling's mother stared at me a moment, then went out with her women, leaving us to take our places while thralls spread the tables. While we drank Erling gave me an eating knife and a spoon of silver, for all Norsemen carry their own. We ate the vile food when it came, flat as the landscape of Jaeder—boiled pork and barley bread and fish; but the ale was good. An older warrior named Hrorek stood up and recited a verse he claimed he'd composed on the spot in honor of the journey—absolute babble of course, even if you understood the Norse tongue better than I did. But

Erling seemed pleased, and he took a silver ring from his arm and had it carried over the fire to him. All the men shouted and stamped their feet, so I suppose it meant something to them.

When our hunger was blunted and the ale was beginning to have its effect, Erling introduced me. There was no friendliness in his mother's eyes (I learned her name was Ragna) as she stared at me from her own high seat on the women's bench at the east end of the hall. I rose and gave them a benediction. There was a lot of grumbling, and I sat down. But Halla smiled at me, and that was worth seeing.

After the meal Erling and the lads sat drinking and comparing tattoos and telling lies and picking fights with each other. I had trouble following after awhile, so I excused myself, going out into the strange, light Norwegian summer night. A serving woman led me to the priest's house. It was built much like the hall, but small, and of turf. It needed no pillars. Benches had been made by the simple shift of digging a trench down the middle for the hearth fire, with flat stones set up to retain the sides. In one corner there was a box-bed, too short to stretch out in, in which I had no intention of lying in summertime.

I was ready to put out the soapstone lamp when I heard the door creak. Halla stood there, and the room brightened with her eyes.

"I want to be baptized by you," she said.

"Right now?" I asked.

"No—whenever it's proper. I've been instructed already, by Father Ethelbald, the old priest. But before he could pour the water on me, he was—he died."

"And you are keen to be joined to Mother Church?"

"I'm eager to do whatever Erling wishes." She sat on a bench and spoke easily, as if we were old friends. "I come of a good family, Father. My father is an honorable *bonder*, but we aren't rich or of the highest blood."

"Bonder?"

"A free farmer. Erling's mother wants him to make a high marriage, but I believe he cares for me, and if I'm a Christian he might marry me. I want him all for myself, Father."

So she would serve the Lord for a husband, as I served Him for my freedom. We were alike in our ill motives, except that she was not a hypocrite.

Still I asked, "Do you believe in the Father, the Son, and the Holy Spirit? Do you believe that Christ died for your sins, and rose again from the dead?"

She frowned. "I don't understand all that Father Ethelbald told me, but I think Jesus is a better god than Thor."

"Then you have more faith than some Christians I know," said I. "We'll see to the baptism when I'm settled in."

As she went out she turned back at the door and said, "May I ask about one of the things I don't understand?"

I said, "Of course."

"Father Ethelbald used a word—'evil.' It's not a word we have in our tongue. He tried to explain what it meant."

"Ah well, evil means there are . . . things about in the world, and in men too, and all they want is to do harm, just for hate's own sake."

She thought a moment.

"What a frightening world you Christians live in," she said.

I said, "And the one around us isn't?"

I thought about Halla that night, wrapped in my cloak on the bench, listening to the sea's muffled threats—poor lass, she had little hope of her heart's desire—and then I was thinking of Maeve, and home, and my parents and Diarmaid and time and miles and the wickedness of men, and I wept like a child woodlost at night, until I slept, shivering.

I woke the next morning to the sound of shouting and dogs barking.

When I came out into the sunlight, I felt eyes on me from every side. They were all around the steading, their black and red and yellow hair cropped short, walking slumped in their shapeless, pale garments, barefoot or wearing wooden clogs. Thralls. Mostly Irish.

I stood and looked at them, and one by one they set down the bowls or spades or forks they carried and shuffled towards me, looking at the ground mostly, raising their eyes to meet mine for a second at a time, then letting them slide away. At last a cluster of them hemmed me in. And suddenly I was afraid of them; because I was free and they were slaves—for that they might kill me, Irish or not.

Then a woman sobbed and fell to her knees, clasping my legs, crying, "Father!" And then they were all kneeling—

"Father! Bless us!"

"Father! Pray for me!"

"Father, it's been eight years since my last confession—"

"Father, how are things in Ireland?"

"Father, do you know my family? They live in Connemara—"

And for a moment I forgot I was not a priest. I reached my hands to them and blessed them. I blessed them and promised them a mass soon. They wept as if truly comforted. Then they went off, smiling, to take up their labors again. I stood for a moment leaning against the wall with my eyes closed, winded as if with digging.

When I opened my eyes, there stood the biggest man I'd ever seen, not so tall as Erling, but broader, watching me. He grinned. There were interruptions in his teeth. He had wide shoulders, and arms like a strong man's legs. He was clean bald over the scalp, with a nasty scar that looked like a burn covering the left side of his forehead and stretching down to the ear, just missing one tufted eyebrow. His beard was short and brown. His eyes were small, and pale, and unfriendly as badgers.

"Will you bless me too, Father?" he asked.

"If you like," I said. "Come closer—I'll lay hands on you."

"It's you who mean to break the power of Thor at Sola? With your holiness and faith?" His hailstone eyes pierced the nooks of my skull, and I had to look at my feet.

He laughed. His laugh was stronger than my whole body. He walked away from me, laughing.

Thorkel came towards me from the hall. "That was Soti the smith," he said. "He was struck by lightning and lived." I crossed my fingers against the evil eye, for even smiths who've not had intercourse with heavenly fire know too many things.

"Erling wants you in the hall," said Thorkel. "There's trouble."

"What sort?"

"His father's dead. Aslak, his brother, too. Killed by Orkney Vikings at Kolness yesterday. Such raids are common—it was just ill luck that Skjalg and Aslak were there. They could have saved themselves by running away, but Skjalg was too proud."

The hall went silent for a moment as I raced in and took my seat. A thrall brought a bowl of water, in which I was expected to wash my face, and a towel. A woman set porridge and fish before me, and Erling passed me a horn. It was a strange horn, with studs set into it, running in a line from brim to tip.

"You drink to where the next stud is uncovered," said Erling. "That way nobody drinks too much in the daytime, when he needs a clear head." He spoke as usual, but there were red spots on his cheekbones that I'd seen before only in battle.

"I've heard about your father and I weep for your loss, my lord," I said when I'd had my measure. "What do you plan?"

"I'll hunt them down and kill them. If I knew where they were I'd be gone this minute. They have a strong force, so I'll need to take most of my armed men. Fortunately I still have the company I took with me to the Baltic. I've sent men out for news, and I expect I'll know more shortly. But I hate waiting."

"Shall I come with you? I'm always glad to fight Vikings."

"You'd best stay here. I didn't buy you for your strong arm. Which reminds me, I haven't shown you my church yet. I want you to set it in order so we can have a mass for my father's soul, and for victory, when I return. I wish I had time for one this morning, but I hope to be gone soon. Pray for us when I am."

He took time to show me the church, and I left most of my breakfast behind. It was a stone building a little bigger than my house, with benches along the walls, but there was a crude stone altar at the east end, and a carved wooden crucifix hung above it.

"I want to build a better one someday, but this will have to do for now," said Erling. "One day I'll raze the holy place of Thor and build you a church on that spot."

"Has she been properly hallowed?" I asked, waving some cobwebs aside.

"We haven't had the chance to get a bishop here for that," said Erling. "But I have some surprises for you." He called in a thrall who bore a small chest, which he laid on a bench. Erling opened the chest with a key and handed me a bundle of cloth. "Father Ethelbald's vestments," he said. Then he drew out an object swathed in linen. He unwrapped it for me.

"A chalice!" I said. "A lovely chalice, in silver!"

"There's this too," said Erling, and brought out a paten.

"Wherever did you get such things? No—don't say it. Prizes from your Viking days?"

"Not as bad as that. The king of Agder had them for his high table. I paid a pretty price for them."

"God will reward you," I said.

"One more thing." From the bottom of the chest he brought a book. "I don't know properly what it is, but the pictures inside look holy."

" 'Tis a psalter," said I, "and a lovely one, though some impious hand has pried the gems from the cover ornaments. But no matter. The true treasure's inside. Many a church in Ireland is less well furnished than yours, my lord. I am grateful for this. I can read— a little."

"What's this—a housewarming?" said a booming voice. Soti the smith strode over the threshold. "A fitting time for a gift. Priest of the White Christ, I give you a thrall for your service."

I stared at the man.

"No, not one of your Irish stoneheads—I'd not insult you with shoddy goods. My gift is a Norse thrall, one you'll enjoy beating."

"You try my patience, Soti!" said Erling. He turned to me. "The thrall he means is a man called Lemming. We call him that after a mad beast of this land, which goes off its head sometimes and runs into the sea to drown. Lemming has said often he means to die. He says he means to be hanged for the murder of his master. Soti is the only one strong enough to control him; partly with his arm and partly through his spells."

"The priest is a big, strong fellow," said Soti. "And surely he has magic of his own, being a servant of your Christ. Such a man need have no fear of Lemming."

"I'll hear no more of this!" cried Erling. "Get out, Soti."

"Hold, my lord," said I. "I accept the smith's gift."

Erling spoke softly. "You don't know what you say. Lemming is half bull."

I whispered back, "I can't let this man call me coward."

"Lemming will kill you."

"I take a bit of killing, my lord."

"I can't afford to lose another priest. You cost me much in Visby."

"And I can't afford to lose . . . we call it losing face in Ireland. It's Christ's honor at stake."

Erling scowled. "May He protect you then."

Soti said, "A word with you, my lord. I've a thing to tell you, but not in this place." They went outside and I locked the chest and went out to join them. It was a wonder how easily I slipped into the priest's role. I didn't know what trouble I'd bought, but I could smell that, Christ's honor or no, I dared not give place to the smith in anything.

"You bear me no love, Soti," Erling was saying.

"But I loved your father, and I'll not see him lie unavenged. I've looked into my forge at white heat and seen the Orkneymen where they beached one of their ships, damaged on the rocks. They lie in Soknasund, not far at all."

"You swear this is true?"

"When have I ever read falsely? And if I'm wrong, what have you lost? As good one way as another when you track your quarry over water."

I may no longer have believed in God, but I was not such a fool as to doubt that there are devils. No Irishman was ever that much a blockhead, nor ever will be.

"My lord, may I speak?" I asked.

"I'd be grateful," said Erling.

"What I say tastes ill in my mouth, for I lost my own father and brother not long since, and I know as well as any man the cry of blood. But this Soti is as great a devil as you'll find even in this devil's land."

"And you think he lies?"

Soti was glaring at me.

"I fear he tells the truth. I'd not have you in his debt. A Christian, my lord, is not strictly required to take vengeance—even, God help us, for a father. Not when it sets his soul in peril."

"Thank you for your counsel, Father Aillil," said Erling with a pale smile. "Pray for me, then come back when you've advice I can follow."

Erling went off with Soti and the ship was gone with most of the warriors in what seemed a few minutes. It was a fine morning for Jaeder, cloudy and blue but not actually raining yet, and the fog was dwindling. Thorkel, who had been left behind with a small guard commanded by Hrorek, met me and we watched them sail away. Then he took me to a place where we could see most of the neighborhood. Sola lies to the northeast of Sola Bay on the sea, above its sand dunes, at the north end of a great crescent of farmland and bogs, ringed by hills inland. He pointed out the various farms nearby, some owned by Erling and rented to tenants, others held in freehold by bonders. To the north, west of the Hafrsfjord, we could see Kolness, and on a hill beyond it Tjora farm, where the jarl's balefire was, and he showed me one or two nearer hills where Erling had his own fires. He explained how the peninsula stretched north into the Boknafjord, and how Erling would round its point at Tunge and sail east to Soknasund. The day being clear, we could see mountains over the hills to the southeast, beyond Gandalsfjord. To the south was the commanding view of Jaeder and Rogaland and the sea lane which made Sola so valuable in the land's defense. . . .

Then I heard a great roar, like that of a beast, behind me, and I knew without looking that the thrall Lemming had found me. I whirled to meet him and ducked under a great swinging arm, spinning aside as something the size of a church went flying by to land rolling in the mud and sit for a second staring at me before heaving itself up to attack again.

I had only a heartbeat to take my enemy's measure and (as my father used to say) he was a man you needed an hour or so just to look at. I saw a shaggy, straw-colored beard, and a badly broken nose, and shoulders that it must have been weary work to carry around.

He roared again and came at me, and I leaped out of his way. I'm no little man, and I'm no weakling, and I like a good brawl as well as any Irishman, but I thought all the biggest bruisers in Norway must be smelling my scent and swarming at me at once.

I had more skill than Lemming, thank God. He counted on his strength, and if I'd let him catch me it would have been over. But I danced about outside his grip, teasing him, tripping him up, even landing a punch in his gut (with no effect I could see) as he went by. My only hope was to tire him. After several minutes I was breathing like a wind-broken horse, and he still came on like a gale out of the north.

Thorkel watched all this standing hipshot with a hand on his swordbelt, a smile on his face. He was too wellborn to meddle in a fight with a thrall of course. A crowd of folk gathered to watch us. Some of them even cheered me.

Then Lemming caught me a punch on the side of the head, and I saw stars, as they say—and they say it because that's what you see—and then he had me about the chest in a bear hug, and I couldn't breathe. And the world began to dwindle and travel rapidly away from me, and I heard a horn and a cry, as if from a great distance—

"Ships are coming! We're under attack!"

CHAPTER IV

I stood in the abbot's cell. I felt muddled because, though being called in for a beating was hardly strange to me, I couldn't recall what I'd done this time. He sat slumped on his hard bed, and he sighed and looked up at me with an old horse's eyes.

"Unlike some people, I know how to do what I'm told," he said, getting to his feet. "I don't like it, but I do it, because without obedience the world falls in. Is that not so?"

"Very true, Father," I said.

"Don't lie to me. A lying tongue like yours should be torn out at the roots and fed to dogs, and the dogs stoned, that our calling be not disgraced. And to think they want you—you don't even believe in God, do you?"

"I suppose not, Father."

"'I suppose not, Father.' You're worse than the rest. You live in this prison, this shambles, this slave pen of earth and you watch the evils that fall on the innocent, and as long as it touches you not it bothers you no more than the death of a bedbug in Babylon; but let the blow fall on you or someone you care about and you shout, 'There is no God.' And the joke of it is that you don't disbelieve in Him at all. You're just trying to hurt His feelings to get His attention. As if God suffered by your disapproval."

"He acts as if He's not there. What am I to think?"

"Think anything you like. It matters naught to me. I only called you here to give you the message entrusted to me."

"Entrusted? By whom?"

"By Authority at the highest level, of course. I act only in the orthodox fashion: I come in a dream, which is not, strictly speaking, me coming to you at all, but only a fantasy of your sleeping mind. The fathers of the church condemned with one voice all attempts to communicate with the dead, although Origen . . ."

I knew he'd go on like this for hours if I let him. "You're saying you're dead?" I put in.

He looked at me as if he'd forgotten my existence. "Of course I'm dead," he said. "You mean you didn't know? The last thing I ever saw on earth was the welcome spectacle of your back heading down the road and away from the monastery, before I fell into the apopleptic fit that killed me. You may add to your catalogue of sins the occasion of a good man's death."

I thought of apologizing, but decided there would be no point. "What's this choice you speak of?" I asked.

He looked disappointed then, denied the chance to throw my "sorry" back in my teeth. "You have a choice," he said. "You may take your martyr's crown now . . . martyr's crown, by God!—you who wouldn't even pay the toll!—or you may go back and continue your mission."

"Martyr's crown. You mean—"

"Yes, the blessings of Paradise. Manna for breakfast. Water sweeter than wine to wash it down. Music by David and Asaph and all the greatest bards. Games on the grass with the Holy Innocents. Hunting with

St. Sebastian, and your evening dinner cooked by St. Laurence. Then a friendly wrestling match between St. Augustine and Job, and dancing led by Mary and Martha. And with all this to do, you let it all slide just for the pleasure of gazing on the face of the Beloved."

"Or I can go back to Jaeder and live among people who hate me, going always in fear of my life?"

"And get rained on. You mustn't forget the rain. And wait till you spend a winter in Jaeder. You'll long for your old cell then, I promise you."

"Is this a test of some kind?"

"Everything's a test. Look, why should we waste time? I know your nature—you'll never choose a life of suffering, however good the cause, when you can have a martyr's crown at a bargain price. So I'll just go and tell them your decision. . . ." He moved toward the door.

"Hold on!" I cried. "You think I'm soft, don't you? You think I've no guts! Well roast you! Send me back to Jaeder. I'll earn my crown—what do you know of martyrdom, anyway—"

And a man came up from behind the abbot—an old, bald man with white hair and keys at his belt, and he reached his hands out to me . . .

I woke with a dull feeling that I'd been had.

Horns were blowing and people were running about, shouting and toting things, but I lay on my back in the mud, looking up at the clouds, trying to decide whether it would be wise to get up. My head ached, and I had an idea that if I tried to move my arms and legs I'd regret it.

At last a thrall running with an empty barrel tripped over my legs and sprawled on his face. I groaned and rolled half over, then sat up slowly. I felt as if my body'd been used as a roller for a ship's portage. The thrall frowned at me and got up and ran after his barrel, which was tumbling toward the low side of the steading.

Very slowly I got to my knees and, bracing myself against a wall, achieved my feet. Then I turned my head carefully to see what was happening.

The thralls and the women were carrying things—barrels, chests, bales of wool, hams—out the gate and down the lane. At its end they headed east, in an ant line toward the higher hills. The fifty or so warriors Erling had left behind were forming up near the gate, and a few bonders who must have been in the neighborhood when the call went out were being outfitted from the armory. Looking down toward the bay I could see the last of three ships beaching itself boldly on the sand, while men disembarked from the other two. There looked to be three or four hundred of them.

I found Thorkel among the warriors and said, "We don't stand a chance."

Thorkel's face was pale behind the nosepiece of his helmet. "All we need to do is slow them down. We're moving the people and treasure to the stronghold on the hill there—" he pointed east. I spotted it then—a tooth jutting up from one of the hills. Clusters of people were running there from every direction. "Hrorek has sent men to light the balefires, and we'll have the more distant bonders joining us with their spears soon after. The thing now is for you who aren't warriors to get to the stronghold fast, so we don't have to die in the open warding you."

"Ward yourself," said I. "I'm getting arms." I ran to the armory and took a leather shirt with iron plates, an axe, a shield, a spear and a helmet. I poked my head inside the church and noted thankfully that the priest's chest had been taken.

The steading was empty now, and we warriors felt it no shame to sprint for the stronghold, given the odds. It was no easy run uphill carrying iron, but our enemies had the same handicap. Those already inside closed the gates the moment the last of us got in.

We posted our little force around the walls. The stronghold was a very plain, circular pen with six-foot banked turf walls and a wooden parapet. One turf-roofed house stood in its center. I stood beside Thorkel on the south side, my spear ready for thrusting.

"A little time, that's all we need," he said between his teeth. "Time for the balefires to be lit and the farther-off bonders to come in. Do you see smoke anywhere? I'd think they'd have the fires going by now."

"Nothing," I said. "No sign of smoke."

"At least we can be grateful Aki won't burn the steading. If it took fire, Erling would see its smoke and come back."

"Is this Aki? The Opprostad hersir's brother?"

"Aye. I know his ships. The plan's plain enough. He sent those Orkneymen to attack Kolness and run away, expecting to draw Erling off and leave Sola to him. You've got to admire his courage, beaching his ships in the surf at Sola Bay. He came from the north, so he must have had his ships behind some island or in some inlet, waiting for Erling to pass."

"But how could he know Skjalg would be at Kolness?"

"That would be luck, from his point of view. Watch yourself."

An arrow flew past my ear with a little *whup* sound and a puff of air. Aki's men were taking their places behind their shields, or behind rocks and boulders, on all sides, their bowmen beginning their work from the cover.

We warded ourselves with our shields for the next few minutes. Someone began to scream from near the gate.

At last a man came around to us and said, "Eystein

says that if they get over the wall, we're all to gather around the house to defend the women and children."

"Eystein?" said Thorkel. "What happened to Hrorek?"

"He didn't make it inside."

"God rest him," I said.

"God rest us all if those balefires aren't lit," said Thorkel. "Has anyone seen any sign?"

"They won't be lit," said the man. "One of the boys we sent to light them got back before they hemmed us in. He said the wood had been wet clean through to the ground. Aki has friends hereabouts."

"That's it then," said Thorkel. "It comes to us all in time. I'd thought to kiss a few more girls, but the Norns decide."

"That's not Christian talk," said I.

"I suppose when it comes to the point, a man finds out what he is. Sorry, Father."

I didn't know what to say to that. The other man went away.

We made them fight for it. Our cover was good, and we had plenty of arrows of our own, if not so many bowmen.

With true Norse perversity, the weather stayed clear. The clouds drifted off, the sun beat on us and dried us, and the women who came around with water moved slowly for fear of the arrows. When they got to us, they never had enough.

"Why doesn't Aki burn the steading?" I asked Thorkel.

"I told you. The fire would bring Erling back."

"Why should he care whether Erling comes back? He could sack the place, burn it to the ground, and be gone before Erling could get here."

"And have Erling come after him? He doesn't want Erling's goods—he wants Erling dead. Otherwise he could have done all this while we were voyaging. I suppose he plans to wait in the steading and surprise him when he comes home. He'd have the high ground then. He knows he can't beat Erling in a fair fight. That would be why he's sparing his men too. They could take us with a rush from all sides, but it would cost them."

"Perhaps. But if I were he I'd be wondering now whether to settle for what I could get."

"To be honest, so would I."

"In that case, there's a chance he might decide to leave us alone up here."

"Too late. The tide's ebbed since he beached his ships. And there's one more thing. He's sworn to take Halla Asmundsdatter to his bed, and we have her."

"So the abbot was right. He always said the lust of the flesh would be the death of me. I'd thought he meant my own flesh."

The shadows were lengthening when we heard someone cry, "The fire! The fire!"

I wondered if they'd decided to burn the steading at last, but someone shouted, "They've lit the Tjora balefire!"

"The jarl's balefire!" said Thorkel. I craned my neck and caught sight of the black smoke to the north.

"Thank God," I said.

"The man who talked the wardens into lighting it will hang."

"Well if I knew his name, I'd not betray it. We should get help now."

"And Aki knows it. So we can expect—here it comes!"

Then was a time. The arrows rained on us until our shields were hedgehogs' backs. One man after another screamed and lay screaming until the arrows finished him, for we were too busy to help. Aki's men attacked on all sides, and we thrust at them with spears, and when one went down another took his place, and if he warded well with his shield he got in close to the parapet and we had to discourage him with axes and swords. I had thought my shield light at first. Now it weighed like an anvil, and my axe like the earth.

The attack ended at last. We knew there'd be another soon, and we were weary and fewer than before. I wondered how long we'd been at it. The light night gave little clue.

"I need to talk to Eystein," I told Thorkel. "Where will I find him?"

"Probably near the gate. Don't go away long—I need you here."

"Maybe I can make it easier for us all," I said, and ran off, keeping to the cover of the wall.

I found Eystein huddled with some of his men, tying a bandage on his arm. He was dark for a Norseman. He scowled at me and said, "I'm busy, god-man."

I said, "Let me arm the thralls."

He said, "You're mad. We've never armed thralls in Jaeder."

"We'll all die if we do nothing."

"Thralls are no use with weapons. Besides, it's wrong. I won't save my life by wrong dealing."

"For God's sake—think of the shame to Aki! Think what men will say if he's beaten in part by thralls!"

Eystein scratched his beard. "I never looked at it that way," he said.

"Well think quickly."

"Oh, Hel," he said. "Do it. I'll probably be sorry, but right now I'd like to live long enough to be."

So I ran to the house and inside. The free women were huddled on the benches, watching a kneeling red-haired woman chant over a pile of sticks near the hearth. The thralls crouched near the entryway. They knelt when they saw me.

"Which of you want to be Aki's thralls?" I cried to them.

They exchanged dull looks.

"Who is willing to fight to keep a better master?" I said.

One man asked, "Do you mean, take arms?"

"Yes! Will you take them if they're offered?"

"You mean they'll let us fight?"

"Yes! But we've got to hurry!"

"What is this?" came a woman's voice from the other end. Ragna, Erling's mother, strode towards us.

"Eystein's agreed to it. We need every man we can get."

"You upturn the world, god-man!"

"Perhaps. But we'll never know if Aki wins through."

She stared at me. "If thralls can fight, so can women," she said. "There were shield-mays in olden times. None of us has the thews for such work, but we can cast a spear or draw a bow."

A cry of "Yes, yes!" came from the hearth. It was the woman with the sticks.

Now I was shocked, but I said, "All right, let's all do what we can," and led the lot of them out. I let them loose in the weapons pile and ran back to my place beside Thorkel.

"I've armed the thralls and some of the women. They'll be with us soon."

"Thor help us," said Thorkel.

When they made their next attack they got a surprise. The women and thralls had gotten bows, and a wealth of arrows lay on the ground. The shooting wasn't of the best, but there was plenty of it, and once again the attackers fell back, leaving a good number dead and wounded.

A wounded man lay near us outside the wall. He cried, "Thor! I'm belly-shot! I have the porridge sickness! Someone help me!"

A woman—somebody's wife judging from her headcloth—shouted back, "Good! I hope you suffer! I hope you linger days! I hope the ants find you and nibble away your eyes and your nose while you yet live! I hope Vikings come and rape your wife and take your children as thralls, and I hope you hear of it in Hel!"

Thorkel looked at me and said, "There are tales of women warriors in old times. Fortunately we're more civilized than that now. Or we were until you came."

When the light faded our bows were of less use. We were all up on the walls then, those who were left, and it was thrust and hack work, and Aki's men came on and on, and we were weary. The woman who had taunted the wounded man fell beside me with an axe-cloven skull, and I wanted to be sick. A man goes to war precisely not to watch his own women die.

Someone shouted, "The hall—it burns!" and we craned our necks a moment to see the smoke go up from Sola, and we knew we were down to the apple core.

Then Aki brought fire and broke the gate, and we fell back to make a shield wall before the house, and the women fled inside but most of the thrall men stayed with us. We stood shoulder to shoulder, arms aching, barely upholding our shields, and Aki's men's eyes glowed in the torchlight, and then falling sparks told us that the house was burning behind us, and the women and children ran out screaming to huddle behind our backs. And somebody began to sing a death-song, and all the men took it up, and I tried to follow it too. Consider it when your day comes. It helps a little.

And then there was a shout from somewhere, and Aki's men looked around, startled, and I saw a spearpoint stick out the belly of one of them.

And they fled before Erling Skjalgsson's warriors. And I saw Erling himself in the firelight, sword in hand, shouting, "Aki, you son of a troll, I'll have your liver for breakfast!"

CHAPTER V

We ran back to the steading to save the hall, but only made it in time to see the last rafters fall. Once the ruin was complete the windows of heaven opened and soaked us all with rain. Not much was saved there, but most of the stone and turf buildings suffered little damage. My church was fine. I trudged around with some women and thralls getting our wounded under a roof, while other women went with knives and cut the throats of Aki's fallen. I bound limbs and fed leek porridge to those with stomach wounds, so we could tell by smell if the gut was pierced. Erling organized the household to march over to Somme, which, like many farms in the neighborhood, was his property. Aki and his men who still walked were locked in a storehouse there.

I got a bed on a bench among the warriors. I was wearier than I'd ever been in my life, but I couldn't sleep. It was the same all around me. The warriors, especially those who'd defended the stronghold, were whispering to each other in the dark, telling what they'd done and what they'd seen done, speculating on what would have happened *if*. They'd been through something they'd tell their grandchildren of, and they wanted to know how it would sound. They'd been given a little horrible beast to carry about with them, and they wanted to build it a cage so they could scare the girls without anyone getting bitten.

An older man named Bergthor, lying next to me, was composing a poem. I couldn't tell you what it said—the usual nonsense about "the flame of the wound" and "Atli's devourer," but I listened to him anyway, and in time I must have slept.

Somebody kicked me awake no more than two minutes later, saying, "Get up or we'll sling you out. The jarl's come to breakfast."

I shook my head, stiff everywhere and feeling five hundred years old. "The jarl?" I asked.

"Jarl Haakon, lord of Norway. He was sailing south, saw the balefire, and now he wants an explanation. So you'd better think of one."

"Me? I didn't start any fires."

"No, but your thrall did. The man they call Lemming. He's under close guard now. By our law the master answers for his thrall's deeds."

Thrall women were setting up the tables, and I pushed by them as I limped out in the yard to find Erling.

Erling was busy, in counsel with a short, broad, brown-haired older man in a rich green cloak whom I took to be Jarl Haakon. They were headed for the hall, followed by the jarl's bodyguard, and when Erling saw me he put a finger to his lips, which advice I heeded. I watched them go inside, then followed, taking a new seat like the rest of the household across the hall from where we usually sat (or would have had this been our own hall), since Haakon had been given the high seat. The men we'd displaced moved to a new bench across the table from us. A fat old thrall in a fine blue shirt hovered at the jarl's elbow, running errands for him and shouting commands to other thralls. I did not join the toasts to Thor, Odin and Frey which began the meal, but I drank when Erling and Haakon *skoaled* each other, and ate some breakfast in spite of my nerves and the pain I got when I tried to raise my arms. I hadn't eaten since the morning before. Erling whispered, "You'll be all right, Father. Just let me talk."

I looked around and missed a face I wanted. "Where's Thorkel?" I asked.

"Didn't you know? He died at the stronghold last night."

"Poor lad. I lost sight of him after we fell back from the wall. I'll bury you as a Christian, Thorkel, and let God judge."

"What's that?"

"Just a thing between us two. By the way, I was wondering—did you actually find the Vikings at Soknasund?"

"Oh aye. We were almost on them when someone saw the fire and we headed home instead. I don't care about them—they were only tools."

"Then Soti is a true seer."

"Yes, though his wife has the real sight. The women usually do."

"But he didn't see the greatest danger."

"No. And he had no good explanation."

"That's the trouble with seers, my lord. They see only what the Devil wants known."

The women of the household mingled with the guests, as was custom, but I missed Halla and Erling's sisters. I asked Erling whether they had come to harm.

"None at all," he said, "and I mean to keep it that way."

Jarl Haakon called across the fire, "Well then, Erling, what's to be done about my balefire? This thrall of yours attacked the wardens when they demanded proper tokens, and they've both got broken bones. I've had to send ships back up the coast to call off the levies, and it's me they'll blame for lost field time."

"In my view," said Erling, "the lighting was justified. This was not a simple *strandhogg*, with a few Vikings slaughtering cattle and stealing thralls. This was a cold stab at my authority, and so the authority of every lawful lord in the land."

"Fine words," said Haakon, "but the kings and landed men of Norway have been stealing each other's rule since Freya was a virgin. That's how your grandfather got Sola. Aki wants satisfaction for the lands your father took. You'd do the same."

"I'd not do it by stealth."

"There's nothing wrong with stealth. There is something wrong with using my balefire for private warfare. That must be paid for. Who owns the thrall?"

"My priest, Father Aillil."

"A Christian priest? That bull-calf there? It gets worse and worse. All right, god-man—what do you have to say for yourself?"

"My lord," I said, "I've seen the thrall but once in my life, and at the time he was trying to break my neck. He was given me as a gift only yesterday, and he's never even slept under my roof. I might add that I never asked for him. I'd as soon ask for a boil."

"Aye, I've never yet heard a Christian priest own the blame for anything."

"I can swear that he tells the truth, my lord," said Erling.

I said, "There's one thing I'd like to say though." Erling shot me a cautioning glance. "The thrall did his best to protect his master's home and person. For that he should be rewarded, not punished. But if you must punish him, you should know that it's his wish to hang."

"What?"

"That's why they call him Lemming, my lord. He's been trying for years, they tell me, to get himself hanged. In a way, to hang him would be to reward him."

Haakon said, "Hmm, I suppose we could flay him . . ."

Erling said, "My lord, this trouble over a thrall is beneath your notice. If you leave him to me, I promise he'll get a rope around his neck."

"Yes, all right, as long as it's done."

"Good, then may I say that I rejoice the fire was lit?"

"What do you mean?"

"So that you might be here for my father's and brother's grave-ale. You and father were always friends. And you can pass judgment on Aki, a matter suitable to your rank."

Jarl Haakon leaned back in his seat. "I wonder if I wouldn't be better served were it Aki hosting me now."

I buried the Christian dead the next day, doing the service as best I could from memory and filling the rest out, I'm afraid, with plain mumbo jumbo. At the same time Erling was sending messengers with invitations to his father's and brother's funeral, a week hence. While they waited he spent handsomely on hospitality for the jarl. I don't think the man was once without a full ale-horn the whole week. We must have all been a nuisance to Odvin, the man who lived at Somme with his family and had to let the great folk use all his best beds, but he was a tenant after all and had no say. Every morning Erling and I and a few others trooped up to the church before breakfast, and I gave them mass, and I said vespers each night.

One of those first evenings I stepped out to take the air. I recognized one of Erling's thralls, a lad named Enda, who came to me and said, "Father, there's trouble among the slaves."

"What trouble, son?"

"It's Kark, the jarl's slave." He meant the fat fellow who followed Haakon like a dog. "He's making hell for the girls. He bullies them and handles them, and makes them lie with him, and then brags about it afterward. The men he beats for the least thing, and no one dares cross him, because the jarl holds him so dear."

"It's often the way, I'm afraid, with us who sit at the world's bottom. When we find someone to spit on, we make the most of it. But I don't know what I can do. This Kark is no Christian; he won't heed me."

"That's just it, Father. He fears you. Everyone's marked it. He makes the sign against the evil eye whenever he sees you. You're magic to him. He thinks you're not a man and not a woman, begging your pardon, and you speak with men long dead through books, and commune with spirits in a strange tongue. We thought you might put the fear of God in him."

The idea had charm. I went with Enda to one of the thrall houses.

"They say he was born on the same day as the jarl, and he's been with him all his life. The jarl treats him like a pet. It's a bitter thing, Father, to be bullied by one who's no better than you."

"Lad," I said, "don't tell anyone I said so, but I've been a slave and I've been free, and the only things I've seen to make one man better than another are how he thinks of himself, and how he treats others."

"I don't follow. You can't mean I'm as good as my lord Erling?"

"Well no, hardly anyone is that . . ."

We found Kark lying in a corner of the house with one hand under the dress of a sobbing girl. I held my lamp near my face and said, "*Morituri te salutamus!*" in my most sepulchral voice.

Kark looked up at me with round eyes. I've heard many tales told of Kark in the years since, and with each telling he grows more stunted and twisted and dark and ugly, the picture of a thrall as the Norse see them. I will do him justice. He was one of the fairest men for his age I'd seen in Norway, with snow-white hair and great blue eyes, pretty as a woman almost.

"*Arma virumque cano!*" I intoned.

He let go the girl now, and cowered in the corner.

"*Vox clamantis in deserto!*"

The wretch went into a fit. He groveled at my feet, and I had to put a hand on him to stop him screeching. This only made it worse, and he scrambled away, cringing back in the corner with his arms over his face.

It had been too easy. I said, "Now leave the other thralls alone, my lad. And if you tattle to your master, I'll turn you into a herring."

I'd been right, I thought as I went back to the hall. There was real pleasure in finding somebody to spit on.

A few days later the guests began to arrive. Chief among them was the head of the family, Olmod Karisson, an actual son of the famous Horda-Kari. He was, I think, the oldest man I had ever seen, with a hairless head as fragile-looking as an eggshell, and a long white beard. They had to carry him on a litter. But, unlike his late kinsman Thorolf Skjalg (whose name had meant "squinter"), his pale blue eyes saw everything. He sat in his place next to Erling, eating little, drinking less, but marking each man and all his actions. It seemed to me he spent no little time watching Erling.

With him came his son Askel, a big, laughing, easygoing fellow whom all liked but no one minded much. And Askel's son Aslak, a pimply, red-haired boy at the teetery age of about fifteen summers. He had the kind of meager mouth you often see on red-haired men for some reason, and he watched Erling with a dog's worship.

There were other relations too, all great men at home, but I have less cause to remember them.

The first day of the feast, after they had laid Thorolf Skjalg and Aslak Skjalgsson in their graves with proper heathen rigmarole and the sacrifice of two horses and three dogs, Olmod crooked a finger to me and I went up and sat by him.

"God-man, I have a question about your religion."

"I'll answer as best I can, my lord."

"I'm told that Christians are expected to love their enemies. Doesn't that make them unfit to be lords and wage war?"

"Not at all, my lord. Think of Charlemagne, and Alfred of England, and Brian Boru. A Christian is commanded to do as he would be done by. Would any lord wish other lords to stop making war? Of course not. It would take half the fun out of life. Besides, our scriptures say that the king bears the sword, for the punishment of evildoers."

"Good. That's useful information."

"Are you thinking of becoming a Christian, my lord?"

"Don't talk hog slop."

On that first day Erling was expected to sit on the pedestal of the high seat (in this case the guest seat) until he had drunk a toast to his father's memory and made a vow. The vow he made surprised everyone.

"I have a debt to repay," he said. "I am told that my thralls helped save Sola for me. Therefore I vow that every thrall I own will be given the chance to earn his freedom."

A buzzing went around the hall. Most people liked this vow little, but the thralls serving us looked suddenly glad. Olmod stared, but from where I sat (further down the bench than usual, out of deference to the great folk) I could not see his expression.

At one point I overheard Olmod saying to Erling, who sat now in his father's seat, "You know how to host great men, my kinsman. It seems to me Jarl Haakon's ale is stronger than lesser men's, and your servants keep his horn ever filled."

Erling smiled and said, "Yes, great lords must be treated as fits their dignity."

I think that by the third day of the feast Jarl Haakon had forgotten all about the balefire.

That was the day one of Erling's men came in and stepped up by his seat to whisper in his ear. Without a word, Erling rose and went out. The messenger went to each of his fellow bullyboys in turn, and they all went out the same way.

They were gone some time.

When Erling returned it was with three tall, well-dressed men. They stood together before Jarl Haakon.

"My lord Haakon," said Erling, "may I present Sigurd, Jostein and Thorkel, the sons of Erik Bjodaskalle of Opprostad?"

"I know them well," said the jarl, looking over the rim of his horn. "You are the brothers of Aki."

"They came under the shield of peace," said Erling. "But they came with three ships."

"I care nothing for their ships. Where I guest there is peace by law."

"We cannot promise future peace, though, unless our brother is returned to us," said Sigurd, the oldest, a very handsome man approaching middle age who wore wide Russian breeches. His only defect was a head too large for his body, but it was a fine-looking head. "He was mad to go out as he did, but he's our brother, and we'll not leave him to the mercy of the son of Thorolf Skjalg. We wish to see him now, and make some kind of peace settlement."

"See him you shall," said Haakon. "It's time I judged this business of arson and murder."

Erling motioned to one of his bullyboys, who went out and came back in a few minutes with Aki, his red tunic dirty and torn, but well cared-for and more sober than we. He was a thick-bodied man with a dark blond beard and eyes full of hate for Erling.

"Aki is my brother, and I am a hersir," said Sigurd. "I demand to know why he is held like a thrall. The law says that a man can be killed when caught in the act of arson, but not held for killing later."

Jarl Haakon stood up, swayed and sat down again. "The matter here is not arson, or not arson only. It is murder. The murder of a hersir. For common men we have *Things* where free men can judge cases. But in these matters of war, between landed men, it falls to the lord of the land to mediate. I am the lord of the land."

The brothers bowed. "We gladly submit to the wisdom of such a man as you, Lord Haakon."

"You sodding well had better. What have you to say for yourself, Aki? By what right did you kill my friend Thorolf Skjalg and his son, and burn the hall at Sola, and try to take Erling's inheritance?"

"By the same right whereby Ogmund Karisson and Thorolf Skjalg took our farms of Oksnevad and Figgjo, to name but two," said Aki.

"My lord," said Erling, "the difference lies in this—that we won the fights, thus proving our rights before heaven. He who loses the fight loses his rights. So it has always been. So it is with Aki."

"Don't listen to this *Christian!*" shouted Aki. "How long do you think you can trust him, when there are those in the land who wish to turn you out and put a cross-man in your place? Whose side do you think he'd take, sitting there with his magic-man on the same bench?"

The jarl's eyes narrowed as he looked at Erling, and at me, and at the brothers. "I've heard that you're a Christian too now, Sigurd," he said, "and that you have famous friends."

"I claim the right to judgment by duel!" cried Aki. "I will meet Erling Skjalgsson in *holmganga!*"

"So let it be," said Jarl Haakon.

"What's this *holmganga*?" I asked Erling as we left the hall. The skies were cloudy, but it hadn't started raining yet.

"A formal duel. We fight in a marked space, and we each get three shields. The man who first draws blood can claim victory, but I think neither of us will settle for that."

"Can you take him?"

"On my worst day. I only wish I hadn't had so much to drink."

He went to put his armor on, and Aki was taken to the armory to get his own back. We trooped out to a nearby meadow, well grazed, where Erling's men cleared all the stones and dung out of a space about ten feet through, laid a large cloak on it and set stones to hold down the corners, then dug three furrows around the edges to make boundaries. Jarl Haakon examined the field and pronounced it acceptable. Erling and Aki took their places on opposite sides, each with a man to keep his extra shields. They had to wait a bit while Olmod was borne up on his litter.

Haakon called for a horn and held it up before us all.

"I hallow this horn to the honor of Thor, guardian of justice. May he watch over this ground, and make the right victorious. Skoal!"

The men cried, "Skoal!" and Haakon drank, then passed the horn to Erling and to Aki. Erling made the sign of the cross over it before drinking.

"Aki," he said, "I offer you peace before this goes further. Admit my rights and swear to let me and mine alone, and you may go home with your men and ships."

"Hear how the coward scrabbles for a bolthole, now that he faces the avenger! Don't think to talk your way out today, Erling Skjalgsson! I've sworn to drink your blood and bed Halla Asmundsdatter. Prepare to meet your southland god!"

They stepped onto the cloak. They took each other's measure, feinting and circling, testing reach and quickness.

"Strike then!" said Aki. "The first blow is yours as the challenged! Don't keep me waiting!"

The next thing I knew, Aki's head was flying through the air, and his body, spouting blood, was collapsed on the cloak with his shattered shield on top of it. The head rolled a bit and came to rest not far from my feet. It had been the fastest thing I'd ever seen.

The men cheered, and Erling took his helmet off.

"We have seen the judgment of Thor!" shouted Jarl Haakon. "I declare before all men that the death of Thorolf shall cancel the death of Aki, and no *mansbot* may be demanded for this day's business. Furthermore, two of Aki's ships will be forfeit—the first to Erling, for his losses, the second to me for the troubling of the peace. Aki's men may go home in the third. Last of all, the sons of Erik will pay a fine of thirty-six *aurar* for the death of Aslak Skjalgsson. Let this be the end of the matter!"

Erling's men mobbed him and lifted him to their shoulders while Aki's brothers wrapped the body in the cloak and the Horder chiefs gathered around Olmod's litter, speaking in low voices.

CHAPTER VI

In the course of the feasting the free men held a *Thing*, or assembly, and acclaimed Erling hersir in his father's place by banging their weapons on their shields and making an ungodly racket.

The men half carried Jarl Haakon to his ship when the feasting was done, and he said he couldn't remember having such a good time in years. Only two men had been killed during the drinking, one of them by accident in a wrestling bout, so the peace had held.

"Thank God he's gone," said Halla as we watched his ships sail off. "Erling kept me and his sisters hidden away all the time he was here." We could hear the sisters' voices, shouting and laughing, as they skipped about like calves turned out of the byres in the spring.

"That was wise. Haakon kept himself to thralls this visit, but I'm told there are a lot of angry husbands up in the Trondelag."

"Why can't all men be like Erling?"

"Who'd sit in the lower seats?"

When the guests were gone, Erling set about

making repairs at Sola. He had arranged to buy timber from a cousin, to rebuild the hall.

We were having supper at Somme one of the first evenings thereafter when Erling had Lemming brought in. Lemming had been locked up since the night of the fires, and they brought him in chains. He stood before the high seat and eyed us like a penned boar.

"Thorvald Thorirsson, known as Lemming," said Erling. "You have been accused of lighting the jarl's balefire in breach of the law of the land. What say you to this charge?"

"Hang me," croaked Lemming.

"Not until I understand better. You did not love your old master, Soti the smith, did you?"

"Bugger him."

"And you do not love your new master, Father Aillil, either?"

Lemming spat.

"And you do not love me, the lord of Sola?"

Lemming only growled.

"Then explain to me, Lemming—why did you take such risks to save the lives and wealth of so many whom you do not love?"

Lemming hung his head like a scolded child and said nothing.

"No answer?" said Erling. "Are you going to leave us with a mystery?"

Lemming still said nothing.

"Then there's nothing for it but to pass sentence. As you may have heard, I promised Jarl Haakon I'd put a rope around your neck."

Lemming raised his head and looked Erling straight in the face. His eyes were cold as caves in a glacier.

"Bring the rope I chose," said Erling. One of the men went out to the entry room and came quickly back in.

Lemming tensed his entire body, never taking his

eyes off Erling, as the man laid around his neck a braided torque of pure silver, then loosed his bonds.

When Lemming reached a hand up and felt what was there, he gasped, and we all did the same.

"No man who saves my home and title, and the lives of my people, will be hanged for it, jarl or no jarl. This is the rope I give to you, Lemming, and with it your freedom. You may go or stay, as you like."

Like an oak felled after a hundred years, Lemming toppled to the floor and lay as a dead man.

Later that night, when most of the men had rolled up in their cloaks on the benches and Erling and I still sat and talked, his mother came in with a sheathed sword. She held it out in both hands and said, "This should be yours now, Erling."

"My father's sword?"

"*Smith's-Bane* was his, and his father's before him. It comes to you."

"I thought you laid it with Father in his grave. Surely he would have wished it."

"It is right that the heir should carry the sword."

"Mother, I am grateful, and I will keep it as a treasure." He took his father's sword.

"And you will bear it in battle?"

"No, that I will not. I have a better sword." He drew Smith's-Bane from its sheath. "Do you see how the steel is patterned along the inside, like wheat sheaves and writhing snakes, and bright on the edges? That's how they made swords in old times—with steel and iron forge-welded together, and pure steel at the edge, because steel was dear. But my new Frankish sword is steel all through. It's lighter and stronger, and it won't be bent as easily."

His mother snatched the sword. "I'll take it back then, and bury it with your father! I thought you'd be glad to carry the weapon your ancestors bore with honor since the day it was found in its maker's dead hand. But I see that you care only for what is new. The old you throw off like worn clothing, whether your father's sword or your father's faith! You think this Christ too is greater because he's new!"

"No," I broke in. "Not because He's new. Because He's true. No other reason, ever."

I don't know why I said that. I didn't believe Christ was true at all. I suppose I was getting accustomed to my role.

She turned on me, her face white. "I didn't ask your counsel, god-man! Never speak to me unbidden." She spat on the floor and went out.

"Far be it from me to tell you your business, Father Aillil," said Erling, "but I gave up long ago trying to convert my mother."

I slumped on the bench. "A man must work at his trade," I said.

Erling was silent for a time, watching the flames on the hearth. "How did you feel when your father was killed?" he asked at last.

I pulled my cloak tighter around me. "It was as if—as if someone had taken a cleaver to the world, and chopped it off sheer before my feet, leaving me teetering on the edge."

"That's it," said Erling. "I felt it, but I couldn't find the words. You must stay with me always, to say these things for me."

I baptized Halla, along with a bonder and his wife and some of the thralls' children, the following Sunday. Erling gave her a brooch as a memento, and she looked happy as a bride in her white gown.

The smiles of pretty women are gall and poison oak to priests. Worst of all is to be an unbelieving priest, who cannot profit by prayer and fasting for the mortification of the flesh. And in fact a true priest can get away with some backsliding, and often does, especially in the outposts of Christendom. As a false priest I dared not.

Besides, she was Erling's woman. I would not touch Erling's woman though she implored me with tears (which was unlikely), and not only out of fear.

But that did not exorcise the memory of her eyes, and the echo of her laughter. I went out that evening and walked about the farmstead in the long dusk (I'd moved back into my own house at Sola now), hoping to lose my itch in weariness of the body. The sky was clear for a change, and the breeze carried a rumor of winter.

"You can't fight it, you know."

"Who's that?" The voice startled me. It was a soft voice, but clear.

"When have you ever curbed your lust? You'll watch her, and watch her, and someday it will be too much for you, and you'll try to take her, and Erling will kill you, or sell you. Do you think you're really a free man?"

"I don't know what you're talking about," I said. It was an uncanny voice. It seemed to come from no direction, almost like my own thoughts, as if someone had wormed into my head and spoke from behind my eyes. I looked around in the red and silver light and saw no one. The only shapes nearby were two hillocks of earth, overgrown with heather.

"You may fool Erling, and you may fool the yokels in the church, but there are those who cannot be fooled."

"Are you God?"

"You may call me 'god' if you like. That would please me. You would do well to please me. The time is coming when you will be much in need of friends."

Yes indeed, there are devils. I ran back to my house as swiftly as I could, stumbling and ignoring it. In my haste I blundered into a large, hard body. I landed on my rump and looked up at Soti the smith, who had come up the path from the other direction.

"Out so late, god-man?" he asked. "Calling to your

spirits? You come from the direction of the Melhaugs. I'd stay away from Big Melhaug were I you, especially at night. There's a dragon under that mound. It's said it was a human once, long ago, and the *haug* is its grave, but it's a dragon now, and it eats men's souls."

I said nothing, but bolted for my house. Behind me I could hear the smith laughing.

I took my meals with the household at Somme, and one evening after the drinking was done, Erling called me to him and said he wanted my help.

"I've vowed to give my thralls the means to their freedom," he said. "I owe them for the night of the fires, and it seems to me a fitting task for a Christian lord. Do you agree?"

"With all my heart."

"Good. Now my problem is that I can't just turn them loose and bid them godspeed. For one thing, they're not prepared. Have you seen Lemming in the last few days?"

"From time to time. He seems to do a lot of dicing with the bodyguard. By the way, you paid me too much for him. I got him for nothing, after all."

"Say no more of it. I like to do things properly. I thought Lemming might have somewhere he wanted to go, and the silver I gave him would pay for it. But he says one place is like another. He bought a fishing boat, but lost it at dice. Now he just drinks from a cask of ale he bought, and hacks pieces off the torque and gambles them away, and when the silver's gone God knows what he'll do."

"And you're afraid the others would do the same."

"I can't afford it. By our law a master answers for the living of any thrall he frees. I need to see that my freedmen have livelihoods."

"Have you something in mind?"

"I have a plan. I want to give each thrall a set

amount of work to do each day. When that is done, each should have a piece of land or a task or craft they can ply, to earn silver. When they earn the price of their freedom I'll sell it to them, and set them up with some land and a cow. That way I can get people on land that's fallow now, and they'll pay rents and my lordship will prosper. And there's something else . . ."

"Yes?"

"You've been to Visby. There's a class of people there, and in other market towns, who are neither farmers nor priests nor bodyguards nor landholders. They're more like Soti. They live by working at crafts, and selling what they make for their own profit. The lords of the towns tax them. I think it would be profitable to have such people of my own."

"But you have no town."

"I've thought of founding a market, perhaps just in the winter. Risa Bay, north of Kolness, might be a good place."

"You want to train your thralls as craftsmen?"

"Do you think they're too stupid?"

"My lord, I was a thrall too not long since."

"Indeed. I apologize."

"There's something else you could do, my lord."

"What's that?"

"The silver they pay you. You could use it to buy more thralls."

"I'll have to. I can't run my farms without thralls."

"And you could offer them the same bargain. You'd have the hardest-working thralls in Norway!"

Erling frowned. "I don't know. It might make me a laughingstock among the landholders."

"It would make you great in the eyes of the Lord. And it would pay you well! How much would the landholders laugh when they saw your fields wide and rich, and your storehouses full of grain and silver?"

Erling smiled. "You could be right. If my vow

works as we hope, it might be worth considering. It might well be. And it would be fitting for a Christian lord. We've never had Christian lords in Norway. Someone will have to show the way."

"Very true."

"I need a man to be in charge. Someone with brains and a heart. You said that you read a little. Can you write?"

"A bit. Not much."

"More than anyone else here. I'd like you to keep records so that there'll be no question about accounts."

"I can work out some kind of system of marks and ciphers, I suppose. I'd need parchment and pens and ink."

"You'll get them."

"I'll see what I can do then, my lord."

"Then God bless us both!" said Erling Skjalgsson.

CHAPTER VII

I called Erling's thralls together in the church the next Sunday after mass and laid out his plan. The scheme, I said, would begin in the spring, with the spading.

"But how long will it take?" asked Turlough, a big, black Irishman who talked, as they all did, haltingly, careful not to misspeak.

"That's up to you. If you work hard in the evenings, perhaps two years—perhaps less. If you don't work so hard it may take three or four years. Or more. And of course the weather will make a difference."

"Can we go home then?" asked a woman named Bridget, no longer young, with a wind-dried, seamed face. How old had she been when they took her from Ireland?

"That's up to you. You'll be free to work and save, and go where you like. Erling hopes that most of you will choose to stay here."

"What about our children?" asked a Norse thrall woman named Thorbjorg.

"Children under three go with their mothers. Those over twelve may earn their own freedom."

"How do we know we won't be cheated?" asked Turlough.

"That hangs on whether you trust me. I'll keep the records. I'll make a sign like this on a sheet of parchment—this will be your sign, Turlough—and when your grain or handiwork is brought in to the stores and weighed or valued, you'll be credited with its worth in silver ounces, and I'll make a mark for each ounce beside your sign. When the ounces reach half your value, I'll take the sheet to my lord Erling, and he will declare you a freedman. You won't be fully free, of course, until the other half is paid or you hold your freedom-feast according to law."

"Why not just pay us and let us hold the money?"

"Two reasons. The first is that we don't trust you. I'll not lie about that. Look at Lemming if you wonder why. The second is that it's too easy to rob a thrall, and I'm afraid you'd have the devil's own time getting justice against the thief if he's a free man. But what you earn is yours, and if you have trouble that requires ready money, come to me, and I'll speak to Erling, and we'll give you the silver if we agree it's needed."

"It's an insult, that's what it is," said Turlough.

"No," said Bridget. "It's a better chance than we ever hoped to get in this land, and I thank God for it. Count me in, Father Aillil, and see how fast I can buy myself."

A knarr sailed in with the timber from Hordaland, and Erling announced that work on the hall would begin the next day. He asked me to be there at the start to bless the building.

As I walked in the mist with a bowl full of what I called holy water the next morning, I found a small crowd gathered about the site, both men and women, with Soti at their head. He led a goat on a rope, and was trading hard words with Erling.

ERLING'S WORD 61

"It has been thus since men first lived at Sola, and so must it be!" he shouted. "The people expect you to uphold the custom, and the gods and spirits will not brook change! You do not know what you dare!"

"I know what I dare," said Erling. He spoke low, but there were red spots on his cheekbones. "I know that my God is greater than all your gods and spirits together, and all men together, and this hall will be hallowed in His name, and His alone! I bear with you, Soti, because of my mother, but on this I stand firm. Now go away, and take your goat with you."

Ragna pushed through the crowd. "If your father were alive, he'd flay the skin off your back!"

"If my father were alive he'd be lord of Sola and could do what he liked. I am lord of Sola now, and I must do what I think best."

"Do not think yourself beyond your father's power!"

The voice was a woman's, and it belonged to Soti's red-haired wife. She was much younger than her husband, a thin woman with a longish nose, but not unlovely. I'd seen her the night of the fires, kneeling and chanting in the house at the stronghold. Her name was Ulvig. She held by the hand a fair, blue-eyed girl, about twelve, their daughter.

"Your father is nearby, sleeping in his howe," said Ulvig. "Do you think he forgets his home and its affairs? Do you think he cares not whether his gods are welcome in their accustomed places? Do you think he will not act?"

Ragna said, "When the gods see the hall built without sacrifice, they will want their gifts with interest. Are you willing to pay the price they will ask, my son?"

"I owe nothing to the gods. Let them howl for their blood."

"They will do more than howl," said Ulvig.

"I fear them not," said Erling. "I have Christ's

messenger with me, whose merest word will put all spirits to flight." He reached a hand out and clapped me on the shoulder.

I felt very cold of a sudden.

They all watched me as I went about the site, sprinkling water and reciting scraps of Latin. Inside I prayed, because I could do nothing else, to the God who had sat and watched while Maeve was raped and my parents and brother killed. To the God who did nothing to protect us from capture and slavery. Who did nothing while wars raged over honest people's farms and wrecked their harvests to starve them, who did nothing while children died of pestilence, who watched the strong and the selfish put their boots on the faces of the weak. I knew what to expect from that God, but where else could I turn?

"*Gungnir.*"

It was Soti speaking. He repeated, "*Gungnir.*" I knew the word. It was the name of Odin's spear.

The people took it up. "*Gungnir.*"

"*Gungnir.*

"*Gungnir.*

"*Gungnir.*"

The chant grew louder and louder, and drowned my baby Latin altogether.

They chanted until I finished, then went silent. The wind came up strong of a sudden, out of the north.

"Odin has heard," said Soti. "Watch yourself at night, Christ-thrall."

The workmen (mostly farmers working out obligations to Erling) had only begun setting the wallposts and pillars into the earth when the rain began. It rained harder and harder, until each man's clothing weighed heavy as a sheep and no one could see, and they had to stop. The rain continued, and the men went home to their farms at last, saying this did not bode well.

It did us no good that lightning struck one of the pillars that night and left it in two pieces.

The next day it threatened rain again, and the farmers told Erling they would do their service in some other way. They would not labor on a cursed building. The red spots appeared on his cheeks, but he let them go.

"Why not let the thralls work on it?" I asked Erling. "They can start earning their freedom now. They're none of them skilled carpenters, but they know how to work, and you must have some Christian workman who can guide them and won't be afraid of the old gods."

"I have Christian workmen," said Erling. "But I'm not sure they don't fear the old gods."

"You're not going to give up?"

"No. Not if I have to raise my hall with my own hands. Say a mass for my hall, Father Aillil."

I almost sobbed. "My lord," I said, "I would God that He had sent you a worthier priest."

"Father Aillil, I've never stopped thanking God for you. I would not trade you for the Archbishop of Cantaraborg."

I said his mass, just as if it would do some good.

I was sleeping badly, and as I lay waking that particular night I heard a tapping at my door.

I lay in my robe for warmth, although I hadn't yet moved into the box-bed, so I sat up on the bench and poked the hearth fire and then went to the door.

It was a young woman who entered, a plump thrall girl of Soti's. I didn't know her name, as she did not come to church. She was pretty in the porridge-faced way you often see in Norway, and her short hair was yellow.

"My master sent me, Father Aillil."

"What does he want?"

"He says I am to lie with you tonight."

I was surprised. I would have expected a better plan from Soti. "Run home and tell him I said no," I answered, heading back to my bed.

"Please, Father, he'll beat me if you refuse."

That was more like Soti. "Wait a moment," I said, while I pulled on my shoes. Then I took her by the wrist and led her back to Soti's house.

I banged on the door until a thrall woman opened it.

"I want to see your master," I told her.

"He's in bed."

"Then wake him."

"I dare not!"

"Then I'll do it." I pushed past her and strode down the hearthway to the box-beds. "Which one does he sleep in?" I asked.

The woman pointed with a trembling hand, then ran out.

I banged on the box. "Soti, you bastard, wake up!" The thrall girl tugged on my hand, trying to get away. I held her fast.

The door opened and Soti's head appeared. "What do you want, god-man?" he growled.

"Keep your thrall girls at home. I don't want them."

"What are you babbling about?"

"You sent this girl to me with a threat to beat her if I didn't lie with her. I'm telling you to leave off, and if I hear that you've laid a hand on her, Lord Erling will be told of it!"

Soti crawled out and sat with his feet on the step, a blanket around him. "I don't know what you're talking about, god-man. You know you can't believe what these thralls tell you. Half of them don't even believe in the gods, so how can you trust their word? This girl has been telling you tales. I'm sorry she disturbed your sleep. She'll be punished."

"Leave her alone, I said!"

"Fine, fine, whatever you want," said Soti, and crawled back into his bed and shut the door.

The girl fell on the floor, sobbing. I patted her head and told her it would be all right, then trudged home and lay down. I could not sleep.

Again, the tapping at my door. "Father Aillil! Father Aillil!"

It was the same girl. I opened to her, and she slumped against my chest.

I led her inside and lit a lamp. She'd gotten the kind of skillful beating that leaves no lasting marks and breaks no bones, but her eyes were blackened, and she bled from a corner of her mouth.

"My master says . . . you must lie with me or he'll beat me again, and say again that it was all my idea. If you go to Lord Erling, he'll say the same, and beat me worse. Please, Father, is it so terrible to lie with me?"

I stroked her hair. "No, child," I said, "you don't understand. A priest isn't allowed to lie with a woman. He may not even marry, not in law."

She wept then, and I told her she might lie the night on the other bench.

She curled up there with thanks, and I listened to her breathing a long time. When I woke in the morning I found her warm against my back, and my male parts were aware. I jumped up and went out to walk it off.

That day the weather was better, and I spoke to the thralls and got several men willing to work for their freedom-silver. Erling had a man to train them, and they began the labor. It went slowly, and the foreman cursed them loudly and often as they fumbled the staves in the rocky ground.

"At this rate the work won't be finished before snow comes," said Erling.

"They'll learn. Once they get the feel of the work,

and know what it's like to do a job well, for their own good, they'll be fine."

"I wonder. We've always believed that there is no chance in life. If you become a king, it's because you were fated to be a king, because you are kingly. If you become a slave, it's because you are slavish, and you run into your right place as water into a hole. Can these things be changed?"

"My lord, we were all born thralls of sin, fated for Hell because we were ourselves hellish. But Christ had mercy on us, and paid a great price to make us sons of God. It seems He believed that people change."

Erling granted that was true, and I walked off wondering if Christ had been too hopeful.

I waited for her knock that night, and it came at last.

"Father," she said, "my master says you must lie with me truly, as a man lies with a woman. Otherwise he'll kill me." She fell on her knees at my feet. "A master may kill a thrall, Father, and there is no punishment. None may interfere. Don't let him kill me, Father!"

She was soft and warm, and she tried very hard to please me. And oh, she did please me. It was sweet as laughter to lie in her arms, and touch her, and do all that was forbidden a priest. It was as if I eased a cramp in my soul, and when I slept at last, I slept better than any night since I'd left Ireland.

I was awakened by another knocking, this time very loud. I opened the door to find a man standing in the morning light. "Lord Erling sent me," he said. "He wants you at the new hall, right away."

I ran there and found a crowd of people gathered around one of the pillars. They were looking up to where a spear had been driven into it, about two men high. A walrus-hide rope was tied to the spear, near its head, and from the rope a man hung. He hung close against the pillar, a dark shape against the pale sky, for the spear had been dragged to a downward angle by his weight.

It was Turlough the thrall.

Soti the smith was there, and he said, "See—Odin has taken his first sacrifice! And it is far from over."

Erling said, "Get a ladder and cut him down."

A raven flapped down, black as blindness, and perched atop the pillar.

CHAPTER VIII

Erling, Steinulf and I walked about the building site after the body had been taken away. The spear still stood in the wood.

"Who could drive a spear deep enough at that height to bear a man's weight?" asked Steinulf. "I couldn't do it. You couldn't do it. Soti or Lemming couldn't do it. Sigurd the Volsung could have done it maybe, or Svipdag, but such men are rare nowadays."

"It happened. There must be a way," said Erling.

"Oh, there's a way. It's on everybody's lips. One of the gods, or one of the underground folk, or a walker-again."

Erling turned and looked at him. "You speak of the newly dead."

I said, "No, my lord, not your father or brother. Their souls have gone to a place far from Sola. If their bodies or anyone's walk again—I'm not saying they do, I'm only supposing—then the spirits that use them are not theirs. Your father and brother were human sinners, no worse. This is demon's work."

Erling said, "Couldn't someone have hammered the spear in—climbed a ladder somehow and—?"

"Can't have done," said Steinulf. "The higher you climbed the ladder, the further you'd get from the butt of the spear. That's a six-foot shaft. No man has that kind of reach. And someone would have heard."

"I'd thought your blessing would frighten the spirits off, Father Aillil," said Erling.

"My lord, the holy apostles themselves found some spirits unmasterable except by prayer and fasting. I'm a weak reed to lean on when you face demons of this power."

"Can you fight them with prayer and fasting then?"

"I can try, my lord, but I'm no apostle. I fear the Lord hearkens not much to my prayers."

"You must do what you can. I ask no more of any of my warriors. You eat at my table, you must stand in my shield wall."

I bowed my head. "As you command, my lord. I've had no breakfast. I will live on water until this business is ended."

"I will have my hall," said Erling. "It will not be hallowed to Odin. Not while I am above ground. Father, I think it would be good for me to join you in this battle. I will fast also. Now let's see Turlough's family."

They shared a low turf house with three other families. There were no box-beds, but there were low stone partitions dividing households. The place stank of sweat and fish and unwashed wool. Turlough's wife, a shapeless, brown woman named Copar, sat leaning against a partition and scrambled to her feet when we entered. Her three dirty, snuffling children clung to her skirts. She bowed, unsteadily. Someone had given her beer.

"I am sorry for your loss, woman," said Erling.

"It's very kind of you I'm sure," said Copar. "It's hard to understand the ways of the Lord."

"Your man fought for me the night of the fires.

By his death he has earned your freedom—yours and your children's."

The woman gasped and fell at Erling's feet. "No, my lord! Don't send us out by ourselves—not now when we've none to protect us! It's a cold land in a cold world, and things walk at night that should not walk—"

Erling put his hand on her head. "No one will send you out. We'll find you a living first. Only I want you to know that your man didn't die for nothing. He would have wanted you free, I think."

"Aye, my lord," she hiccupped. "He was a hard man, and he beat me when he was drunk, but it was because he was shamed to be a thrall, you see, and mad at the world. We're in your hands, my lord. Do what you will."

Erling spoke to each of the children, and asked their names, and gave Copar some bread from the hall. Then we went out and breathed fresh air again.

"It's best to believe in fate, Father Aillil," he said. "I must think those people different from me. If they're not, 'tis almost beyond bearing."

"What now, my lord?"

"I'll see about getting the thralls out to build today. You will go to the church and say masses. Then get some sleep. Tonight you and I will watch together at the hall."

I sleep badly when I'm hungry, and worse when I'm frightened. When the voice began to speak, I wondered who had come in without my hearing; then I knew it for the voice from Big Melhaug.

"It all comes from the sin you call superbia, *overweening pride."*

"I am many kinds of sinner," I muttered, "but I don't think I'm especially proud of myself."

"No? You talk of your god as if he were your father; as if he felt and pitied."

"God help us if He does not."

"Why should he? On what grounds do you assume his love? On the word of a Jew a thousand years dead? Who could believe such things?" Did I see eyes—unblinking, yellow snakeish eyes? *"Does the hawk pity the rabbit? Does the wolf pity the sheep? Where in all the world is there mercy for weakness except in the ravings of your religion? When has this mercy ever been shown? And what use is mercy unshown?"*

"Then what is there but despair and death?"

"There is courage! Face the darkness! Be strong enough to make the sacrifices. Harden your heart. Life can be a wonderful thing, but you must seize it by force!"

"My Lord Erling believes. I can at least believe in his faith a while yet."

"Don't think that you will thereby prevent the sacrifices. The sacrifices will be made...."

"There's a saga of a hero named Bjovulf," said Erling as we sat under the stars and purple heavens that night amid the ribs of the hall. He was in full armor and had two casting spears at hand. I was armed with the crucifix from the church. "He came to Hroar, King of Denmark, to rid him of a troll who broke into his hall each night and killed men."

"What happened to him?"

"Oh, he killed the troll. Ripped his arm out of the socket and let him run away to bleed to death. There were great men in those days. Are you my Bjovulf, Father Aillil?"

"You need no heroes, my lord. This Bjovulf can have been little ahead of the man I saw fight Aki."

"Even Bjovulf couldn't fight all the heathens in Jaeder and all the gods of Asgard together."

"How did you become a Christian, my lord? What keeps you firm? I've heard of your king Haakon the Good. He tried to live as a Christian, but the lords made him sacrifice and he was buried as a heathen, they say."

"We went a-viking in Ireland," said Erling, "my father and I. I saw a man—a priest—die for Christ. We were holding him and others for ransom, and some of the lads were having a lark and thought it would be sport to make him eat horsemeat. He refused, and the lads took offense at his manner. They tied him to a tree and shot him full of arrows. He died singing a hymn. I thought he was as brave as Hogni, who laughed while Atli cut his heart out. My father said not to talk rot, that a man who dies over what food he'll eat dies for less than nothing."

"I've never seen a true martyrdom," I said. "I'll wager it wasn't like the pictures."

"No," said Erling. "It looked nothing like the pictures in the churches. Martyrs die like other men, bloody and sweaty and pale, and loosening their bowels at the end."

"So I'd feared."

"What of it? The pictures are no cheat. Just because I saw no angels, why should I think there were no angels there? Because I didn't see Christ opening Heaven to receive the priest, how can I say Christ was not there? If someone painted a picture of that priest's death, and left out the angels and Christ and Heaven opening, he'd not have painted truly. The priest sang as he died. Only he knows what he saw in that hour, but what he saw made him strong.

"I saw a human sacrifice once too, in Sweden. When it was done, and my father had explained how the gods need to see our pain, so they'll know we aren't getting above ourselves, I decided I was on the Irish priest's side."

"And you're sure our God doesn't need to see our pain?"

"Not in the same way. I serve a God who will not have human sacrifice. You've never believed in human sacrifice, but I did once, so I can tell you it makes no little difference."

I said nothing for awhile. A cloud bank was moving in from the northwest. I hoped we wouldn't get rained on.

"They tell me you've taken a leman," said Erling.

I jerked my head up. I'd almost fallen asleep. I said, "It's often done."

"Father Ethelbald said the Irish church was strong in forbidding such for priests."

"We are, we are. But the nights are long, and the flesh is weak, and many think it's better to cleave to one woman than to lust after the whole race of them."

"It's one of Soti's thralls, isn't it?"

I didn't want to talk about this. "Yes, as it happens," I said.

"Is there some trouble, Father Aillil? Does Soti hold anything over you? I'll help if you ask."

"It's . . . it's between Soti and me, and nothing you need trouble over."

"Be that as may be, remember I'm ready to help. As you yourself said, Soti is as great a devil as you'll find in this land. He does nothing in sport."

"I'll remember, my lord," I said.

Why didn't I tell him? Did I think he couldn't protect the girl? Was I ashamed of my weakness?

The true reason, I think, was that if Erling helped I'd have no further excuse for bedding her. I didn't want to stop, and a small surrender to Soti seemed worth it. A mere sin of the flesh, after all, and all in the open, would put me under no great obligation to the smith.

Someone screamed in the night.

It was a loud scream, and a long scream. A man with a belly wound, or a woman in fouled childbirth, screams like that sometimes.

"Down by the byres," said Erling, and set off running.

I followed, all the hairs on my back lifting.

People came tumbling out of houses to gape at us, the men carrying axes. We reached the byres and ran around them, then poked in the grass and among the stones, finding nothing.

Half-dressed men came to join us, and no one found anything.

"Oh God," said Erling at last. "My hall."

He raced back as fast as he had come, with me at his heels.

It was a different pillar this time, but the same kind of burden. Erling seized the man's legs and lifted him, but he was already dead.

CHAPTER IX

Erling spent the night praying in the church, knees on cold stone. I tried to keep vigil with him, but fell asleep.

"This has gone far enough!"

The voice of Ragna woke me. She swept in followed by a serving woman.

"What kind of troll's cavern is this place? Give us light!" The serving woman had come prepared with a soapstone lamp, and she went, very irreverently, up to the altar and lit my tallow candles.

"Mother, this is a church," said Erling, rising stiffly.

"That means nothing to me. I have words for you, and they will be said. And you will listen!"

"Of course, Mother." Erling sat on the bench.

"Do you know what they say out there?"

"I suppose they're saying that the gods are against me and my luck is gone."

"They say that. They also say that the ancient kings of Rogaland have heirs in Ireland, and perhaps it's time to call them back."

Erling stretched his neck. "I thought it was something like that."

"And what do you intend to do about it?"

"I will catch whatever's doing this, and kill it."

"Even if it's your father?"

"Not my father. His walker-again. Just a devil in his body."

"Slowly, one bit at a time, you cast aside everything that ever you believed, everything your father and I believed."

"I must do what is right."

"People are dying, Erling! *Your* people are dying. First it was a thrall. Last night it was a free man. Tomorrow night it will be a warrior, or perhaps one of us. When you are dead, who will look to my welfare?"

"We have many kin, Mother, if it comes to that, but it won't come to that. I will stop this thing."

"Bait not the gods, my son! You are strong and brave, but you are not stronger and braver than fate! You are proud—like your father and his father, and Horda-Kari and all the rest of that blood. And my blood too—I come of proud stock also. But there is such a thing as too much pride. Ask your priest—is there not a sin of pride?"

Erling said, "Please go now, Mother. I want to speak to my priest."

"I'll go and sew your shroud. If you are set on making me weep, I must be prepared."

She gusted out, and Erling remained sitting and ran his hands over his face. "I've prayed most of the night, Father. I thought there'd be a sign from God."

"And?"

"Nothing. Not a word. Am I too proud? Was my father right? Is it folly to hazard your life over a footling matter like food, or a goat buried under a doorway?"

The man fed me to be his priest, so I answered him as a priest.

"My lord, when the early Christians were martyred in Romaborg, all that was asked of them was to sprinkle a little incense on an altar. They didn't have to pray to or believe in the false god, just go through a ceremony that even their enemies didn't believe in. But they would not. They let themselves be burned alive, and torn by wild beasts; they let their flesh be ripped by pincers. They accepted it not only for themselves, but for their wives and children, and they shouted encouragement to them as they watched them die. It was a stubborn thing they did, and wrongheaded from any sensible point of view. But it was not pride. And in the end they won, although they never lived to see it."

"Yes," said Erling. "That's what I learned from the sagas when I was a boy. That it matters not when you die, or by what means, but only how you face it. A young man in a tight place, facing deadly odds. Such was Christ himself, at the battle of Calvary."

What would he have done had I counseled him to be sensible? Why didn't I counsel him to be sensible? I truly do not know.

Erling said, "I must find a place to sleep or I won't last the night."

I said mass for the two of us, and he went out. I snuffed the candles and went to my own house to sleep. My stomach whimpered like a dog at the door, and sleep, along with a draught of well water, was the only relief I could offer it.

Halla called to me as I was going inside, and I stayed to greet her.

"You've got to stop him," she said.

"I cannot. I wouldn't if I could."

"He'll be killed!"

"If you wanted a man unlikely to be killed, you should have chosen a herdsman or a farmer." Or a priest, I might have added, except that in this land priesthood was risky.

"If it were only men, I wouldn't be afraid! Erling can defeat any man!"

"Well you should be afraid of men. There are such things as arrows."

"Fighting the gods is different!"

"We fight the gods every day, my daughter. Odin with his deceit, Thor with his anger, Frey with his lust—they all live within us, and they threaten terrible things if we deny them their sacrifices. A Christian must learn not to believe their lies, even when they seem truth of all truth. Even when it means death . . ."

"I'll be glad when you're dead!" she shouted. "If you have to be a martyr, good for you. But my Erling!" She ran off, weeping.

Cold eyes, yellow-green and round. *"Why do you say such things? Why are you so cruel? You are no martyr. If you had lived in those early days, you'd have sprinkled all the incense they asked for, and thanked them. Whom do you look to impress by this self-slaughter?"*

"No!" I said through clenched teeth, and covered my ears to keep out the voice of the dragon.

"It's time."

Erling, standing in my doorway, woke me. I shook myself and got up to join him.

"Are you hungry?" he asked.

"I could eat that old cheese you Norwegians like."

"Then let's be done with this, and we'll eat till we burst."

"It'll be Friday in the morning."

"Then we'll eat all the fish in the sea."

We set out together for the hall site. No work had been done there that day. There was a sliver of moon. The sun balanced on the horizon, ready to tip off for the short night.

We sat facing each other, our backs against two of the pillars.

"What are those birds you have painted on your shield?" I asked him.

"Eagles."

"Why did you choose that emblem?"

"I watched two eagles battle once. I thought it the grandest thing I'd ever seen. Soaring and spinning, talons and beaks, far above the earth. If men could fight that way, would they have the courage?"

"I think you would, my lord. That's not flattery. I've seen you fight."

Erling laughed. "Everyone talks about my duel with Aki Eriksson, the easiest of my life. He fought like a sheep. My mother could have killed him. But folk tell the story as if I did something great. I think some day I may regret killing that half-wit."

"Why so?"

"Sigurd Eriksson, his brother, is a good man, and a Christian. They tell a tale about him. They say that when he was serving King Valdemar in Russia he visited a marketplace in Estonia. There he saw a handsome thrall lad. He thought the lad looked wonderfully like his own sister Astrid, widow of King Trygvi Olafsson of the Vik. Astrid had disappeared years before, fleeing Norway by ship. When he spoke to the boy, he learned he was indeed Astrid's son Olaf, and that they'd been caught by Vikings and sold into thralldom.

"He bought the lad and set him free, and they say he's a man grown now, a great warrior and a Christian. I'd like to meet this Olaf Trygvesson. I think Jarl Haakon may have come to the end of his thread—

"What's that sound?"

I listened. "Footsteps. A lot of them. Coming towards us."

"Do you think all the gods are coming?"

I began the Pater Noster as we stood and faced the noise, trampings up the walled path. Erling held his shield before him, spear ready, and I held the crucifix high.

It was dark now, and they were shapes in the

dimness as they approached, twenty, fifty of them. Starlight glinted on helmets, spear points and shield bosses.

"Lord Erling!"

"Steinulf!" shouted Erling. "I told you men to stay at Somme!"

Steinulf stepped forward. "We talked about it, my lord. We decided that you had no right to demand it. If you die alone, we are shamed for life. You have the right to command us to die. You have no right to command us to live."

"Not all of you are Christians. Did you all come?"

"Every man."

"Then it seems there's nothing I can do. Watch with us. We mean to end it tonight."

The wind blew colder, and clouds rode in on it, shrouding the stars. The men sat back to back, sharing warmth. It was black as Judas' grave.

"Three knots bind the heart;
Three links chain the mind;
Three words make a man a craven.
These are the knots that bind the heart:
Never to touch the fair girls again.
Never to drink the brown ale again.
Never to do the deeds that men remember."

I thought I'd heard the voice before. It sang on the wind, and it sang against the wind, and it sang under the wind.

"Three knots bind the heart;
Three links chain the mind;
Three words make a man a craven.
These are the links that chain the mind:
Never to hold your son in your arms.
Never to see your son raise a beard.

> *Never to sit by his side in the hall with
> the warriors."*

The wind came up stronger, and raindrops fell, cold as a river under ice, and I began shivering to rattle the flesh off my bones.

> *"Three knots bind the heart;*
> *Three links chain the mind;*
> *Three words make a man a craven.*
> *These are the words that cravens make:*
> *'Sometimes the arrow leaves you blind.*
> *Sometimes the spear will leave you lame.*
> *Sometimes the sword will geld you*
> *   and not kill you.'"*

"A hymn, Father Aillil! Sing us a psalm!" It was Erling's voice, but it seemed very far away. I tried to sing, but my teeth were chattering. I bit my tongue.

The world was very black.

There was one light in all the world.

It came towards us, over the meadow, from the direction of Thorolf Skjalg's grave.

We all saw him. The men groaned. They wept. They yammered like dogs. Some shouted, "Thorolf! 'Tis my Lord Thorolf come out to walk again!"

He was a tall man, dressed in full armor, with shield and spear and sword at his belt. He glowed all over with blue fire. He was coming to us.

The men began to beat at the earth, and at the pillars, and at each other. "He walks again!" they cried. "He comes to make the sacrifice!"

"Run!" someone shouted. "We've got to run!" But no one ran. No one stood on his feet. A few tried to crawl, but most stayed in their places, kneeling or sitting, watching the walker-again come nearer and nearer.

"It's the battle-fetter!" someone cried. "Odin has set the battle-fetter on us!"

All the men groaned and rolled on the ground, and I rolled with them.

Thorolf came ever nearer. I could see his eyes now. They were green-yellow, round and cold.

"Death!" cried a man. "It is our death, each and all of us!"

The wailing rose like steam from a bog in winter.

Then a hand fell on my shoulder. I could not see the face of the man, but I knew his voice. Erling said, "A psalm, Father! I don't ask you to fight, but sing me a psalm that I may fight—that one about the mountains falling into the sea, and shaking!"

I set my forehead to the stones and tried to gather my wits. I found I still had the crucifix in my hands, gripped so tightly it was wet with my blood. I tried to moisten my lips. I licked the blood from my hands.

"*Deus noster refugium . . .*" I croaked.

"*God is our refuge and strength, a very present help in trouble.*

Therefore we will not fear, though the earth be removed, and though the mountains be carried into the midst of the sea.

Though the waters thereof roar and be troubled, though the mountains shake with the swelling thereof.

There is a river, the streams whereof shall make glad the city of God, the holy place of the tabernacles of the most High.

God is in the midst of her; she shall not be moved: God shall help her and that right early."

I could not see the fight that Erling fought. Only now and then the witchlight of the walker-again flickered, and I knew that flicker for Erling's shadow. I saw the demon cast his spear, and saw his mouth open in something like laughter. I saw him fend what must have been Erling's spears in return. I heard the whacking of blades on shields, and saw the dead man leap and whirl; and his leaps were head-high, and his whirls faster than birds' wings. I spoke my psalm again and again, gripping the crucifix as a drowning man clings to driftwood, and I wept for my lord, and all the men wept for him, and they cried, "My Lord Erling! My Lord Erling! I'd come to you if I could, but I am only a man, and not a hero, and I weep to see you die alone, as heroes always must."

And I found I was saying the same.

Faces blossomed before my inner eye.

My father saying, "Sparrow-heart! Stop wiggling or I'll leave the splinter in your flesh, and you'll carry it to your grave. Crying too? Such a baby! Are you my son or a heifer-calf?"

The abbot saying, "Hold still. You weren't afraid to transgress, now take your licks like a man!"

And a boy named Aoife who put his red face close to mine so I could smell his breath and said, "Now admit you're a liar or I'll break your finger. I'll do it too—you know I did it to Dathi and I'll do it to you. I like the sound when the bone snaps. So say it. Say, 'I'm a filthy liar.' Say it now...."

I do not know how long it took. We watched—we could not do otherwise—and it went on and on. Parry and thrust and leap and slash. Strike with the sword and strike with the shield boss. Circle and watch, then in with a flurry of blows.

But at last we knew that the morning was coming. And as the sun edged the eastern mountains, the battle-fetter was loosed. And we looked at one another, crouched and kneeling and wet and filthy, useless weapons flung about in the stones and dirt, and we were filled with shame, and groaned aloud. And we scrambled to our feet and rushed into the meadow.

Two bodies lay on their backs in the stubble.

One had once been Thorolf Skjalg. It was ugly and putrid but no longer a danger. Steinulf struck its head off with his sword so that it might not walk again.

The other was Erling, bloody and pale. We knelt

about him, weeping. "Bjovulf can have died no better," I said.

"Sigurd died not so well," said another.

Someone else said, "He breathes!"

CHAPTER X

We bore Erling to my house on a shield (not his own—that was smashed) while some of the other men reburied Thorolf with his head at his hip.

Two men had to hold Erling still as we carried him. He thrashed about and cried, "Father!" or "Jesus!" or "No, no!"

Ragna arrived from Somme about the time we got him into my box-bed. No one had told her her son was hurt; no one needed to. She sent everyone out but me.

She leaned into the bed and began pulling off his brynje. "Lie still, my son, your mother's here. All is well. It is good that courage is passed along in the blood," she sighed. "I think few women could bear what we heroes' mothers must."

Erling had another fit then, and she held his shoulders and spoke soothing words, and he grew calmer at last, but he did not know us. He babbled to himself, and his eyes rolled.

"I should not have buried Smith's-Bane with Thorolf," she said as she continued stripping him. "A blade turned against kin is unlucky, and borne by a walker-again it can be venomous."

"He's very strong," I said. "And there's no serious bleeding."

"There is a wound though. Here—do you see? Near the heart. That it bleeds not is the unhealthiest thing of all. When did you ever see a wound this size—three fingers wide—that did not bleed? Don't say it; I will. Only on a corpse. This is a deadly hurt, a fey sore. Hardly or never is a wound like this healed."

"There must be some medicine—"

"Oh aye. Battlefield herb. Little Hero. A paste of stinging nettle. We can get them and try them, but they won't be enough for this. We need help from the gods, and will the gods help my Erling?"

I had no reply to that.

"What of your god, priest? Does he heal the sick?"

"It's said He does. For great saints. I'm not a great saint."

"What good are you, god-man?"

I slumped on the bench. "God knows," I said.

I could not forget my terror in the night. It had been like a long fall; it had been like slow smothering. There was a wound near my heart too—having been mastered so utterly by fear, would I ever master myself again? Something had broken inside me. Would it heal?

Someone came in the door. I looked up to see Ulvig, the red-haired wife of Soti. She carried a goatskin bag. "I have herbs and runes of healing," she said.

Ragna flew at her. "Out! Out! Get away from my son, you witch!" She bore the woman out the door and told the bullyboys, "Don't let her near the house! Take her bag and burn it unopened! Do it now!"

"Don't stare at me," she said when she came back. "I'd be glad of Ulvig's skill were it honest. She's been a help to me often. But in this we are not allies. She would kill my Erling for the gods' sake. Her herbs would be nearly right, but only nearly. Her runes would be cut just on the edge of wrong. Only a master would know the difference. But they would sicken my son. I know Ulvig too well.

"I have none to lean on but you, god-man. My gods and spirits are of no help here. So do your magic. Go hungry, and pray, and sing over your holy meal. Light candles. Do you want to ward your only protector? Do you want to show all Jaeder the power of your god? Then save my son. Because I promise you, if he dies there will be none to avenge you when you die, and you will surely die."

I had not broken my fast. I did not break it in the days that followed, days of impassioned, craven pleading to a God I had denied, broken only by spells when I lost my senses and fell on the stones of the church floor for hours at a time.

Later that first day I woke to find Halla giving me water, holding my head in her lap like a child's. I crawled to the altar and prayed when I was refreshed, and she knelt beside me and kept me company, nor left me except to fetch more water.

I prayed all the prayers I knew. I opened the psalter and went through it from beginning to end, then began again at the first page. The colors of the illuminations shimmered before my eyes, and the misshapen people who dwelt in them seemed to walk about and speak like living men.

I forgot how to count the days.

I don't know when it was Halla said to me, "You must eat, Father, or you die."

I took a sip of water and went back to my prayers without answering. To look on her beauty would be a kind of food, and I refused it.

God, all-knowing and craftier than any man, had found the hook to draw me back to Him. The hook was fear, cold as a January night. No, more than fear. Cowardice. The whining cowardice of a dog too much beaten.

God did not care for my love. All He asked was that I bow my neck like a defeated soldier, that He might put His foot on it.

"*Salvum me fac, Deus. . . .*"

"*Save me, O God; for the waters are come in unto my soul.*

I sink in deep mire, where there is no standing; I am come into deep waters, where the floods overflow me.

I am weary of my crying; my throat is dried; mine eyes fail while I wait for my God. . . ."

I thought one of the patriarchs in the illuminations in my psalter looked wonderfully like my old abbot. He had the same face, and the same stooped back, and when he walked about in his painted rectangle, he had the same stiff shamble.

He said to me, "It must be true that the mercy of the Almighty is boundless, for here you are, still above ground, while better men and women are in Hell. I know not why they send me to you a second time, except that such menial errands are salutary for a soul in Purgatory. But what good it can do a child of perdition like you I cannot guess.

"Nevertheless, I bear you a message, which you will doubtless misconstrue, making your last state worse than your first, and filling your cup of iniquity to the brim.

"Here is the message I bring—if you wish your foreign lord to live, do as I tell you. . . ."

When I came to my senses I found that I'd fallen asleep on my knees, the psalter on the stones in front of me. It was dark in the church.

I tried to stand, but could not raise myself. A hand took my arm and helped me up. I looked into Halla's eyes, hollow with hunger and sorrow. My leg bones felt as if they'd been sharpened at the ends.

Turning to go out, I was amazed to see the church

full of people. There were thralls, and free men and women, and several men of the bodyguard. They all looked at me as at some monster.

I tottered out between them, supported by Halla, scattering blessings out of habit. The night air felt like a cold bath when we got outside. We went slowly toward my house.

A tall man approached us as we went. He wore a dark cloak and a dark hat.

"There are other ways," he said.

"You come late with them," I mumbled.

"Not to save the Squinter's son. You don't need him. I can make you great in this land. You will do wonders, and speak oracles. Men will fear you. Women will not refuse you. Remember, you're a fraud. How long do you think he'll defend you when he learns the truth?"

"He's the best man I've ever known. I'll not betray him."

"Suppose I offered you this girl at your arm? Would you do me a favor for her? I don't ask you to raise your hand to him; only let him be a little longer."

"You talk like a madman. They deserve each other. It's good to see them side by side, the brave and the fair. It makes me feel there's justice in the world."

"What if I offered you another girl? A girl called Maeve? I could find her for you, and bring her to you—nothing easier. Your friend has had a good life. He's done great deeds. Men will sing of him for generations. Could you not trade a little time of his— how long do warriors live after all—for some good years for your sister? To loose her bonds and lift the yoke from her shoulders? Soon she'll look like an old woman, bent and gray, living as she is now."

I groaned. "You speak to the wrong man," I said. "If I were free, or brave, I might strike hands with you on that bargain, but I'm a slave and a coward, and I fear the God of Abraham."

Then we were at the door of my house, and the man was gone.

"How is he?" I croaked to Erling's mother, who sat by the bed.

"He moves not at all. He doesn't even struggle. Little is left."

"One thing remains," I said. Lightheaded, leaning, I bent and poked my thumb in a soapstone lamp that hung from a spiked sconce in one of the bed pillars. With the oil I marked a cross on Erling's brow and on his breast.

"In the Name of the Father, and of the Son, and of the Holy Ghost, come out of him," I said. "You know who I mean."

Erling went into a gagging fit, and a great black beetle scuttled out of his mouth and tried to run away across his shoulder. I reached my hand out and grasped it before I knew what I'd done. It made high, screeching sounds and waved its many legs.

"Enough of you," I said. I held the thing over the lamp flame. It screamed high and loud enough to hurt my ears, and it bit at me, but I held it there until it was a taper of blue flame. The pain seared my nerves from fingertip to heart, but I heeded it not. In a few moments all that was left was a smudge of black on my fingers and a smell something like burnt hoof.

"He sleeps the healing sleep. It is well," said Erling's mother.

I sank onto my bench. "Halla," I said, "that man who met us as we came—do you think he could have been—"

"Man? I saw no man. You spoke as if answering someone, but there was no one there, and I couldn't understand your words."

"That's right," I said, wrapping my cloak about me and lying down. "I hadn't even marked it. Odd that he should speak Irish. . . ."

CHAPTER XI

We took it in turns to watch through the nights with Erling the first week, his mother and Halla and I. Sometimes he wrestled hell-things in his sleep, and then he'd wake, staring and sweating, and we'd have to hush him like a child ridden by the nightmare.

Once when this had happened, and he knew at last that the voice with comforting words was mine, he said, "Father Aillil—your father was killed."

"Aye, my lord."

"If someone had asked you to dig up your father's corpse, and look on his face, would you have done that?"

"Never."

"No. No man would, willingly. A rotting corpse is not your father. If an enemy had cut him up after he died, it would anger you, but you'd not feel his honor had been touched. Decay is the same, a foul desecration of a corpse, but no harm to him.

"I saw my father walk again though, Father. The eyes that watched when my first arrow hit its mark, the mouth that smiled when I wrestled my cousin Thorgeir to the ground and made him yield, the tongue that called me a fool and a woman when I was baptized—they were all there, in that hellish blue light. They mocked me. They shamed my father. They told me that everything I believe—and everything he believed—is a lie. They said that life itself is a lie, because it promises goodness and hope and love, and all that awaits is death and rot. They said that the real rulers of the world do not think and do not feel and care nothing for good or evil—they merely are. And someday even they will not be. They said that those who build high and those who dig deep are the same, because all will end in a level ruin."

"This was the wickedest of devils, my lord."

"Aye. But I did not let it defeat me."

"No, my lord."

"That's all you can do with a walker-again, you know. Not let it defeat you. You can't kill it. You can drive it from its corpse, but it will find another. Then someone must fight it again. The fight goes on all our lives. We shall not see the end of the battle before Judgment Day."

"We need not be fighting all the time," I said. "God gives His beloved sleep."

"You mistake me. I'm not weary—not in my soul. In my father's walker-again I saw that thing you priests call evil—a twisting, a decay of what was noble. I hate evil now. I hate it with a pure hate. I will be strong for the Lord, and I will plant His church here, and woe to any man who stands in my way!"

The Norse call the time between mid-August and mid-September "Corn-cutting Month." It brought the finest weather I'd seen in Jaeder (it only rained half the time). The haying was done; all the grass on the farm had been cut and ricked for the winter, along with heather from the hills. Now the free men and thralls worked together to cut the oats, rye and barley with their sickles. The air was dusty and sweet, the skies occasionally blue, and nobody expected me to join in the work. People said I had mastered the gods, and they bowed when I passed. My little church was full every Sunday. Even Ragna asked for baptism. Perhaps God was pleased with me after all.

Erling had dragged himself out of bed, over our protests, the second week. He had walked three steps and fallen, but each day he went a little further, and before two more weeks were done he was swinging a sword in the yard and wrestling short bouts with Eystein. He laughed and drank in the now-completed hall with his men as before, except that he was short with Soti, who took to eating in his own house.

Erling's new hall stood bright and handsome, carved and painted in red and gold, a landmark from anywhere in the neighborhood. He had replaced the old box-bed-in-the-corner sleeping arrangement for the master with a loft room above the entry room, reached by an outside stairway. When Halla was not standing in the steading, spindle at work, eyes on Erling, you could generally find her in the weaving house, working on a tapestry of David and Goliath for the wall.

There was a stranger who lived in my clothes, who heard confessions and said masses and preached little homilies and comforted the sick. He seemed a decent fellow, sincere and faithful and compassionate, though oddly unlifted by his success. But at night, when he closed up the church and went to his house to lie in the arms of his leman, he vanished quite, and a carnal Irishman named Aillil took his place. Only, when he lay in the darkness with her warm in his arms, he imagined she was Halla.

I'd best give my leman her name, since by now she was becoming a human to me, and not just "that woman." Her name was Steinbjorg. She came from a long line of thralls, she loved honey and being tickled, and she was terrified of thunder.

I'd done one thing for the sake of my conscience, lest I be an utter hypocrite. I changed the tonsure the Vikings had given me on the thrall-ship. I let the crown-hair grow out, and shaved my skull forward of a line across my head from ear to ear. This was the ancient Irish tonsure—the tonsure of Patrick and Columcille. It had been out of use for generations, and wearing it made me feel somehow less an imposter before God.

I was paring the tallow out of the candlesticks in the church one morning when Soti walked in. He stood by the doorway, arms folded.

"I've seen your holy place," he said. "It's only right you should see mine. Or would that frighten you?"

"Those that are with me are more than those that are with you," I said, setting the sticks aside and getting up. I followed him out.

"True enough, true enough," he said, as he led me down the lane. We walked in a light drizzle. We could not see the sea, although we could hear it. "It seems everyone wants to be a Christian now."

"I was speaking of the unseen world. One of our holy men said those words to his servant, then opened his eyes so he could see the armies of God camped around them."

"If your god has these great armies, then why did he let men kill him?"

"For the same reason a father would die for his children—to save them."

Soti shook his head. "No. It goes against decency. We must not think of the gods as our parents. It sets us too high. Your god humbled himself, let himself be shamed, and you glory in his shame. Do you not see that it eats all law? If the great are to be low, and the base are to be high, then someday thralls will bear swords, and lords will carry dung. This cannot be."

"Christ came to satisfy the law, and fulfill it."

"No. This thing of yours is the end of law. My gods uphold the law. When they are gone wolves will swallow the sun and moon, and winter will last a hundred years."

"Law is good," I said. "It keeps us from tearing each other to bits. But there is a better thing than law."

"Yes there is, but it's not a thing for men. Look there—there you see my holy place!"

It was outside the walls, at the west end of the hill, overlooking the sand above Sola Bay, a stone house with a turf roof.

Soti opened the door and led me inside. It was much like any other house in Jaeder, except that there was a sort of dais built at the far end, topped by a number of carved and painted wooden posts—three large ones at the center and a number of smaller ones grouped around them. The light from the hearth fire was poor, but that only made the images more threatening, full of imminence.

"Sticks of wood," I said. "When the swallows soil them they cannot clean themselves, and when the rats chew them they cannot shoo them off. Your gods are rotting, Soti."

"And does your god float in the air if you drop him during your magic meal?"

"The Eucharist is a mystery. You wouldn't understand."

"These images are mysteries also. Do you think I believe these posts are all there is to my gods? My gods are far greater than these posts! But in the images I meet them, and they speak to me. They speak truly."

"They speak half truly, perhaps. Enough to get men killed, and damned."

"If the gods wish a man dead, is that not their right? Does your god ask leave when he takes a life? You call your god trusty, but in your heart you know him ruthless and forsworn as my gods. Look—here is Odin—" he pointed to the tall post furthest to our left, a figure with a hole for one eye, and a long beard and a spear in one hand. "—Odin is the wisest of the gods. He knows all that happens in all the worlds, and he knows all that happened in the past, and all that will happen to the end. He works magic by unspeakable rites. He gives victory to his favorites, but he betrays them all in the end. I say it openly, for it is true. Are any people so wise as the Norse, who trust not even their gods?"

"You are to be pitied," said I. "Your chief god is a liar."

"Odin is not chief god. Oh, some will say so. Kings and jarls and hersirs and poets. They think they see one of their own in Odin. But the bonders know better. They know that when you choose a god, it's plain power you want. Have you ever seen plain power, god-man?"

I thought of my scrap with Lemming.

"Whatever you're thinking of, it's not even close. I have felt power. I was struck by Thor's hammer. He left his mark on me to carry to my grave. If they dig up my bones a thousand years hence they'll trace its black stain on my skull.

"Look on Thor!" He pointed to the image at the center, built wider than the other two, with a spiky red beard and great round eyes and a hammer in one hand.

"It was when he struck me down that I saw how little I was, and how great is the sky. I saw myself less than a gnat, less than a grain of dust that the breeze carries off. It was in kindness that Thor showed me this. I, who have felt his power, can never fear a man again—even you, god-man—and I know that when Thor takes time to notice you and your insults to him, he will crush you as a man crushes a louse between his fingernails, and with less concern.

"But even if you should somehow evade the hammer, you are not safe. Look on the last of the great three—his name is Frey."

Frey was the worst. In Odin's and Thor's images there had at least been some hint of majesty—the kind of glory you found in the ancient gods whom worthies like Virgil and Alexander had worshipped. But the round little eyes of Frey were the eyes of a swine, and he grinned an idiot grin on top of the long beard he stroked, and with the other hand he grasped an enormous phallus, fully the size of one of his legs. Most idiots I've known have been decent fellows, but if you can imagine an evil idiot, he would look like Frey.

"Any man who could worship that would be happy in Hell," I said, looking away.

"Yet I think if you are likely to bow to one of these three, it will be Frey," said Soti.

"You lie."

"And how is Steinbjorg these nights? I always found her most warming when the weather grew cold. There was a thing she used to do with her toes—"

I wanted to flee that place of abomination. Instead I said, "All right, how much?"

"How much for what?"

"For Steinbjorg. She serves you days but sleeps in my bed. It's unhandy for both of us. Name a price and I'll buy her."

Soti smiled. "No, I think not," he said. "You just go on enjoying her, god-man—or turn her out, it's all the same to me. I'll name my price when the time is right."

"You're trying to put a hook in my mouth."

"I have a hook in your mouth. You've taken it and run with it. I'll pull you in in my own time. Enjoy the bait, but remember who holds the line."

"Lines can be broken."

"By big, strong fish. Are you a strong fish, god-man?" Soti stepped nearer. "I know your secret wound, man of Ireland. I can't say who it was—someone close to you—a woman or a girl, I think. You wonder why there was a miracle for Lord Erling, and none for her. And you fear the answer your heart knows, that she was lost because she was nothing to your god. Like mine, he cares for the great ones, not for the little ones. They fall and he marks it not, for his eyes are on great dooms and high deeds. But he has said it is not so, and that makes him a liar, and you cannot bear that."

I said, "If I understood all I would be God, and I am not. He who would believe must endure to have a few questions unanswered." And I turned and left the shrine before he could reply, as if my answer had been a strong one.

Coming out into the pale light, I saw Soti's daughter Freydis racing towards me along the path. Whatever the smith's and his wife's sins, they must have been good parents, for their daughter was as smiling and sweet as she was fair. She wore a green frock this morning, and she beamed at me.

"Father Aillil!" she cried. "See the pretty stone I found!"

She held it out for inspection, and I pronounced it a pretty stone indeed.

"Is my papa in the shrine? I want to show him my stone."

I said, "Do you go to the shrine often?"

"Oh yes. Is papa there?"

"Do you like the shrine?"

She laughed at me. "It's just the shrine. It's where the gods live. You don't believe in the gods, do you? They'll kill you some day."

I sighed. "Yes, your papa is in the shrine," I said, and walked back to the steading. I spent an hour in prayer.

CHAPTER XII

Mid-September in Norway brings what they call Autumn-month. With it comes a Thing. Erling summoned Soti for manslaughter and arson by witchcraft.

"I care nothing for Soti," I said to Steinbjorg in bed one night, "but it seems a weak case to me. The laws against witchcraft in Norway can't be very strict. Of course I know nothing of heathen law."

Steinbjorg laughed. "That's not the point." Her arm lay across my chest and her hair tickled my face. The nights were colder now, and we lay curled in the box-bed, her warmth a comfort. "The law is in how you use it, like any other weapon. Lord Erling has friends and kinsmen, and he's hersir of the district. No one will deny his suit. Soti isn't even a Jaederer by birth—he comes from Halogaland. Some say he's part Lapp."

"Why doesn't he flee?"

"Soti has never fled anything."

I believed her.

I said, "I can't see Soti as a folded-hand martyr. He's planning something."

"Of course he's planning something. He's always

planning something. But you have the great god, so what is there to fear? Now pay attention to me. I don't want to think about Soti. I have something to tell you."

"What?"

"I'm going to have a baby."

I wept then, as if a baby myself. All I could say was, "If it's a girl, her name is Maeve."

Soon folk began to come in, by ship or boat or riding, and set up tents in the Thing-meadow, near Soti's shrine. Erling set up tables loaded with food for everyone twice a day. When I said mass I was surprised at the number of strangers who partook. I hadn't known there were so many Christians in Jaeder, if any Norseman could be truly called a Christian (saving my Lord Erling, of course).

On the other hand there were men, especially the older ones, who looked quickly away when I came near, and did something with their hands behind their backs. Often Soti could be found deep in talk with such men.

On the first morning of the Thing some men went to the meadow with hazel poles and set them in the earth in a large ring around several rows of benches near the shrine. To these they knotted a rope, called the "Peace Rope," and made a barrier within which the twelve judges took their seats.

After saying mass I followed Lord Erling, carrying the crucifix as I'd been instructed, from the church out to the Thing-stead.

Erling stood near the Peace Rope and cried, "In the Name of the Father, and the Son, and the Holy Spirit, I declare the Peace of the Thing. Any man who breaks this holy peace, let him be outlawed, turned away from God and good men; outcast as far as wolves run, or fire burns, or earth gives grain, or children call to mothers, or ships sail, or shields shine, or the sun rises, or snow falls, or Lapps skate, or fir trees grow, or hawks fly—"

A voice cried, "Unlawful! The Thing is unlawful and the Peace is unlawful! I appeal to the judges—is this the law of Sola-district?"

And there was Soti, dressed all in black, coming from the shrine, and in his hand he waved a great gold ring of twisted strands.

The oldest of the judges cried, "What business is this, smith?"

"Since the law first stood, the Thing has begun when the hersir sets the ring of Thor on his arm and proclaims the Thing-peace! Never has the peace been declared under the sign of the White Christ!"

The old man scratched his beard and said, "What say you, Lord Erling?"

"The gods of the lord are the gods of the land," said Erling. "One lord holds by Thor, and cries peace in his name. Another holds by Odin, another by Frey. I worship the White Christ. I've told no man whom his god should be. No man will force me to take up Thor's ring."

"So spoke King Haakon the Good, when the times for sacrifice came," said Soti. "He would not honor custom, for he'd picked up the Christ-worship in England. But the bonders and lords, who loved him, would not be satisfied, and in the end he sacrificed, and there were good harvests and good fishing all the years of his reign. And after him came the sons of Erik Bloodaxe, and they too called on the White Christ, but they would not be persuaded, and stiffened their necks, and all the time of their rule there was foul weather and bad harvests, and unpeace in the land. And I say to you that the same will follow here if Lord Erling calls not on Thor!"

"The true God rules earth and sky and sea, and gives or takes their bounty at his pleasure," said Erling. "You all know what has occurred here at Sola these last months. In all my dangers, I have had beside me the priest of the White Christ, Father Aillil" —here he pointed to me and my crucifix— "and neither man nor devil has overcome me. At the same time the priest of Thor here has given twisted counsels and caused much death and loss, of which I shall say more later."

"I am no priest," cried Soti, "only a poor smith, who must care for the holy fires since the proper ward, our hersir, will not do so. But even in my weakness, I dare risk the iron-ordeal. Does the Irish priest, who came here as a thrall, dare so much? I challenge him!"

Erling looked at me then, and everyone looked at me, and what could I say? I said, "I accept!"

The crowd broke into excited shouting, and I whispered to Erling, "What's this iron-ordeal?"

The abbot had often told me that rashness would be my downfall.

This is the iron-ordeal:

Everyone goes to the forge, where the smith takes an old iron kettle or whatever lies to hand, and heats it red-hot. Then he takes an axe and chops the iron into bits, which are dumped in another kettle (in our case, as we were having a sort of competition, there was a kettle with scraps for each of us). Then the one being judged washes his hand and plunges it into the kettle, takes up a handful of the scraps, and carries them twelve paces to a trough, where he must toss them in. A mitten is bound on the hand, and four days later the judges examine the burns and judge his truthfulness.

We stood there, Soti and me, side by side before the judges, arms outstretched, and waited for the word to start.

Erling said, "Wait! The smith has hands like a turtle's back from years with hammer and tongs. My priest has hands like a child's. This is not an equal test."

"We will bear that in mind when we view the burns," said the chief judge. "Prepare yourselves."

"I am ready," said Soti.

"Any time," said I (I should have stuck my tongue in the kettle).

"Proceed," he said.

I looked into the kettle, where the air swam like water, and thought, *No man can do this*, and then I was reaching down and taking up the iron.

There is no pain like burning. I wanted to watch Soti and hold the iron at least as long as he, though my fingers be singed away, but I couldn't see him. I couldn't think of him. There was room in the world for nothing but burning, blistering, biting, boiling, melting pain, and the need to walk my twelve steps as quickly as ever I could. The one thing I remember seeing in the crowd is a very fair, pale-haired woman with great, wide-set green eyes, a stranger. I don't know how long I held the iron. It can't have been long. I made it to the trough after a journey of a thousand miles and dropped my torment, and I was surprised to see that my hand still had its shape, though the skin was not whole. I heard the shouting of the crowd as if through three inches of wool, and there was a not unpleasant smell of roasted meat in the air. Someone grabbed my arm and jammed the mitten on, tying it tight.

I swayed, and Erling caught me. I whispered, "Get me away from here. I'm going to faint."

When I came to myself I lay in my bed, and my hand was singing to me, and an unfriendly song it was. I looked at the mitten. Its ties had been sealed with wax. Ragna sat on the edge of the bed, looking at me. Halla and Steinbjorg peered in over her shoulder.

"You're quite mad, you know," Ragna said.

"That is very clear to me just now," I answered. "Give me something to drink."

She put an arm around my shoulders and lifted a cup of something foul-smelling to my lips. "Get it past your nose and all will be well. You'll sleep a long time. And have no fear for your hand. God wouldn't let an honest man's burns mortify."

What a cruel thought to sleep on. . . .

I dreamed of the fair woman in the crowd. I can't have seen her more than a few seconds, but I remembered each pore of her skin, and where each lock of hair hung, framing her face and tumbling to her shoulders. I also dreamed of things I had not seen— breasts and thighs and long, shining length of leg, and I dreamed of doing with her everything a man can do with a woman, and everything beasts do with one another, and sometimes she enjoyed it, and sometimes she cried out in fear or pain, but I didn't care, because all I did only filled me with a starved-wolf hunger to do yet more and more to her.

Do you understand me when I say that that dream filled me with fear when I woke to find its memory in bed with me? Or that I laid penance on myself for it greater than ever I had for lying with Steinbjorg?

The wait for a decision on the iron-ordeal didn't delay the regular business of the Thing. There were cases to try, and fines to be decided, and taxes to be paid, and wares to be bought and sold, and wrestling matches and horse fights to watch and wager on.

I had a pastime of my own—sitting alone and staring at my mitten, imagining the foulness inside. The pain was such when I tried to flex my fingers that I wondered whether I'd lost their use for good.

I didn't stay in bed after the first night. The pain was just as bad in bed or out, except when I bumped the hand against things, which I seemed to do every minute or so. And gradually the pain got better, at least while I kept my fingers still, and I took more interest in the goings-on around me.

I couldn't help looking for the woman I'd seen. She would have been hard to miss, but I did miss her. Since she wasn't from the Sola neighborhood, she must have come with some party or other, which made it unlikely she'd just gone home. I even asked Lord Erling whom she was, but he said he'd never seen such a woman, and would have remembered if he had.

"Perhaps she has a jealous husband," he said, "and he's keeping her shut up in the tent."

I said, "She wore her hair loose."

"A protective father then. What concern is she to you?"

"Just curiosity."

"I don't like to criticize, Father Aillil, but I've noticed in you an interest in the women I hadn't looked for in a priest."

I sighed and said, "Well, I'm Irish after all."

The day came for the examination, and Soti and I stood before the Peace Rope, bare-handed at last, while the judges paraded past us and studied our hands. I sneaked a glance at Soti's, and it looked as if he'd handled nothing less gentle than a baby. My own looked like something the ravens would be interested in.

"Have either of you anything to say before we pass judgment?" the chief judge asked.

Soti said, "I am Thor's man. Anyone can see how he has guarded me from harm for his own honor."

I opened my mouth to say something, but heard Erling's voice break in.

He stepped up beside me and said, "It is customary for men to bring witnesses to attest to their truthfulness. I challenge Soti to bring forward any free man who will call him true. Father Aillil, though, has many to vouch for his word—look! Here are men of Sola to speak for him!"

And we looked about us, and there were something like two hundred men in a circle around the meadow, fully armed.

Soti cried, "Unjust! He tries to sway the court by force! Thor has force too, my neighbors—don't think he'll forget what you do today!"

Erling said, "My men have done no violence here, nor will they if good order is kept. As hersir, it falls to me to keep a guard. Carry on, judges, and don't even think about these men."

The judges mumbled among themselves, but it didn't take them long to judge in my favor. "It is doubtful," said the chief judge, "that any man could hold the iron as long as Soti did, unburned, except by black witchcraft."

Soti bellowed and threw himself upon me, but many hands pulled him off, and I was only a little bruised.

"Now," said Erling, "I wish to bring my suit against Soti for the deaths of my father and brother by witchcraft. I have witnesses to bring in this case."

And Erling told his tale, and many men vouched for his honesty, and Soti got his turn, and spoke bitterly.

"Well I see that I'll get no fair hearing today," he said. "Therefore I beg Lord Erling to accept self-judgment in this matter. I will pay whatever fine or penalty he lays on me, even up to outlawry."

"This is the penalty I demand," said Erling. "I wish Soti to be given into my hands for torture, until he shall receive the true Faith."

"THOR!" Soti shouted, face to the sky.

CHAPTER XIII

Torture wasn't a usual penalty among the Norse in those days. Erling told me he'd heard of it from Father Ethelbald. It hadn't appealed to him at first, but his mother favored it, and for Soti it seemed just the thing.

I said I could appreciate the thought, but what use would a forced conversion be? You can't twist a man's arm to believe.

Erling said, "I don't care a fishbone for Soti's soul. If he burns in Hell, so much the better. I just want him to stand before the people and deny Thor. We'll find our work much easier when that happens."

"Take care you don't kill him then."

"That's where you must help. You must be there to watch when we torment him, so we don't overstep."

I could think of ways I'd rather spend an evening.

The Thing broke up. We'd chained Soti in his forge, and kept men watching him, and each day after supper we'd forgo the drinking bout and go down to see to his education. One of the men of the bodyguard did the actual work. Erling didn't want to leave obvious marks, so we tried this and that and settled on applying the flat of a red-hot axeblade to the soles of his feet.

"You haven't the calluses there that you have on your hands," said Erling.

Soti said, "Thor is great."

I said, "Only God is great, and He waits with a father's love to welcome you into His family. This burning can become cool ease, and your thirst delightful freshness, if only you will accept the mercy He offers."

I'd often been disgusted with myself. Not until now had I been disgusted by my office.

Ulvig, Soti's wife, stopped me one night as I trudged back to my bed, weary as never in my life, my hand itching.

"Do you think you will break my husband?" she demanded.

I said I didn't know.

"My husband has defeated you already."

"How so?"

She smiled. "You'll see soon enough," and she was gone.

As the nights wore on, and Soti remained obstinate, Erling took to going to him later and later; sharing a few skoals with the lads before beginning his work. Before long he would not start before he was well drunk, and I thought it a good plan and followed his example.

My right hand will never be fair to look on again, but I'd not trade it for Soti's feet. There's no pleasure in sitting in red forgelight, seeing hot iron pressed to flesh until it smokes, smelling the burning, hearing a man's screams, and hardening your heart to pity.

At length people complained that the howls in the night troubled their sleep, and we moved the business to the daytime. This forced Erling to get drunk before supper, which had never been his habit.

I stayed in the forge one afternoon when Erling had stumbled out, and I crouched in the dirt near the stinking man and said, "For God's sake, be baptized and make an end of it! You can't bear this forever. Your heart will burst. I'm not sure I can take much more myself."

Soti croaked, "Give me water," and I dipped some from a bucket and held the dipper to his mouth.

"I am—almost—finished with my work," he said when he had drunk. He licked his cracked lips and smiled. "Soon I will have you where I want you."

"You're mad," I said, getting up. "You're a prisoner on the point of death. Be sensible. Freedom is there for the taking if you only will."

"Would you have so counseled—one of your holy men of old?"

That hit home. " 'Tis not the same thing," I said.

"No it isn't. Not nearly. Your holy men—so far as I can tell—suffered to be like your weak, tree-hung god. I suffer to defeat you!"

"How can you defeat us?" I asked. "You're powerless."

"I can make you—I am making you—what I am."

I went out into rain, suddenly sober and loaded with truth heavy as lead. There was a crash of thunder and blue lightning close by.

Erling and I were late waking the next morning, and I found him in the hall eating a solitary breakfast, in which I joined him. Ragna sat nearby on the bench.

"It has to end, my lord," I said to him. He looked at me with hollow eyes.

"It will end. When Soti receives baptism," said Ragna.

"No, my lady," said I. "This has been his plan from the first. He knew he couldn't defeat us in law. He accepted this ordeal as his service to Thor."

"Then let him die screaming."

"Then he wins most surely. He'll fling it in our faces as he dies. When you try to do Christ's work by force and cruelty, you deny all that Christ taught. You speak Christ's name, but it's Thor you serve, for it's Thor who rules by the strong arm."

"I am a hersir!" cried Erling, standing and turning his back to me. "Do your Christian lords at home spare their enemies when they have them in their hands?"

"Such matters are too great for me," I said. "But I know this. You cannot build Christ's church with the hammer of Thor. Soti is counting on that."

Erling turned to me and his eyes shone. "I have one more arrow in my quiver. It came to me before I slept last night. Wait for me at the forge, and see if I don't win this game."

I went, and sat on a block of wood, and stared at Soti.

"What's on today?" he asked. He looked like a devil, a thing from underground.

"Erling is coming. He has something new to try on you."

"Good," said Soti. "This foot burning was growing wearisome."

Erling came in. "I have a new tormenter for you, Soti," he said.

"Einar lost his stomach, did he?"

"All work is best done by men who love it. There is one man who dreams of torturing you. . . . Come in, Lemming."

The giant walked in, stooping through the door. Soti's face went white. We left the forge.

Then the screaming began. Everyone on the farm—the thralls digging peat, the fishermen tarring their boats, the bullyboys whacking each other with blunted swords for practice—all stopped and shuddered at the sound.

I've known despair. I've stood in the place where

hope is seen for fraud, and all that remains is death—
the sooner the better. So I recognized the screams
of Soti.

I went to the hall and found Erling slouched in
the high seat, an empty horn in his hand, calling for
more ale. His eyes were puffy; his mouth hung open;
he stared as if he didn't know me.

"It must end," I said.

"I struck Halla last night," he said. "Why would I
do that? I don't even remember how she angered me.
She looked at me like a hurt child. I've become . . .
some man I don't know."

"Let Soti go, my lord," I said. "Or kill him. But
while this wrong continues you are not lord of Sola.
You're not even lord of yourself. Thor rules here."

Erling groaned. "What does Christ want? If you
serve him weakly, He's angry. If you serve him too
strongly, He's angry again."

"It isn't easy, my lord. The right thing is never easy.
When you shoot with a bow, there's only one bull's-
eye, and six hundred hundreds of ways to miss."

"So I'm beaten this time."

"You've not often been beaten."

"Almost never."

"No man wins always. If you learn something,
you've made a profit. Be satisfied."

He smiled and pulled himself up. "I suppose it's
like this when you die," he said. "At the very end,
it's a relief."

Inside the forge we found Lemming standing over
Soti, a glowing poker in his hand. One of Soti's eyes
was out, and there were burn marks all over his naked
body, especially in the male parts.

"*Mercy!*" he screamed. "*Get him away from me!
I'll be baptized! I'll do anything!*" He twisted in his
chains and tried to draw his knees up. His grimed,
marred face ran with tear channels.

We stood and stared at him.

"Blessed be Jesus!" cried Soti. "Blessed be Jesus and his father, and his mother, and their ghost, and the holy bread, and that fellow in Romaborg, and that other fellow in Cantaraborg, and—"

Erling placed a hand on Lemming's shoulder, and the giant turned. I thought for a moment he would strike Erling, but he lowered his hands.

"Set him free," said Erling. "Let him serve Thor in peace. I never looked for this. I am shamed before God."

CHAPTER XIV

Soti was awhile in bed, but he came to me in the yard one bright October morning, halting and leaning on a stick, grinning and peering at me with one unbandaged eye.

"Good morning, god-man," he said.

"Good morning," said I.

"Have you heard the news? Erling offered me a mark of silver to move away from Sola."

"I heard. When do you go?"

"Oh, I wouldn't leave here. After all I've been through to serve my gods here, how could I? No, I'll stay close at hand, and be ever in your sight. You've made me—what is your word?—a martyr."

"You denied your gods."

"That's your story. I don't recall it that way at all. As I remember it, when the pain grew fiercest and I was all but on the point of death, Thor himself appeared in the smithy and commanded Erling to set me free, and Erling fell on his knees in fear and did as he bade. At least that's the story people tell in the countryside."

"You'd serve your gods with lies?"

"Why not? Do you actually believe the stories you tell? Virgin births, and rising from the dead, and walking on water?"

I tried to think of an answer that wouldn't be a lie.

"Come," he said, "I'm not a man who bears a grudge. We've scored off one another, back and return, since you came. Why be enemies? I'll make you an offer—we'll set up an image of your Christ in my shrine, and we'll worship all together. We've seen that we believe in the same things—why should we be fenced by the names we call the great powers? We'll join forces!"

"When pigs play pipes," I said, turning away. Whatever I thought of Christ, I knew He didn't belong in the same shrine with Frey.

"You couldn't have killed me, you know!" he shouted to my back. "I'll tell you a secret! I am not as other men! I have no heart in my body! If you put your ear to my chest you'd hear never a beat! I keep my heart in a locked casket, and the casket is in a secret cave, and the cave is in a magic mountain, high up in Lappland, and no man may come to it but by the death of his firstborn!"

Soti laughed then, and he laughed a long time. Ulvig came at last and led him home.

I went into the weaving house and watched Halla standing at the loom, working with the beater and colored yarn, building her tapestry of David and Goliath.

"Tell me of this David," she said. "Did he have a wife?"

"He had many wives, for he was a great king," I said.

"Did he have a leman?"

"Quite a few, truth to tell."

"The Jews must have been much like us."

"I suppose they were, in many ways."

"Did King David have one wife he loved best?"

"Well, there was one named Bathsheba—"

"That's a funny name."

"I fancy they'd have laughed at our names too."

"What about this Bath—this woman? Why did he love her more than the others? Did he pay a high bride-price for her? Was she more beautiful than any other woman? Did he have to fight her father and brothers to take her?"

"Ah, the price he paid was high indeed. And I have to think he must have loved her more than the others, because he chose her son to succeed him, though he wasn't the oldest. And if he loved her most, it must have been because they suffered most together.

"It was like this. The king stayed home while his armies went to war, and one night he stood in a high place and saw this Bathsheba, a warrior's wife, in her bath. He sent for her and lay with her. We aren't told what she thought about it. Then, when she told him she was with child, he tried to get her husband to come home and lie with her; and failing that he made shift to have him killed in battle. Then he wed the widow.

"The child was born, but the Lord slew it, although David wept for mercy. And the Lord laid a curse on David's house, so that there was rape and murder among the children. But another of Bathsheba's sons inherited."

Halla's hands were swift with the beater. "The Lord is very hard on those who sin, is He not?"

"I—I suppose. But then David was pretty hard on Bathsheba's husband."

"And this thing David did—this is what you priests call 'evil'?"

"One kind of evil, yes."

"Are there not stories of God closing a woman's womb because he was displeased? I think Father Ethelbald said something such."

"Well, yes, but it's not always because—"

"I think I'm barren, Father." Her hands did not pause.

"Have you talked to the older women about it?"

"Yes. They think I'm barren too. I've been with Erling two years. There have been times when I thought there was a baby, but it came to nothing. Is God angry at me because I'm with Erling and not his wife? Am I evil?"

Of all questions she could have asked, that was the one I was worst fitted to answer. I opened and shut my mouth a few times and tried to think.

"Why don't you speak? Is the answer so terrible?"

"I just don't know what to say," I said. "The Church teaches that men and women should be married or celibate, one or the other. But as it works out, we don't usually make much fuss if a man—especially a great man like Lord Erling—takes a leman. And here in Norway it's thought highly honorable. I haven't noticed that lemans are more often barren than other women—"

She stopped her work then, and covered her face with her hands. "He'll never marry me. Not if I can't give him sons."

I put a helpless hand on her shoulder, and she turned and wept against my chest.

"When are you going to marry Halla?" I asked Lord Erling a few minutes later. It was an impertinent question, but I felt impertinent. I had found him standing amid the stubble in the home-field, exercising his best falcon. He squinted as he stared into the blue, watching its trackless path, living in faith. A gaggle of bullyboys stood around to lend moral support. Everyone wore heavy cloaks, and the sun was no match for the breeze.

He answered in a voice that told me Halla was not foremost on his mind just then. "Marry her?" he asked, still staring upward. "When did I ever say I'd marry her?"

"Well, why don't you? What better wife could you find?"

"Excuse me a moment, Father. Whitefoot's stooping."

The bird fell like a hailstone and strangled a hare. All the men whooped and cheered, and we ran together, leaping a fence, to the kill. Erling retrieved the bird, and one of the men set to dressing the hare, making sure that Whitefoot got his share.

"Now what was this about Halla?" Erling asked as he hooded the bird.

"You ought to marry her. She wants to be married, and God would be pleased."

"Pardon me, Father, but did I promise to marry her? I don't recall that I did."

"I haven't heard of any promise."

"And have I treated her in any way shamefully, or failed to give her the respect due a lawful leman?"

"Of course not."

"And did she bid you come to me and ask for marriage?"

"No. She knows nothing of this."

"Then I fail to see why I should marry her."

"My God, she's the fairest woman in Norway! She loves you more than her life! What else do you want?"

"She's not the fairest woman in Norway," said Erling with a smile. "The fairest is Astrid Trygvesdatter, whom I saw once and can never forget. I fear she'll never have me though, since I slew her fish-wit cousin Aki. But even so, fairness has little to do with it. Walk with me, Father, and I'll tell you how I mean to marry." He strode away from the bullyboys, bearing the falcon on his arm as if it were no heavier than a poor man's lunch.

"The sons of Horda-Kari have been hersirs for generations," he said. "We take pride in the title. We like to say that a hersir out of Kari is worth any jarl and most kings. You've heard of Klypp who slew King Sigurd Sleva?"

"Oh, aye."

"It's a fine story. But I think the time for our kind of pride is over. Norway isn't what it was. Like it or not, we'll be one land under one king in the end, like the southern lands and Denmark. Then there'll be a long tug-of-war between the lords and the king. And we lords will have to gather all the power we can under his rule. That will be a time for jarls, and I fear no hersir will be left with enough turves to roof his house.

"I need to get the name of jarl, Father. The best way I can figure to do that is to make a high marriage. Maybe I'll never have Astrid Trygvesdatter, and maybe the woman I get will have a walleye and a humpback, but be a jarl I will, and I cannot look lower, even to comfort Halla.

"I know she dreams of marrying me, Father. I'm not blind. And it pains me to disappoint her. But it cannot be. More than her happiness, or mine, is at stake."

It was mightily sensible, and I hated the sound of it. I muttered, "I see," and shambled off.

"By the way, Father," Erling called after me. "When are you going to marry Steinbjorg?"

I wondered how much mansbot would be laid on a priest who strangled his lord.

I stomped around the steading and thought, and the more I thought the angrier I grew. Soti was sure he had a hook in my mouth. Erling judged me of little account, it seemed, and comical to boot. Halla looked to me for help, but I could do nothing for her.

I needed to put my hands to something, something I could break, or I might kill somebody. Then I thought of one thing I could do, a thing that would give me joy and remind people who was priest around here.

I got an axe from the toolshed and laid it on my shoulder, then ambled down the path to the shrine of the old gods.

Inside, it looked as I remembered it. I marched to the dais, laid the axe on it, spit on my hands and took the axe up again.

Frey first, I thought. I swung the axe back over my shoulder . . .

"Stop!"

I knew that voice. Where had I heard it? I turned around—

And there was the fair woman I'd seen at the Thing, of whom I'd dreamt shameful things. Have you ever seen a beauty that is almost deformity—the eyes too great and wide-set, the mouth too large and soft, the figure too lush? Almost a kind of jest? And yet desirable—a thing—"thing" seems the right word—to lust after?

She walked toward me, the sway of her hips rousing me in a moment, as if I were a stallion with the mares in heat. Did I smell something? I seem to remember that I did.

"There are pleasanter things to do, Aillil," she said.

Then I knew the voice.

It was the same voice I'd heard speaking from Big Melhaug—the voice of the dragon.

I fled, leaving the axe behind.

'Tis a fearful thing to meet the gods on their own ground.

CHAPTER XV

Winter in Norway starts in mid-October. In late October you can pick bearberries in Jaeder if it isn't raining. Rich men can go hunting if it isn't raining. Poor men thresh grain if it isn't raining. And the swallows fly south, proving that God gave more sense to them than to us.

It's a cold rain, the rain of Jaeder in October. It blows in from the sea with the ocean's lungs behind it, and it soaks through your cloak and your shirt, and works in around your ankles and down your collar, and drives an icy spike next to your heart, so you're a long time by the fire getting warm again.

"This country isn't fit for men," I said one evening in the hall. "It's fit for rats and gulls and toads, but not for Adam's sons."

"Well, it's no worse than Ireland," said Erling.

"Slander," I said. "Ireland is fair and green, with gentle breezes and warm sweet rains, and the children go barefoot even in February."

"Only because they're too poor to get shoes. I spent a year in Ireland, remember, and some of the lads thought it colder and wetter than Jaeder, and others said not, but we all agreed it was no better."

He had passed me the horn while he spoke, so I was swallowing when he finished and didn't get a chance to reply right off.

"Has anybody gotten a look at the Milky Way?" asked old Bergthor. "You can tell how the winter weather will be by studying the different parts of the Milky Way. I used to know how to do it when I was younger."

"You have to get a look at the Milky Way first," said I. "I'm not sure I'd know it if I tripped over it, it's been so long."

"God is good to us," said Erling. "He gives us winter that we may better enjoy the summer's warmth, and hunger that we may relish our food, and thirst that we may get drunk with a good heart."

"If you put it that way," said I, "that could be what the Lord meant when He said that the poor are blessed, although I doubt it."

That was when one of the men came in and said, "There's a balefire lit, my lord."

Erling sat up, aquiver like a hound. "One of the jarl's, or one of ours?"

"One of ours. To the north, at Randaberg."

"Then it must be Vikings. Sound the horns for a levy. Send runners to question the watchmen, so we'll know whether to expect company by land or sea." He called to the men, "Get some rest! It'll be an early morning, whether we march or sail. The wind's northerly, so if it's ship business we'll have to pull for it."

The men scrambled up and those who slept in the hall began rolling out their beds, while the thralls dismantled the tables.

I went to my own bed then, and it was still dark when Erling's shoeboy shook me awake. Erling stood in the doorway.

"We're sailing; you might as well come too," he said

to me. "You've been owley lately—I think you need the excitement."

Out into the black rain we went, down to the fjord where *Fishhawk* was being launched from her house. The moment I stepped up the gangplank I knew I'd be sick, and I was hard tempted to beg off; I wasn't much practical use after all. But pride prevented. I kept trying, without success, to find a place to stand where I wouldn't be in somebody's way. 'Tis a fine thing to be part of a well-drilled team, where every man knows his job. It's less fine to be a stumbling stone.

At last the weapons were stowed, and the lines secured and the first shift of rowers seated on their sea chests, and as the western mountains lightened the lead man started the rower's song, and we pulled away from Somme. I did not row. I puked.

Imagine a world made entirely of water—all of it black, all of it moving against you. The water in the air flies in your face and blinds you and soaks you; the water below you lifts your ship the height of its masthead and then slides suddenly from under, letting you drop. And this goes on over and over, through a pale morning that does not end. Is this Hell, O Lord? If so, I repent all my hard words and thoughts. Anyone who could create such a sweet thing as dry, solid land must be good beyond imagining, and if You'll only bring me back to it safe I'll never blaspheme again, I swear it.

My clothing weighed like the turf roof on the hall, and it was woven of ice. A man who has only a suit of ice to warm him is miserable indeed. And yet it might not have been so bad if only my stomach had kept still....

I sat in the stern near the steersman, and I had to tug my robe loose where it had frozen to the deck. I'd had the sense to wear boots, but the wind wormed in underneath and painted my shins blue. I got to my feet and stomped, blowing on my fingers. Our ship looked like an angel craft, rimed all over with ice. The wind had calmed somewhat overnight and fog walled us in; we sat quietly in the water, the men dipping their oars from time to time to keep us in place. I thought I'd be all right for the time being if I didn't eat anything.

"Ready for breakfast?" asked Erling, coming up behind me and slapping me on the shoulder.

"Today's a fast day," I said.

"Really? What's it in honor of?"

"I'll think of something."

"Well I'll explain where we are, since you're a stranger hereabouts. We're facing northeast as we sit. Aft is Tungeness. It's the northern tip of Jaeder, where the jarl's balefire is. East and south, though you can't see them for the fog, are the Boknafjord and Sokn and Bru islands, and between them runs Soknasund, where I chased the Orkneymen. Our watchmen tell me our visitors were headed in here, so they'll probably have overnighted somewhere in the Boknafjord, and if they're headed south along the seaway they'll tumble into our arms like a newborn into a midwife's. We'll see their sails before they see us."

"And until then we wait?"

"Until then we wait."

"They could have gone past in the night."

"Unlikely. It's bad enough sailing in the daytime this time of year."

"Is it indeed?"

Erling said, "The wind's picking up again. It's almost due north. That's good." Then he called to the steersman to keep us headed into it.

He settled his elbows on the rail. "It's odd about Soknasund," he said. "I keep coming back to it somehow. Like a dog who's always underfoot, no matter where you walk. I killed my first man there—an outlaw who'd raped a 15-year-old girl. We ran him down like a mad dog, but it was I who put the first spear in him. They made much of me for that, and a good thing too. You need a lot of assuring the day of your first kill."

I found no reply to that. My first kill had been during the sea fight rounding Jutland, and I'd never been troubled an eyeblink by it.

I said, "It's a kind of mercy to kill a man that sunk in evil."

"A hard mercy, Father. Life has too many hard mercies, I think."

He roused himself. "Well, come on! Somebody do something! This waiting makes a man heavy-hearted."

Someone shouted, "I see something!"

"What do you see?" yelled Erling.

"Two ships—coming our way!"

We all stared to starboard through the wall of mist. At first I saw nothing, but then there was the glint of silver or steel through a rent the wind tore in the fog, and soon we could make out a pair of sails— one striped in red, the other a solid yellow.

"They're coming to us," said Erling. "Hold steady, lads."

It seemed to take forever for the strangers to approach, close to the wind as they sailed. As they drew nearer we could see that these were warrior ships, nothing else, white with ice like us. They sailed heavily under men and steel. I went to the arms store and got me an axe, shield and helmet.

Erling was about to hail them when the call came from their side.

"Who are you?" came a ringing voice. "Where are you from and what do you want?"

Erling told the steersman to cut them off and shouted, "That's for me to ask," as our oars dipped and rose. "I am Erling Skjalgsson, hersir of Sola and north Jaeder. If you come in peace, you're welcome to guest at my home. If you come for a fight, we're ready for that too. Who are you?"

"No one for so great a man as you to fret over. I'd hoped to come and go unmarked, and no man the worse. My name is Ole, I am an honest Viking out of Russia and England, and I only wish to go home."

"And where is home?"

"The Vik."

"You're off course if you come from England."

"We sailed directly oversea, and made land at Moster inside Boml Island. Yesterday we got this far south and thought it best to overnight in the fjord. We put ashore on an island and had morning mass."

"Are you a Christian?" Erling called. "Have you a priest with you?"

"I have six priests from England. Are you a Christian?"

"I am that. I have a priest too. I know he'd be glad to meet yours."

Don't be so sure of that, thought I.

"Perhaps another time, Erling Skjalgsson. As it is, we're late in the season, and we must make sailing time. Let us part as friends, and I warrant we'll meet again."

"But surely you can take a meal with me!"

"Nothing would please me more, for I know your name and reputation. But today it cannot be. Will you be so good as to give us seaway?"

Erling ordered the men to row us out of Ole's course, and we sat and watched as the two long ships sailed by. They were a tough-looking crew, and well outfitted. I waved at the English priests, who looked sour when they saw my Irish tonsure. And we all stared at this man Ole, who wore a red shirt and a fur hat and cloak, and stood very tall and handsome.

"What is your farm?" cried Erling. "Who is your father?"

"I have no farm now," said Ole, and his blue eyes sparkled even at that distance. "My father is dead.

But I'll have my inheritance one day, and you'll hear from me."

We watched them disappear in mist, and somebody said, "That's a lot of priests for two ships."

CHAPTER XVI

A day came when the herds and flocks were brought in from the outpastures and Erling and his foreman looked over the cattle and the pigs. The foreman marked with tar the ears of those least worth feeding through the cold months, and the next day thralls took axes and knives and did the winter slaughtering.

It was my job to gather all the children, free and thrall, and lead them down to Somme, where the slaughtering was done another day, and keep them occupied. Halla came with me. For luck, it did not rain while we walked, and we got a dry place in a guest house.

We played games until I was tired, and then I told stories with good success, for of course Irish stories are better than Norse, and they were new to the children. I was getting well along when Halla, who had disappeared a moment, came inside dragging two screaming children by the ears.

One was a bullyboy's son, and the other was Soti's daughter, Freydis.

"Guess what I found these doing?" Halla cried.

"They were in the hay, with their clothes off, playing with each other."

"Take your hands off me or my papa will skin you alive!" shouted Freydis. She looked less pretty than usual, with a red face and stalks in her hair.

"No such talk," said I. "What will your father think when he learns what game you were playing?"

She shook herself loose and crossed her little arms. "He knows I play the game. He says I may do anything I like, because I am the gods' gift. You play the game with Steinbjorg, and you'd like to play it with Halla. That's what my papa says."

My face felt hot and I could not look at Halla, and all I could think of to do was to swat the boy.

"What's happening to the sun?" I asked Erling one evening in the hall.

"Don't tell me you never noticed winter nights are longer?" Erling replied.

"Within reason, yes. But as late as the dawn is coming now, there'll be no day at all left by Christmas."

"Be comforted. We never lose our day altogether. They do lose it farther north, up in Soti's country. The night lasts months on end up there."

"Christ have mercy," I sighed. "I've come to the gate of Hell. No wonder there are so many devils in Norway."

Erling said, "I've seen good men from Lappland, and wicked men from Arabia. And the other way around. Tell me, are North Irishmen wickeder than South Irishmen?"

"Ireland is a blessed land, hallowed by the bones of ten thousand saints," I said. "Devils fear to approach Ireland."

"Then we Norse are mighty indeed," said Erling, "for we fear not to attack where devils quail."

"Only a Norseman would be proud of out-deviling the devil," said I.

❖ ❖ ❖

I haven't said much about Erling's sisters. It's not that they weren't charming and lively lasses, darting in and out and chattering at the tables, but their lives turned on things that mattered little to me, and I rarely spoke with them except in confessions, and of course I couldn't tell you about those even if they'd been memorable.

The older one was called Thorliv, the younger Sigrid. They were both fair and tallish, as I've said, and almost like enough to be twins. Thorliv had a rounder, merrier face, though she was dreamy and quiet by nature. Sigrid had a longer, graver face, masking a devilish humor.

Sigrid came to me one day while I was shooing out some chickens that had got into the church through a door left open. She sat on the bench fidgeting, with the face of Cleopatra forced to wait for her dinner while the slaves cleaned up a spilled kettle.

"How long is this going to take?" she sighed.

"It'll be quicker if you help me," I said, waving my arms and trying to herd the squawking birds toward the door.

"No, I'll watch you."

"Very wise. Good for your education."

"Maybe it would help if you made noises like a dog."

I ignored her advice and finished the exorcism. "All right, darling, what's on your mind?" I asked, sitting down.

"First you have to promise me you'll never, never tell anyone we talked about this."

"I think I can do that."

"Do you think Erling will become a jarl?"

"I think he can be most anything he wants to be, and a jarldom is what he's after."

"How long do you think it'll take?"

"That's hard to say. From what I hear, there are big changes coming, and soon."

"Would you marry a man and woman without the blessing of the bride's family?"

"Never, unless she'd lost her family, like the thralls."

She scowled. "Even if they'd die if they were kept apart?"

I said, "What's this all about? Do you want to get married?"

She sighed. "You won't tell anyone?"

"Not a soul. Unless you run off with him. Then I promise I'll tell the world, and lead the hue and cry after you."

"I want to marry Halvard Thorfinsson."

I paused. "He's a good lad, one of the best in the bodyguard, but he's only a bonder's son."

"But he could marry a hersir's daughter! That's not impossible. What I'm afraid of is that Erling will become a jarl, and then I can never marry Halvard."

"Have you talked this over with your mother?"

"How could I talk to her about it? She'd promise me to a king's son if she could." She made a face as if that were a fearful fate.

"What about Erling? He might understand."

"Halvard says no. He says he wants to do great deeds and earn me."

"That's probably the wisest course."

"But what if he gets killed?"

"I think a girl like you isn't likely ever to choose a man who'd die in bed."

"No," she said. "I've thought about it. I think we should all do what the Gospel says, and turn the other cheek and love our enemies, and never fight a battle."

"If you really feel that way, perhaps you should be a nun."

"I'll become a nun if I can't marry Halvard."

"Well, you're not yet fifteen summers old. Perhaps you'll feel differently in time."

"That's what I'm afraid of!" she said. "I want to make my life before I get old and stupid, like the rest of you."

CHAPTER XVII

"Bless me, Father, for I have sinned," said the lad Enda.

"I know it, my son," I sighed. "Whatever possessed you to do such a thing?"

Enda knelt at my feet in the mud of the steading. His hands were tied behind his back, his face was tracked with tears and grime, and the wet snow fell on us. There are no trees in Jaeder high enough to hang a man on, but someone had fixed a beam to the peak of one of the storehouses, and we spoke in its shadow.

"It was a bonny knife, and the man has many knives. I only thought it would be pleasant to carve something with such a knife, and sell it maybe."

"You knew it was death for a slave to steal," I said.

"Father, don't you see—sometimes a man's got to reach for the thing he wants or he'll go mad. And if he can't—well then why not die and be done? What's the use of living this way?"

"I've pled for you with Lord Erling, but he says there's naught he can do."

"I expected nothing more, once they found the

knife in my bed," said Enda. "Please hear my confession, Father."

As he recited his little sins for me the crowd grew impatient and took to murmuring. Lord Erling told them to be quiet and gave us our time. Lemming stood nearby, a coil of rope over one shoulder. Hanging was thrall's work, but Erling had had the kindness to hire the big man rather than force one of Enda's friends to do it. If Lemming felt one way or another about the job, he showed no sign.

I shrove the lad and he said to me, "One last thing I ask, Father."

"Anything."

"Pull out the thong about my neck."

I fumbled at his collar and fished up a small wooden crucifix. It wasn't expert work, but it showed promise (dear God, what a word!). It was also unfinished, Christ's feet melding into the uncarved wood at its base.

" 'Twas the thing I was working on," said Enda. "I know it's incomplete, but I'd take it as a favor if you'd wear it when I'm gone. It would be . . . as if a part of me went on in the world."

Blinking back my tears I said I'd be honored to wear his cross. Then I patted his shoulder and turned away as they strung him up. I pushed through the men and women staring up at the last struggle, and took the path down to Sola Bay. The snow, melting as fast as it hit the ground, soaked through my shoes. Still, I thought, I'm not as cold as Enda. I wanted to cry, or punch somebody. I walked along the sandy shore and watched the gray waves, and let the gray sound of them wash over my soul.

"An unpleasant business," said a voice. I turned to see Lord Erling behind me.

" 'An unpleasant business,' " said I. "We'll raise a stone to the lad and carve on it, 'An unpleasant business.' "

"I take no pleasure in hanging thralls," said Erling. "There's no glory in it and it's expensive. But the law's the law. For God's sake, if he'd only been patient he could have earned his freedom. Why in the name of all the saints must thralls always act like thralls? If they're my brothers, as you say, then why don't they behave with honor?"

I rounded on him and yelled in his face. "Honor! Honor is something for a man with a home, with family, with friends! You act with honor because you've a place you must go where they'll drink to you if you're brave and shame you if you're a coward. But the thralls—you drag them from their homes and their land, you pen them up with strangers in a place where all despise them, and you expect them to act with honor? Where was Enda's father, where was his uncle, to teach him honor? How can a man have honor without a clan?"

Erling sighed. "I did not make the world. If God makes some men thralls, what can I do, except treat them with the best justice I can?"

"Justice! Would you hang a free man for stealing a knife?"

"I've never heard of a free man stealing anything. I suppose his own family would kill him, out of shame."

"What if it were a woman?" I asked. "Would you hang a thrall woman for stealing too?"

"No. We'd cut an ear off her."

"And if she did it again you'd take the other ear?"

"Of course. The third time we'd take her nose. After that, she can steal as much as she likes."

"Most amusing, your law," I said, and plopped down on a wet rock.

"I'm not making it up. Actually, the law for a foreign-born thrall who steals is flaying alive. I refuse to do that."

"You're too kind."

"Answer me this then, Father. What could I have done other than what I did? Give me your counsel."

"I don't care, my lord. This morning I don't give a herring's nose about your duties, or your honor, or what you can or cannot do. I heard the confession of a lad not yet twenty, and now he's rotting meat. Pardon me for being judgmental."

Erling reached a hand out and jerked me off the stone, pulling my face up close to his. I'd never felt his strength before. My feet dangled in air.

"You are my priest," he whispered, and his face had gone red. "I found you in a slave pen and set you free. I gave you a life and I gave you honor. You've no right to speak to me that way!"

"String me up then!" I screamed back. "You're so high and mighty and righteous, you've no need of a priest anyway!"

Erling tossed me backwards onto the sand, turned and went home. I sat on an icy rock and watched the sea.

And it was thus I caught the fever that kept me in bed until nearly Christmas.

CHAPTER XVIII

They call Christmas *Jul* in Norway, and it used to be celebrated in mid-January, but Haakon the Good, who failed in so much, at least got most of the Norse to change it to December 25 and the eleven days following.

The thralls ran about, cleaning and washing and airing beds, cooking, fetching and carrying, but they did it with a good will, because Jul was a good time for them as well as the free folk. Ragna rousted me from my bed Christmas Eve and set some of them sweeping my house out. "We'll have to get you a house thrall," she said. "That slut of yours is never here in the daytime, and you keep house like a bear. How long is it since you've had your clothes washed?"

"I don't want a thrall," I said.

"Well, you'll get one anyway. Set him free if you like and pay him wages, but you can't go on living like this."

"I haven't been well."

"You're fine now, and you need a thrall." She gusted out the door, then poked her head back in. "We will have mass tonight, won't we?"

"Yes, of course."

I wasn't keen for Christmas. I was still angry about Enda, whose crucifix now hung about my neck, and the thought of spending the festival among barbarians and far from home did not set my heart singing. It occurred to me, for no particular reason, that I didn't know when Easter would fall the next year. I wondered how I'd find out, and if I really cared.

I poked my head outside and saw Erling walking through the steading with his red-haired cousin Aslak Askelsson, who had come to guest with him for the feast. Aslak had brought news that Jarl Haakon was dead, and everyone was waiting to hear the story.

We got to hear it the next day, after I'd said the high mass and the toasts had been made and we'd all honored the Lord with drunkenness and gluttony. Erling said, "Aslak, tell us this tale of the fall of Jarl Haakon. I liked him when he was sober—did he make a good death?"

Aslak, seated in the guest seat and looking a little shy of the honor and attention paid him, coughed, and Halla brought him a horn of mead, which made him blush. He said, "Sad to say, he was unlucky in his dying. It happened this way—

"Haakon was feasting at Medalhus in Gaulardal, but he'd left his son Erlend with his ships at Viggja. The drink must have addled him, because he sent his thralls to Orm of Leira and demanded Orm send his wife Gudrun to him."

"Orm wouldn't take that well," said Erling.

"Indeed. He sent the war arrow out and soon the whole district was in arms. Especially the smaller bonders, because Haakon had often done the same to them, and they'd no protection. But Orm of Leira is another sort of man altogether. He blocked the roads so Haakon couldn't get back to his ships. Haakon sent his men away to fend as best they could, and to try to get word to Erlend to sail home to

Hladir, and he fled across the Gaular River to his leman, Thora of Rimul. He drove his horse into a hole in the ice and left his cloak close by so men would think he'd drowned. Then he went to Thora, and the thrall Kark was with him.

"Meanwhile, as Erlend sailed out of the fjord, he was met by a man named Olaf Trygvesson—"

"Olaf Trygvesson!" cried someone. "Is he in Norway?"

"Aye. He sailed from England this autumn, and met with his kinsmen at Opprostad, and then sailed north with five ships to kill Haakon. He must have uncanny timing-luck. He killed Erlend and took his ships without trouble, then came ashore to find that every man in the district was eager to join him.

"Well, naturally they looked for Haakon at Rimul. The dead horse in the river didn't fool them a bit—Haakon had left too many tracks. They marched up the valley and held a Thing at Rimul, and Olaf stood on a big rock and shouted that any man who killed Jarl Haakon would be richly rewarded. But nobody betrayed him, so they finally went to Hladir, which Olaf seized for his own.

"The next morning up came Kark, and in his hand he carried Jarl Haakon's head."

"I can't believe it," I said. "I knew Kark. He hadn't the kidney for that kind of work."

"It happened this way—" said Aslak, "—at least this is how Kark told it. Thora had had him, I mean Kark, dig a large hole in the pigsty at Rimul. Then they laid boards over it, and Haakon and Kark went underneath with a lamp, and Thora covered the boards with dirt and ran the pigs over them, and no one could tell their hiding place.

"But when Olaf had come to Rimul, the rock he had stood on to speak was hard by that pigsty. And Haakon and Kark had heard every word. And Haakon had whispered to Kark, 'You're not thinking of betraying me, are you?' and Kark had denied it, and Haakon said, 'We were born on the same day, and I think it likely we will die on the same day. Remember that.'

"And when Olaf left and evening fell, they slept, and towards morning Jarl Haakon cried out in his sleep. Kark tried to wake him but could not, and he was afraid because he didn't know whether some of Olaf's men might still be about, so he took his knife and cut the jarl's throat."

"A bad death for a great man," said old Bergthor.

"And what reward did Olaf give Kark?" I asked.

"The reward he deserved. He had his head cut off and set the two heads side by side on the gallows out at Nidarholm. Every man who goes by throws stones at them."

I got up to go outside, afraid of what I might say.

"Stay, Father," said Erling. "This needs talking of."

"I don't feel well," I said.

"Still. I want your counsel. This matter of Olaf Trygvesson is a tangled one."

"Jarl Haakon is dead. Olaf rules in the Trondelag now. What concern is it of yours?"

"Haakon was lord of most of Norway. Olaf wants no less, I'm sure. That's why he went to Hladir, not to his own inheritance in the Vik. If he's to be another Harald Finehair, every landed man in Norway will have to decide how he stands towards him. Aslak, what do Olmod and the cousins think of all this?"

Aslak said, "Olaf is kin to the Erikssons of Opprostad. There's little likelihood he'll come to us in peace."

"Yet Olaf was friendly enough when we met," said Erling.

"When you met?" asked Steinulf.

"Don't you remember the tall Viking from Russia with the two ships at Tunge? Who do you think that was?"

A murmur coursed through the hall. Everyone

wondered to think they had come so close to the great Olaf Trygvesson, and not a blow struck.

"Then he must have sailed south to Opprostad to get support from his kinsmen, then shot north to Haakon," said Steinulf.

"That's what I think," said Erling.

"Yet you made no move to stop him?"

"I didn't know it was he at the time. I thought it possible. Perhaps I failed in my troth to Haakon, but Olaf made no attack, and I don't care to molest fellow Christians and priests on mere doubt."

"And Haakon had about come to the end of his thread," I muttered. Erling stared at me.

"He looked a king from head to foot," said someone. "He wore an embroidered shirt of scarlet, and a rich fur cloak, and his arms were loaded with rings."

"He has the blood of Harald Finehair—I should have known it," said old Bergthor. "So many of them have that height, and those bright eyes."

"Are you saying that because you parted from Olaf in peace we might make terms with him?" asked Aslak.

"I think there might be hope," said Erling. "Or are you fitting out a fleet to go against him?"

"No point in it. He's sticking to the land this winter—taking the road to the Vik to rally his kin there. We'll be boxed between the Tronds in the north and the Vikers in the east, not to mention the Erikssons, before we get our chance at him."

Then they began the game of "What If?" which means so much in war and state, and my mind wandered. I thought of Kark, and I thought of Erling, and it seemed to me there was little to choose between them.

Then Steinbjorg came in and whispered in my ear, "Gunnlaug is come to her time. She's calling for you. She says she knows something's wrong, and the child must be christened."

❖ ❖ ❖

We went to the house where the woman Gunnlaug lay, with other women about her. No man was there but me; even her husband, one of the bullyboys, feasted in the hall. We heard her cries before we got there, above the patter of the rain, and I could smell her sweat when I got inside.

Someone told her the priest was come, and she cried for my prayers between her screams. Yet today I can see her face, drawn to the skull with pain, the hair pasted to it like seaweed on a rock, her mouth stretched to bare the gums as she cried again and again, and it never seemed to end. I prayed my prayers and prayed them over, and the women made her walk about the room to loosen the child's grip, and still it went on. I looked at Steinbjorg, kneeling at her head or holding her arm, and thought that she would suffer so as well, a few months hence. I wondered how it was for the blessed Virgin, nearly a thousand Christmases before. Could it have been easy to bring the Son of God into the world? Must not her body and all of nature have protested the invasion, shrinking in wonder and fear from the fullness of time?

But this child was nothing like Mary's, when at last she came forth. She was red and shriveled and slimy of course, like all babies, but this one cried strange, bubbly cries, and her mouth was wrong. The women tried to hide her from Gunnlaug, but she croaked, "I know it's ill-formed. Let me see it. I want to hold it." So they wrapped her in a cloth and gave her to her, and she held her and cooed to her, weeping. Then she said, "Father, you must christen my child now."

I said, "I think she'll live. She can be christened in the church."

Gunnlaug looked at me, and her eyes were miles deep, with all the misery of Eve's curse in them. "She will not live, Father. You must christen her now."

There was water there, so I christened her Maria, as her mother wished. I had barely finished when the door burst open and Gunnlaug's husband came in, followed by Soti, a halting and fearful shadow.

"Let me see the child," said the father.

Wordlessly the mother gave her up to one of the women, who passed her to him.

He looked at the face and cursed. Then he turned and carried the child out.

"Where's he going?" I asked.

Soti answered. He stood before the door. "He goes to expose it on a hillside. That is our way with the deformed ones. It keeps the race strong."

"This is an abomination!" I shouted. "Lord Erling will hear of it!"

"It's the law," said Soti, smiling. "A strong law for a strong land, and strong gods."

"It's murder!"

"By no means. That thing is no human. It cannot walk. It cannot talk. It cannot even feed itself. It's a beast like other beasts, and if it's not worth its feed we put it down. It's the decision of the father, or of the owner if the mother's a thrall."

"Get out of my way, Soti."

Soti stepped aside, still smiling.

I'd not known how much of the night had passed in Gunnlaug's labor. When I got to the hall everyone was dozy with drink, and Erling nodded in his high seat.

"Gunnlaug's child is born," I said, shaking him. "She has a harelip. The father took her out to expose her. You've got to send men to stop him."

Erling stared at me with fuddled, sad eyes. "I'm sorry," he said, "but I can do nothing. It's the law here. Soon, perhaps, we can change it, but—"

"Sod you," I whispered. "Sod you and your law and your land."

I rushed out into the rain and wandered paths

through the night, listening for a cry, tripping over stones and stone fences, getting mired in icy bogs. I never found the baby.

At last I followed the smell of smoke back to the steading in the dark, a long stumble that left my feet slashed and my shins bloody. In my house Steinbjorg waited. She rushed to strip me of my wet things and said, "Where have you been? Have you gone mad? You could have sunk in a mire, or been taken by wolves, like that poor baby. What's gotten into you?"

I shuddered like a horse's flank. Steinbjorg bustled me into bed and wrapped herself around me, and blankets around both of us. Through chattering teeth I said, "Don't you see? Don't you see what Soti meant?"

"What are you talking about?"

"You're his thrall. When our child is born, he'll find some flaw in it. He'll expose it, unless I do his will."

I stood in bright sunshine in a patch of meadow somewhere in the Sola neighborhood, although I don't know how I knew that, since nothing I saw looked familiar. The ground wasn't very promising: boggy and full of rocks.

I heard a noise behind me and turned, and for a terrifying moment I thought it was the black giant with the axe, but then I saw that it was only the abbot. He held in his hand an iron-shod wooden spade, such as the thralls use to break up the fields in spring. As usual he looked at me as at something a maggot had vomited up.

"This is your patch," he said.

"My patch?"

"Your patch, lumpkin. 'Tis here you must work and raise a crop, to earn your freedom."

"I'm free already!"

"You? As far as I can see, your useless head remains on your shoulders. Or don't you remember, you would not pay the price to enter the land?"

"There's little point in paying such a price," I said. "What good is freedom, or entering the land, or catching the white hind, if I lose my head?"

"A head like yours would be little enough loss, but be that as it may you've made your choice, so nothing remains but to work your patch. Sow the seed, cultivate it, harvest it, and we'll give you credit for the value of the crop." He extended the spade to me.

I said, "Do you mean I may enter the land after all, and pursue the white hind, if I do this?"

"If you buy your freedom. But be warned that freedom is not cheap or easy, and, as you yourself have observed, yours is a pretty poor patch."

"You just watch how fast I can buy myself!" I cried, seizing the spade, and I turned from him and set to work with a will. I manhandled the rocks out, and dug ditches to drain the boggy places, and spaded and planted. Faster than I could ever have imagined the shoots began to sprout.

I watched the shoots with love and fascination. They were not like any plants I'd ever seen. They were pink instead of green, and as they matured I saw that they were not plants at all, but small, perfect children.

Looking on them, I loved them. I felt tender care for each precious, precarious little soul. "How will I harvest them? How will I sell them?" I wondered. "How can I endure to part with the least of them?"

And then I heard a flapping sound behind my head, and spinning round I saw, against the sun, great black wings. Ravens were raining from the sky, coming to snap up my precious babies. They were large as a man, these ravens, with red eyes and golden beaks sharper than shears, and there were hundreds of them. I flailed my arms and swung my spade, trying to drive them away. They came on as if I didn't exist, and began to grasp my little ones in their beaks, and they pulled them out of the earth, threw their heads back and gulped them down. It was done faster than it takes to tell. All my sweet innocents were slaughtered, and the ravens, with one contemptuous look back at me, took to the sky again, blocking the sun out with their shadows, leaving me alone on the desolate ground.

"*GOD!*" I screamed.

CHAPTER XIX

My fever came back of course, and I missed most of Jul. By little I grew aware of a presence in my house, and when I came to myself I saw an old man sitting on the step of my bed, staring at me. He had thick black eyebrows and a sloped forehead below his cropped white hair, and there was no valley between his forehead and his nose. I recognized him as a thrall named Caedwy, a Briton.

"What are you doing here?" I asked, hoarse.

In reply he stood up, pulled down the skin under his right eye so that I could see the crescent of red flesh beneath, and scratched his crotch with vigor.

"You're mad," I said, turning to the wall. My muscles ached.

"No use to deny it, I can tell one of the Brotherhood when I smell him," I heard him say. "How could you do the deeds you've done without you were one of us? Eh?"

I said, "I don't know what you're talking about."

"The men with the long ears. Long, long ears, like rabbits. They hear everything that's said in all the worlds, and if only we'd feed our horses on wool, they'd live to be a hundred. Iron makes a bonny pillow. When they burned men in wicker cages you could hear the screams fifty miles, and the gods were pleased. The great god shone in those days, and it didn't rain all the time like now."

Dear Lord, I thought. *They've given me a Druid for a thrall, and mad to boot.*

Ragna granted, when she came in to check on me, that the old man was daft, but she said he was too bent for field work and ought to do something for his feed. As we spoke he sat by my fire, picking lice out of a blanket and saying a prayer for each as he flicked it into the flame and heard it pop. I asked why I couldn't have a Christian, and she said it would breed jealousy; the priest's servant would put on airs. "Anyway, you should convert him. That's your job."

When Erling looked in I pulled the blankets over my head and pretended to sleep.

"I'd not have sold you," he said.

At first I couldn't think what he was talking of.

"In Visby," he went on. "At the time I was serious, but when I'd thought it out I knew I'd never sell a Christian priest back to the heathen. If you'd refused I'd have taken you somewhere where there was a church."

I'd known that for some time, but I wouldn't give him the satisfaction of saying so.

Halla came the next day. "Erling is hurt that you won't speak to him," she said, sitting on the edge of the bed with an easiness that troubled me.

"Good," said I.

"You've been like the wrath of God ever since they hanged that thrall."

I held the crucifix up where she could see it. "He made this," I said. "His name was Enda. He was about your age. He was young and rash, and he tried to better himself by stealing from his enemies. If he were Norse they'd call him a Viking and skoal him in the hall."

"So what would you? Should Erling make a law that thralls may steal?"

"He needn't hang them."

"Most men say he's too kind. They wanted the boy whipped to death."

"I'm sure Enda was most grateful as he strangled."

"Are the laws so much gentler in Ireland?"

I rubbed my eyes. "It's the whole way of things, the waste of lives, using people like cattle. Keeping them down because you know that if they get a fair chance they'll have plenty of their own to get back from you. Look at what happened to that bastard Kark."

"He murdered Haakon. You're not condoning murder, surely?"

"Olaf had sworn an oath. He saw no need to keep it to a thrall."

"The oath wasn't meant for Kark. And it wasn't meant for as craven a deed as Kark did. Kark knew that. He betrayed his lord, who'd given him gifts. Even a free man would be despised for that."

"And is Erling different? He let Haakon's enemy sail out of his hands, just because he thought Haakon was doomed and Olaf might make a better friend."

Halla stood up, her face pale. "Do you believe such a thing of Erling?"

"I don't know what I believe of anyone in this country. I thought Erling worthy of my trust. Now I wonder."

"You think like a thrall," she said, and went out.

"Perhaps I do, perhaps I do," I muttered.

Erling came to see me again soon after. He stood for a while a few feet from my bed while I ignored him.

"You're free to go," he said.

"What do you mean?" I asked, surprised into speech.

"When the spring comes and sailing's good, you're free to take the first passing ship bound for Ireland. You've repaid your price and more since you've been here. I'd thought you'd like to stay and see the thing through, but perhaps it's best you go home. If that's what you want."

Don't be generous!, I screamed inside. *I don't want your generosity!*

Aloud I said, "I want to see my child born."

Erling went out.

And finally came Steinbjorg, a shape in the darkness, a warmth and weight against me in bed. I could feel our baby kicking at my ribs.

"I think it was wonderful, the way you tried to save the child," she whispered, putting her arms around my neck.

It was good to be praised. I kissed her cheek.

"And afterward, when you said you were frightened for our child," she said, "that made me very happy."

I muttered something.

"And I thought, 'If he loves the baby, perhaps he loves the mother, too. . . .'"

I said nothing. We lay unspeaking, with no sound but the wind and the muffled surf. I could have lied to her. I'm not sure why I didn't.

"What did Lord Erling say when you told him of the danger?" she asked finally.

"The danger?"

"To our child. Soti's threat."

"I didn't tell him."

"Why not?"

"Is he the father of the child? Is he God? Do I have to run to my master with my every fear and beg him for protection? Can't I guard my own flesh?"

Steinbjorg turned away from me. "You talk just like the thralls."

CHAPTER XX

The next day I rose a couple hours before the morning meal. Steinbjorg had gone, the peat fire burned low, and Caedwy lay on the bench curled up in a blanket, arms wrapped around a cur dog he'd adopted when he came to me. He slept by himself, and needed the animal for warmth. The dog twisted its neck and stared at me as I pulled on breeches and socks under my robe and tied my shoes on.

Caedwy's head turned too, and I could dimly see their four eyes reflecting. "Feeling better, master?"

"Yes. I'm going out."

"Cold morning."

"I'd noticed." I went to my chest, fished out the key I kept on a cord around my neck, and unlocked it.

"Anything you want?"

"No. You needn't get up." I took out a hefty sealskin pouch. Inside was the silver I'd gotten as my share of the Vikings' plunder that day off the point of Jutland, plus the price Erling had paid me for Lemming. I hadn't had a use for it until now.

"I've heard you talking of that boy Enda," said Caedwy.

"What of him?"

"A good boy, that. 'Twas a shame."

"Yes."

"I can see why you're cross. We of the Brotherhood, we who've seen the great mysteries, we know that such laws as hanged poor Enda, they're nothing. We've seen the true law, and men like Lord Erling are blind to it, and will always be."

"For the last time," said I, "I am not of your Brotherhood, and I know nothing of your mysteries, nor wish to."

"That's how I know you're a Master, master. In these times a true Master would never reveal it but to another, and I, the gods help me, have never attained mastery."

I went out saying, "Go back to sleep."

There was an old turf house on Sola, half fallen in from rot, and there Lemming lived by himself. I left tracks in virgin snow as I walked there, and I couldn't see the house at first for the fog. The air was as still as inside a chest.

I stood outside the door and knocked. I feared he might anger at being wakened, but he answered right away and bade me come in.

He had a fire going, and by its glow I saw him sitting on a pile of skins. He didn't look like a man just wakened. He might have been sitting there all night, power at rest, staring into his fire.

I drew the pouch from my bosom and tossed it down in front of him, making a clatter. "I want to hire you," I said.

He stared at the pouch as if he'd never seen one before, then raised his eyes to me without speaking. One scarred eyebrow rose, and I took it for a question.

"You'd probably do it for nothing," I said. "This is a job you'll enjoy. But I want you to do it for my need, not yours."

He said one word: "Soti."

"I helped stop you killing him once. I repent it now. I thought I was saving my soul, but I sell it today anyway. I've no wish to hang, nor to see you hang. It must look like an accident."

Lemming gazed at me as an animal would. It unnerved me. His look might have meant anything, or no more thought than a skull's.

" 'Tis a pity Jaeder has no cliffs," I said. "Cliffs are wonderful for accidents. They're often deserted, one push and he's over, and who's to say he didn't slip?"

The look did not change.

"I don't know why you hate him so," said I. "I'm sure you've good reason. My reason is that he's threatened my unborn child. I wish I could kill him myself, but I don't think I'm a match for him, even crippled. I'm sure God—my God, that is—understands that. But whatever guilt there is, I take on myself. By paying you I take the guilt. At least that's how I see it—"

I saw I was babbling and stopped my mouth. Why justify myself to this heathen beast? We stared at each other across the fire for a moment.

Then Lemming grinned at me, showing broken teeth.

I went back to my house and found that Caedwy had rearranged my few bits of furniture. My chest, my stool, even the pile of peat turves near the hearth, had all been aligned parallel to each other and at a shallow angle to the walls and benches. A small enough thing, but I didn't like it. I went out to find him and ran him down in the church, where he was doing the same thing to the chest and the altar furnishings, all the time droning some song about an ash grove.

"What are you doing?" I cried.

Caedwy looked at me with Christmas eyes. "The perfect conjunction!" he cried. "East and west, the path of God. We do all in humility, that we may right ourselves with the ways of the heavens. When the stars were sheep, their beards fed the fish. These northerners know not the true path of God, but I can always tell, even in the dark, even in a fog, even a hundred miles under the earth. Why don't men have breasts?"

"Put everything back the way you found it," I said. "Do it now."

"Of course!" said Caedwy. "I see! How wise you are, master!"

Erling greeted me when I went to the morning meal, my first in the hall since Jul, but I answered coolly. He left me to myself then, and spoke to others.

A singular thing happened before we were finished. A strange man rushed into the hall with a spear in his hand and cast it through the body of one of the men at the table across the hearthway. Everyone was up in a moment, and I vaulted our table, leaped over the fire and pushed through the bodies to the stricken man, whose friends had already laid him out on their table. At the same time several of the bullyboys seized the intruder and began knocking him about. I couldn't recall whether I'd seen the wounded man in church or not, and I was asking him if he was a Christian and wanted last rites, but the noise was too great for me to hear his answer. Erling's shout finally brought quiet.

"Silence!" he roared. "Stop hitting that bastard—hold him until we know more. Father Aillil—how is he?"

"Nearly gone," said I. I spoke to the man. "Are you a Christian, lad?"

"No," he said. "I go with Thor. But I need to know—why?"

Erling needed to know the same thing. His face was bright red. He had the attacker brought before the high seat.

"My name is Arnor Baardsson," said the man. "I come from Thornheim farm near Randaberg."

"Randaberg is Kar's home," said Erling, referring to the man bleeding under my hands. "What's your quarrel with him?"

"I was trying to say, my lord, before these men stopped my mouth, that I have slain Kar Thorsteinsson lawfully in daylight, and before witnesses, in vengeance for the death of my brother Bjorgulf."

Kar whispered, "I know nothing of Bjorgulf's death."

"He says he knows nothing of it, my lord," I said to Erling.

"What say you, Arnor?" Erling asked.

"Within the last week feud has broken out between Thornheim and Randaberg," Arnor answered. "It began with the killing of my cousin Asmund. Since then two more men are dead of my family, and now three of theirs that I know of. I've been a day traveling."

"Kar had no part in any crimes against you."

"He's the greatest warrior of his family. It was more honorable to kill him than some weakling."

"Did you think that it might make you a powerful enemy, to kill one of my bodyguard before my eyes in my own hall?"

"I know you for an honorable lord, Erling Skjalgsson. You will not have a man slain out of hand for a lawful killing."

"Don't chop law with me," Erling almost whispered. "You've killed a man of mine in my own hall, without giving him any chance to defend himself. I can take you out and have you hanged, and never pay a ounce of mansbot."

"My lord, may I speak?" asked Halvard Thorfinsson, who sat on our bench down near the women's end. When I heard his voice I couldn't help glancing at Sigrid, who watched her love with great eyes.

"What has this to do with you, Halvard?" asked Erling.

"Arnor is kin to me. I too knew nothing of this feud, but I beg you to accept self-judgment, and ask you to name what price you'll take for the offense."

"It's unwise for young warriors to make pleas for the enemies of their lords."

"Arnor's no enemy of yours, Lord Erling, unless you'll have it so. His fight is with the Randabergers. He has acted rashly, but it was a bold deed nonetheless. There will be blood enough shed before this business is over with. You can leave the killing to us."

Erling's face had gone back to its wonted color. "The mansbot for killing a lord is thirty-six *aurar*," he said. "I'll have no less for this offense to me."

"Our kin will pay it."

"I do not like these feuds in my lands, Halvard. They waste men and wealth."

"A man must have vengeance for his kin," said Arnor.

Kar died then. There was blood everywhere.

I looked at Sigrid again. Her eyes shone like blue stars.

They let Arnor go his way, and carried Kar out. I hadn't finished my breakfast, but had no stomach left.

I was just walking out into the steading under a leaden sky when I heard the cry of "Fire!"

Everyone looked for the smoke, and we saw it coming from the direction of the smithy.

I was one of the first there, and only had time to glance at the man who knelt over a charred body outside the door before we were all scooping snow up in our hands and throwing it inside. The smithy had stone walls, and the beams inside were already aflame, so there was little we could do. Men started bringing up buckets of water from the well, but the fire only died when the turf roof fell in and smothered everything.

Then we turned to see Lemming kneeling by Soti's black body, heaping snow on him to cool his burns. The smith's big chest rose and fell, but he did not move otherwise.

"He must have caught a spark from the forge in his clothes," said someone. "Did you pull him out, Lemming?"

Lemming nodded.

"Will he live?"

Lemming shook his head.

"Soti always kept water nearby to douse himself," somebody said.

"Perhaps he couldn't move fast enough on his bad feet," said the first. "Anyway, he caught fire."

"Strange Lemming would try to save him," said someone else. "He hates Soti."

Lemming widened his eyes.

"When you see a man burning," I put in, "you just act. You don't think whether he's your enemy or not." Lemming turned his eyes on me, and I walked away.

Caedwy awaited me at my house. " 'Tis good, 'tis good!" he cried. "A wicker cage would be better, but we do what we can. You're all black with soot and blood, master, like the men who lived on the moon when the stones fell up. I'll bring water to wash you with."

CHAPTER XXI

They bore Soti to his house in a blanket to die, and his burial was the following day. I watched from a distance. That night when I came in from the hall I found Caedwy sitting beneath the lamp in my house, staring into a small basket he held on his knees.

"Tell him to stop it," said Steinbjorg from the bed. "He makes my skin prickle."

"What are you doing?" I asked.

"Telling our fortunes, master."

"What's that mess in the basket?"

"The guts of a pig. I got them from the kitchen."

"You're divining from pig guts?"

"A horse's or a man's would be better, or a black cat's best of all, but we make do." He blinked his large brown eyes up at me.

I sat down on the bench, weary and not a little drunk. "And what do your guts tell you?" I asked.

"You will live long and see great things," said Caedwy.

"I'd prefer to live long and see little things. Great things have a way of coming out bloody and bitter."

"You'll be offered your heart's desire. But you'll cast it away."

"That sounds like me. And what of you?"

"You'll set me free."

"Not if you keep up this soothsaying. It's devil's work, and puts both our souls in danger. Get rid of those guts. I want to go to bed."

"He said I'd die," said Steinbjorg.

I reached over and grabbed the man by his shirt and shook him. "What did you tell her?"

"I didn't say she'd die. I said I see darkness before her and darkness within her."

"If I ever catch you playing this Hell's game again, I'll twist your head off. Do you understand me?"

Caedwy threw the mess to his dog, who attacked it with relish.

"He tells the truth," said a voice at the door. I jerked my head up in fright. My door usually squeaked loudly on its leather hinges when opened. How Ulvig got through it in silence I'll never know.

"What do you want?" I asked.

For a reply she walked to me and slapped me across the face. I leaped up, raised my hand, then stood poised.

"If I were a man, you'd strike me," she said.

"So?"

"You think you're safe now that you've killed my Soti. Think you I don't see your hand behind it? But you've missed the mark by a long span. You'll find that of the two of us, Soti was the gentle one."

She left, leaving the door open to the bitter wind. Caedwy and his cur huddled in a corner, whimpering, and the guttering light made the room sway like the sea.

Ragna came to me one day and said, "You must go and speak to Halla."

"What's wrong?"

ERLING'S WORD 159

"She's gone mad. I've tried to talk to her, and so have all the women, and she's raving. It must be a devil."

I put on my cloak and followed her to the hall. As I started up the stairs to the loft, I looked back to see Ragna still standing below.

"Aren't you coming along?" I asked.

She shook her head. "The old gods speak through madness. It's not right I should see their faces. I'm too lately out of their worship."

"She's a fair woman and I'm a priest. It's not right we should be alone in a sleeping chamber."

"Just go to her before she does herself harm. We've taken all the steel from the loft, but the mad can always find ways."

"Call your daughters or a serving woman then."

"They won't come near."

A scream from above decided me. I clattered up to the balcony and in to Halla.

Loft rooms are always smoky, but my first thought as I entered was that the place had caught fire. I couldn't see anything, and my nose and mouth clogged with something that stopped my breath. I staggered out the door and found I was covered in down. Halla had slaughtered a cushion. When I went back in I found her laughing at me in a swirl of drifting feathers.

"It's snowing inside!" she cried. "It's Fimbul Winter, the end of the world!" She wore an everyday overdress and shift, and they were disarranged, besides which she was covered from head to foot in feathers.

"What's the matter with you, lass?" I asked.

"What's the matter with you, Father Aillil?" She shook her long hair in a spray around her head.

"Ah well, we haven't time enough for that, and you're the one making a fuss."

"I'll be good," she said. She sat down on a chest and folded her hands on her knees. She blew a feather off her nose and giggled. "I always do what's expected of me, and I never, never, never make a fuss. When my father says 'You'll go with Lord Erling and be his leman,' I go. When Erling takes a wife, I'll welcome her and not make a squeak, or go home to my father if he sends me. I'm a good girl. Aren't I a good girl, Father?"

"You're a rare girl, my daughter, but I fear you're making a fuss nevertheless."

She looked around at the settling feathers. "It's my cushion. I sewed it with my own hands. Why shouldn't I set it free? I want to see it fly away!" She ran to the door, opened it, and stood trying to shoo the feathers out into the breeze.

I got up and closed the door to keep her off the balcony, and she sighed. "They won't go," she said. "They like it here. They love me, and now they can't understand why I tried to send them away. I'll gather them up and sew them a new cushion if that's what they want. I didn't know. I thought they might like a change."

"Did something happen to trouble you?" I asked.

She knelt at my feet and took my hands. "Do you think me fair, Father?" she asked.

There was a bench behind me and I sat on it, still holding her hands. "I think you're as fair as a summer morning with the sun rising over Lough Erne. The grass is dewy and fat, so a man could live on it, and the flowers open their mouths and praise God with a song of sweet odor, and the birds raise a hymn they learned from Solomon two thousands of years since, and have passed on in secret to their children ever after. And far across the water you can see swans swimming, and the sunrise tints them pink, and the breeze is so mild and gentle it's like the hand of your mother on your forehead when you're a child, and sick, and she fears to lose you." Unfit words for a priest, but they came out of me like the feathers from her cushion, as easy lost and as hopeless to recall, once the fabric was torn.

She pulled away from me. "How am I like a lough?" she asked, shaking her head. "Am I flat as water? Do I make waves when I move? How am I like grass? Am I green?" She began to struggle out of her overdress, then lifted her shift saying, "Where am I green? Tell me where I'm green!" I covered my eyes, sweating with the hunger to look on her.

"Why do you stop your eyes?" Halla asked. "Am I so ugly—flat like the water, green like the grass? Perhaps I have legs like those swans. Perhaps I am a swan. If I could fly away, I'd know better what to do than a lot of stupid feathers—"

I had to open my eyes then, for I could hear her footsteps toward the door, and I feared she might run out on the balcony and leap. I caught her as she worked the latch, and held her naked in my arms. Her skin was very smooth, her bones very small.

"Put your clothes back on, Halla," I said.

"Why?" Her eyes were wide and innocent.

"Because your clothes love you, and it hurts them that you cast them off."

"I wouldn't want to hurt them. I wouldn't want to cast anyone off." I let her go and she got her shift and slipped it on again, unashamed as a child. I couldn't take my eyes off her. Then she put on her overdress and sat on the chest. I sat across from her.

"You look at me with angry eyes, Father," she said.

"I'm not angry, daughter. I just wonder what brought you to this."

"You mustn't wonder about things. When you wonder about things you think about the future, and when you think about the future it makes you sad, but you can't help anything. I'm never going to wonder about anything again."

"The future shouldn't make you sad. God holds you in His hands."

"There's much road to walk between today and Heaven. It's what I'll meet on the road that frightens me. I wish I could fly to Heaven this moment. If I ran out and jumped from the balcony, maybe—"

"You'd probably only break some bones. And if you died you'd be a suicide, and God wouldn't have you."

"I don't think God's fair."

"You're not the first nor the last He'll hear that from."

"You have something on your face."

"What?"

She laughed. "You have something on your face. It looks funny."

"Where?" I rubbed my nose and cheeks.

"Not there."

"Where then?"

She got up and came toward me. She leaned down near my face and peered closely. "Right there," she said, and kissed me quickly on the lips.

I couldn't move. She put her hands on my shoulders and kissed me again. "If I lay with you," she said, "and I had a child, we'd never know if it was yours or Erling's. Wouldn't that be funny?"

I stood up and pulled away. "Don't say such things."

"Don't you like me?"

"I'm a priest!"

"You lie with Steinbjorg."

"Steinbjorg isn't Erling's woman."

She plumped down on the floor. "Yes, it should be Erling's child. I want it to be Erling's child. That's why I went to Ulvig. I'm getting sleepy, Father."

I gaped at her. "You went to Ulvig?"

"I know it's wrong. To go to a witch. But I want to have Erling's child, and she can give you drinks to open the womb."

"Is that what she gave you? A drink to open your womb?"

"Yes."

"And when did you take it?"

"This morning. Before breakfast." Her head was nodding now.

"Don't go to sleep," I said.

"I can't—I can't keep my eyes open."

I took her in my arms and half carried her outside and down the steps to find Ragna. "Ulvig gave her a potion for barrenness," I said. "God knows what was in it. Get your daughters and some of the women and we'll keep her walking in the snow until it wears off."

And that's what we did through the rest of the day, and long into the night. She was sweaty and pale, and she shivered and screamed, but I loved walking her about when my turn came, and I could not forget the sight of her body in the loft, or the curve of her back under my hands.

CHAPTER XXII

Erling was furious with Ulvig and threatened to bring suit at the next Thing, but she told him to wait and see what harm had been done; and, God help us, in time it became plain that Halla was with child. I thought no good could come of such a conception, but the lass was happy; and what could I have done anyway? I made Erling promise to let me christen it in its birth hour though.

"Why did she do it?" he asked me in private.

"I'm not free to answer that," I said.

"Then just tell me if I'm wrong. Does she think I'll marry her if she has my child?"

I said nothing.

"I see. I never knew she took it so much to heart. I must think on this."

The rains came and washed away the snow, and then it snowed again, and then the rains returned. We had thunderstorms in February, which is a pleasureless thing. I took a wild guess on when Lent should begin, and proclaimed the fast.

In mid-March the thralls began carrying manure out of the byres in baskets on their backs to spread on the fields with seaweed. And in April the cranes and wild geese came back, and the heathens made sacrifices in secret places, and the thralls put on wooden clogs and began spading late in April (or early in Cuckoo Month, by the Norse reckoning), and then I had my hands full setting up the freedom plan. Those thralls who had no crafts got plots of land to work, and there was a lot of grumbling and comparing, and I had to knock a few heads together before everybody was happy.

A ship sailed in one day from Hordaland with a summons from Olmod and the Horder lords for Erling to meet them and discuss Olaf Trygvesson. He sailed off in *Fishhawk*, leaving a strong guard (strengthened by conscripted bonders) under Eystein, and plenty of watchmen along the coast. Along with Erling went Halvard Thorfinsson, to be dropped off near his home and join the feud. No one saw Sigrid weep, but she went about with reddened eyes. I said a special mass before they left, but Erling and I did not bid each other goodbye.

The following day one of the thralls came to me and said, "I can't work that plot you set me on."

"What's wrong with it?"

"Nothing wrong with the land. The land's fine. But a man can't go out in the countryside these evenings. The troll'll get him."

"Troll? What troll?"

"Haven't you heard? He's been seen by many after dark. Sometimes skulking around Ulvig's house; sometimes out in the fields or the hills. I can't go out and work that land in the evenings with him around. What use is freedom when you're eaten by a troll? And if it's not the troll, it's the underground-woman."

My ears pricked up. "You've seen an elf-woman?"

"You mustn't use that word. They don't like it. I haven't seen her myself, no. But she's been seen. And there's nothing more dangerous than an underground-woman. I'd rather face a troll than an underground-woman."

"What does she look like?"

"What do you expect? She's beautiful. She's—how do you say—ripe. A man looks at her and hears her voice, and he forgets who he is. The next thing he knows it's forty years later, and he thinks it's been but a night, and he's shaking all over and his hair's white."

I said, "I'll tell you what. You get some sticks and carve yourself a crucifix. Then come to me and I'll bless it, and that should protect you from trolls and . . . undergrounders."

"Will it really, Father?"

"Without a doubt."

It was worth a try. I went to the hall for supper mulling over the fact that someone else had seen my elf-woman. This was good from the standpoint that I might not be mad; it was bad from the standpoint that she might really be around, and would have to be dealt with. I had no illusions regarding my strength in spirit. I believed in God again, but I did not love Him, and if He'd done things through me it was only for want of a proper tool.

And there was a part of me that thought, "It might be worth forty years and white hair to put hands on that creature."

I crossed myself and said the Pater Noster.

The mood in the hall was cheerless, as most of the bodyguard would have liked to have gone with Erling, and the bonders wanted to be home for planting. This was worsened by the knowledge that there would be red meat to eat in Hordaland and most of their homes, while we made do with fish because of Lent. Lent was my fault, and some of them let me know it.

"The trouble with your god, god-man," said Bergthor, "is that he acts like any other king. He comes along and does something that he says is for you, and you're expected to thank him for it and pay him back for it, even though you never asked for it in the first place. I'd just as soon face the Devil myself, man to man, and make a fight of it without any meddling from priests or kings."

"It would be no fair fight," said I. "The powers that oppose us are not so great as God, but you and I are less than fleas in their sight."

"Well, size and strength aren't everything," Bergthor replied. "A man can kill a bear or an aurochs because he's smarter than they."

"Devils are also smarter than we."

"I don't believe it."

"It's true," said another man further down the bench. "I know a thing that happened—it happened to a man I knew—well, I didn't actually know him, but my cousin knew him. He lived up on Kormt Island, and was a fisherman."

"Not a fishing story!" said Bergthor.

"It proves how much shrewder the spirits are than we. This fisherman went out in his boat one day and set his lines, and when he tried to pull one line up, he felt a heavy weight at the end. He thought he'd caught a fine big fish, but when he pulled it up, what did he see but a man's face! He pulled further, and saw he'd caught a merman. Of course he knew that a merman can tell you anything you want to know, so he caught him fast and bound him with the fishing line. 'Now, tell me how I can be sure I'll always make good catches,' he told the merman, but the merman wouldn't answer. So he rowed home as fast as he could and carried the creature, struggling, on shore.

"As he climbed up from the strand his young wife came down from the house to greet him, and she said, 'What have you caught, husband?' and he said, 'I've caught a merman, and I'll force him to tell me how to make good catches, and we'll be wealthy folk,' and his wife kissed him and made much of him. The farmer liked this, and when his dog came up and began jumping about them he kicked the beast so it ran away howling.

"And the merman laughed.

"As they made their way to their house, the husband carrying the merman, he had trouble watching his step because his prisoner struggled so, and he tripped over a tussock of earth and almost lost his grip.

"'Curse you, you stupid tussock!' he cried. 'I don't know why a thing like you was put there to trip up honest men!'

"And the merman laughed.

"When the fisherman got home, he set the merman in a corner of his house and told him, 'There you'll sit, my good fellow, and neither food nor drink will you get until you answer me every question I wish to ask you.' But the merman said nothing.

"A little later the fisherman's thrall came in, and the fisherman told him he needed him to make him a new pair of boots. 'And do it right this time,' he said. 'The last pair you made had soles much too thin. I don't want these wearing out in a season, like the last pair.'

"And the merman laughed.

"The merman said not a word for a full week. At the end of that time, he said to the fisherman, 'Row me out to the spot where you caught me, set me free, and I'll squat on your oarblade and tell you all you wish to know.'

"The fisherman knew the merman would not lie, so he carried him down to the boat and rowed out to the very spot where he'd caught him, and cut the cords that bound him. The merman leaped out onto the oarblade and squatted there, saying, 'Ask now.'

"The farmer said, 'How can I be always sure to catch all the fish I want?'

"The merman said, 'Use a three-barbed hook, forged from new iron and tempered in blood. Bait one barb with fish, one with pork, and the third with human flesh. Use a fishing line made of a man's gut, and you will always catch all you can row off with.'

"'Good. Now explain to me. Why did you laugh when I kissed my wife and kicked my dog?'

"'Because you're a fool. Your dog loves you, and would die for you, while your wife hates you and has a lover, and wishes you were dead.'

"'And why did you laugh when I cursed the tussock?'

"'Because you're a fool. There's a Viking treasure buried under that tussock, and it's destined for you. You cursed your own fortune.'

"'And why did you laugh when I told my thrall I wanted thick soles on my boots?'

"'Because you're a fool. Those boots will last you the rest of your life.' And with that the merman leaped off the oar and down into the sea, and was seen no more.

"Well, the farmer rowed home as fast as he could, and ran and got a spade, and he dug up that tussock, and there was a heavy chest buried there, just as the merman had said. He carried it home, and his wife said, 'What's this, husband?' and the fisherman said, 'This is our fortune, my dear,' and they broke it open and it was filled with gold and silver. And the fisherman was so happy he forgot all the rest the merman had told him, and he and his wife drank and were merry till early morning.

"And when he had passed out drunk, his wife stole away to her lover's house and she said, 'The old man has found a treasure, and no one knows it but I and you. Let's kill him now, and flee with the money.'

"They crept up to the house, and as they came near the fisherman's dog began to bark, and the lover killed him with his axe. And at the sound of the barking the fisherman awoke, but was too drunk to get out of bed, and the last thing he ever saw was his wife's lover coming towards him with his bloody axe.

"And they buried him in his new boots.

"So you see, it's no use thinking we're smarter than the devils. They always laugh last."

"That's an uncheery story," said Bergthor.

As we sat thinking about it, Ulvig came down the hearthway.

"You are all prisoners," she said. She said it to all of us but her eye was on me.

"What rot is this?" demanded Eystein.

"The kinsmen of Soti have come for revenge. There are more than a hundred of them, and those not stronger than he are greater magicians than he. We have the wardens, we have the balefires, we have the thralls, we have the children, we have the armory."

"Codswallop," said Eystein. "No hundred men could come on Sola unseen."

"Soti's kinsmen can. They can cross new snow without leaving a mark. They can steal upon a rabbit in broad daylight and seize it with their hands. When you think you see them, it's only the shadow of a cloud, or a wolf prowling. When you see them not, then they are surely there."

"Why do you come to us like this," I asked, "instead of just firing the hall?"

"We want only one man's death—yours, god-man. But your death is not enough. You will sacrifice to the old gods first."

"Never," said I.

"We have Steinbjorg. We can cut her child from her belly and offer it."

I reeled. Eystein said to me, "Don't listen to her. We'll fight our way out and kill these heathen."

"Not before the woman and child die," said Ulvig.

"I'll sacrifice," I said.

"It's not worth it—not for a thrall!" said Eystein.

"Before God she's my wife, and the child is my flesh!" I said.

"Let's be clear," said Ulvig. "Let's see that all is understood. Your holy ones who died in Romaborg, they let their wives and children be tortured and killed rather than sacrifice to other gods, did they not?"

"Aye," said I.

"But you will sacrifice to save your woman and child?"

"I will."

"And your god will surely send you to Hel for it?"

"Without a doubt."

She beamed at me. "Good. Very, very good. All you men, and you women too, leave the weapons behind and follow us."

She led the way out into the night. *Enough, God. You've asked of me all I can give. There is an end to endurance.* I said to Ulvig, "Do I have your sworn word you'll spare Steinbjorg and the child, and kill none but me?"

"Unless they threaten us, all may live."

I knew she'd keep her word. I'd have done this for Maeve, given the chance. At least I could do it for Steinbjorg and the babe. Then to Hell with me. What did I matter anyway?

The men who ringed the hall bore torches, and some of them were tall and broad, like Soti, dressed all in furs, and others were small and dark, with odd tasseled caps and shoes whose toes curled up. The big ones carried spears and shields, and the small ones had bows and arrows.

Ulvig led the way, never looking back, sure of her power. We took a path I knew well. It led to the Melhaugs.

We had a full moon for it. We could make out Big

and Little Melhaug far off—just humps of earth, grown with heather. The same good earth that feeds us, and will cover us someday, only this earth was not good. Drums were beating, a rhythm like the thumping of a coward's heart.

As we drew near, someone lit a fire near the bigger mound, and I saw what looked like a huge, long-legged insect rise up in its light. I had a brief terror that I'd be fed to this thing like a fly to a spider; then I saw that it was a platform, twenty feet high, and the small men from the north were raising it on six poles and lashing its supports tight. And they had built an altar of stones nearby.

They ranged us, men and women, in a wide circle about the mound and the platform, and Soti's kin stood armed behind us. Ulvig took a place near the fire, and this is what she said:

"This night belongs to Frey, and to Freya his sister. On this night the gods say to us, 'Men, be as we are.' The laws were made by the gods for men to obey, and it is good that we should submit to them; but the laws do not apply to the gods. The gods are in the earth, and the earth is cruel, miring men in bogs, breaking them in rockslides, bringing forth poisonous plants. The gods are in the air, and the air is cruel, bearing sicknesses, sending hails and snows and lightnings. The gods are in the water, and the water is cruel, withholding its fish when men starve, and drowning them far from home. The gods may lie, as Tyr lied to Fenris. The gods may murder in secret, as indeed they do each day. The gods may couple, parent with child and brother with sister, as Frey and Freya do.

"The gods will be with us tonight. What does it mean when the gods are with us?"

Soti's kin cried out together, "ALL IS PERMITTED!"

I shuddered. Bergthor, beside me, said, "I'd heard of it, but I'd never seen it. This wasn't our custom here, even under Skjalg. In the old days yes, but it'd gone out of use before my father was born."

"What are you talking about?"

"The great summer sacrifice."

The little men from the north piped on pipes in time with the drums, and Ulvig began a dance around the fire, slowly at first, then faster and faster. She wore a heavy black robe with fur trim I'd never seen on her before, and soon her face glowed with sweat and her eyes glowed with joy. There was a kettle cooking over the fire, and one of the little men brought her a dipper of whatever was in it, and when she'd had it she cast off her headcloth and let her long red hair fly free, and it spun out a rain that looked like blood in the firelight.

And then a man came from somewhere, and I'd have sworn it was Soti if Soti weren't dead, but I couldn't see his face as he wore a woolen mask, and on his head was a ridiculous bronze helmet with horns, and he too wore black, and they danced together in the moonlight, and the dance was shameful.

And the little men piped and drummed, and they sang a song in a strange tongue, and danced in place with small steps.

And one of them brought the dipper to me, and I saw and smelled that it was some kind of meat stew, and I thought of Erling's martyred priest as I drank it.

Then Ulvig staggered to the platform, and she began to climb, unsteady as if drunk. When she had gone up a few feet, she stopped and cried, "I see all the Northland! Everywhere the gods walk unseen, and they mark who keep the sacrifices, and who have set them aside for the White Christ. And they send pestilence and bad seasons and unpeace to their enemies!"

She climbed a little further and cried, "I see all the world! The gods are everywhere—called by other names, but remembered, and honored, and fed. I say to you, men of Jaeder, the great world is not Christian as you think! Our gods are mighty, and they remember their friends!"

And she climbed yet again, and came at last to the top, and she stood on the swaying platform and spread her arms in the moonlight and shouted, "I see the heavens and the nine worlds! I see Asgard, where faithful warriors go when they die, and there they battle by day, and at night their wounds are healed, and they feast on pork and drink sweet mead, and listen to brave songs, and lie with the fairest virgins! But the followers of the White Christ go down to Hel, and there the trencher is called Hunger and the knife Famine, and they lie down at night on a bed called Sickness."

And the little men piped and drummed, and sang their song, and there was a company of folk dancing in the firelight, men and women.

Ulvig cried, "Bring now the god's gifts!" And there were brought a ram, and a boar, and a hound, and a stallion, and last of all Freydis Sotisdatter, wrapped in a white bearskin and carried on a pallet, seeming half asleep. They laid the child on the altar.

And the beasts began to roar and bay and rear and kick, so that those who led them had to hold tight to the ropes. And then I saw what had panicked them, for dancing with the dancers was my elf-woman.

"As was done with me, and with my mother, so it will be with my daughter!" cried Ulvig. "She is twelve summers old, and she will be made one with Freya by coupling with a thrall, and a ram, and a boar, and a hound, and a stallion, and so she will be mother and wife to all things in the earth! Then the thrall, and the ram, and the boar, and the hound, and the stallion will be sacrificed! Bring the thrall!"

Then came the elf-woman, smooth as water, to take my hand and lead me forward.

And as she came to me, soft and silken and rosy and filling my nostrils with a scent like flowers and rain and moldy wheat, I thought, *What could be more right? The horse is happy because he's a horse, and does not try to be an angel, and he runs and he eats and rolls in the grass and he fornicates with any mare who'll have him. He is not good or evil—he's just a horse. But a man chokes his head with a thousand puzzles of right and wrong, and for all his trouble he never feels right. Except for these heathens—they're happy, like beasts. They don't wage war on the world they live in. Why have I wasted all these years wrestling myself? I could be happy right now, this moment . . .*

And God help me, I went willingly. I'd forgotten right and wrong like a tale heard years since, and a dull one. I think not one man of Erling's knew shame at that moment, or would have done otherwise.

I've never been so ready. I was ready as any beast who smells the female in heat. The hand of the elf-woman felt hot on my arm. I almost ran to the altar where Freydis lay, fumbling to pull my robe up. My own sacrifice meant nothing to me if only I could plant my sacred seed.

And then Halla was before me, and I swear I didn't recognize her at first as she screamed in my face, "NO! THIS IS EVIL!" and struck me.

And I blinked, and suddenly I knew her, and I remembered who I was, and I looked at Freydis and saw a little girl with tears on her cheeks. And I shouted, "NO!"

The elf-woman clutched at Halla, and Halla slapped her face. The elf-woman swung her arm, and Halla flew ten feet backward, landing against a man of the bodyguard and bowling him over.

Then the music faltered, and everyone looked up, and we saw the platform sway, and under was Lemming, lifting one of its legs, every sinew straining, and we watched in silence as the whole structure toppled, and Ulvig fell with it, screaming, to land in a heap that did not move.

And I turned and tore an axe from the hand of one of Soti's kinsmen, too stunned to resist me, and I brained him with it. And Lemming killed another with his bare hands, and then Erling's men came to their senses and followed our lead. Then there was bloody work, and many dead on both sides, but the heart was out of our enemies, and we slew every last one we found. If any of the little men got away we could not know.

But before it was over I found Halla lying in the grass, and I held her in my arms and asked her if she was all right, and she wept and said, "Father, I think I'm losing the baby."

I sat crouched in the furrows of my patch, weeping over my lost children. As my sobs died, stifled in mere exhaustion, I looked up and saw the abbot there again, leaning on his stick.

"Gone are they, all your pretties?" he asked. "You've found the work harder than you expected? Your strong arm and your clever brain aren't quite up to the work?"

"No man could save my crop," I sobbed. "The ravens are too many, and too strong; and the crop so precious... I can't bear to plant another."

"Are you ready to pay the toll then?"

"My head? What good would that do, you bloodthirsty bastard?"

"And is it thus you speak to your betters who mean naught but your welfare?" His face twisted in anger and he raised his stick to strike me. I awaited the blow unmoving; I was past caring. The moment hung suspended like a water drop at an icicle's tip, but the smiting never came. At last I looked up to see him standing above me, stick hanging from his hand, face turned to the sky. He seemed to listen to words I could not hear. At last he shook his head, crossed himself, and lowered his gaze to me.

"Very well then," he said. "My advice to you, and it is the advice of a man both old and wise, is to dig."

"Wait a moment," said I. "What's happened now? Who spoke to you? Did they tell you not to beat me?"

"You ask too many questions."

" 'Twas Himself, wasn't it? He took my side! He took my side and you've not the guts to tell me!" It was as if a small, pale light had been struck in my heart. Much as I'd pitied myself through the years, and deeply as I'd felt my grievances, I'd never before been able to believe that God might truly side with me even once.

"What of it?" the abbot cried. "A blind hog finds an acorn now and again, and even such as you can't be wrong all the time. It doesn't change the fact that I'm your superior, and your digging remains to be done!"

He was right of course. A just God would not punish me more than I deserved, but my deserving was plenty enough. "Dig, you say?" I asked.

"Dig. Take your spade and dig. There is a treasure hidden in the field. Dig and find."

I stood and picked up the spade. "Where shall I dig?" I asked.

"Where you stand will do as well as anywhere."

I set my foot to the spade, dug it in and levered up a bladeful of stony earth, then another. "How deep do I dig?" I asked.

"As deep as necessary."

I dug and dug, until I had dug myself down waist-deep. "I'm not finding anything," I complained.

"Then I suppose you must not have dug far enough."

I dug and dug until my head was below ground, and yet I found nothing. I asked no more questions, but kept digging. With each spadeful I had farther to pitch the dirt over my head and out of the hole;

often the clods and stones came back down on me. But I dug on. My hands grew blistered, my arms and legs cramped and aching, but on I dug.

I looked up at last, forced by weariness to rest myself. The sky was a small blue eye looking back at me, the abbot's head its pupil.

"Find anything?" he asked.

"Nothing," I panted.

"Then carry on."

Stifling a curse I stamped the spade once more into the earth, put all my weight on it, and with a sudden shudder and uprush of air the ground beneath me gave way, and I fell for the time it takes to pray three Pater Nosters (and believe me, I prayed them) before I came down with a splash into water.

I plunged deep and came up again floundering, gasping for air. I swam for shore, dragged myself onto sand, and looked about me.

It was Jaeder again; I stood on the sands of Sola Bay. I was puzzled for a moment, but one never troubles much over such things in a dream. The light might have been stronger than a real Jaeder day, the colors somewhat brighter; otherwise the only difference from the land I knew was the presence of one huge fir tree on Sola's high ground. "I'll go see this marvel," I said, and took the path to the farm.

I stopped outside the steading to stare. The farmstead was deserted. No warrior, free man or woman or thrall was there, no pig, no horse, no hound. In the center of the steading the fir tree grew, its boughs filling the yard.

"There's a hawk's nest at the top of the tree," said a voice behind me, and I turned to see the abbot.

"Is there indeed?"

"In the nest is an egg of gold. Inside the egg is a hawk who can protect your crop from the ravens. But you must find the hardest thing in the world to break the egg, else the hawk can never come forth."

"It's a very tall tree," I observed, cocking my eye at the top.

"Better get started then."

So I pushed my way in among the fir boughs, rough and resinous and cool in the shade, and set my foot on one of the lowest limbs, and began to make my way up, scaling as if on a ladder. It was easy climbing, but it never seemed to come to an end. Climbing inside the tree, as it were, behind the sun-loving needles, I couldn't well make out how far I'd come. Hours—even days—might have passed; the light never seemed to change. Only very gradually did the limbs grow smaller and shorter, and a moment came when my head emerged into the sunlight. The day seemed no further advanced than when I'd started. So either I hadn't climbed near as long as I'd thought, or I'd climbed a full day. Or two or more.

I turned my gaze upward, and now I could see the nest above me, still a long way up, where the tree seemed dangerously narrow and whippy. But I climbed on, and the further I climbed the further the crown bowed out under me, so that we were bent almost flush with the horizon when at last I reached the hawk's nest.

And there, just hanging under the nest's brim, was my golden egg. I took it in my hand with a shout, and as I shouted I lost my grip and fell toward the earth.

I fell in a strange calm. *If I'm to break the egg, I thought to myself, I might as well fall on top of it; perhaps one of the stones on the ground will do the job.*

And then I struck the ground, face down. I felt nothing, but knew my body had been shattered. I heard the abbot's voice above me. "A bad fall," he said. "Very poorly done." I felt his hand on my shoulder as he turned me over.

"The egg," I croaked when I could see his face. "Did it break?"

For an answer he held the thing up, shining and unmarred.

"You've got to heed the instructions," he said. "Only the hardest thing in the world may break this egg."

"What's harder than this cruel northern land?"

"Your heart, of course." And he reached his hand into my crushed chest and drew forth my living heart. Only it didn't look like a heart, it was only a rounded gray stone, like thousands you could find along the sea strand.

He took my stony heart and struck the egg with it, and the shell shattered like a sunburst, and a beautiful white hawk with red wings shot forth and soared into the bright bosom of the sky.

CHAPTER XXIII

The morning after Erling's return he came to me in the church and I said to him, "My lord, I must confess to you."

"I have no power to absolve you," he said.

"Still I must confess. I've judged you harshly, and I've no right to judge. You've heard what I did the night of the sacrifice?"

"I pray God I'm never tested as you were."

"I failed at every point."

"You did not do the thing at last."

"I ate horsemeat. Your martyr priest died rather than do that. But I can forgive that in myself, because I wanted to save my woman and child. I'm not a hero. But when I think that I was on the point of raping a twelve-year-old maid—I, who bled for my sister! I could dwindle to a mayfly, and fly away to Eastland and be eaten by an elephant, and the elephant be eaten by a hundred men, and all those men and all their descendants would die of my shame.

"I know what you'll say—there was magic at work, and the elf-woman, and the music and dancing, and the moon, and whatever they put in that stew. But they couldn't have called me if I hadn't known their tongue. I've seen—it's as if a man looked at his reflection in a pool, and saw a troll's face there."

Erling went to the altar and straightened a candle. "I know too little of God's teachings," he said, "but isn't this what they call repentance?"

I could not answer. No, it wasn't repentance, or not full repentance. I still hadn't told him I was no priest. I'd thought I might at first, but my courage failed.

"Lay a penance on yourself," he said. "Suffer and be done with it. I can't have my priest going about moaning over his sins. What I liked in you from the first was your spirit, and you'll not get far in Norway without it."

"How can I stand before the church when everyone saw me at the sacrifice?"

"Those with any sense will be as ashamed of themselves as you are. Those who blame you I'll mark, because I've noted that most men condemn loudest those sins they themselves haven't mastered. Perhaps that's why God is so merciful. Having no sins of His own, He finds nothing unforgiveable."

I shook my head. "That poor child. They brought a stallion! She'd have been killed, surely?"

"Most times they are, or so I've heard. But the ones who live are accounted mighty souls."

When I'd heard his confession and absolved him, Erling said, "Come with me to Lemming's house. He has a story, and I'll get it from him if I have to hold his feet to a fire, like Soti."

The big man was sleeping when we walked into his hovel, and he jerked up and nearly struck Erling before he saw who had shaken him.

Erling and I sat on the other bench as he stretched and scratched, wordless as a bear.

"I'll have your story," said Erling, "and I'll have it now. There are limits to our patience. You can't act as you have without explaining yourself."

Lemming leaned back against the wall and stared at us from shadowed eyes.

"What do we know?" said Erling. "We know you served Soti for years, and that you came to Sola with him from the north. You hated Soti—hated him as a man hates death. And you showed no special love for anyone else. Yet you lit the balefire at the risk of your life. Why? It seems to me there must have been someone at Sola for whom you did care."

Lemming stared and said nothing.

"Then came the great summer sacrifice, and again you put your life at risk. For whom? For Father Aillil? Not likely. But who else was in danger? If the sacrifice went on, none but he would have died."

Lemming's mouth twisted, and the cords of his neck stood out.

"But there was one in danger of another kind. The child, Freydis."

Lemming looked away.

"Ulvig said, I'm told, that the ceremony was performed on her when she was the same age. So she would have coupled with a thrall. And I ask myself, was that thrall Lemming? Is Lemming the father of Freydis?"

The big man stood of a sudden and spread his arms and bellowed. Then he collapsed, like a burst bladder, into a pile of flesh and bone unaccountably small, and lay sobbing.

"He can't be her father," said I. "The father would have been sacrificed, unless the custom was different then."

"Who was Freydis' father, Lemming?" asked Erling.

The voice came up from the sobbing heap as from a grave. "My brother," he said.

Erling rose and put his hand on the man. "You are her only decent kin," he said. "You shall raise the child. You shall have Soti's house, and work his forge—you know the work—and have his property.

Only this I demand—the child shall be christened, and brought to church each week. You need not be a Christian if you want it not, but Freydis has seen too much devilment."

Lemming made a lunge and caught Erling by the hand. "I'll die for you," he croaked.

We found Halla in the same women's house where Gunnlaug had given birth, propped up on cushions in a box bed. Erling walked to her, bent in and kissed her.

"I've brought Father Aillil," he said. "Will you marry me, Halla?"

Halla looked pale. "Now?" she asked.

"If you like. Or we can wait and do it properly, with feasting and music and rich gifts all around. I'll marry you any way you wish, if only you'll be my wife."

"It's very sudden."

"From God's point of view it's too long coming."

"But why?"

"Because I heard the tale of what you did the night of the sacrifice. And it came to me, like a blind man walking into a wall, that I'd never seen you as you are. I'd looked on you as a toy and a playmate, but you're a fine woman, equal to any in the land. If I marry any other, I'll rue it the rest of my life. Will you marry me, Halla?"

Halla passed a hand over her forehead. "I need time to think," she said. "Forgive me—since losing . . . since what happened I've thought new thoughts. I'm honored, and I love you very much, but will you let me go to my father's house awhile, and think and pray?"

Erling looked disappointed but said, "Anything you wish. I make you a promise, Halla. While you live, and while you are unwed, I will marry no other woman." He took her hand in his.

She drew the hand against her cheek. "Don't promise that," she said, her eyes shining.

"It's done, and I never break my word. Now eat, and rest, and go to your father when you will, and come back to me ready to be mistress of Sola."

"Not quite the outcome I'd looked for," said Erling when we were outside.

"I'm glad nonetheless," said I. "I've prayed for this."

"Yes, you saw Halla's worth from the start. You stung me, Father, I'll not deny it, when you questioned my word. I feel no shame in the matter of Olaf Trygvesson and Jarl Haakon, but my heart puckered as I thought of Halla. Father Ethelbald once told me that a man and woman who lie together become one flesh, and I saw of a sudden how much Halla had become a part of me. Then I came home and heard what she'd done, and I knew what I must do.

"Tell me, Father, what's it like when a man finds that the woman he's played with as a toy is a human soul to whom he owes the same honor and fair dealing he gives a fellow warrior?"

"Ah well, I'd say it's like finding yourself working and fighting among the grown men one day, and it comes to you that you're one of them, though it seems yesterday you were only a boy."

"Yes. As always, you have the words. In fact it may not be like becoming a man—it may be the thing itself. Perhaps I've never been a man till now."

"What does your mother think?"

"She doesn't know yet. She'll be none too pleased, but she likes Halla for all that and will get used to the idea. I hope I can say as much for my kinsmen in Hordaland."

"Do they disapprove of Halla?"

"No, but they greatly approve of Astrid Trygvesdatter. That was one of the matters we discussed up north. They want to wed me to Astrid to make peace with the Sigurdssons and Olaf Trygvesson."

"But Astrid's the lass you've dreamed of for years!"

"I heard a priest preach on a text once that said, 'When I became a man I put off childish ways.' Astrid was a dream. Halla is a real woman, and my wife before God."

That left but one thing for me. I walked to my own house, where I knew I'd find Steinbjorg. I'd tell her we were safe—Soti and Ulvig were dead, Lemming had Soti's property and would surely sell her to me. I'd tell her I was not a priest, and that when a true priest came to Sola I'd confess to him, give up my office, do the penance he laid on me, and marry her. She wasn't Halla, but she was more than I deserved.

The moment I stepped over the threshold I knew something was horribly wrong. Blood has a smell. As my eyes made peace with the dimness, I could see the body by the hearth, and there was blood everywhere—gallons of blood—a sea of blood—

"I made the sacrifice, master."

There was Caedwy in the corner by the bed, hiding like a naughty child, eyes wide, still holding the bloody sickle, his clothing soaked in gore. I gaped at him.

"They stopped the sacrifice," he said. "But the sacrifice had to be made. I knew that's what you wanted. That's what the troll said too. We'll make a big basket and burn her properly—"

I ran at him and knocked the blade from his hand, cutting my own to the bone. I took him by the shirt and dragged him out into the sunlight and shouted, "A rope! Somebody get me a rope now!"

A thrall brought the rope, and I knotted it around Caedwy's scrawny neck, and I dragged him to the storehouse where they'd hanged Enda and flung the rope over the beam, and I hoisted him with my own hands, and held tight until his kicking ended and his breeches filled, and a while longer, while his cur dog leaped about me and barked.

Then I let him drop, and I went back to my house and took the horrid thing that would have been my wife in my arms, and I whispered secrets to it until it grew cold.

CHAPTER XXIV

He came to me in the darkness, a moving shadow, a whisper of stirring in the air, somewhere between waking and sleep.

"Yet another plant plucked up," the abbot said, in a voice uncommon soft for him.

"Two plants. The dearest of them all," said I.

There was silence for a space, and I spoke again to him, at once angered that he'd come and fearful he might have gone. "Are you to be a Job's comforter to me then, explaining how these innocents had to die for my deserving?"

His answer came slowly; so slowly that for a time I thought I was alone indeed.

"I'm sent to beg your forgiveness," he whispered at last.

It was my turn to be silent.

"It seems I've been overhard on you," he went on. I tried to imagine the expression on his unseen face, but couldn't fit one to the features. "The opinion at the ... the Highest Level is ... Och! You've got to understand."

"Understand what?"

"You've got to understand about Heaven. Heaven isn't what we thought. Or rather it isn't what I thought."

"So you're in Heaven now? Well out of Purgatory already?"

"I'm outside of Time. The question has no meaning."

"And what's Heaven like?"

"That's what I'm trying to tell. There's no words in Irish or Latin. 'Tis a shocking place, Heaven. There's things here—things encouraged, that'd never be allowed below. I can't say what; I can't even hint it, because it would put thoughts in your fleshly mind that would be like to get you damned. But here it's permitted—here all is permitted. '*Love God and do what you will*,' said Augustine, but you can't really do that below because your nature's diseased. It's like Adam and Eve. It was good for them to be naked, but it wasn't good after the Fall. We're not exactly naked here, but . . . it takes some getting used to.

"I spent my whole life mastering the rules. I thought it would please God, and it did. But early on I lost sight of the weightier matters of the Law.

"You though—with your recklessness and wanton ways—I find that God . . . God likes you better than He likes me. He loves me no less than you or anyone, but some . . . many . . . He likes better, and you're one of them.

"When He put on a body and walked among us, He wasn't like me. He was like you. I studied the gospels my whole life, yet I missed that plain fact, near enough to my face to singe my eyebrows. He went to weddings and parties, and played with children and spoke to loose women. Men like me He showed the back of His hand."

Can a blessed spirit sob? I could swear I heard him sob then, but the sound was so soft it might have been the roof settling.

"It's the risk He loves!" cried the abbot. "It's the

mad, devil-take-the-hindmost rascality of the saints who throw away their gold or their shirts or their very lives and value it all at a feather for love of Him. God help me, in my whole life I never did one incautious act, and now I repent my respectability; I repent it in sackcloth and ashes."

Long silence then. The world had stopped; the night might linger forever if I gave it no push with a word. I outwaited him; humbled him by forcing him to ask the question once more.

"I've come to beg forgiveness," he said. "Will you give me it?"

"With all my heart," said I. "Just as soon as God gives me my woman and child back."

My memory of the weeks and months that followed is smoky. That we celebrated Easter I know, but whether it was done well or poorly I cannot tell. I baptized and buried, heard confessions and pronounced banns, and did the work of a priest generally. As before, the priest Aillil and the man Aillil were two separate souls, only the man Aillil had died.

Even anger can be pressed to death. I knew the cause of Steinbjorg's murder, and our child's—the judgment of God on my sacrilege in feigning His priesthood—but I was too weary to rail at Him for it. "You are mightier than all the world and slyer than a Scot," I said to Him in a rare moment of plain speaking. "There's no use arguing with someone who kills the innocent to make a point." Then I asked forgiveness and did quick penance, and thought no more such dangerous thoughts.

A man came with a ship to buy grain one summer day, and in the hall that night he declared himself to be, not a merchant, but an agent of Svein Forkbeard, King of Denmark.

"Svein will make you a jarl, Erling Skjalgsson," the man said. "He has heard your name and your deeds, and it's men such as you he seeks for retainers in his Norse domain. Denmark is a richer land than Norway, a civilized and Christian kingdom, and to steer your lands under Svein is far to be preferred over serving whatever sea king thinks he can hold a few woodlots in Norway for a month or two."

Bergthor said, "Does Svein think to send the Jomsvikings to conquer us again?"

Everyone laughed, and the agent reddened. Someone explained to me that Bergthor was harking back to an attack from Denmark years before, which had turned out badly.

Erling smiled, turning the gold ring the agent had brought from Svein in his hands, and said, "It's good to know the king of Denmark invites me if I need him, but all in all I prefer a Norwegian lord."

"Do you think you're likely to make peace with Olaf Trygvesson, whose uncle you slew?" asked the agent, and after that things were unfriendly, and the man went on to the next district unsatisfied.

I was giving the host to Ragna one day at mass when I noticed, as one suddenly notices a cobweb that's been flourishing in a house corner for days, that the woman had grown thin, and the skin hung loose and pale on her jaw and neck. I went to her in the women's house later and asked her if she was unwell. She smiled at me from her seat and said, "No, I've only been fasting much lately."

"Is there some matter I should have in my prayers?" I asked.

"No. I mourn my old sins, and the days of heathendom. My husband was a heathen and so was I, Father, and I loved him much; but now I see that our lives were wicked, and he burns in Hell, and I am only saved, if saved I will be, by God's mercy. When I walk about this farm, I sometimes think how I miss Thorolf, and then I tell myself it's wicked to miss so evil a sinner, so I do penance. And sometimes I think how great have been my sins, and how short a time I have to atone for them, and I do penance that my stay in Purgatory may be the less. So with one thing and another, I've been eating little. And truth to tell, I find I want food less than I did. I suppose that lightens the value of my fasts, so I must fast even more."

"You shouldn't abuse your body so as to break your health," I told her. "The body must serve us as a horse serves his master, but only a fool would starve his horse."

She smiled a small smile. "I think what time I have left will not be shortened much by penances. I have thought that when I've seen my son married, and a new mistress in place at Sola, I will find a convent in England or Germany, and take the veil."

I said that would be an honorable undertaking.

"The great thing is to get Erling wed to Astrid Trygvesdatter," she said. "When I see that done I can bid the world farewell with a good heart. And in Heaven I can tell my ancestors I have left the family higher in the world than I found it. Only my ancestors won't be in Heaven, will they? Ah, me."

One morning in June I was awakened by somebody beating on my door. I stepped out into a blue and shining morning, and the bullyboy who'd roused me said there was a stranger in the steading, and that Erling wanted me. As my head cleared, I realized a voice was shouting, and shouting in Irish.

I hurried to the gate, where a crowd had gathered around a tonsured man in a tattered monk's robe, accompanied by a huge wolfhound which snarled at Erling's hounds. The man stood with his arms stretched out and his face turned to heaven, crying, "Now, Lord, let thy servant depart in peace; I have finished the course, I have kept the faith; let the arrows of the heathen pierce me through; let their spears transfix my bowels and their axes hack my corpse, still in my flesh I shall see God. Though I walk through the valley of the shadow of death, Thou art with me; I shall not be afraid for the terror by night, nor for the arrow that flieth by day; from the end of the earth I cry to Thee, when my heart is overwhelmed; lead me to the rock that is higher than I; for Thou hast been a shelter for me, and a strong tower from the enemy. . . ."

He had to take a breath some time, and when he did I put in, "I'm sorry, brother, but if you're seeking martyrdom you'll have to look elsewhere. We have a few heathens left here, but we keep them on a leash."

He opened his eyes and stared me in the face, and had I not known better I'd have thought from his look of joy that we were long-lost kin. He was a long, ginger-haired fellow with a crooked nose, thin to the point of unhealth, and his chin and tonsure needed shaving. "Praise to the Beloved, a Christian priest!" he cried, and he leaped on me and grappled me to his breast, giving me ample proof that along with food and a shave he needed a bath (it didn't occur to me until later that I'd dwelt in heathen lands so long that I'd come to despise the honest stink of a holy man). His rangy hound leaped about our knees in brainless sympathy, and Erling's hounds put their ears back and growled at the sight.

Erling stepped nearer and said, "Now that we've eased your confusion, brother, may I offer you the hospitality of my house? I am Erling Skjalgsson, lord of Sola. The fellow whose back you're trying to break is Father Aillil, my priest. Breakfast is nearly ready, and I beg you to join us and tell us how you came so far by yourself."

"Fishermen found him wrecked on the reef this morning and brought him here," Erling told me when I'd gotten loose and we were all headed for the hall. "He was sitting on the rocks, singing, they said, with the dog howling at his side. When my men took charge of him he assumed they were going to kill him."

"A natural assumption, if you're from Ireland," said I. "He must be a White Martyr."

"A White Martyr?"

"White Martyrdom is when you go off by yourself, far from your homeland, to live or die by God's providence. It's not so common anymore, but in times past many a monk set sail in his curragh and was never heard from again. Somehow this one got carried here."

Once we were seated and I'd blessed the food, and our guest had refused the washing bowl, I began to question him, and there was whispering as the Irish speakers translated for their friends.

"My name is Moling," he told me, "and I am a man of Armagh, a wicked transgressor before God, guilty of sins of the flesh and sins of the spirit." He spoke cheerfully though, as if the memory of his sins troubled him not at all. He ate a bite of the food set before him and passed the rest bit by bit to the dog who sat with his muzzle on his knee.

"It's not horsemeat," I said, recalling my own sins.

"What? Oh, of course not." Moling's eyes had gone dreamy, and he snapped back with a smile. "I had no such unworthy thought. I've no wish to insult the hospitality of Christian brothers in an alien land. It only seems I've less need of food than I did, since I've been spending much time with God, and my friend Conn here, God bless him—" he patted the hound "—he's a purely carnal being, as God intended him to be, and better able to appreciate these things. So I enjoy spiritual food, and Conn enjoys fleshly food, and we praise God according to our kinds."

"What led you to take up the White Martyrdom?"

Moling smiled. "I killed my father and mother," he said. "I killed my wife and children, and I raped my neighbor's daughter, and I robbed the church and I betrayed my king, and I took the homes of the poor and drove them weeping into the road. I broke fasts and labored on Sundays and lied to my confessor and slandered the Blessed Virgin and spit on the crucifix, and stole the sacramental wine and got drunk on it. I moved my neighbors' boundary stones, and accused them falsely and perjured myself at their trials. I lent money at interest. I burned down houses, and stole cattle, and took slaves, and—"

"You kept busy," said I.

"I? Oh yes, it's rather a lot for one life, isn't it? And I'm not as old as I look. But then perhaps it wasn't me at all. Perhaps it was some other fellow. Or perhaps I only dreamed of doing them, and so sinned in my heart. What does it matter?"

"It must matter somehow, else why are you wandering the earth to earn forgiveness?"

He stared at me. "To earn forgiveness?" he asked. "You can't earn forgiveness. Surely you know that."

"Then why this penance?"

"For the Beloved, of course. When a man as wicked as I has all his sins forgiven and debts paid, he must love the One who forgave. And love wishes to be with the Beloved. If I could suffer a thousand thousand White Martyrdoms, and a thousand thousand Red Martyrdoms, they wouldn't begin to repay what He spent on me. But as I let go everything that separated us, I am drawn closer and closer to Him, and my joy is sometimes such that I think that this world, where I seem to range as a starving stranger, is Paradise itself, and I wander in blessed groves and eat the apples of Heaven and hear the music of angels. Did you hear them this morning? They sang the strangest song to me as I sat on the reef. 'Maeve lives,' they sang. It was beautiful, but I don't know what it means. I know a couple lasses named Maeve, but why shouldn't they be alive?"

I reached out and took him by both shoulders. "What else did they sing?"

"Nothing. Only 'Maeve lives.' Is this Maeve someone to you?"

I let him go. "My sister," I said. "Taken by Vikings. But what use is it to tell me she lives without saying how it is with her?"

Moling laid a hand on my arm. "In the end, we none of us ever know how it is with another, even our dearest. We must leave each of them in God's hands soon or late."

"I don't mind leaving her in God's hands. It's the hands of some greasy Viking master I can't bear to think of."

"There are many kinds of White Martyrdom, my brother. Embrace it as a bride, and find your true love."

"Let's speak no more of this," I said.

Moling spent the day playing with children and watching Lemming in the rebuilt forge until supper, which he fed again to his hound. Then he passed the night in a byre, refusing absolutely to sleep in a house, and after I had said mass the next morning he made ready to set off north overland. We told him it was a long, dangerous journey, sometimes roadless, pitted with mires and unfriendly men, and the Boknafjord only the first of many waters he'd have to cross. These things only made him more eager. "I've heard tales of heathen Lapps in the far north," he said. "I must go and preach to them."

"Wait a bit," I said to him, and I ran to Erling, who was in the horse pen, gentling a colt.

"Let me go north to Tungeness with Moling," I said.

"I don't see what help that would be," said Erling. "You don't know the way any better than he."

"I want to speak with him. There are things I can talk over only with him."

ERLING'S WORD

"What sort of things?"

"Irish things. Churchmen's things."

"I could send one of the men with you, I suppose. I'd hate to have you end up sunk in a bog."

"Send no one. I must be alone with Moling."

Erling searched my face, then called a thrall. "Get some food together for Father Aillil—sausages and cheese, dried fish—traveling fare."

CHAPTER XXV

The land way north was not an easy one, as Norwegians prefer to go by water if they're traveling any distance, and we had water on both sides. The paths varied, being now wide and easy, now narrow and stony, now low and muddy; sometimes they forked without any hint as to where they'd lead, sometimes they'd disappear altogether in a bog or a grassy waste, and you'd have to go carefully around, or push your way through with the sun as your guide. Sometimes we'd stop at farmsteads for directions, and the farmers and their wives looked at us as if at walkers-again, often slamming their doors shut in our faces. Moling didn't seem to mind anything. He swung his staff and paced along at a remarkable speed, leaving me puffing to keep up. He sang most of the time, songs I hadn't heard for long and long. His hound traveled twice the distance we did, racing ahead, doubling back to see why we came so slowly, then racing ahead again.

It took to raining in the afternoon and I began to look about for friendly shelter, but Moling paid it no mind. We slogged along, waterlogged, cold, and mired with mud to our knees, and it occurred to me that Moling, not understanding the light nights, would go on like this until autumn. I finally said, "We have to find shelter for the night! It doesn't get dark until close on midnight this time of year."

Moling looked at me as if I'd found the answer to the problem of Free Will.

"Is that so?" he asked. "Where shall we look?"

"Well there's a farmhouse up there. We can only ask."

The farmer was heathen, and paled at the sight of our robes, but he respected the name of Erling Skjalgsson, which I dropped with a thump, and grudgingly let us have a place in his byre, empty this time of year. We found straw to spread our cloaks on and opened our scrips, he for his hound and I for the beast within.

"Remarkable, these long summer nights in Norway," Moling said as he fed the dog and scratched its belly. "Are the winter nights short in proportion?"

"Aye. The winters here are like a foretaste of Hell."

"I've spent a lot of nights in the open, watching the moon and the stars. I've come to a conclusion about them."

"And what's that?"

"I think it can't be true that the sun travels around the earth. It must be the other way around."

I nearly choked on my cheese. I'd had no idea how far gone the man was. "That's the maddest thing I ever heard," I said, and I said it to his face. I mean, there are limits. I'd had enough of this kind of nonsense from Caedwy.

"No, think about it. How could the earth be the center of the universe? This is a fallen place, a cursed place. The sun, on the other hand, is glorious and gives us life. The sun is a symbol of the Beloved. The earth must be the sun's dog, running about it as Conn does with me."

"Look," said I. "The earth is down, and it's flat. The sun is up, and it's round. The sun flies. The earth just sits there."

"I've heard that the Greeks believed the earth to be round like a ball."

"It makes no difference. If the earth moved, we'd all fall off it."

"I suppose that's true. It's a pity. It would be much better theology for the earth to go around the sun."

"I hate to spit in your beer, brother, but real things seldom make good theology."

"Ah well, it's no matter. In any case the sun will rise in the morning whatever we think. Now tell me, Father Aillil, what is it you wanted to talk with me about?"

"How did you know I wanted to talk with you?"

"Am I wrong about this too?"

I closed my scrip. "No, you're not wrong. I need to confess to you."

"I'm not a priest."

"If I wait for a priest I may wait forever," said I. "First thing, I'm not a priest myself . . ." and I went on and confided to this madman all my secrets and my whole history at Sola, all I'd wanted to tell my Steinbjorg. For all I knew he'd babble it to the world. When I was done I sat silent.

"I cannot shrive you," he said.

"WHY?" I shouted, and the farmer and his family must have been wakened.

"Because there's no place in your heart for my forgiveness to rest. See here, the Beloved is like a loving father who comes to his child each day and says, 'I have a gift for you,' and offers him some treasure, but the child is holding on to the gift he was given yesterday, and so cannot take the new gift. You must let go yesterday's gift, my brother Aillil."

I shuddered. "I cannot," I said. "My hands are iron. They will not open."

"Then they must be heated in the forge, and hammered open. The Beloved will do it, for He loves you."

"I'm sick of His love. I'm crushed and crippled under the lead weight of God's love."

There was no answer. I looked and saw that Moling was sleeping, easily as a child, with his dog curled up against his belly.

We went on the next day in much the same way. Again I had trouble keeping up and got no chance to talk. But now I doubted whether there was much use in talk. Moling was like the adults I'd watched as a child, secure in their growth, knowing everything and sufficient for all, whose world I could neither understand nor enter.

There was rain and then fog, and as the fog burned off we heard a sound of shouting and clanging some distance off, but in the direction we were headed.

"There's a battle!" said Moling, and the ring in his voice made me wonder if he hadn't been a warrior once.

"What about it?" I asked.

"Let's go see!" He hitched his skirts up in his belt and set off like a greyhound, catching his dog up, and the two of them raced ahead of me, growing smaller and disappearing over the crest of a low ridge.

When I finally drew up to them we were halfway down the other side, and in the dale below two gangs of men were having it out with swords and axes. There were about twenty in one group, and only six in the other.

"Bad odds," said Moling.

"What can we do?" I sighed.

"We have our staffs. We could fall on the larger group from behind, and the Lord might give us victory!"

"Or they might brain us with their axes."

"Yes," said Moling, and from his eyes I realized

that being brained with an axe didn't seem to him an awful thing at all.

And suddenly I thought, *What the Heaven? Let's die here today, saving lives, and go home to the Beloved.*

So I shouted, "Columcille!" and Moling shouted something or other, and we fell on the fighting men like a thunderbolt.

And I swear to God, the moment those men started getting thumped from behind, and turned to see two roaring Irishmen with bare legs and flying staffs, they screamed and fled, nor looked back while we could see them.

Three from the other side still stood. They let their weapons sink, and one of them sat down, and another said, "Are you Valkyries?"

I wish Moling had understood the question. It would have given him a laugh.

I said, "No, we're not Valkyries, we are men and servants of the White Christ. I am Father Aillil, priest to Erling Skjalgsson, and this is Brother Moling, a holy man of Ireland."

"If you're Erling's priest you're well met," said the man. "We have one of his men here, a Christian, and he's dying."

And I looked down and there lay Halvard Thorfinnsson, with blood soaking the belly of his shirt.

"Oh Lord," I said. "Have pity on little Sigrid."

I stepped toward him but Moling was ahead of me. He took Halvard's head in his lap, and gave him water to drink from the skin he carried, stroking the pale hair of the young warrior.

Halvard said, "I want to confess, Father."

I heard his confession and shrove him, silently praying God, as I always did, to accept the faith of the dying in place of my ordination.

"There's much pain," said Halvard when we were done.

"You're a brave lad," I said. "You'll do as well as any."

"It's strange to die this way, and me a Christian. If I were heathen yet, I'd know that Odin would welcome me to Valhalla. What welcome has Christ for a warrior, Father?"

I had no quick answer, and Moling must have seen my trouble, because he asked what the boy had said. I told him.

"Tell him I've had a dream about Heaven," said Moling. "The teachers tell us that the Beloved lives outside Time itself. He goes back and forth in it when He wills. And when we go to be with Him, we too will be outside Time.

"It seemed to me in my dream that at the last day the Beloved called together all the great warriors who had been brave and merciful, and who had trusted in His mercy, and He mustered them into a mighty army, and He said to them, 'Go forth for Me now, My bonny fighters, and range through Time, and wherever there is cruelty and wickedness that makes the weak to suffer, and the faithful to doubt My goodness, wherever the children are slain or violated, wherever the women are raped or beaten, wherever the old are threatened and robbed, then take your shining swords and fight that cruelty and wickedness, and protect My poor and weak ones, and do not lay down your weapons or take your rest until all such evil is crushed and defeated, and the right stands victorious in every place and every time. We will not empty Hell even with this, for men love Hell, but I made a sweet song at the beginning, My sons, and though men have sung it foul we will make it sweet again forever.'"

I said these words to Halvard in Norse, and he died smiling.

I hired a boatman to take Moling across the Boknafjord to Aarvik the next day, and we said our goodbyes, and I got a ride back to Sola in a fisherman's boat.

And then I had to tell Sigrid about Halvard.

I stood in my patch among my children, working with a hoe to keep the weeds from them. A bird shadow swam the earth at my feet, but I looked up without fear, for I knew it was my white-and-red hawk, and although the ravens might fly by in the distance they knew better than to venture closer.

"Doing well now, are you?" asked a voice, and I knew it for the abbot, for who else spoke to me in these dreams? "Getting along fine, no problems?"

I worked on in silence.

"Are you ready to forgive me?" he asked.

"Still on that?" I asked. "You harp on it as if my forgiveness were worth the wealth of Dagda."

"What do you know of worth?" he cried. "If you knew the value of one word of forgiveness, you'd be all day coining indulgences like the king of Ulster at his mint! To have such wealth at your fingertips and never to touch it . . . if you could see things from my side of the river, you'd think yourself a pauper living on a mountain of gold, and all unknowing."

"I'm just being holy, as my Heavenly Father is holy. He doles His forgiveness out in jealous dribs and drabs. Why should I be prodigal with mine?"

"All saints and blessed angels! Did I teach you so badly? Think you really God is a hammer-tongued old *fir darrig* such as I was? Think you all the praises and thanksgivings of scripture are but flattery to a tyrant?"

"I know how God has used me. I know nothing more."

"You know nothing at all! You've never seen, and you will not look, and you haven't the sense to—" Then he fell silent, as if a hand had stopped his mouth. I plied my hoe until he spoke again.

"Would you hear a jest from Heaven?" he said. "A thing to make you laugh? I've learned I was never meant to be an abbot, nor even a monk. I was born to be a married man and a father. There was a girl I grew up with, whom I used to dream about, and I always thought those dreams a torment from the Devil. As it turns out, 'twas she God had intended for my wife. And my cramped nature came from being a man out of place in the world, trying to make shoes with a cooper's tools, so to speak.

"You, on the other hand—you'll laugh when you hear this—you were born to be a priest. Isn't that rich?"

I didn't laugh, not at all.

"You've overlooked one thing, you know," he said at last. I didn't want to listen. I wanted to toil here among my children, looking at their bright faces, hearing them laugh, watching them grow. I would never sell them. I would keep them forever, and if I never earned my freedom, so be it.

"What you fail to consider is that your whole prosperity depends on the white-and-red hawk. But no hawk is forever."

I whirled to face him. "What are you getting at?"

"Behold," he said, and with a long finger indicated the sky.

I turned unwilling eyes upward, and I saw that another bird was approaching from the west, a great white eagle, larger than the hawk.

"Does he come as an enemy?" I whispered.

"Watch."

The two great birds circled each other for a minute, then the white-and-red hawk stooped before the eagle, and flew his circle lower than before, while the white eagle circled above.

"They watch together!" I cried. "Instead of one guardian, I now have two! You're a poor prophet, Father."

"Yet watch."

Then came a great flock of ravens, all the ravens in the world, so many they blocked the sun out like a thunderhead, and they attacked the eagle and the hawk. And great was the battle then: the noble birds fought like hurricanes and thunderbolts; one after another the ravens fell in blood like rain, and yet there were so many of them that still they came on, and the hawk and eagle were wearied. And as they fought, the battle moved off, drifting eastward before a westerly wind, until all the birds were gone from sight.

"So fine, so brave; can they both be lost?" I cried.

My answer was to see the white-and-red hawk return alone. He took up his watching post above my patch, and the white eagle was seen no more.

"Thank God this one was spared me at least," I said.

"Yet watch."

Now came a red eagle, greater even than the white one. This time the hawk did not greet the larger bird with obeisance—he flew in his face with rage and flashing claws, and great was their battle, so that the blood fell down in my eyes. But at last the red eagle struck the hawk down, and he fell like a hailstone to land among my children and lie unmoving, his eyes gone lightless.

I knelt and wept for the white-and-red hawk, for whom I had suffered much, and who had repaid me well.

"Now see who wards your patch," said the abbot. I looked up and saw that the red eagle had grown to even greater size, and was circling as the other noble birds had done. But all the birds of the earth, eagles and hawks, ravens and crows, even bluebirds and gulls, gathered together against the red eagle. He fought valiantly, but I thought they were too many for him.

I lowered my eyes. I no longer cared.

"Erling is the white-and-red hawk, isn't he?" I asked.

"You worked that out all by yourself? Perhaps there's hope for you yet."

"Why should he fall before that bloody red eagle? What do I need with the red eagle? I was well suited with things as they were."

"Perhaps God has purposes beyond what suits you. Perhaps there are more patches in Norway than yours alone, and just as dear to Him."

I looked at the sky. All the birds were gone. "They must have slain the red eagle," said I. "Who will guard my patch against the ravens now?"

"There are no more ravens. They will never come again, or not for a very long time. But there are other dangers."

And suddenly he was the Black Axe-man again, towering over me with his weapon swinging. I turned and ran from him, and as I ran I crushed my children underfoot.

CHAPTER XXVI

"There it is, the Gula Thingstead," said Bergthor, pointing. I'd come to the ship's rail for other reasons than the view, but I raised my throbbing head and saw a sloping, south-facing meadow with mountains at its back above the narrow sound where we rowed. Sogn and Hordaland are unlike Jaeder—tree-covered in their lower parts and rugged in all their parts, and it was no wonder that holding Jaeder's field country meant much to those who lived here.

We'd endured another winter, and it was now the spring of the Year of Our Lord 997, and time for the great regional Thing. We were having a mercifully dry week.

We disembarked at the jetty, and our ships anchored in the harbor. We climbed to the meadow and to Erling's family booth, a foundation dug out of the earth with low walls of piled turves. It needed only the striped woolen awning roof we'd brought to make a comfortable temporary house. As the thralls raised the tent, Erling stood beside me outside and stretched his arms wide, as if summoning the steep green mountain slopes and the bright Gulafjord, thick with ships, as witnesses in a lawsuit. "Is Norway not a fair land, Father?" he asked.

"As Lucifer was fairest of the sons of the morning," I answered. "It's the heart that counts, and it's a wicked, heathen heart this land has." My gaze turned eastward toward the temple, a tall, steep-roofed stave building with dragon heads at the roof peaks.

"Perhaps that will change soon. And we'll help change it by our work here. Look—do you see that company?" He pointed to a line of folk climbing the hill below us and to the east, not one of the larger groups.

"Yes," I said. "What of it?"

"That's Asmund Fridleifsson's household. Asmund is father to Halla. I think—yes, Halla's there!"

"Perhaps they want to accept your marriage proposal."

"I hope you're right. But they could have done that without sailing all the way to Sogn."

I offered to go and inquire, but Erling said to let it be for now.

That evening the Horder lords met in Olmod's booth. Erling asked me to come along.

Olmod sat propped up by cushions and wrapped in blankets in the high seat, the light from the hearth fire shining on his spotted skull. His voice had worn thin, and we strained to hear him.

"The issue stands thus," he piped. "Olaf Trygvesson is lord of the Trondelag, the Uppland districts, the Vik, and Agder. Now word has it he's sailed to Rogaland, and the Rogalanders, urged by the Erikssons, too are submitting to him, being baptized, and acclaiming him king. Our bonders have already invited him here so as to hear what he offers. We can expect him any day. He promises friendship and great gifts to those who bow to him, but he's bloody-handed with those who resist.

"So the question is this, kinsmen—shall we gather

our forces as the western lords did in Harald Finehair's day, and meet this Olaf Trygvesson in battle? We might hope to have better luck than they did, who had their lands seized, to the profit of my father Horda-Kari and my older brothers among others."

"We need to know what the Sognings and Fjorders have to say to that," said someone.

"And they're waiting to hear what we say," said Olmod. "It's come to this—that of all the kins of the Gulathing-law, our word bears the most weight. That's a good thing, but it won't last if we say nothing, and what we do say had better be wise."

"It seems to me we'd be wise to follow Horda-Kari's example," said Erling. "He and his sons threw in with the king and made their fortunes thereby. I've met this Olaf Trygvesson, and I'll stake my head he's born to rule."

"It's no surprise you'd lean to Olaf," said another man. "You're a Christian, as he is. Harald Finehair never forced any man to change his faith. Make Olaf king and we end our way of life. We'll be like the southerners, and as weak as they."

"Weak as Brian Boru?" I asked. "Weak as Alfred of England?"

Erling put a hand on my arm and said, "My priest speaks out of turn, but he has a point. The southern lands are rich, and they grow rich by work, not just stealing the wealth of others."

"This is Norway!" said the man. "We haven't any broad fields like England, unless our names are Erling Skjalgsson, and even your fields aren't as fine as theirs, Erling. We haven't their long summers, or their mines of metal. Their god gave them these riches for profit, and our gods gave us strength that we might share the profit!"

"Going a-viking isn't what it once was," said someone else. "In the old days Horda-Kari could take a few ships and catch the English asleep. Nowadays it's harder to surprise them. You've got to join some great army and march up and down the country and beat them down until they pay you Danegeld. As long as that half-wit Ethelred sits on the throne we'll make do there, but he'll die someday, and suppose his heir is another Alfred? And it's the same in France. Even in Ireland and Scotland they've taken to standing together against us."

"If Olaf Trygvesson and his god come to rule, we can say goodbye to harrying forever. Christians teach that all men are on a level—that an Irishman has the same worth as a Norseman, if you can believe it!"

"Still they say Olaf fed the ravens well in England," said someone else. "They say there hasn't been a warrior like him since Haakon the Good. Haakon was a Christian too. Maybe there's something in it."

The man who'd spoken of broad fields said, "Norway is great because we're wolves in a world of sheep! If we turn sheep as well, we won't even be sheep among sheep. We'll be the poorest, skinniest sheep of all. We'll starve on our frosty mountainsides, and the world will pay us no heed, even to pity us."

"It's well to speak of what should be," said Olmod, "but let us consider what is. Can we, do you think, with the combined force of Hordaland, Sogn and the Fjords, defeat Olaf Trygvesson with the men of Trondheim, the Uppland, the Vik, Agder and Rogaland behind him?"

"Have we come to this?" asked Broad Fields. "Do we judge now based on whether we may succeed or not? If to submit is to lose our honor—and I say it is—then let us die, each man, rather than submit. Remember Horda-Kari! Would he have asked such a question?"

"He did," said Olmod.

A hush fell over the company.

Olmod said, "My father and brothers had no wish to be Harald Finehair's men. Why bow to a king when you can be rulers free and clear over your own lands, however small? But they saw how many lords had bowed, and how many were left to oppose the king, and they asked themselves, 'Would it be such a shame to be Harald's men? Do the lords of the southern lands blush to lay their hands on the king's sword pommel and pledge troth? And would we not be better off with one king and one law for all the land?' And they turned their backs on their neighbors and sailed to Harald and offered him service. This I had from their own mouths."

There was quiet for a while.

"How do we approach Olaf?" someone asked.

"There is one among us who is known to Olaf Trygvesson by face and reputation, and who is a Christian as well," said Olmod. "I have proposed before that we bid for Astrid Trygvesdatter's hand for Erling Skjalgsson."

"Will he wed his sister to a mere hersir?"

"Let him be made a jarl."

"Shall Skjalg's son be advanced above the rest of us?"

"Who else among us will Olaf make a jarl? Do you think he'll promote a worshiper of the old gods? And do we want to live in Olaf's Norway without a jarl from our kindred to stand before the king? Suppose Olaf promotes some kinsman of his own over us?"

"Won't the other families have candidates too?" someone asked.

"Most of them owe us favors. And they buy grain from Erling."

"There is one hitch," said Erling.

"What?" asked Olmod.

"I've sworn to wed Halla Asmundsdatter, and as a Christian I may have but one wife."

Olmod settled deeper in his robes. "We would never ask you to break your word, Erling. We all know your word is sacred, as it should be. But there are other counters on the board, and they may be more changeable than your honor."

I broke away from Erling as soon as the meeting was done and ran through the encampment, asking the way to Asmund Fridleifsson's booth. A word to a thrall brought Halla out to speak to me, and I suggested we walk to a more private place. Privacy was difficult to find, but we finally found a spot on the strand. The sun still glowed in the west, and a hundred ships' prows, stripped of their figureheads so as not to offend the land spirits, gleamed in its light.

"You may be in danger," I said.

Halla took my hand and I shivered from crown to footsole at her touch. "What do you mean?" she whispered.

"Erling's kin want to wed him to Astrid Trygvesdatter—"

"I know. They've sent men to speak with my father."

"Don't be afraid for that—Erling refuses to break his word to you. But Olmod hints that there are other ways. And it comes to my mind that your death would be a happy chance for them."

"Surely they wouldn't go so far?"

"They feel this wedding is their best hope of favor with Olaf. They're jockeying to keep their power. A woman's death more or less would be little to them."

"Erling would never consent to their will if they killed me."

"It could look like an accident. Or sickness, if they worked by poison. I'm not saying it'll happen thus—no doubt they'll start by leaning on your father. How strong is your father?"

"His strength is no matter, Father." She looked at her feet and then back up at me. "Father, I think you care for me."

I was grateful for the dim light. I hoped she didn't see me redden. "Of course I care for you, my daughter."

"I don't mean that, Father. A woman knows when a man wants her, and I've seen it in your eyes. I mean no shame to you—you've ever been the decentest of friends. And now I tell you with no shame on my part that I'll be your leman—if you still wish it."

The earth bucked beneath my shoes. I had to clutch at something to steady myself, and Halla was the only thing to hand. I put my hand on her neck, and ran my thumb across her cheek.

"Erling cares for you," I said. "He'd never forgive me."

"He must marry Astrid, Father. Olmod's men spoke to my father and me, and we're agreed. How could I live with Erling, knowing he'd be a jarl but for me?"

"You're worth a jarldom, daughter. Never disbelieve that."

"It's for the land, too. The bonders, like my father, who need a lord in the king's favor. There are always lords, Father—we don't often get the chance to have a part in making them, and to advance a good . . . a good man." Here her voice caught.

"All my life," she said, "men have decided for me. This decision is mine alone to make. Why should Erling be the only one who gets to be a hero?"

I might have kissed her then, but a shadow suddenly approached and took the shape of Erling Skjalgsson.

"Go back to the booth, Father," said Erling. "I want to speak to my betrothed."

I left them embracing by the water. "Well, Aillil, old son," I said to myself, "you've just fulfilled that bastard Caedwy's prophecy. You were offered your heart's desire, and you cast it away."

✧ ✧ ✧

I was stooping to enter the booth when a sound caught me up short. I'd know that voice if I were deaf—I'd know it if I were dead and in Hell. The elf-woman.

I hurried around the corner of the booth and saw her in the twilight, talking to Sigrid, touching her hair.

"Begone, devil!" I cried, and, to my horror she ran laughing, holding Sigrid by the hand. Sigrid laughed too as she ran, and they flitted lightly through the encampment. I shouted "Stop! Kidnapper!" but the people we passed only stared at me as if I were mad, pursuing a quarry that was not there.

They led me up the mountainside, they nimble as shorebirds, I puffing and hulking my way, falling further and further behind at each step. They neared a gray wall of rock that rose sheer above us, and I labored to pump my legs faster, for I guessed what was there.

As they drew closer the elf-woman cried a word out, and a great door, tall enough for a giant, opened silently to them. Once they were through it began to shut itself. I strained my heart near breaking to reach it before it closed, and threw myself through the crack at the last moment, feeling the brush of the stone on my heels. I lay panting on my face and looked about me.

It clutches my heart to this day to remember what I saw there. Tir Nan Og, the land of youth, must have the look of the country I saw inside the mountain. The sky was fair and blue, with a sun of its own that gave light and warmth but would never burn you. The hills and meadows were green as Ireland (oh, sweet memory!), all soft grass and moss with never a prickly or noxious weed. The breeze was gentle, bearing soft melodies just outside clear hearing. Rivers ran through the dales, so clear you only knew there was water in them because the bright things that swam there were fish and not birds. And here and there parties of fair folk in bright raiment danced and played on instruments, laughing and careless, and ate dainty food from silver platters.

Yet there was a strangeness to the place as well. I once saw a book in the monastery on a subject called Geometry. It had drawings of things that weren't objects, but only pure shapes—cones and cubes and what do you call those round things? It seemed to me that whenever I turned my attention away from any particular thing in the land inside the mountain, it resolved itself, at the corner of my eye, to one of those pure shapes. But when I fixed attention on it again, it returned to the form of a tree or a flower or a butterfly, or what you will.

I do not know how long I wandered in that beguiling place, seeking the elf-woman and the girl. At last I found them, lounging in a meadow under a blue and yellow awning, not hiding from me at all, and why should they? I was in the other world now, the door shut behind me.

"Welcome, Aillil," said the elf-woman. "Sit beside us while I call for refreshments."

"I'll not drink anything in this land, or eat anything either."

"Speak not so quickly of that you understand not. Think you you barely made it through the door? It would have closed you out, or crushed you, had I commanded it to. I let you in so you'd see where Sigrid had gone. All this fair land is hers to dwell in; rich clothing and sweet foods will be hers. Are you so in love with your world that you'd force her out of all this to return there?"

I turned to the girl. "Is this what you want, lass? Never to see your mother or sister or brother again? To cut yourself off from the Lord and His salvation?"

Sigrid smiled at me as a child would, her head tilted. Her blue eyes were empty as a crone's womb. "It's lovely here," she said, "There's music and dancing, and good food, and soft garments to wear, and the winter never comes, and no one ever falls in love...."

"You can't take a christened soul," I said to the elf-woman.

"But she can stay with me if she wills, and she does will."

What could I say? What could I offer in God's world that would match this place? I racked my brains for an argument and found none.

"What of you, Aillil?" the elf-woman asked. "You've naught to hold you at Sola. If you renounce your faith you may remain with us here. We can become ... close friends."

There was that smell again I'd smelled in the old gods' shrine. Something tingled at my groin, unruly as another man's dog.

Never had I been so alone. I had no ally—not God (did He hear prayers from this place?), not even myself. I wanted to stay. I wanted this fair creature. Had I ever wanted anything—Halla, Maeve, my freedom, my child, God Himself—as much?

Desperately I clasped my hands, trying to pray, and pressed them against my chest. And there beneath my hands I felt Enda's cross that hung about my neck. Its touch was like a bucketful of cold water in my face.

I lifted it and looked on it. Wonderful work it was, for an unskilled hand—you could read the pain and patience on the Lord's face, almost feel the agony of screaming nerve and outraged muscle. Down at the foot where the carving ended unfinished, it was as if Enda had left his name behind—his and the names of all those who lay down the promise of tomorrow for the dream of eternity—and the name had been taken up into the Beloved's own passion.

And in that moment all my seeing changed. This was not a wide, fair land—it was a great, knobbly cave at the roots of the mountains, lit only by a few fissures in the rock, and the air was cold and damp, and there were bats about, and those who danced were starveling, hollow-eyed mad children in rags who jerked or rocked to tunes inside their heads. And the food they ate was dirt and leaves and rocks and bat dung.

"It's a seeming, every bit of it!" I cried. "A lie, a fraud and a madness! Not a thing here is real!"

"Real!" the elf-woman cried. "What use is reality? What good has reality been to you? Your real world is cruel and bitter; it swallows all your dreams, then it swallows you! Do you think these children here would go out into that world again, even if you could make them see as you see? Lay the wooden Jew aside and join us again! In this world no one ever suffers as its maker did—there are no meaningless sacrifices like his!"

"Meaningless?" I looked on the lovely thing in my hand. Curious how an image of such suffering can be the most beautiful thing in the world. " 'Tis the risk," I said. "This thing is beautiful because it was made in danger. All real beauty is risky. All love is risk. Sigrid said it—'Here no one falls in love.'

"I see Christ in this carving, not just because it's a man on a cross, but because the One who chose the cross is present whenever men and women give their lives for something greater than themselves. At the cross God entered our danger and our failure, and at His rising they rose as well. I wouldn't trade this cross for all your country!"

"But we can give you that too!" said the elf-woman. "You want to feel danger? We can make you feel danger such as you've never imagined! You'll feel a hundred times alive when you've done!"

"With what? A dream? A mummer's show? Not for the sons of Adam. 'Tis the rocky truth—the very risk of very loss—that makes the beauty! The risk God Himself took when He made things that could say no to Him! If Enda's danger had been only a seeming, the beauty would be only a seeming too. But Enda carved his name into the bedrock of the cosmos, into the place where the cross is planted. And there it will remain when the world is ground to dust."

"Great talk!" shouted the elf-woman. "But who is equal to it? That's God's failure! He asks too much. The followers of the old gods sacrifice their food, their beasts, their goods and even their children rather than make the sacrifice He demands. Even you won't pay that toll!"

"Perhaps I will," said I. "But even if I cannot, I'll not settle for your safe world."

"I'd not walk blindly into the danger you've chosen, not for all of Heaven," said she.

"I know. Therefore you are damned."

She was silent a moment. "You say the sons of Adam need the truth. I say the sons of Adam—and Christians in particular—cannot bear the truth. I'll make you a wager on it."

"I've no reason to play games with you."

"I'll give you a reason. I'll let the girl return with you to the outside. But I can always call her back, now she's tasted the life we offer. Win the wager and I'll let her alone."

I frowned. "You leave me no choice."

"This is the wager. Erling Skjalgsson will soon be offered the hand of Astrid Trygvesdatter. To wed her he must break his vow to Halla. I'll wager he breaks his word. Will you wager on his Christian troth?"

"If you can foretell the future, what's the use in wagering?"

"I see you have your doubts about Erling's word. Fear not, I do not know the future. I only speak aloud what I sense in men's hearts."

"Erling is the truest of men. He'll not break his word to Halla."

"Then it's a wager?"

"It's a wager."

"And not a word of this to Erling!"

"No. Not a word."

"Done!" And Sigrid and I stood in the dark outside the mountain.

"Here is how Olaf Trygvesson bore himself in the Vik," said Arinbjorn Thorsteinsson, a hersir of Sogn. "He went about the country and called Things, and there he cowed the people with his armed men and demanded that all be water-sprinkled in the name of his god. And any man who spoke against it was killed on the spot, or tortured, or had a hand struck off, or his eyes gouged out." The assembly of bonders and lords murmured over these unlawful carryings-on. We all stood in the rain, facing the great boulder on which Arinbjorn stood to address us. Near him the judges sat on their benches, with Olmod the Old, who was lawspeaker, chief among them, and around them the Peace Rope had been strung.

Askel Olmodsson spoke for his father. He was no great speaker, but everyone listened carefully because they knew his words came from Olmod. Beside him his son Aslak stood, much grown and filled out since I'd seen him last, taller than his father now. "Everyone knows Olaf picked up outlandish customs in Russia. We can't help that just now. The question is whether we can meet his fleet in battle and defeat him. If not, we must do our best to make him welcome and hope to remind him what conduct befits a Norse king."

"The sons of Erik Bloodaxe were Christians like Olaf," said a bonder. "While they reigned the winters were hard, the summers were dry, and the herring never came."

"And Charlemagne of France was a Christian," said Erling. "So was Athelstane of England, who fostered

Haakon the Good. I haven't heard that their lands suffered bad seasons because of it."

"France and England are not Norway," said the man.

"And which land has most reason to regret that?" asked Erling.

"They say Olaf is as great a warrior as Haakon," said another bonder. "They say he can juggle three knives, and cast a spear as well with his right or left hand, and run outside his ship on the oars. He's been lucky in all his battles, and won much booty. Do the gods give such gifts to a man who displeases them?"

"No one denies that Olaf is a great warrior, and well fitted to lead an army," said Arinbjorn from the rock. "But if we submit to him he'll demand that we cast off our old faith, as he has everywhere else. He's not content to worship his own way and leave us alone. He says every man must pray as he prays, or suffer for it. This is the point. Will we submit to that?"

Olmod whispered to Askel, who said, "Do we have a choice? Have we the ships? Have we the men? Have we the luck? The lords who defied Harald Finehair and got away sailed west, to the Shetlands and Orkney, to Ireland and Scotland, to Iceland. I haven't heard that there are untilled fields in those lands awaiting new settlers today. Erik Thorvaldsson has found land west of Iceland, but the word is that's filling too. Where will we go if we cannot live in Norway, under the king? Flee where you will, you'll find the kings Christian."

No one spoke for a time.

"What do you propose then, Olmod?" asked Arinbjorn at last.

"Let us hear what Olaf has to say. Let us talk to him. We will say to him, 'Olaf Trygvesson, we respect you, but we do not fear you. Show yourself our enemy, and we will fight you and cost you ships and men. Be our friend, and we will serve you and take your god.' Other regions have met this man with defiance and poured blood out for nothing. Let's ask him what he'll do for us if we give him what he wants."

A bonder cried, "I like that! I don't mind being sprinkled if there's some profit in it."

The crowd seemed to agree, and Arinbjorn was calling for quiet when a man in a blue cloak came striding through the crowd to the Peace Rope. He turned and faced the crowd and said, "Hear me! I come from Olaf Trygvesson. He has received the call of the Gulathing bonders to meet with them. His answer is that before he speaks to the bonders he will speak with the lords. He will come with one ship tomorrow morning. He says he wants to greet you all, and will show you how generous he can be to his friends, and how hard he can be with his enemies."

CHAPTER XXVII

They had a handsome ship, painted red and gilded, with a sail patterned in red and gold diamonds. They disembarked at the jetty and climbed the hill, a double line of fair folk dressed in the brightest hues and richest fabrics to be had from the eastern trade. They looked like summer birds, or butterflies, and the sun shone for their convenience. I'm sure I wasn't the only one who suddenly felt himself a mud-daubed, homespun-covered, louse-ridden yokel squatting in the world's remotest nook ... which will have been the intention.

First of all came the bishop and all six priests, in vestments so pure and lovely you'd think they'd sprung from the earth on flower stalks that morning. Then came twelve tall, handsome men whose high heads and easy bearing marked them more clearly than the pommel calluses on the heels of their right hands as warriors, undefeated and in their prime, young enough to think their prime would last forever.

Then came Olaf, a face and blazing blue eyes I recognized, not so tall as Lemming but easily as tall as Erling. What is it that sets kings apart from other men? Even in the Estonian slave market he must have had that look about him. The slavemasters must have beaten him often. At his side walked two golden-haired young women, very tall, very lovely.

"There," said Erling, beside me, "is Astrid Trygvesdatter. The taller one."

I felt cold as I thought of Sigrid. "She's very fair, but not as fair as Halla," said I.

"How can you compare the sea and the sky?" asked Erling. "Does the best wine taste better than a loaf of fresh bread? Each is fine in its own way."

"How stands it with you and Halla?" I asked pointedly.

"She's being stubborn, but let's not talk of it now." His eyes followed the women.

Then came the Erikssons from Opprostad, Sigurd and Jostein and Thorkel, and about fifty more warriors, all lovely to look on, and none of them anyone you'd want to tangle with having nothing more than the right on your side.

Olaf and his party trooped to the law rock. Olaf climbed to its top alone and said, "I greet you, lords of the Gulathing. I am Olaf Trygvesson, by God's grace king of Norway."

Olmod stood, supported by Askel, and said, "We bid you welcome, Olaf Trygvesson. Your fame comes before you. We have long awaited the chance to see your face."

"I rejoice to be here," said Olaf, "to see your honest Norse faces and hear your plain Norse speech. Many years I spent in strange lands, in king's halls and on muddy battlegrounds, but whether I slept on scarlet silk or a cloak thrown on the ground with my brynje on my back, I always dreamed of home, and the light nights, and the glaciers, and the fjords, and eating lingonberries and flatbread, and watching towheaded children play in the heather. There are those who call me an enemy of Norway, but that I can never be. No man loves his mother more than he who has lost her, and Norway is my mother, whom I have found again as I found the woman who bore me, against all hope."

I hadn't heard before that Olaf's mother had been rescued too. I knew a moment of envy, hot as an abscessed tooth.

"I say it again—no man could love Norway more than I do. But because I love her, it pains me to see the sad state she stands in today. There is no high king, and where there is no king the law is weak and divided. Men fear to travel by land, and they fear to travel by sea, for the landway and the seaway are infested with thieves, and so trade is leashed, and everyone made poorer. And lords fall upon each other like wolves to steal each other's property, and there is no one above them to knock sense into their heads. And foreign lords like Svein of Denmark look at this land and lick their lips, saying, 'She has no king; her lords are divided; she is ripe for the picking.'

"But saddest of all is this—on every hill and in every grove I see the temples of devils, the old gods who are no gods, who have eyes but see not, and hands but feel not, and feet but walk not. I want to weep when I think of my own people bowing down to blocks of wood and slabs of rock and offering to them the beasts of their flocks and the fruits of the soil, and yes, sometimes even their fellow men. I weep for the folly of this worship of senseless things, but even more I weep when I think of the hatred and cruelty of the devils who lie behind those images, who have bought the souls of my people for little price.

"It is my dream—it is my purpose—to see Norway brought out of its darkness of ignorance and foul custom, and into the pure light of the Christian faith, to stand beside England and France and other lands the true God has blessed in the brotherhood of Christendom. I offer my love and my shield of defense to all who will be baptized and accept me as king. To those who cling to the old ways I promise only steel, and hemp, and fire. That is the word of Olaf Trygvesson."

Olmod Karisson stood up again among the judges and whispered to Askel, who spoke for him, "Your words, Olaf Trygvesson, are both hard and fair, as a sword is hard and fair. We know that this is your way when you come to any district, and we lords have given much thought to how we should answer you. We are proud men in the west—the first ships to take the Viking road to England came from here. An ancestor of mine sacked Lindisfarne, and brought back such treasure as had never been seen in Norway. It follows that if a man comes to us demanding to be made king, and telling us to break our laws and change our ways just because he has a force behind him, well, we know something of force ourselves. On the other hand, if a man comes to us offering himself as king, and promises to advance our interests and promote our kinsmen, well then such a man we will welcome, and we will swear to him undying loyalty. Forgive me, I am an old man, and my ears are not as sharp as they were. What sort of speech did you make us, Olaf Trygvesson? Was it a threat or an offer?"

Olaf said, "The answer to that lies with you. Will you accept the baptism of Christ, or cling to the worship of devils?"

The lords began to whisper to each other, and Arinbjorn the Sogning hersir stood up and said, "As for me and my family, we have decided to give up the old gods and worship the White Christ. Indeed, we have turned our temple, which you see yonder, into a temple of Christ, and placed an image of him inside, such as you Christians worship. It is a very holy image, my lord, for if you watch it carefully, it can be seen to move."

"We do not worship images," said Olaf, "but it would be outside reason to expect you to understand that so soon. We would see this temple of yours, and this image, so that my bishop may judge whether what you say is true, and if so, whether it is of God or the Devil."

I was surprised by Arinbjorn's sudden conversion, and it struck me as odd that I'd heard nothing of this image before. I said as much to Erling, and he whispered that we must watch Arinbjorn closely.

When Olaf came down, Olmod called Erling to them and presented him. Olaf said, "We've met before, Erling Skjalgsson, and I know you are a Christian. I'm pleased to meet a civilized man in this place."

Olmod said, "We think Erling the most hopeful young man in Norway."

Erling introduced me to the king and I mumbled something polite. The bishop and priests were nearby and I preferred not to make an impression (I'd donned a cap to cover my tonsure). Kings don't mind if you mumble. They don't care about anything you have to say anyway.

We trooped up to the temple, and the king's twelve bullyboys went in first. Then followed the king and his priests and Arinbjorn, then Olmod (leaning on Askel), Erling and me.

As my eyes adjusted to the dimness, lit only by the hearth fire, I could see a strange crucifix planted in front of the gods' dais. It seemed to be life-sized and very lifelike, but why was Christ wearing a tattered robe, and why—dear God!—why had a dog's head been fixed at the top of the upright?

Then I forgot the image, for there was a sudden shout and struggle, and I saw Erling grappling with Arinbjorn, each with an arm around the other's body, right arms raised high. In Arinbjorn's hand a knife gleamed, and Erling's hand gripped his wrist.

The king's bodyguard leaped upon them and had them separated in a moment. "Thor lives!" shouted Arinbjorn. "The gods have cursed you, Olaf Trygvesson! You'll die far from home, forsaken by your Christ!"

"Shall we hang him?" asked one of the guard.

"No," said Olaf, looking around him. "He comes of a high family. Let him be outlawed." There was a sigh from the onlookers, and outside we could hear those who had seen telling those who hadn't.

"I swear none but Arinbjorn knew of this," said Olmod.

"Erling Skjalgsson," said Olaf, "it seems I owe you my life. You've a good eye and a quick hand. What reward can I offer you?"

"Let's speak of that in counsel with my kinsmen," said Erling.

"So be it," said Olaf. "Now, what of this crucifix?"

I looked at it and said, "That's no crucifix, my lord, that's a living man. Where's that knife? Cut him down!"

The guard who'd taken the knife ran forward with me and leaped on the dais to slice the ropes that held the wretch on the cross. Many hands lowered him to the floor, and I said, "I know this man," and knelt beside him. It was my friend Moling. "Get him water," said someone, and footsteps ran off.

Moling breathed in shuddering gasps; he was pale as parchment and weighed no more than a baby, and his skin felt cold. "Brother Aillil," he croaked. "Can't see your face. Know your voice. It seems I've turned my White Martyrdom to Red after all." Then he fell to coughing.

"How long have you been hanging there?" I asked.

"Can't tell. Dark in here, even when I could see. But there's light in my—in my heart."

"Will you be cheerful even now, madman? You can't tell me this is God's good will."

A cup of water was pushed at me, and I put it against Moling's lips. We spilled most of it, but I think a little got down his throat, because he spoke more easily.

"It's the difference between us and them, brother," he whispered. "They sacrifice and carve their runes and chant their spells to bribe their gods to give them what they want. We pray and fast and subdue our flesh so that the Beloved might give us..." And Moling died in my arms.

"Here dies a saint," said Olaf Trygvesson.

CHAPTER XXVIII

"I've a shameful thing to confess, Father," said Erling to me. It was the morning after Olaf's meeting with the lords, and Moling's death. Erling had called me away to talk under four eyes, and we'd climbed the hillside and sat on a large rock overlooking the thingstead. "Last night I dreamed of Astrid Trygvesdatter."

"Show me the man who can put a bridle on his dreams, and I'll show you a man who needs not God's mercy," said I.

"She's very fair," said Erling. "Have you seen her, walking with Olaf? She's as graceful as a hawk on the wind. And when she smiles—"

"Don't torment yourself, my lord. You're not the first man to want a woman he can't have."

"But I can have her, Father. All I need do is break my word to Halla. Halla would understand. My kin would cheer me, since it wasn't a proper betrothal after all. My mother would be so glad her hair would go gold again. And it would be good for the land, so everyone tells me."

"But you won't break your word," said I with a dry mouth.

230

"No."

I sighed. "Halla's worth it, my lord," I said.

"Aye."

We fell silent for a while. It troubled me that Erling didn't agree with all the fervor I'd have used.

"Astrid Trygvesdatter's not perfect," I said. "Her upper lip is too short. And she has a proud look. Any husband who wants to rule his home will have to wrestle her for it, I'll wager."

"Any horseman knows that a beast with spirit is best for the true rider."

"I'm a peasant, my lord, with peasant tastes. I can't see things through a lord's eyes. But it's a sin against yourself to dwell on her like this. If you've made your choice, be done with it. Don't put your hand to the plow and keep looking back."

"I know that," said Erling. "And that's what I mean to do. But I had to talk to someone about it. The priests are right, you know. A man should lie with one woman in his life, and she his wife. Otherwise it ends in unfair deeds."

We went back down to the booths, and I thought in my heart, *You take Astrid, and I'll take Halla, and the whole world will be a happy place.* Then I thought of Sigrid and asked forgiveness and laid a penance on myself.

We went to Olaf's booth, where the Horder lords were gathering. Olaf's priests stood outside. I winked at one of them and he looked away quickly. I had found with pleasure that, far from being eager to question me and object to my haircut, they were snubbing me altogether, as English priests are wont to do with the Irish. Even in the heart of heathendom they wouldn't lower themselves to talk shop with a man of my tonsure. I hadn't had a chance to test Bishop Sigurd, but I assumed he'd be worse than the priests.

We all went inside and sat on the benches. Olaf

had the high seat, and Olmod sat across from him in his blankets.

"I have two matters to discuss with you," said Olaf. "One is a lesser thing, though great in itself, and that is my debt to Erling Skjalgsson for the warding of my body. The second is what terms we shall make in exchange for the baptism of all the men of the Gulathing-law. You men of the west are lucky to have a leader as wise as Olmod Karisson. Wherever I've gone in the land, no lords until now have had the wit to meet me in this businesslike way."

"These two matters you speak of are one in our view," said Olmod. "We have taken counsel, and we have but one wish as to what you shall do for Erling, and for us. We wish you to wed Astrid Trygvesdatter to Erling Skjalgsson, so that we may ever be certain of a place near the king's heart."

"You ask a great thing," said Olaf, scratching his beard. "Kings' daughters and kings' sisters are born for high matches, profitable marriages to kings and the greatest lords."

"We have no objection to Erling's advancement," said Olmod with a smile.

"I need to warn Erling, too, that Astrid will make a formidable wife. If she lacks any virtues, they are that sweetness and biddability which are a woman's greatest charms."

"I must speak," said Erling. "There is no woman alive I'd rather wed than Astrid, and no man I'd be prouder to have for a brother-in-law than you, King Olaf. But I've given my promise to another woman, and I mean to keep my word as a lord and a Christian."

"Well then, there's no point to this," said Olaf.

"Let us set it aside a moment," said Olmod. "Arrangements are being made which may change Erling's mind. In any case, you'll want to set the matter before your sister."

"I would not give Astrid's hand without her consent," said Olaf. "I'm not sure I could if I tried. But it seems we've gone as far as we can in this business for today."

"There is one other thing," said a man. We turned to see that Sigurd Eriksson had stood. "My brothers and I have endured much shame over the years through Thorolf Skjalg's holding of our odal lands. Now we're told we may have to look on Erling Skjalgsson as a kinsman. If this is to be, we must settle once and for all who holds what land in Jaeder, and who shall be lord there."

One of the Horders said, "Will we never hear the end of this Jaeder business?"

"An end to it is exactly what I ask," said Sigurd.

"Do you think I'm going to turn my property over to you?" asked Erling.

"I think you will if the king commands it."

"And would the king command such a thing?" asked Erling, turning to Olaf.

"The king will do what's best for the peace of the land," said Olaf. "Any lord who opposes him will know he has an enemy."

"It would ill become you, O King," said Jostein Eriksson, rising, "to set aside the rights of your near kinsmen for the profit of the sons of Horda-Kari. Don't you see how sly they are? We haven't taken a step since we got here that hasn't been foreseen by Olmod Karisson. He says he knew nothing of Arinbjorn's plan to kill you, but we've only his word on that. If we don't watch ourselves, they'll steal the ships from under our feet as we sail away and leave us swimming in the fjord, wondering how it was done."

"If you've some charge of false dealing to make, let's hear it," said a Horder.

"None of your kin has ever dealt fairly. Your women trade off nursing babies so you'll all learn to suck what's not your own!"

Then the two of them were at each other's throats, and in a moment Olaf was down among them, taking each by the scruff of the neck and shaking them like puppies. The tales of his strength were no lies.

"Now sit down and keep your mouths shut," he said when they were quiet, "or I'll sew you in a sack together and dump you in the fjord. This is not how civilized men act in the presence of the king. Do you understand me?"

The two men bowed their heads and mumbled apologies.

"All right. Don't let it happen again."

He went back to his seat and said, "Thorkel Eriksson. You're a halfway bright man. Set your case before me. Why is Erling's advancement an offense to you?"

Thorkel stood and said, "It's all right for Sigurd. He has Opprostad, and he's hersir. But Jostein and I, as younger sons, must make do with lesser inheritances. Ogmund and Skjalg took some of our best farms. If we held them, we'd be great men as our ancestors were great. While Erling holds them we are that much the less, and the poorer, and we feel the shame of it. It galls us."

The king frowned. "So your complaint is that your lands are too little, and you have to look on Erling Skjalgsson's prosperity."

"We are uncles to the king, my lord. We should not be smallholders in the land."

Olaf nodded. "There's truth in that. Yet I can hardly give Astrid's hand to Erling, if that's what God intends, and then take estates from him. Be silent for awhile, everyone, while I think."

And Olaf set his chin on his knuckles and thought for several minutes while we watched him, quiet as well-behaved children.

At last he sat up and said, "Let me make a proposal. In my business in the Vik, I was forced to outlaw several lords and take their estates. Suppose I were to give the finest of those estates to you brothers, Jostein and Thorkel? The Vik is better land even than Jaeder, and its lords have long been the richest in Norway. Would you be willing to be lords in the Vik, and live far from Erling Skjalgsson?"

Jostein and Thorkel said "Aye" without hesitation. They'd been in the Vik with Olaf and seen the property there.

"Then so be it," said Olaf. "Erling and Sigurd will divide overlordship in the west. I think the two of you can get along without cutting each other's throats, can't you?"

"May I speak, my lord?" asked Sigurd.

"Of course."

"I want to rule no lands but my own. It is my wish to stay at the king's side always."

Olaf leaned back in his seat. "How great a lord does that leave you, Erling Skjalgsson?" he asked.

"I am your man, my lord," said Erling. "How great do you want your man to be?"

We broke up the meeting soon after that. As the others were going out, Erling went over to Olmod. I nosed over to hear what he'd say.

"If any harm comes to Halla Asmundsdatter," he told the old man softly, "I swear I'll go abroad and become a monk."

Olmod said, "What ugly thoughts you have, kinsman."

Murder defiles a holy place, even among the Norse, and after the meeting everyone agreed that it was time to carry out the king's will. A company of men went to the temple and brought out the images of Thor, Odin and Frey, and the smaller images. They broke off all the gold and silver and piled the wood together, and Olaf himself set a torch to the pile. A wailing from the crowd went up with the smoke, bonders and their wives seeing their faith torn from them by the king's word.

"It's a sad sight, in a way," said a voice beside me. I looked and gave a start, for it was Bishop Sigurd. He was young for a bishop, though his hair was iron gray. He had a pleasantly homely face with a long chin and the eyes of a sick man, at once sunken and puffy.

"I'm surprised to hear you say so, my lord," said I, with caution as I knelt. He bade me rise.

"On Sunday we'll dunk all these people in the fjord and call them Christians, but in their hearts Jesus will be just another god they've heard of, less interesting, perhaps, than Thor. And any who refuse we'll torture or kill, although there shouldn't be much trouble of that kind here, as the people generally follow their lords. Still it's not very Christlike, is it?"

"We tried torture at Sola once," I said. "It did us more harm than it did the man we pained."

"I know well what you mean. My hair was brown when I came to Norway."

"Then why, my lord?"

The bishop stared at the fire.

"Come away with me to a place alone," he said, and I led him up to the rock where Erling and I had sat earlier. The bishop seated himself and said, "Do you know what the sin against the Holy Spirit is?"

"I know it's unpardonable. I've never understood what it means."

"The theologians wrangle over it. I have my own idea. In the Gospel, Christ speaks of it after His enemies have seen Him work miracles, and they've said He does these things by the power of Satan. I think what the Lord means by the sin against the Holy Spirit is a state of mind like theirs, in which a man looks at good and calls it evil, or looks at evil and calls it good.

"I must confess to you, my son—I couldn't say it

to my own priests—that sometimes I fear I've committed that sin. Much as I study the scriptures, I find in them no word permitting me to force men to be baptized through violence. The screaming! The smells! I dream of them at night. And a voice says to me—'God would give you hearing ears, to listen to the voice of His Spirit, but day by day you make your ears deaf to the cries of men, and one day they will be deaf even to Him. And then you will have committed the unpardonable sin.' And you cannot shrive me of this sin—not you or any priest—because I cannot turn from it."

"Why not?"

"You're Irish, aren't you—Aillil's your name, am I right?"

"Aye."

"In Ireland, did you ever see a Viking raid?"

"Oh aye. That I did. Up close."

"The Norse tell jolly tales about their gods, and I enjoy hearing those tales. But those same gods teach them that might is right, and that Norsemen are people and foreigners are beasts, and that as Norsemen they have a right to catch and herd and brand and slaughter and sell foreigners as livestock. Only Christ can teach them differently. Ethelred of England said to me when I was commissioned, 'Do your work well in Norway and you'll be more protection to my people than ten thousand warriors.' God knows we men of Christendom are brutal enough with each other. But when we slay our brothers we at least know them for our brothers. In time we may learn to act like brothers. But men who worship Thor will never learn that in a thousand years. Every image I burn, every heathen I baptize, may mean one house unburned, one man unkilled, one child not enslaved."

His words brought back memories of Maeve, and my imposture, and the death of Steinbjorg; and thinking of Steinbjorg made me think of Halla. If she were free of Erling, and Erling free of his vow, and I were free of my lie—

"My lord," I said, "I've not made a confession in more than two years. I've grave sins to be quit of." I knelt as I spoke, and I told all, and I remained kneeling for some minutes after I'd finished, wondering if the bishop had fallen into a trance.

"How very strange are God's ways," he said at last.

"I wonder each day that He slays me not with fire from Heaven."

"I didn't mean that. Oh, you've sinned, and you'll have to do heavy penance. But I was thinking of how the Lord plucked the unlikeliest man in the world out of Ireland and brought him here to do His work. That's so like Him. He never uses a sword when he can do the job with the jawbone of an ass."

"Ass is a fitting word," said I, "but I can hardly say I've done God's work."

"What do you call it then? If I'd gone to Sola I'd not have lasted a week. I'd have been martyred like Erling's first priest. It's fine to have martyrs, but somebody's got to be alive to say the masses."

"My masses weren't effectual! And when I think of the babes I've christened, all still heathen, and the couples I've wed, living in ignorant sin—"

"A layman may christen if there's no priest to hand and the need is great. And marriage is a complicated issue. . . .

"From what you told me, you seem to have been ordained by the greatest bishop of all in a vision. I'm inclined to accept that vision. Ordination by vision is irregular, but what's not irregular in Norway? I've burned men's flesh in the name of Christ—who am I to carp at your ordination?"

"You wish me to live in my sin?"

"No—if your conscience is troubled, we can't have that. Bow your head."

And he placed his hands on me and absolved me,

then said the last words I'd expected to hear—the words of ordination.

"There. You are now a priest ordained by a bishop. And as your bishop I declare all your priestly acts efficacious retroactively. I'm not sure I can do that, but I'll chance it. If this is sin, I take it on myself. That way I can also claim some merit in your victories. Because when you look at it straight on, Aillil my son, you've been a very successful missionary. So stand and take up your cross again. And for heaven's sake, come with me now and get a proper tonsure."

"I'm not sure I even believe in God," I said, numbly. I'd had dreams of wedding Halla, and instead I found myself condemned to priesthood.

"Believe in God? You who've seen the walking dead and Odin and the elf-woman, who've done a miracle? Do you think the healing of Erling was by your own power? If you don't believe in God, I don't know who does."

"All right, I believe in Him," I cried. "But I hate Him! I'm as heathen as the worst of the Norse. God is my enemy. He let them kill my family and enslave my sister. He let my leman be killed, and my unborn child!"

"Does that make Him your enemy? Does God give pleasant lives to his friends, and pain to his enemies? I haven't seen that to be true."

"I hate Him, my lord. I hate God. If that's not the unforgivable sin, what is?"

"You miss the point. You've seen evil, and you called it evil. That's not the unpardonable sin. You're mistaken in thinking all this makes God your enemy, but that's an error, not apostasy.

"Think of this, my son. God's love is a light. It shines brightly on His children in this dark world. What happens to a man who stands in the light in view of his enemies?"

"He becomes a target, I suppose."

"That's what you and I are. Do you know the story of Job? God's love, shining bright on Job, made him an easy mark for the enemy. Granting that we have an enemy, it's natural we'll be attacked. Or don't you believe in devils?"

"Oh, aye. I believe in devils. I believe in God too. But I don't love Him."

"Do any of us love Him worth the use of the word? He loves us—that's the point. Even the best of us raise our pitiful love to Him as a child raises some dead thing he's found in the field and brought home to his father, and the father pretends it doesn't stink and says thank you because he loves his child. When your friend Moling died, what was it he said? 'We fast and pray and whatnot that the Beloved would give us—' You know what he meant, don't you?"

"Aye," I said. "I know what he meant." It was the end of the game—God had cleared the board.

Just then we heard a woman's scream down in the camp, followed by a stream of loud and furious name-calling.

"What's that?" I wondered.

"It sounds like Astrid Trygvesdatter," said Bishop Sigurd. "I would imagine she's just been told that Erling refused her hand."

CHAPTER XXIX

Erling and I sat outside our booth with the others, eating our evening meal. I had to run my hand over my head from time to time, feeling my strange new tonsure. "The tonsure of St. Peter," the English call it. Our old Irish tonsure they sneeringly call "the tonsure of Simon Magus." As if we weren't serving God in our tonsures while their fathers were kissing mares and licking sacrificial bowls.

"Have you talked to Sigrid, Father?" Erling asked me.

I peered at him. "Why do you ask?"

"She seems so strange these days. I find her wandering about among the tents, singing to herself. She doesn't hear when she's spoken to. I brought her to the Thing in hopes I could make her a good marriage, get her mind off that boy who was killed. But it seems she's distracted with grief. Perhaps I should keep her away from steel—"

"No," said I. "Keep her always near steel."

Erling's voice lowered. "The underground folk?"

"I can say no more."

"Sigrid is my sister. I must know."

241

"Trust me in this, as we all trust you. I've said all I can. Tell me how it goes with Halla and Astrid."

Erling looked at the ground and said, "All is well. Astrid utterly refuses to wed me. She says she wouldn't marry a mere hersir in the first place, and certainly not one who has the cheek to refuse a king's daughter's hand." He was putting a good face on it, but it hurt him.

"What of the settlement with Olaf?"

"I can be a jarl without marrying Astrid. Olmod and his plotters will be disappointed, since they say there's nothing like a marriage to make a peace. But when you think of it, how many peaceful marriages have you seen?"

"So you'll wed Halla?"

"Aye. I'll have a fine wife. A fine wife."

I said, "Here comes Sigurd Eriksson. I wonder what he wants."

Sigurd was alone, and when he stopped and stared at the man on the bench across from us, the man got up and walked away. Sigurd sat in his place. "A sweet evening," he said.

"Aye," said Erling. "Sogn is a fine place for beauty."

"Not as good as Jaeder for grain though."

"Not nearly."

Sigurd said, "The king has told us we must live at peace, Erling Skjalgsson. So we're at peace—by law. But there's never a real peace until men make it in their hearts. Can we make true peace now, at last?"

Erling said, "I've never wished trouble with you, Sigurd, nor any of your family. I didn't wish the death of Aki—he left me no choice. I'm sorry you feel cheated by the deeds of my fathers, but it's too late to change that without uprooting my life and wrecking my fortune. Nevertheless, I offer you self-judgment. What penalty should I pay you, that the bloodshed may cease and bad feeling be buried?"

Sigurd leaned his elbows on his knees and stared at the ground awhile. "We're Christians now," he said, "but this Christianity is hard to master. The priests say a Christian must love his enemies, and turn the other cheek to a man who strikes him in the face. How can a man do these things and keep his honor? As far as I can see, no one's worked that out. They talk about it, but no one practices it, not even the priests themselves.

"Still, I say to myself—when a feud has gone on for generations, and there's nothing to be gained, and my family is now better off than yours thanks to Olaf's bounty—what's the use in carrying it on? Yet my kin will not accept peace, I think, unless you pay some price."

"Name the price."

"You'll be a great man in Norway. Everyone knows this. You have property; you have the king's friendship. In these things you are my equal. I don't begrudge it. I think my kin would begrudge it, though, if you were raised above us as a jarl. When the king offers you a jarldom, refuse it."

"That's a high price."

"Your reason need be no secret. Say it's to please us. My kin will be satisfied then."

"I've turned down the sister of the king. Now you bid me turn down his jarldom. I might as well slap Olaf's face and see if he'll turn the other cheek."

"I'll speak for you with him when the time comes. He listens to me."

"I gave you self-judgment, and I must abide by your wishes. But it's a hard thing you ask."

"You gain my friendship with this, Erling. I am no worthless friend."

Sigurd went away, and Erling said, "A man's word should be a cable of steel. But he mustn't be surprised if that cable hangs him one day."

✧   ✧   ✧

The next morning a messenger came asking Erling to come to the king's tent. We went together, with Erling's bullyboys following.

Olaf stood before his booth, wearing a red linen shirt. He had a horn of ale in his hand, and as we came near he said something that made all the men standing around laugh.

"Erling Skjalgsson!" he cried when he saw us. "It's good to see you this fine morning! I've something to ask of you!"

"Anything I can give in honor is yours," said Erling, going to him.

"As my men and I drank together last night, someone got to talking of your adventures. He said that when it comes to strength and skill with weapons you are my only equal in Norway, perhaps in the world."

"I've never made such a claim," said Erling.

"That's not the point, you see. The point is that some men have bet on me, and some have bet on you, and it's up to us to decide the thing for them."

"I'd rather not compete with my king."

"Well, your king commands it." Olaf's eyes were red—I guessed he'd drunk his breakfast. "And he commands that you not hold back to let him beat you, as if you would. We will run, we will cast spears and we will wrestle. And if I'm not winded and bleeding when we're done, I'll lay a heavy fine on you."

The king's bullyboys cleared a course across the Thingstead and set a spear in the ground at each end. The idea was to run down the course and back, rounding the further spear before returning to the near one.

Someone brought a horn of ale for Erling, and as he drank it I said, "I mislike this. A king's pride is touchier than a mortified wound. He'll not punish you for obeying, I expect, but you might lose your favor."

"Has it ever occured to you, Father Aillil, that I can be beaten?" asked Erling, wiping his mouth with his sleeve. "Anyway, I've no choice. Perhaps it's God's will I be a small man in Norway."

"Just be careful."

The footrace, run carrying an axe and a shield, was quickly done, and Erling won it easily. Speed was one of his gifts, and although he and Olaf were nearly of a height, he was built along the lines of a stag, while Olaf was more of a bull. He reached the goal several strides ahead of Olaf, and wasn't even breathing hard.

"Ale for the victor!" cried Olaf, and a horn was brought to Erling. "Drink it dry!" the king commanded. Erling had already had more than his morning measure, but he did as he was told.

A reindeer skin with a bull's-eye on it was next stretched between two spears a distance away, and Erling and Olaf took turns casting three spears each. Olaf's first cast was a little off, while Erling's was clean on the mark. The king ordered a drink for each of them before they cast again. This time both struck the mark. Again the king called for drinks, and the third time both missed by a finger's breadth.

"Now with the left hand!" shouted Olaf. They both missed the first cast, but Olaf was closer. Olaf called for ale. Both missed the second, but Erling was even further off. On the third, Olaf's spear just touched the mark, and Erling was a hand's breadth off.

So the spear throwing was called a draw, and the king called for more ale.

In that moment I understood Olaf Trygvesson, although I dared not say a word to Erling. Olaf was addicted to ale. Like all men so enslaved, he actually grew steadier in the morning when he'd gotten a few measures in his belly, while Erling's senses were dulling.

"Now we wrestle!" cried Olaf. "I warn you again, Erling Skjalgsson, don't hold back a finger! I'll know it if you do!" He pulled off his shirt and crouched, and Erling took his own shirt off, handed it to me, and made ready to meet him.

I gasped when I saw Olaf's back. I'd guessed that he must have been a headstrong slave, and his skin bore witness to it. I'd seen thralls who'd been beaten savagely and often, but I've never, before or since, seen a back as scarred as Olaf's on a man who yet walked. Every color known writhed in its knots and furrows, with white and brown most common. He had to suffer constant pain from the ruined nerves. No wonder he drank so.

The two men approached one another and took the Norse wrestling stance, which involves standing breast to breast, each man looking over the other's right shoulder, his right hand on his opponent's trouser waist, the left grasping a bunch of his trouser leg. They circled, swinging their legs to try to trip the other, for the first few minutes, never looking down (which is bad form). Olaf attempted a tricky hip maneuver, but Erling twisted free. Erling then tried to lift Olaf and drop him off balance, but Olaf avoided that. Then they circled some more, breathing heavily.

Erling tried a cross-hook with his right leg against Olaf's, but Olaf countered with a lift and a knee maneuver. Erling stumbled and nearly fell, but managed to keep his feet. I didn't think he looked well, and he swayed a bit.

"Come on, come on, you'll have to do better than that!" said Olaf. "You want to be a great lord, you'd better learn to fight! You want to scorn kings' sisters, you'd better learn to fight like a troll!"

"I never scorned your sister," said Erling, panting. "I only keep my word, as I mean to keep it to you. Besides, I'm not good enough for Astrid. Ask her."

Olaf kicked out with his heel to hook and trip Erling. Erling stood firm and they grappled a moment, until he got an outside legstroke on the king, which the king struggled out of with a leap and a jig. Then they circled some more, moving slowly now.

"Astrid's changed her mind," said Olaf. "Last night I took her favorite hawk, plucked its feathers out, and sent it to her. She took the hint. She says she'll marry as I will. What's the use being a king if I can't make a jarl of whomever I like?"

"About that jarldom, there's something I should say—" said Erling, but Olaf got a hip under him just then and lifted him high, then threw him to the ground. Erling lay winded a moment, his mouth open, and as he did so Olaf threw himself down and got his legs around Erling's neck (which was not strictly within the rules).

"So what about my sister?" cried Olaf. "Will you marry her, or shall I break your neck?"

Erling croaked, "I cannot break my word to Halla Asmundsdatter."

Olaf said, "Askel, speak your piece!"

Askel Olmodsson stepped out of the crowd and, like a child reciting before his elders, said, "I have offered betrothal for my son Aslak to Halla Asmundsdatter, and her father has agreed to it."

Erling said, "What?" and Olaf took his legs away. Erling sat up, rubbing his neck. "Halla would never agree."

"She has agreed," said Askel. "It's a high match for a bonder's daughter."

"Aslak's just a boy."

"He's nearly a man now—taller than I am. And Halla is little older."

"I think," said Olaf, "that this absolves you of your vow to Halla."

Erling fell backwards on the grass and lay with his arms stretched out a moment. "This is Olmod's doing," he said.

"It's the head of the family's business to arrange marriages."

When he sat up Erling looked like a man loosed from a chain, and his face shone like his honor.

"I'll be very happy to wed your sister, my lord," he said.

Somewhere up in the mountains a scream—from no human throat—rose and died. No one seemed to mark it but me.

CHAPTER XXX

I found Halla walking with her distaff near her father's booth. I asked, "Is this what you're settling for then? This stripling? Do you think you can ever care for him as you do for Erling?"

Halla smiled at me, sweet as the Mother of the Lord. "It's different for women than for men, Father. We like to love, but what we need most is to be loved. Erling will never love me as he loves Astrid, but I think Aslak will. And I think I can make a man of him. Perhaps not an Erling, but a good man still."

"Erling has chosen the lesser woman."

"Don't undervalue Astrid. She's no fairy story princess living her life in a garden. She lost her parents young, and she's known exile and poverty and danger."

I shook my head. "The truth is—I'd hoped that I could . . . see you about Sola each day, as I used to. If I were free—but I'm a priest now for life, and I'd not have you as less than a true wife—"

"You weren't meant for marriage, Father. You have the love of God, the best love of all."

I only looked at the ground.

Halla said, "I remember once when I was a girl, there was a family of cottagers living near us, and they never really made enough of the ground to feed them. In the end they went away, but one Jul before that my mother took pity on them and took me with her to carry a basket of fresh barley bread to their cottage.

"The woman thanked us, and one of the children grabbed a piece of bread the moment he smelled it. He took a bite, then spit it out. He said, 'It's bad!'

"You see, they'd done what many of the poor do. They mixed ground moss into their flour to stretch it. There's no good in the moss for food, except to fill your stomach awhile. But those children had never known anything but moss bread. When they tasted real bread, they thought there was something wrong with it.

"A woman's love, even the best woman's, is only moss bread, Father. When you get used to real flour you'll like it, and it'll feed you as moss never can."

"Is that how you really feel? I would God I had that peace."

"I'm not made of stone. It hurts to say goodbye to love. But I have faith. I learned it from you, even if you didn't understand the lesson."

"He'd better be worthy of what you've done for him," I said. "If he isn't, I swear I'll break his neck."

Tears ran down her cheeks then. I wanted to hold and comfort her, but there were people about.

"I was Erling Skjalgsson's woman once," she said. "They can't take that from me."

"You're Father Aillil's woman, too," said I. "And that you'll always be, for whatever it's worth to you."

CHAPTER XXXI

The Gulathing broke up at last. Aside from acclaiming Olaf king, they made one change in the law that amused me. From that time on, when the land was attacked, thralls were compelled to take up arms.

When I bid the bishop farewell I spoke to him in private. I said, "My Lord, would you be offended to receive the counsel of a man poor in wisdom but rich in scars and bruises?"

He gave me smiling permission to proceed.

"Lay down the iron and steel," I said. "Do the Lord's work the Lord's way. Don't build His house on sand."

I left him with tears in his eyes and no words in his mouth.

Once we returned and gave Ragna the news she'd hoped for, that Erling would marry the king's sister, she began taking her food again and there was no more talk of convents. Like an old king called out to use his life's skills in one last battle to defend his realm, she threw herself into the task of preparing food and drink, finery and bedding for the largest wedding ever seen in Jaeder. "I'm too old for this;

I should be sitting close to the fire and knitting mittens," she told me, but she loved it all. I laughed secretly at first, until one evening in the hall I got to talking to Steinulf and learned that he was Ragna's brother. I don't know why I'd never learned this before—it made sense. The maternal uncle always keeps a wing over his nephew in Norway as in Ireland, and who better to lead your bodyguard than the man who, next to your father, made a warrior of you?

"It's a wonder Ragna has a life at all," he told me. "She was the oldest of us children, and our father's only daughter. Our father was a strange man. You could probably say he was mad, though a son shouldn't speak so. When our mother died, he was still young enough to take another wife, but he didn't even take a leman. He just turned all his love on Ragna. I don't mean he did anything improper to her. I never saw any sign of that. But he thought of her as his wife reborn—in fact he changed her name to Ragna because it was Mother's. In the old religion, we believed that if you gave a child the name of a dead relation, the dead one would live again in the child. And he did a very queer thing to make sure she would never leave him alone. An evil thing, when you look at it straight on. He told her she was ugly.

"Now you and I know that even today she's not a bad looking woman. She wasn't as beautiful as Astrid Trygvesdatter or Halla Asmundsdatter, but she was a handsome girl who could have brought a rich dowry to a husband as well. But Father didn't want her to marry. So every day, almost whenever he saw her, he'd say something like, 'You're a good girl, Ragna. It's a pity you're ugly as a troll, because otherwise you'd make someone a fine wife.' I should have tried to tell her otherwise, I suppose, but when did you ever see a younger brother build up a sister? I'm afraid I joined in the game.

"Then came Thorolf Skjalg. Aside from his squint he was a handsome young man, and rich, and from the day he came to buy horses from our father and saw Ragna, he swore he'd have her. He sent kinsmen to Father and made suit, offering a generous bride-price, and Father refused, saying Thorolf must be a squinter indeed if he thought Ragna fair. Thorolf sent his kinsmen back, naming a richer price, and still Father refused. When he made his third offer, it was so high—high enough for a king's daughter—that our uncles came and threatened to thump Father if he said no. So Ragna was married at last. The day of her wedding she told me, 'I looked at my reflection in a bowl of water this morning and asked myself, "Is this an ugly woman? This woman who has brought the highest bride-price ever known in our family? No, no one pays such a price for an ugly woman."' And from that day she walked with her head high, and she was fairer to look on than I'd thought she ever could be."

"It must have hurt her to lose Thorolf," I said.

"You've no idea. It's a wonder she didn't try to rope Erling to her in Father's manner. She's lost four children over the years, between illness and adventures. It must have been agony to her every time she watched Erling sail off in *Fishhawk*, her treasure floating on a wood chip out where the great serpents play."

"Little wonder this wedding means so much to her."

"Erling is all her hope."

The wedding was set for a day near Midsummer, in June by the Christian calendar, and I'd made sure to check the notches on the stick calendar I'd kept against Bishop Sigurd's so that we'd have no confusion.

If you love ships you'd have loved our neighborhood the day before the wedding. They anchored them in Hafrsfjord so that you'd swear it was a winter forest from all the masts; they even anchored some latecomers up in Risa Bay and drove them overland in wagons to Sola. When they arrived Thursday the guests found a freshly painted hall and garlands of summer flowers everywhere. Pipers and harpists played loudly if not elegantly, and everyone danced. There was food and ale for all, and masses morning and evening. My church had been whitewashed within, and there were golden candlesticks and beeswax tapers, gifts from the bishop.

Olaf and his following, a couple hundred people, made a handsome procession from the jetty to the hall, even more gorgeous than they'd looked at the Gulathing. I'd like to tell you how the bride looked but she'd been veiled against bad luck. Olaf headed the company, looking like a man who had come through blood and steel to take what he wanted from the world, who knew he was living in a saga and was proud of it. I heard someone whisper as he passed, "A king—yes, that's a king." The Erikssons were there too, and Olaf's bent mother, and Aslak Askelsson, looking proud of his new wife, the grave and graceful Halla.

Halla went straightaway to speak with Erling's sister Sigrid, who was looking more beautiful than I'd ever seen her, but had not smiled as far as I could tell since she'd come out of the mountain.

When he got to the steading, Olaf unstrapped his rich swordbelt and handed the weapon to Erling. "I declare the wedding-peace," he said, and then all his company gave up their arms to thralls, who carried them off for storage. Erling and Olaf embraced, and everyone went inside, the men in the great hall, the women in a couple of the other buildings, to begin the business of feasting.

There was food in plenty—porridge and wheaten bread and four kinds of fish and pork and ham and beef, and angelica stalks in honey for a sweet, and there were oceans of ale and mead. The more fighting there is at a wedding, the luckier for the bride and groom, they say. They also say it's a shameful thing to go home from a wedding sober. Not to mention unlikely.

"Organization!" cried Olaf Trygvesson from the high seat, a horn in his hand, barely heard above the arguing and calls for ale. "Organization is what I mean to bring to Norway. Think of the length of the country—from the green fields of the Vik to the icy headlands of the North, where mists shroud the end of the world. A man from the Vik can barely understand the speech of a Halogalander, if at all. And do they think of themselves as Norwegians? Never, unless they're talking to some Englishman who's ignorant enough to call them Danes. They think of themselves as Vikers or Halogalanders. If we're to be a real nation, like England, we must have one king, one faith, one law.

"The land will be divided into regions. Over each region I'll place a jarl, who'll be my representative and collect my taxes, of which he'll keep a part. Under him will be hersirs, keeping watch on the districts and ship levies."

"And the tithes," said the bishop. "Churches must be built, and monasteries and convents."

"Of course," said the king. "I'm going to build a town up on the Nid River, in the Trondelag, and in that town there'll be a cathedral. I'll build it there because the Tronds are the strongest heathens in the land, thanks to Jarl Haakon. They've acclaimed me king, but they've not been christened yet. They won't like it, but it will be done."

"The cathedral or the christening?" asked Erling.

"Both. The Tronders are as good as Christian already. I'll save them if I have to kill them all to do it."

I saw Olmod the Old smiling and nodding in his

seat. This new religion was turning out much to his liking.

"What about going a-viking?" someone asked. "Are we to raid no more, now that the English and the Irish are our brothers?"

Olaf took a long pull from the horn. "There's little I can say about what men do when they sail out of the land. If they try it here I'll hang them by their own guts, but I can't be expected to ward Ethelred's land as well as my own. I'd prefer that men find honest livings, but I fear it'll take time to wean Norsemen from raiding."

"The king was a great Viking himself in England," said someone else, and then he launched into one of those endless, riddle-packed songs. While he sang, two men challenged each other to climb up into the rafters and race about on them. Both fell, being tipsy, and had to be carried out. Then Olaf grabbed the eating knives of two neighbors and juggled them and his own, to a storm of cheers and table thumping.

"Every king must be a juggler," he said when he sat down again. "He must juggle three things—his own struggle against sin, his struggle against lawlessness in the land, and his struggle against the enemies of the land."

"Yes," said the bishop, "but all these enemies are twofold—there is sin born in the heart and sin born in Hell. There is earthly lawlessness and spiritual lawlessness, such as heathendom and heresy. And there is the foreign king, only a man like you and me, and the king of Hell, whom none of us can fight in our own strength. That is why the church must guide the king's counsels."

"Yes, the power of the old gods is not broken yet," said old Bergthor. "Even here at Sola, where we've had a church for years, there's still a troll who lives in the wastes and comes to steal chickens or lambs sometimes. He's been seen haunting the outpastures and you can hear him howling nights."

"A troll?" asked Olaf. "That would be something to see. I wonder how you'd hunt a troll."

"If the truth were known, it's probably just a wolf," said Erling.

"No wolf ever sounded like that," said Bergthor. "I've heard plenty of wolves in my time."

Then a marvel occurred. I can only describe it by saying that the colors in the hall changed. Everything that was bright—the weaving in Halla's tapestry of David and Goliath, the red and yellow paint on the high seat pillars, the reds and blues and greens of the guests' shirts—all grew brighter, as if in sunlight, while all the dull things—the unpainted wood, the sooty rafters, my robe—seemed to darken almost to invisibility, as if at dusk.

And there was the elf-woman, in a gown of green, her eyes as large as a cow's but more fair, her golden hair drifting over her slender shoulders. Not a man breathed.

She glided to the high seat and stood before Olaf. "I have a plea to set before the king," she said. Her voice was like the call of a bird—an evening bird, sweet and unseen.

"Are you of God or the Devil?" he countered. I won't say he looked frightened, but he was pale.

"Does everything have to be one or the other?" she asked. "Do you ask this question of the horse you ride or the dog you hunt with? I am not of your race—your Christ did nothing for me."

"What are you?"

"Your neighbor. Are you not commanded to do well to your neighbor? I bring a plea."

"Have her seized and burned," said the bishop. "This creature is evil. All spirits that will not name Christ as Lord are of the Devil."

"Am I a spirit?" asked the elf-woman. "Do I not

have a body? Look—" and she took a piece of bread from the king's table and ate it.

"This proves nothing," said the bishop. "Spirits can deceive our eyes."

"Will the king hear my plea?"

"What is your plea?" asked Olaf. His eyes had not left her.

"Some time ago a neighbor of mine began to annoy me. He was ever trying to get me into his bed, but he was old and ugly and I did not want him. So I flayed a calf from neck to tail, and left its skin dragging behind it, and I fed it strong herbs mixed with dead men's blood until it grew mightier than a sea gale, and I sent it to haunt my neighbor. Whenever my neighbor left his house, the bull would run to him, invisible, and throw him with its horns. And whenever he went to bed my bull would lie upon him and smother him. Soon my neighbor died.

"But now the bull has turned upon me, and it follows me wherever I go, and I have all I can do to master it. So I beg you, give me some of your holy water, that I may pour it on the bull and kill it at last."

"You've earned the fitting reward for your witchery," said the bishop. "Before the king can consider your plea, you must answer me a riddle."

"We never refuse a riddle."

"The body. The human body. Is it good or evil?"

The elf-woman smiled, spread her arms, and swayed gently before us, and there were sighs from every side. "The body," she said, "is good—very, very good."

"Wrong," said the bishop. "The body breeds pains, and illness, and weakness leading to temptation, and it grows old and dies and rots, and makes mockery of our hopes. Guess again."

"I suppose you'd say the body is evil," she sneered.

"Wrong again. Our blessed Lord came in a body,

and it was a true man's body in every way. Since there was no evil in Him, the body cannot be evil."

"Then there is no answer!"

"There is an answer, but you cannot know it."

"I speak to the king. What is the king's word?"

"I want to lie with you," said the king. The words fell heavy as a man from a masthead. I smelled that mare smell again, as I had in the heathen shrine.

"Renounce Christ. Worship Thor and Odin," said the elf-woman. I wanted to speak, but my mouth was dry as a shinbone a hundred years in the sun.

"I will renounce Christ," said Olaf.

The elf-woman smiled. It was glorious to see (How odd, now I think of it, that I remember her smile. I was sitting on Erling's bench, behind her).

"TO HELL WITH YOU, THING OF EVIL!"

It was the bishop who cried out, and with one motion he snapped the chain of the crucifix from about his neck and sent it flying at the elf-woman.

This is what we saw then. Every man who was there will tell you the same:

The elf woman began to sink down, to shrink in size before our eyes, and her whole body flattened as she sank, from the crown of the head downward, until she was two flat pink disks, the smaller atop the larger.

And then the two disks began to rise again, and there was a white, rounded mass pushing up beneath them, poking up and up from the earth. It rose before our eyes, a hill of white, soft and quaking, towering ever up.

"A breast!" someone cried. "A woman's breast, as big as a house!"

The woman followed the breast, clambering out of the earth, bracing hands the size of ships to pull herself up, elbowing the benches out of her way. And at last she stood free and towered naked above us, and shattered the roof as her head broke it through.

She was a hugely fat woman, as white as milk, with jutting globes of breasts and wide expanse of quaggy hips, and her hair was a mass of black ringlets falling past her shoulders, and her eyes were round as moons and much the same size, and thick, black blood poured with men's dismembered limbs from her gaping mouth.

She screamed, and she was gone, and the hall was as it had been.

The bishop reached out to Olaf, who sat unmoving in his seat. "Bring ale!" he shouted, and a horn was passed, and the bishop poured it down the king's throat.

Olaf coughed and spewed the ale out, then sat for some time with his hands braced on the table, looking down and shuddering.

"I have sinned," he said at last. "Erling, my host, forgive me. I must go to the church and speak with my bishop. The rest of you, carry on with the feast, and pardon me."

These were uncommonly humble words from Olaf, and no one spoke as he made his way out, the bishop holding his elbow, and for many minutes we only sat and stared at each other, wondering.

At last Bergthor said, "This bodes ill, but whether for the king or the wedding I cannot say."

"No," said Erling. "It bodes well. No man attacks another unless he either fears him or knows he has something of value. When the enemy lays on most fiercely, then we know we are dangerous to him, and treasured by God."

"What I can't understand," said someone, "is, if our God is so much more powerful than the old gods, why do all the wonders seem to come from their side?"

A voice said, "Because a marvel is like a sword." Strangely, the voice was my own. "Or like torture. There is no answer to it. The Beloved prefers to woo."

Where did those words come from? I've no idea to this day—I know I'd never thought them. But I pondered them all night, in my bed, until I slept.

I sat on my patch of earth, alone. My children had matured at last, and once mature they had run away from me, with barely a goodbye, and never returned.

I saw a shadow and looked up to see the abbot in his Black Axeman guise.

"Do you forgive me?" he asked.

"Of course," said I.

"Have you done and seen all here that you need to do and see? Are you ready to pay the toll and cross the river?"

"I don't know what I've done and I don't know what I've seen," I said. "I've learned that God pitches camp in the place of pain and danger. Does that mean that evil is good, and God depends on the Devil? Is there no joy without sorrow; no right without wrong? I seem to remember that was heresy."

"And so it is. It's not the evil we need, nor the pain. But we need the risk. The risk we cannot do without. It was God's risk to make the world, and to give Man a choice. All love is risk, and salvation the most dangerous thing of all."

"A man will do anything rather than die. The Lord isn't opposed to that. He's made self-slaughter a sin. Yet the road leads finally to a place where He says, 'Hold still while I kill you.'"

"It's the Death He wants to kill, son. It's your Death you've been clinging to from the day you first popped from the womb and shut your eyes and screamed against the light. Lay the thing down at last."

"It's no easy task. Even Death wants to go on living."

"I didn't call it easy. It's nothing at all He wants from you; but sometimes nothing at all is the hardest thing to give."

"I'm not a hero. I'm not the kind who laughs while they cut his heart out. He says He sees the sparrow fall; but it seems to me He cares only about eagles."

"Aye, it's a thing for heroes, to lay down your right to your safety. Great and small; free and slave; we're all made heroes in the end, or we go to Hell."

"I haven't that to give Him."

"It's not a thing to give. It's a thing to receive. Bow your head now."

I bowed my head. I barely felt the slice of the steel.

The next thing I knew there was golden light, and I was riding again, and the white hind was my steed and we flew over the fair green land, barely touching the ground, steadily approaching a far-off, white-robed figure. Even at infinite distance I knew the face—of all faces in the world most beautiful, most Beloved.

CHAPTER XXXII

On Saturday morning we pulled our throbbing heads out of our beds, or whatever place we'd collapsed in, at Sola or Somme, got some ale inside us to dull the pain, and donned our best togs for the wedding. The day did its duty by bringing out its Sunday weather. The only ill omen I saw was Lemming, watching us motionless as a carrion bird from the roof peak where Enda's gallows was. Erling and his bullyboys and I, singing, trooped down to Somme, where we found Astrid waiting in her veil and bride's crown, and Olaf placed her hand in Erling's.

"With this my sister's hand I make you a jarl, Erling Skjalgsson," said Olaf, "and I make you my man to guard and husband the land of Norway from the mouth of the Sognefjord south to Lindesness."

Everyone gasped, for this was fully half the west coast south of the Trondelag. North of the Trondelag was hardly considered, except for hunting and fishing.

"I thank you with all my heart, and pledge to you my loyalty to the death," said Erling. "But I cannot accept the jarldom."

Everyone stood stock-still. Olaf's face went pale and he clenched his fists. "You despise the honor I offer?"

"Never," said Erling. "I decline with sorrow only. I have promised this as a peace offering to your uncles, the Erikssons."

Olaf turned to Sigurd. "What means this?"

"It is as he says," said Sigurd. "If he remains a hersir he throws no shadow on our house, and it is his mansbot for the death of Aki."

"You made this arrangement behind my back?"

"It was the will of the family."

"So what will I do for a jarl? Shall my sister be wed to a mere hersir?"

"I would have no objection," said Erling, "to being made the highest of that title in the land."

"And so much for my well-planned organization! Well, it seems I've no power in this. Be a hersir then, Erling, and wed my sister and steer all the land I named. It seems the king's will counts for little enough when the lords put their heads together."

"Say not so," said Erling.

And the procession moved back to Sola and to the church, where the Bishop waited outside for us. The vows would be made there, and we would all go inside for the wedding mass after.

Halla moved to my side as we made our way along the road, looking splendid in flower garlands and an overdress of green Chinese silk, though her rich hair had been veiled by the married woman's head cloth.

"You've changed, Father," she said when we'd greeted one another. "Forgive me for saying so, but you used to walk like a thrall, and you never met my eyes when we talked. Now you hold yourself like a jarl, and look me fair in the face. Do you love weddings so much?"

"I'll tell you about it later, daughter," I promised.

We were gathered in the yard before the church and Bishop Sigurd was just saying, "Dearly beloved," when a pile of leaves and dirt I hadn't noticed by the church door stirred of a sudden and rose to become a great, ragged, leathery thing in the shape of a man. With a roar it reached out a long arm and grabbed Astrid, slung her over its shoulder, and ran. It had an uneven, shambling gait, but it was not slow.

The thing had happened so fast, and was so unthinkable, that none of us, even Erling, had time to react. The man-thing was heading towards the gate, Astrid screaming, and although some of the men further back had the presence of mind to pursue, they hadn't the speed to catch the pair.

The creature was well ahead of them going out the gate, and then we could see, sprinting across the homefield and going fast enough to cut off its escape, a man with a sword.

The man was Lemming, and the sword, unless I was much mistaken, was Smith's-Bane, the blade of Thorolf Skjalg, which no one had seen since the night Erling laid the walker-again.

Lemming leaped the wall into the lane and stood full in the thing's path, sword in both hands and cocked over his shoulder.

The thing drew up sharply, looked forward at Lemming and back at the crowd of us coming at it. After a second it turned and came back our way. It was more afraid of Lemming than five hundred men, almost as if it had been—

"Soti!" someone shouted. "Soti's walker-again!"

"No!" I said. "Walking in the daylight? It can't be—"

And then the thing was among us, throwing men left and right, pushing through the crush of us, one free arm dealing thunder and broken bones left and right.

If we'd had our weapons we'd have been able to hurt it, but we were bare-handed all, and though we crowded round we were afraid to strike it even with our hands because of Astrid. At last it stood in a cleared space in our midst, roaring and baring its ragged teeth, one broad arm around the woman's throat, the threat in its single eye plain.

Then it spoke. "Erling Skjalgsson!" it cried hoarsely, and it was Soti's voice.

"Give me my bride," said Erling, pushing near. "Give me my bride and be gone from here."

"Give me my wife!" said Soti. His eye was large and yellow in his blackened face. "Give my wife back to me!"

"Your wife is dead, and justly so."

"Your bride will die, and justly so!" He flexed his arm, and Astrid cried out.

Then Lemming pushed his way through the press, and stood facing Soti with Smith's-Bane raised.

"I'll kill her!" cried Soti.

Lemming laughed.

"Spare her," said Erling, "and I'll give you anything you ask!"

"Revenge!" roared Soti.

"Take my life then," said Erling.

"Come!" said Soti, beckoning with his free hand.

"Let her go first."

"No!"

"How can I trust you?"

Soti rumbled a laugh.

"Very well," said Erling. "Lemming, put down the sword."

Lemming shook his head.

"Lemming, as you love Freydis, I ask it."

Lemming bared his teeth, but laid the sword on the ground.

Erling walked to Soti, and Soti put a big hand around Erling's neck. Soti smiled broadly, a terrible, lipless smile like a skull's, and as he did so Olaf Trygvesson, who had worked his way behind him, swung a huge fist at his temple.

The blow rang like a whip crack. It would have dropped another man, but Soti only reeled a moment, and in that moment Erling seized Astrid and swung her out of harm's way. A hundred hands reached to Soti, but he swept them aside with a roar and pushed his way through the crowd toward the hall. When he got there he swung himself up onto the roof slope, ignoring clutching hands, and began to climb the turf up to the peak.

Erling pushed through and grasped the eaves to follow, but a hand on his shoulder stopped him. He turned and saw Lemming, whose cave-eyes spoke for him. Erling stepped aside, and Lemming began to climb, the sword Smith's-Bane in his belt.

Soti was on the roof peak now, shouting, *"Thor! They say you are dead, but while I live you cannot die! Your hammer killed me not; their torment killed me not; their fire killed me not; I have borne the shock of all the world's weight against me, and still I live, and so I know that you live also! Curse my enemies for me! Let Erling Skjalgsson die as I do, alone, one against many, and let him die at the hands of Christians and kinsmen! Let Olaf Trygvesson die far from home, young, betrayed, his work unfinished, his life unlived, and leave him no son to wear his crown! And Aillil the priest—let him never find the one who is lost to him! Grant me this, great Thor!"*

Then Lemming was up in reach of him, and Soti kicked at him, and Lemming caught his foot, and twisted it, and Soti nearly fell and had to jump backwards. Lemming gave a hop and landed on the peak. He drew Smith's-Bane and they stood facing each other high above us, dark as shadows against the bright sky.

Lemming took a step, and Soti stepped back.

"And you, my thrall, who works my forge now and dandles my daughter on your knee, what curse shall I lay on you? I curse you with years of wolf-living in the wilderness!"

Lemming stepped forward, and again Soti moved back.

"I curse you with the hatred and fear of your fellow men. You shall become a thing like me—a shadow in the night, a bogey to frighten the children. And when you come forth to stand with men again, you will die in hopeless battle, and you will be a traitor to your lord, standing in the shield wall of those who slew him. A fitting death for a thrall, who has no honor. They call you a free man, but I call you a thrall. Thrall born, thrall living, thrall in death. Not a man, even less than I am a man."

Lemming stepped forward again, and again Soti shrank from him. The crowd of us pushed back towards the rear of the hall, to watch their progress.

Soti looked down on us, and he spat. "I curse you all!" he cried. "And I curse all of Norway! This religion you have taken as a gift from the southern lands will be a sickness in you that saps your strength and withers you! You will see the priests grow fat while you grow thin, and as you work to feed them you'll have smaller and smaller strength to go forth and do deeds as your fathers did. And in the end you'll be little men, unaccounted in the world and feared by none!"

Lemming crowded him, and Soti backed up. He was getting near the gable end.

"I would not see the Norway you will build! The Norway you will build is not fit for a man with ribs and a backbone! Heroes will find no place to dwell there—they'll flit from bog to woodland, pursued by all, and hunted down in the end, and their blood will be lost, and all who remain will be thrall stock, with bowed backs and big feet, who'll kiss the backsides of the priests and say thank you when they're smacked in their ugly faces. You've chosen, Norway, and good luck to your choice, but spare me the sight of it!"

And with a shout of *"THOR!"* he ran along the roof

ridge and sprang into space, spreading his arms like a hawk's wings.

And he flew.

I swear on my mother's bones—I was there and I saw it. Instead of arcing earthward, Soti arced skyward, and as long as his cry to his god lasted, he soared like an eagle, into the sun.

Then his voice died, and he dropped like a stone. We felt the jar of his landing in our footsoles.

He lay where he fell, black blood pooling about him, and we gathered around. Olaf Trygvesson stepped near to him and said, "Was this a living man, or a walker-again?"

No one could say for sure. "Bring me that sword!" Olaf cried.

Lemming was there suddenly, and he gave Smith's-Bane to Olaf.

With a blow, Olaf struck the head off Soti, and laid it at his thigh.

"Every man go and get a stone from the fields," said Olaf. "Heap them on him where he lies until he's covered by a cairn that won't be moved till Judgment Day."

And it was done.

As the men moved out to obey, a wailing was heard from the crowd. For one moment I thought Ulvig must have come back also. But when I turned I saw Bishop Sigurd, in his gorgeous vestments, mouth open and tears streaming down his cheeks.

CHAPTER XXXIII

The vows were spoken, and the mass said, and we went into the hall to feast, and when the night came on, not really a night in midsummer, we escorted the couple to the loft, tucked them into bed together, and went down to the hall again to drink and sing and tell dirty stories.

And I grew weary of it at last, for despite the joy of the day and a fair measure of ale and mead, the death of Soti had left a mark on my heart, like the black stain he'd once told me the lightning left on his skull. We were killing the old, wicked Norway—no question of that. But what of the new Norway? The king was a drunkard. The bishop, I was certain, was going mad.

So I wandered out and took the path down to the sea, and as I drew near I wondered to hear a roaring, as if from an angry bull. Approaching with care, I saw a man in a cloak picking up great, rounded stones from the beach and, with spins of his whole body, casting them far out into the waves. It was Erling Skjalgsson.

"My lord!" I said, startled. What was I to say? *I didn't expect to find you here?* An understatement.

Erling stopped and turned to me, a stone in his arms. He panted, and his eyes were as deep and dark as Lemming's. "Just the man I need," he said.

"I'm at your service, my lord."

"I've a bit of a problem in my marriage." He whirled twice and the stone soared out to sea, landing with a great plunk and throwing up a blossom of saltwater. Erling remained standing in a crouch, watching the waves, which leaped at his feet like dogs.

"I've heard men say they're sometimes nervous on the first night—"

"Not that. I'm ready enough. I've never been more ready. But Astrid won't have me."

"Won't have you?"

"She says I may take her by force, but not otherwise. I can't do that."

"No, of course not."

"She says I'm a bonder in a bog, and not fit for a princess. She says refusing the jarldom was a slap in her face. She says if I want her I must either rape her or earn her love."

"Alas, I feared she'd be willful."

"You were right in that."

"Of course she's had a difficult day. Being carried off by a troll, so to speak, isn't what a girl looks for at her wedding."

"Yes, roast Soti. What think you of his curses?"

"It says in the Proverbs, 'As the bird by wandering, as the swallow by flying, so the curse causeless shall not come.'"

"He was a seer though. Perhaps he told me my death indeed."

"What of it? A young man in a narrow place, fighting deadly odds, that's a saga death, you said. What other death would you ask?"

"It's a thing a man shouldn't know, especially on his wedding day."

"And you don't know it. Soti mixed lie and truth

so that you can be sure of nothing. And we'll each of us die, one way or another. No Christian dies alone though. Remember your martyr priest."

Erling stood straighter and pulled his cloak tighter about him. "Thank you, Father. You're right. Someone walked on my grave, but I can endure it."

"What will you do about Astrid?"

"I'll make her love me, Father. If it takes me years, I'll make her love me. I am Erling Skjalgsson, and that's my word."

AFTERWORD:

A note to the reader

If you read historical novels with any historical sense, you know that most authors cheat a little. To get your sympathy, they put social and political opinions into their heroes' mouths which would have gotten them run out of town at best, and burned at the stake at worst, if they'd spoken them in the real worlds they lived in.

Erling Skjalgsson's "self-help" program for his thralls looks suspiciously like this sort of thing. "He wants us to like this slaveholder," you may think, "so he throws in a spot of social consciousness to soften the picture."

To anyone harboring this understandable suspicion, I offer the following extract from the *Heimskringla*, the saga of the kings of Norway, written by the Icelander Snorri Sturlusson (1178–1241):

> "Erling . . . set his thralls to daywork and gave them time afterwards, and allowed every man to work for himself at dusk or in the night.

> He gave them acres to sow corn thereon for themselves and produce crops for gain. He set a price and ransom on every one of them, and many freed themselves the first year or the second; all who were thrifty enough had freed themselves in three years. With this money Erling bought himself other thralls. Some of his free men he turned to herring fishing and some to other trades. Some cleared woods and built themselves farms there, and to all of them he gave a good start in one way or another."

Some modern historians point to this passage as evidence that this was standard practice among Viking Age nobles. I'm not a professional historian, but I make so bold as to doubt that. I'm sure the legal opportunity was always there, but to encourage it strikes me as inconsistent with the Viking temperament. In any case, Snorri thought it unusual enough to make a special note of it.

Of course the fact that I didn't cheat on this point doesn't mean I avoided cheating in other places. . . .

A number of the characters in this book come from history, by way of Snorri. Erling and his father, and Olmod the Old and Askel and his son Aslak were real. Jarl Haakon, Kark and Olaf Trygvesson, of course, lived also, as did Bishop Sigurd and Olaf's sister Astrid. Olaf's kinsmen, the Erikssons of Opprostad, are also documented, except that Aki Eriksson seems to have escaped the record. Historians believe that Erik Bjodaskalle, their father, lived at Opprostad in Jaeder, but Snorri insists that his sons had their estates in the eastern part of Norway. I have ventured to resolve the inconsistency (rather neatly, I think).

There is an ancient stone cross in a museum in Stavanger, Norway, with an inscription that says it was raised in memory of Erling Skjalgsson by his priest. We have the first two letters of the priest's name: AL.

From those two letters (and trusting to the variability of spelling in the Dark Ages) I have raised up the Irishman Aillil.

Regarding the dangerous issue of spelling: due to the complicated nature of the Old Norse language, there are about as many ways to spell Viking names as there are authors. I have adopted an exacting and rigorous policy of spelling each name however I bloody well pleased. Linguists inform me that Olaf should end with a "v," and Erik should be spelled "Eirik." I've tried, but I just can't.

I've chosen to refer to the indigenous minority people of northern Scandinavia as "Lapps" in this book. I'm well aware that this name is offensive to them, and that they prefer to be called "Sami." I have not accommodated them for two reasons: a) Most Americans have never heard of the word Sami, so that I'd have had to add a footnote; and b) Erling and his contemporaries would have called them "Finns" which is equally offensive and confusing to boot. My apologies to the Sami, who are fine people and possibly among my ancestors.

Special thanks are due to Jim Baen for his constructive and insightful suggestions on the manuscript. Thanks to Richard Lane for reading it, and for his comments. Also to my father Jordan Walker and my relatives Oddvar and Hjørdis Rygg; Dagfinnn Kallevik, Unni and Louisa; Thorleif and Gerd Andreassen; Andreas and Gjertrud Andreassen; Einar Andreassen; Kjell and Torbjørg Andreassen; Olaf and Ingeborg Rygg, Ragnhild Rygg and Kjell-Egil Hovlund, who (among others too numerous to mention) were long-suffering with, and helpful to, me as I pursued a man a thousand years dead across the landscape of Norway.

—Lars Walker
Malabar, Florida

The Ghost of the God-tree

Book II of the Saga of Erling Skjalgsson

To my brother Bob—
One of the sworn men

CHAPTER 1

"By what right do you bind and hang free men without trial or offer of ransom?" asked the Viking captain. He was a bold thief, I'll give him that—looking Erling fair in the face, trembling not a whisker, perhaps a touch pale, but all the Norse are pale. "I am the son of Brusi Arnfinsson, a hersir in More."

"Small credit to him," said Erling, still in his fighting gear—gilded helmet with nosepiece, and brynje—rubbing his sword down with a piece of sheep fleece to clean and oil it. "Norway is infested with the younger sons of landed men, sniffing along the borders like wolves, preying on the weak. You burned three farms, killed ten men and took the women and children for thralls before we caught you."

"And you've never gone a-viking and plundered?"

"Not in my own land I haven't. And that was your mistake, son of Brusi Arnfinsson. This is the west of Norway, and Erling Skjalgsson is the law in the west."

"And you're Erling's dog?"

"I am Erling."

The man said no more then, for there was naught to say. Everyone knew the name of Erling Skjalgsson, brother-in-law to King Olaf Trygvesson, and everyone knew he never changed his word. I found no Christians among the pirates to shrive, so Erling had them strung up without further fuss. There were trees here, unlike in Jaeder—a grove of oaks probably sacred to one of the old gods.

Erling went to comfort the liberated women and children, and I looked to our wounded, who were few. We'd made good use of surprise that morning.

Then I took a walk down to the sea, because I dislike the company of hanged men for some reason. Our two ships lay at anchor in a broad cove. A boat not of ours was there as well, a four-oared fisherman's craft. A woman and a boy were drawing it ashore, up to their calves in water. Men lay in the boat, I could tell, but I could not see them clearly.

When he saw me, the boy called, "Are you a Christian priest?"

"That I am," said I. I still felt surprised to be able to say it truthfully.

"And whose ships are these, can you tell me?"

"These are Erling Skjalgsson's of Sola. He's here keeping the peace."

"Then Thor has led us aright! We've come from Moster Island off Boml. We flee Thangbrand the priest."

I scratched my tonsure over that. "Erling is a Christian," I said. "He'll not welcome heathens gladly."

"But he'll not turn us away. All we ask is a place to live in peace. We've heard Erling compels no one to be baptized. We've left all our property except the silver we could carry. If we can buy a piece of land here and live our own way, it's all we ask."

"Is Thangbrand that hard then?"

"He's sworn to rid Moster of all heathens, by baptism or death."

I remembered Thangbrand, whom I'd met at

Erling's wedding that past June. A big, broad-shouldered fellow with the tiny little tonsure you see on priests whose hearts are in this world, never seen in a robe except for divine services (but that wasn't uncommon. I myself had long since taken to wearing laymen's clothes, except for worship and the bishop's visits). He'd seemed a brainless, personable enough lout, more of a courtier than a clergyman, but this wasn't the first I'd heard that he took his missionary work very seriously indeed.

"Do you know any leechcraft?" the lad asked. "My father is badly hurt. We cut him from his bonds in Thangbrand's storehouse and carried him senseless to the boat. My uncle's there too, but he bled to death."

"I'm no great hand, but perhaps I can help. If we can get him to Sola, Erling's mother can look to him." I rolled up my trouser legs and waded into the water to look at the living man in the boat.

The moment my gaze fell on him, lying cheek by jowl with the white corpse as with a sleeping-bag mate, a kind of shroud passed over my eyes, and I nearly dropped in the salt water.

I knew this ugly face well. I could never forget it. A part of the nose was missing, running the left nostril halfway up its length.

He was one of the Vikings who'd stolen Maeve and me from Ireland. One of the gang who'd raped her and killed our family.

Had I thought about it, I shouldn't have been surprised to see him turn up here. There's no breeding ground for Vikings like West Norway, and Ireland is the Norwegians' staked ancestral hunting ground.

My duty was plain. I'd a knife in my belt, and it would be but a moment's work to open the wretch's throat and let him bleed out like his brother. No doubt his kin here would resist, but they were only a boy and a woman, and even if they should kill me, what of it? My kin would be avenged.

Yet I held back. A man, when it comes to it, must work at his trade, and my trade was forgiveness. I'd been a greedy sucker of mercy from Heaven's breast myself. I'd had no inkling, when I accepted God's gift, that He'd test my gratitude so cruelly so soon, but here I was, a servant with his debt forgiven. Would I be a merciful servant or not?

I made fists of my two hands and turned back to shore. I pointed and said, "Erling's camp lies near that grove. See him." Then I all but ran toward the hills inland.

Lord God! Do you ever tire of testing the sons of men? In all my life there was but one sore spot, one unhealed wound, and that was my sister. That I lived a free man, friend and priest to Erling Skjalgsson, only shamed and unmanned me when I thought of her fate.

I walked where my feet took me, cold all of a sudden on a warm August day, pulling my cloak tight around me. After a time I found myself in a low dale with a peat bog at the bottom, the water standing in the diggings. Any Irishman feels at home with peat. I kicked my way through low brush, getting sticking things on my clothing, and sat on a large, lichen-covered boulder by the bog edge, looking away east toward the mountains inland.

I sat, too tired to pray, too tired to think. I settled into a passionless watching, like a beast. There was nothing to see but the birds in the marsh and the flying insects which I swatted unthinking.

I fell into a state halfway between waking and sleeping, and it was thus that I saw the procession.

They came riding eastward through the dale, their beasts treading as lightly on the mud as on a king's highway. Their clothing was bright, their hair shining and golden, but their faces pale as death. Their chief must have been ten feet tall when he stood, and he was dressed all in blue, and he rode a horse without a head.

I've been inside the mountain, and I am a priest of the One God, so I felt within my rights to call out, "Who are you, and where do you ride?"

"We are the old lords of the land, and we move house today, for we're evicted," said the giant in blue. His voice was deeper than an earthquake.

"Evicted? Who put you out?"

"You."

"You may stay for me," said I. "If you harm not my flock, as your underground woman did, I care not where you live."

He reached with his arm, and it seemed to span twenty feet to hover, pointing, in front of the carved wooden crucifix on my chest.

"We cannot live with that thing," he said. "That thing is a bridge between this and the Other World. It puts the High God's print on the fields of men. Our seemings and visions cannot abide alongside that thing."

"I'm an Irishman," said I. "Ireland grows crosses like shamrocks, yet the fair folk dwell in every dell and hillock."

"The small powers can live in Christian lands," said the giant. "Sprites and little old men who sour milk and pinch sleeping servant maids. Such beings have no honor to preserve. They'll live on whatever scraps you throw them. But even in Ireland the Daoine Sidhe are a passed race. They fled but yesterday in our reckoning, and now we too must go."

"I do not wish this."

"Your wishes weigh as little with us as your faith," said he, and they rode on, fading as they went, gorgeous as the summers of childhood.

I unstrung the crucifix from my neck and sat and studied it for the hundredth time. It had been carved by my friend Enda, an Irish thrall lad who'd been hanged for stealing the knife he carved with. His gift had stood me in good stead the day I went into the mountain, for it had revealed the world of the underground folk as a cheapshow seeming, without weight to balance the Lord's flesh-taking, death and resurrection.

Yet I was not blind to the beauty of the fair folk, and I'd have lived in peace with them if I could. There are those who say the undergrounders have no souls and cannot be saved. I do not know. They never let me close enough to learn.

I shook my gloom off at last and trudged back up to the Hangman's Grove. Angry voices grew louder as I approached. I came into the encampment to see Erling's bullyboys binding the woman and the boy, and the boy was shouting, "Foul! Your priest gave us peace!"

When I asked what went on, Erling turned to me with red spots on his cheeks. "Did you tell these heathens I'd shelter them from the king's law?"

I paused before I answered. I suppose I was growing wiser, for I'd not have done so a year before. I said, "May I speak to you under four eyes, my lord?"

It would profit nothing to squabble before the men. We went beyond the grove, out of sight, and Erling said, "Well, what are you about?"

"My lord, 'tis a Christian's duty to take in the helpless and homeless, be they believing or heathen."

"Yes, but if they go back to Father Thangbrand he'll make them Christians. That's God's will, surely?"

"That they'll become Christians I hope; that Father Thangbrand will do it I doubt very much."

"Father Thangbrand is carrying out the king's command. Do you question the king's law?"

"Aye, when the king sets himself to do the Holy Spirit's work by the devil's means. How is Thangbrand's labor on Moster different from what you and I did to Soti, to our shame?"

Erling fumed silently for a moment at that.

"I suppose I'll have to back down this time," he said uneasily. Erling backed down rarely. A lord who changed his mind lost a measure of his warriors' respect, and was liable to lose their loyalty when matters came to a pinch.

"I've another way," I said. "Talk with me as we walk back in sight of the men."

Erling raised his eyebrows but came along. "I never know what to expect from you, Father Aillil," he told me as we walked. "Sometimes I think you're mad, and sometimes I think you're holy, and sometimes I think you're just another kind of beast altogether, like my hounds or one of the underground folk."

"This is far enough," said I. We'd come in view of the men; a hundred eyes turned curiously toward us. "I'm going to shout at you," I said. "Then you strike me down. Afterwards you can give me these heathens' freedom as mulct for striking a priest."

"You want me to strike you? In earnest?"

"Your men are no fools. They'd know if we were playacting."

"A blow from me is no slight thing."

"I know that. I accept it."

"You love these heathen so much?"

"I love them not at all, and one of them I hate more than the devil. But I'll pay any price to keep such blood off my soul as I have of Soti's." I raised my voice. "I SPEAK THE WORDS OF THE LORD! YOU MUST SUBMIT, OR BY GOD I'LL FORBID YOU THE SACRAMENT!"

I remember no more before I woke on the ground, in the grass. The entire side of my face was feelingless, as if it had been snatched off.

A woman was cradling my head in her lap, and I looked up into blue eyes and white hair. There's no sight so lovely as a fair face when you're coming to your senses, and I've been lucky enough to see a couple such in my time. I recognized the heathen woman from Moster.

"I've never seen such a thing in my life," she said. "You risked your lord's displeasure to protect us, who are not even of your faith. Can you move your jaw?"

I tried and wasn't sure whether I'd succeeded, so numb was I, but she smiled as if satisfied. She was a delicate, slender woman, her nose perhaps a trifle long, but very womanly for that, and womanliness is a quality I value (in women). Her eyes were very large.

Then I recalled that lying in a woman's lap, admiring her beauty, was not what the best counselors advised for priests, so I sat up, with only a moment of nausea, and let her help me to my feet.

"I beg pardon for the blow," said Erling (such an apology did his honor no harm, once he'd shown his strength). "As mulct for the respect due you, I give these folk into your protection. But mark this—you'll answer for their conduct."

"Have no fear on that score," said the boy, who stood nearby. "We'll see you don't regret taking us in. I am Arnor Ulfsson. This is my uncle's wife Asa. The men in the boat are my father Ulf, living, and my uncle Thorstein, dead. We're no beggars—we have some wealth. And if you have horses, I'm no worthless man to have about."

"You're a breeder?" asked Erling

"My father was."

"Come talk with me," said Erling, and they went apart together, friends of a sudden.

That left me with the woman.

"I thought you a shade young to be his mother," I told Asa.

She smiled, a little sadly, and said, "Can you come and look at Ulf's wounds? I fear for his life."

I looked away from her. "I'll see if there's someone here who can help."

"Can you not?"

"No," said I. No need to say why just now.

The heathens' boat in tow, we sailed *Fishhawk* south along the coast back to Hafrsfjord.

I love the sight of the entrance to Hafrsfjord. I love it because it means the journey is over, for I hate the sea and all boats. They keep telling me I've only to get my sea legs, but I think I left mine back in Ireland, so little time I had to pack.

We needs must row down the broad fjord against a contrary wind (I mean the men rowed—I row only at great need, and poorly) to Erling's boathouses and pier. They'd seen us coming, of course. Two parties awaited us at the landing—a large procession of women and servants led by Erling's wife Astrid, and a smaller group led by his mother, Ragna.

I clambered gratefully onto the stone pier after Erling, feeling a little better the moment I got it under me. We trooped down (I, as priest, was second) and were greeted by the two groups. Erling took the welcome horn from his tall, fair wife's hand and drank deeply after her greeting speech. I moved quietly over to Ragna's side.

"And how have things jumped since we've been gone?" I asked her.

"Astrid plays the queen as always," said Ragna. "She sneers, she puts on airs; nothing at Sola is good enough for her. God forgive me that I ever wished my son wed to that shrew."

I knew not what to say to her. Ragna had been ready, nay eager, to worship the king's sister when she'd come to Sola two months since, but they'd soon grown unfriends. Astrid thought Erling a match beneath her. In her heart she felt herself a hawk caged with crows, and had no mind to let us forget it.

And there was one thing more. Something only I

beside Erling and Astrid knew, but I thought Ragna guessed.

Every night when they retired, Erling made himself a nest of furs in a corner of the loft they shared, and Astrid lay alone like an abbess.

You'd never have guessed this, of course, from her treatment of him before the people. While never what you'd call affectionate, she always treated her husband with exacting, even exaggerated, respect. To us who knew the truth it was only another kind of gibe.

"We have a guest, my lord," Astrid was saying to Erling. "May I present Eyvind Ragnvaldsson, a wise man and a great traveler?"

A man stepped forward whom I hadn't marked before, though he was remarkable enough. He was passing tall, almost as tall as Erling, and the palest man I'd ever seen in this pale land (I keep saying that when describing Norsemen, but I was forever meeting men who were paler than the last impossibly pale man). His skin was near albino, though his eyes were blue. His hair was white. He was thin but not weak-looking, and the only man I'd seen in the north, outside of priests and monks, who wore no beard. He was also very old—but one only saw his age after studying his face. At first glance he looked no more than two score or so years old. His movements were those of a youth.

"Greetings in Christ's name," said Erling. "The traveler is always welcome at Sola, and the farther he's come the happier the meeting."

"I've heard Erling Skjalgsson named farther out in the world than most men, and am honored to meet you at last," said the guest.

I felt a tug at my sleeve. The heathen woman Asa was there, and she whispered to me, *"There are no trees here!"* Behind her was the boy Arnor, white-faced as a corpse.

I said, "No. This is Jaeder. Treeless from shoreline

The Ghost of the God-Tree

to mountain slopes. Doesn't everyone know that in Norway?"

"You never told us!" the boy blustered. "Who ever heard of a place without trees?"

"One gets used to it," said I.

"You don't understand!" cried Asa. "Sacrifices must be made! They must be hung from the tree limbs, and ale must be poured over the roots, so that Yggdrasil is preserved!"

"Yggdrasil? The tree of your myths?"

"It holds up the nine worlds and the heavens! Without the sacrifices, all may collapse!"

I took them aside so that no one would hear.

"Listen," I said. "Are you the only folk in Norway who make such sacrifices?"

"No," said the boy. "Everyone makes them back home, except the Christians."

"Well even if all this was true, which it isn't, you folks have been making your tree sacrifices for ages, and the people in Jaeder haven't, because they couldn't. And the sky hasn't fallen yet. What makes you think your moving here will change things? Let your friends back home keep the sky up."

"But we can't be sure!"

"We could go barefoot," said Asa.

"That's true," said Arnor. "And we could make sure never to look at a smith."

"Tell me this is a joke," said I.

Arnor said, "What kind of priest are you? Don't you know anything?"

I felt another hand on my arm and turned to see bad-nosed Ulf staring at me.

"Father came to his senses," said Arnor.

I looked into that hated face and felt the blood drain from my own.

"I know you," he said slowly.

"Oh yes, that you do," said I. I braced myself, ready to strike him down for whatever cruelty he spoke.

Instead he gave me a smile, the smile of a five-year-old child, the sweetest baby smile you could imagine from a face so ungodly ugly. Drool ran down into his beard.

"Well, he came to his senses after a manner of speaking," said Arnor.

I turned my back to them suddenly, my chest tight, and mounted the pony that had been brought for me (we great folk all rode). We trooped southwest up the road to Sola, which was a bit of a trek. Sola stands atop a low hill (there is no other kind there) at the north end of a great crescent of low swampy land, hills and farms. The hilltop meadow was ringed with a wall of piled stones to protect the home-field, and a walled way led up to the steading. Near the gate stood my church, raised in stone where the old heathen shrine had stood. We'd burned it and hauled its stones away and brought stones of our own back to build God's house with. I'd sprinkled the place with holy water and prayed the devil out of it before the bishop came to consecrate it.

Then up the lane and into the steading—I swear, the cleanest, brightest steading in Norway (granted, that's not saying much). Astrid kept the thralls at it all day long, and Erling had spent richly on paint and carving and gilding to make it worthy of a princess. Not that she cared.

Then into the hall, a long, massive timbered and raftered building, hump-backed and boat-shaped like most Norse halls, with benches built up along the walls and a hearth-way down the middle where the longfires burned. This was the "old hall," which stood end-to-end with the longer "new hall" Erling had raised since the wedding, for the large-scale entertaining expected of a man of his rank. Erling and Astrid still slept in the loft of the old hall, and we used it for ordinary meals like tonight, when half of Norway hadn't come to dine. It was big enough, even with the household increased to ninety men at all times of the year. We drank while we waited for the food. A lot of drinking got done at Sola those days.

And there was Erling Skjalgsson in his high seat, in the middle of the north bench, between the two great carved pillars, with his tow head and red beard, tall and strong and handsome and honored and rich, a man they made songs about, and all he wanted was to drink himself stupid.

At the women's table, crosswise at the east end, sat Astrid Trygvesdatter, fair as a thousand sunrises with her golden hair and great blue eyes and short upper lip, wanting God knew what—probably just to get away. And on her right Ragna, Erling's mother, much aged and wanting her wishes unwished.

And on Erling's right me, God's priest, feeling duty-bound to find a solution to all this, and clean out of ideas. Not eating much either, because my swollen jaw still ached from my lord's punch.

Our feasts had long since become mummery. As Erling and Astrid pretended to be husband and wife, we all pretended to be the happy household of the second man in Norway.

We drank, we ate, Steinulf roared out a poem about "Ottar's ransom" and "the horse of Aegir's meadow." (Who comes up with these things?)

And Erling asked if the guest had a tale to tell, and Eyvind Ragnvaldsson stood. It's always murky in a hall, and in the gloom Eyvind seemed to glow like a fata morgana. He said:

"King Harald Finehair celebrated Jul in Uppland one year. As he sat at the table, he got word that a Lapp named Svasi was at the door and wished to see him. The king knew Svasi of old, and he accepted his invitation to come out and take meat with him in his tent.

"When he came there he found a woman inside,

Snaefrid, Svasi's daughter. She was beautiful, uncommonly tall for a Lapp, with raven hair and flashing black eyes. She bade him sit and gave him a cup of mead to drink. Their hands touched as he took it, and from that moment Harald could think of nothing but taking her to bed.

"But Svasi had learned to bargain hard, as every Lapp must. He would not grant Harald to have his will without a lawful contract of lemanship. And so Harald gave Svasi rich gifts, and took Snaefrid to himself in law.

"Before she died she gave him four fine sons—Sigurd, Halvdan, Gudrod and Ragnvald, who was called 'Straight-leg.'"

"Of him I've heard," said Erling.

"He was a great soul," said Eyvind. "He was ruler of Hadaland under his father, and much respected.

"But he fell out with his brother Erik Bloodaxe, and Erik was ever Harald's favorite. So when Erik burned Ragnvald in his own hall, it weighed little with the king, by then in his dotage. And that his grandchildren were driven out into exile, scattered to the fence-corners of the world, meant nothing at all to him.

"Ragnvald had a son called Eyvind, a promising young man. He made his way to Sweden and joined a Viking crew, taking the river way to Constantinople. In that great city he talked with men of many races, and heard of far-off lands where there was wisdom unknown even among the Greeks. He befriended a man of the east, who took him morningward across the deserts, and everywhere he spoke to the wisest men, and learned new tongues that he might make friends to take him ever farther. And at last he reached a distant land of which no man from the north had ever heard. There he saw wonderful things, and learned to see the truth at last."

"And what truth did he see?" asked Erling Skjalgsson.

"Our ancestors guessed at it," said Eyvind, "when they said that the soul of one who dies is reborn in a child named for him. The truth is that every living thing, from a man to a horse to the fish in the sea and the louse in your beard, is a soul. According as they live well or ill, they are reborn after death into higher or lower beasts. Thus there is no injustice in the world. If you see a beast or a child suffering, and there seems no reason why they should suffer, you may be sure they did evil in an earlier life, and are paying for it now. In time, after countless circles of rebirth, all will achieve perfection and become gods."

"What of the One God?" I asked.

"Those who have true light say that there is one god indeed, because all souls, and indeed all things that are, are a part of god. And when at last we finish our rings of rebirth we will be united with him."

I'd never met a pantheist before. I'd heard of them, in the monastery, but only as a curiosity out of the past.

"You say that all things are part of God, and returning to God," said I. "But how can that be true of things that do not live? Rocks and water—how can they be reborn to godhood?"

"Things without life do not exist at all, my friend," said Eyvind. "They are shadows. They have being only in our thoughts. That is why those truly enlightened can command their bodies and the world around them. They can suffer pain without concern, and travel great distances in a moment, and appear and disappear at will."

"This is heathendom, surely," said Erling, glancing at me.

"It's like a catalog of heresies," said I.

"We serve the Lord Christ here," said Erling. "You have the hospitality of my house, so I'll not put you out. But I warn you, do not speak of these things here again."

"There are fences round your thinking, Lord Erling," said Eyvind. "You huddle in fear behind them, afraid of thoughts that might disturb your peace. But your peace will be disturbed. The peace of all in Norway will be disturbed."

"You are grandson to Harald," said Erling. "As such you are a threat to my lord, Olaf Trygvesson. As a teacher of falsehoods you are a threat to the souls of my people. I will lay no hand on you for hospitality's sake, but you must speak no more."

"The day has not dawned when a rightful king of Harald's house need mind a hersir out of Horda-Kari. Your kin were always cowardly, and liars."

"You pass the bounds!" cried Erling. All the men were roaring from the benches.

"It is as I said; you fear the truth."

"NO MORE!" Erling rose from his seat. "Be silent, or you break hospitality!"

"I need no hospitality from Rogalanders."

Someone from the opposite bench—I don't know who—lost his temper and threw an eating knife at Eyvind.

We all saw it fly at him, and he saw it too. But he did not regard it. He showed no reaction when it struck him, and I wondered at his self-control. Then I saw that the knife had not struck him after all. Had it missed? No—I'd seen it flying straight at him. And then—I could see this because I was on the same bench, on the other side from Erling—I saw the knife shivering in the wall behind him.

Directly behind him.

If he'd shifted to avoid the weapon, he'd moved so swiftly I'd not seen it at all.

If it had passed through him, then he must be—

"A ghost! You're no man, you're a ghost!" I cried.

"You've all seen me eat," said Eyvind. "I am no ghost."

"You've deceived our eyes in some way!" I said.

"Not at all. I use my knowledge. I've done nothing you couldn't do, if you only embraced the light."

"Begone, thing of Satan!" I cried, my hand on Enda's crucifix.

And he was gone. As if he'd never been there.

"What have we seen here?" asked Erling.

"God knows," said I. "I pray I never do."

Erling said, "Olaf must be told of this."

Erling set the heathens up in a little house hard by the horse byre, near the northeast corner of the steading. He made Arnor his stableman, giving him the place of old Thorvald, whose joints had gone stiff on him after a lifetime of broken bones. The boy commended himself to Erling the first day after his arrival by gentling Ravn.

Ravn was a tall, black horse of foreign blood, probably of mixed breed, but still he towered over the short, stocky, light-coated horses the Norwegians grow. Erling had set his heart on riding a tall horse like an English lord. I'd asked him what was the point, since there were hardly any roads in Jaeder and he went everywhere by boat. Erling had replied that he planned some road-building.

In any case, Ravn had thwarted him thus far by refusing to be ridden. Erling had bought him full-grown, and just between us he'd been skinned in the deal. The beast laid his ears back and bared his yellow teeth at the approach of any man.

But Arnor worked a miracle. He walked out into the pen with a bridle in his hand, and approached the horse somewhat sideways, his head turned, staring off across the fields.

Ravn skipped shy as usual for a start, quivering and snorting, but the boy's strange behavior seemed to soothe him, and he allowed himself to be approached. Arnor began to sing a song, a lilting, repetitive thing such as Lapps sing, and the beast only looked bemused as Arnor slipped the bridle over his head. Then he ran his hands along Ravn's neck, back and withers, and when he was calm, mounted him bareback.

Ravn simply stood in place, and when Arnor shook the reins and spoke, allowed himself to be directed.

Everyone broke into cheers then, and Ravn panicked, and the boy had all he could do to keep from being thrown.

Afterwards Erling declared him a magician. Arnor said, "You only need to think like a horse. A horse is a quarry beast, an animal preyed upon, like an elk or a hare. All he needs to know is that you don't mean to eat him."

"Then he ought to love Christians, for we never eat horses," said Erling.

I'd been watching and listening as they talked, and when they were done I turned to go and was startled to see bad-nosed Ulf, my enemy, standing up against me, smiling.

"Jesus loves me," he said with that childish smile.

"Yes, I suppose He does," said I.

He pointed to his head. "Water? Jesus water?"

I said, "No," and turned away.

He showed up in church the next morning, and never missed a mass thereafter, though I made him stand outside with the excommunicants and the new mothers.

CHAPTER II

A fortnight later Erling set out south on horseback, by appointment to see his wife's kinsman Sigurd Eriksson south at Opprostad. Outside harvest-time Sigurd rarely left his chosen place at the king's side, and the king lived in a year-round progress from one to another royal farm through the length and breadth (such breadth as Norway has) of the land.

In any case Sigurd had sent word to Erling to meet with him. They'd grown middling friends since the wedding, though the old blood-quarrels still rankled.

But that made Erling all the more eager to show goodwill whenever he honorably could. He'd also found it prudent to pass news and appeals to the king through Sigurd—Sigurd was as careful as he in doing right by his former enemy. He was also the man Olaf trusted best, even more than the bishop.

I came along, not to visit the Opprostad folk, but to see my friend Helge of Klepp, who lived not far north of them. I'd only met him at Erling's wedding, and had I known him earlier I'd perhaps not have judged Jaeder so backward and heathen as I had. I liked Helge much for himself, but I must be truthful—

he owned a thing I lusted over and loved to put my hands on.

Erling's sister Sigrid came with me. She'd become my shadow in the past year, keeping by me like a colt with her dam. I wasn't sure what to make of this. Mostly it pleased me but I feared her fear. I hoped I'd not be her crutch for life. She was about seventeen years old then, slender and tall and fair of face like all her family, but she showed no interest in marriage. Sometimes she spoke of taking the veil, but it never came to anything.

With her came Freydis Sotisdatter, who clung to Sigrid as Sigrid clung to me. Fourteen years old now, plump of figure and large of eye, she had uncanny moods, and sometimes could be found staring into space, whispering to unseen confessors.

And because Freydis came, Lemming must come too. He bore the sword Smith's-Bane at his hip, a gift from Erling for high service.

Lemming had only two frets that I could see in those days—keeping watch on Freydis' fancies and putting up with Asa and Arnor, who built their lives around not looking at him.

So in that company we took the road, such as it was, south. It took two days due to the bad going (the trouble between neighbors had strangled commerce) and we put up at a farm along the way. A trip by sea would have been faster, but Jaeder was niggling for harborage. The Opprostad folk themselves, great as they were, had to keep their ships in the Gandalsfjord to the east and cart their goods and folk overland to get to them.

Lemming and I and the girls rose early the second morning and set off by ourselves on foot to Klepp, ahead of the main party.

It's even flatter around Haa and Klepp than around Sola. The distance to Klepp wasn't long, and the morning was fair with only a whisper of autumn. We had a merry walk along the higher ground, past the meadows stone-walled to keep the grazing animals out of the home fields. Seagulls called out over the sea, and cranes swooped down onto Orre water ahead of us. In some places the barley was being cut already by thralls with sickles.

The sky turned gray and began to curl at the edges, like parchment in a fire.

I closed my eyes and shook my head. When I looked again, it was blue and clear, unremarkable as the shining firmament painted by God on the second day of Creation always seems. I wondered if I were taking sick.

"Hard to believe it will all burn in less than two years," said Sigrid.

"You mean Bishop Sigurd's Judgment Day?" I asked.

"The Lord's Judgment Day. It's coming, in the one-thousandth year after the birth of our Lord."

"You shouldn't put too much faith in dates," said I. "Our Lord said no man knows the day or the hour."

"The bishop explained all that. He says no one knows what day it will be, but we can be sure of the year. There are seven ages in the world. The first was from Adam to Noah. The second was from Noah to Abraham. The third is from Abraham to . . . David? Yes, David. Then from David to—well, I forget, but anyway the sixth is from John the Baptist to the Judgment Day, and it lasts one thousand years and the thousand years are up soon. The Lord will come in the sky with His army of angels, and He'll punish the wicked, and the seventh and last age will begin, the Kingdom of God. You respect the bishop, don't you?"

"I respect the bishop above all men. But I think he may be wrong in this. I've talked to farmers who say they don't plan to plant that spring. Let the bishop's calculations be just a year off and we could see famine."

"The bishop says many who do not watch and pray will be left outside the Kingdom."

"I don't lack faith in God. I lack faith in this particular teaching."

"But it's the bishop's teaching! He's God's prince."

"Aye. But bishops have been wrong before."

"I don't understand. If the bishop can be wrong, how can we be sure what God says?"

Before I could answer, Freydis said, "The world we know will end in the year One Thousand."

I sighed. The child was always saying things like this, and the worst part was that her augurings were so foggy you weren't sure what she meant, and so could never prove her wrong. Either she was a little mad (which would be sad if not surprising), or she had the Sight as her mother had (which would be worse).

"What do you mean by that, child?" I asked, confident it would do no good.

"I don't know," she said.

If you want to be thought a great soul, always talk in riddles and never explain. I've used the trick myself.

"Of course you have to have the year right," said an unfamiliar voice in a strange accent.

We looked around to find that a stranger had joined our party. He was a long, fit-looking man, roughly dressed and unarmed except for his staff (a thing unknown among free laymen). He was no Norseman—his dark skin, hook nose and raven hair marked him as a man of the great southern sea.

"Who are you, pilgrim?" I asked.

"Just a wanderer, a singer of songs and a teller of tales, uninvited guest at every house." The stranger smiled, showing white, white teeth.

"I'd say you're a long way from home."

"And I could say the same of you—or am I wrong in thinking I hear the music of Connaught in your voice?"

This man was very good.

"What do you mean about the year, friend?" I asked.

"I happen to know that Jesus Christ was born a few years before the year you call One. So the thousandth return of His birthday has passed, and if He were coming back on the bishop's schedule, he'd be walking among you now."

"Are you a Christian?" I asked the man. "A Greek, perhaps, or an Egyptian?"

"I don't think you could call me a Christian."

Freydis walked up beside him and put her hand in his. "I love you," she said.

He stopped and placed his free hand on her head. "I love you too, child. But I'd want to be first in your heart, and you love all the same." Lemming, always careful of his chick, moved up to them, hand on sword hilt, but the stranger only smiled at him and he relaxed.

"We go to visit Helge of Klepp," I said. "He's a great man, and always welcomes strangers, especially those with tales to tell."

"I know of Helge, and will see him in time," said the dark man. "But not today. I've other errands just now. God bless you all, and give you a good day."

And he set off downslope, carried away from us at remarkable speed on a pair of long legs.

So we came to Klepp, which is a hard place to describe except in terms of what it isn't. It's on a hill in a place not hilly, and it isn't quite as grand as Sola, but it was kept every bit as neatly—a rare thing in Norway. We followed the lane up the low rise into the steading, and there found Helge, sitting at peace on a bench in a sunny place along the south wall of his hall.

Helge was not a big man, but sturdily built and strong. He had a squarish head, and his whitening yellow hair receded from a sloped forehead. And if you wonder why a strong man, old but not feeble, should be sitting at leisure in the sun in harvest-time, it was because of the liverish sword-scar that ran at an angle across his forehead before slashing down to ruin his left eye.

Helge was blind. After the left eye had been destroyed, he'd told me, the right one had endured but awhile before dimming out of loneliness.

"Hello, Old Bear!" cried Sigrid as she and Freydis ran together to plump down on either side of him on the bench and hug him as he stroked their hair. Helge beamed. He adored the girls, though no more blind to their faults than I.

"Where Sigrid and Freydis come, Father Aillil and Lemming cannot be far behind," he said.

"We're here," said I. "You'll have to take my word about Lemming—you know his closed mouth."

"But I know his footstep as well as yours. You are welcome, all of you. I give you joy of the day, and a sweet one it is. Can you say mass for me in the morning, Father?"

"Yes, we'd planned to stay the night if you'll have us."

"Well, I'm not sure I've food enough in the stores for these two gluttons, but I suppose we can all take our belts in a notch."

Helge called a thrall to bring the particular chest, and the man came a few minutes later with my heart's darling. He opened the lid, and I took out the Gospel of Matthew, parchment cased in brown leather with brass furniture and a single ruby in the cross on the cover. I kissed the cross.

"What will you read today?" asked Helge.

"In view of our talk on the road, there's a passage along here I want," said I.

I translated Latin to Norse:

"But of that day and hour knoweth no
man, no, not the angels of heaven, but my

Father only. But as the days of Noah were, so shall also the coming of the Son of man be. For as in the days that were before the flood they were eating and drinking, marrying and giving in marriage, until the day that Noah entered into the ark, and knew not until the flood came, and took them all away; so shall also the coming of the Son of man be. Then shall two be in the field; the one shall be taken, and the other left. Two women shall be grinding at the mill; the one shall be taken, and the other left.

"Watch therefore, for ye know not what hour your Lord doth come. But know this, that if the goodman of the house had known in what watch the thief would come, he would have watched, and would not have suffered his house to be broken up.

"Therefore be ye also ready: for in such an hour as ye think not the Son of man cometh."

"You see?" said Sigrid. "Not a word about the year."

"I think the year is implied, daughter. It's never wise to be too clever with Scripture, finding shadow meanings against the plain sense."

"But the bishop is very close to God. If God has a new thing to say, He'll tell the bishop."

"God is also One who keeps His Word. If a man is shamed to deny his own word, you can be sure God would not do such a thing."

"So you say you understand better than the bishop?"

I had no answer for a moment. It doesn't pay for a priest to backbite his bishop, especially in the presence of children who shed words as a dog sheds hair.

Helge said, "The bishop is not a lord. There are no

lords in the church. The bishop serves the church, and is subject to God and His Word. You know the bishop, and you know as well as I that he's a very humble man. Ask him sometime whether he can be wrong."

I silently blessed Helge for that speech, though I'm not sure the bishop would have put it quite that way. But it satisfied Sigrid for the moment.

After the girls had gone to pick flowers (with Lemming to shepherd them), I told Helge about Eyvind Ragnvaldsson. "He says the world is an illusion, subject to shaping by those who've trained themselves in secret truths. It's heresy, of course—but that knife passed straight through his body. I saw it. It jarred me, friend. I'll say this to you, and to no other living man: Suppose we misunderstood our Lord? Suppose He rose from the dead because He knew that the world of things is but a dream and so was able to impose His will on the dream?"

"That's easier to believe, I think, when you live by sight. For me, who must meet the world by ever barking my shins on it, it's hard to shrug off bodies so lightly."

"But suppose we can't trust any of our senses?"

"Then why believe what you saw Eyvind do? The knife that passed through him cuts both ways."

"You're right, of course. I never thought of it so."

"But it goes further. You must decide what you believe. Do you believe that our Lord spent three years with His disciples, and they learned *nothing* from Him at all? Absorbed not an inkling of His real teaching? If so, He was the worst teacher ever born. Can you really believe that?"

"No. No, I can't."

"There's a place we must all come to, my friend, somewhere in life. It came to me the day I awoke to find my box-bed full of fog, and I opened the door to let the fog out, and the fog had filled the world.

"There's good news—that is that the world is real.

"But there's bad news too—the world is in the power of the evil one, and is full of enemies. That places each of us in the shield wall, and makes of each a warrior or a traitor."

"Yes. I saw that when I went inside the mountain to take Sigrid away. I thought I'd learned the lesson."

"We never learn. Not in this life. We have to remind ourselves every day. That's why I'm so glad to have my gospel book, even if I can't have it read to me as often as I'd like."

"I envy you that book."

"You have your psalter, and the plenarium the bishop gave you. I'm happy with things as they are—it keeps you visiting me."

"I'd visit you anyway."

"I know you would. Did you know that the bishop offered me two marks of silver for my gospel?"

"Really?"

"He thinks it unfitting that a layman own the Scripture. I told him the only person who can read it to me is a priest, so that seemed to soothe him. But I wonder. I'm not sure the Bible was written just for shaven men. Surely Paul's letters at least were written to ordinary folk."

"Well, one sees his point. Can you imagine if every cottager and fisherman had a Bible and thought himself fit to dispute with his priest about it? It would set an axe to the world's roots."

"Or perhaps the blind would receive their sight, the lame would walk, the lepers would be cleansed, the deaf hear, the dead be raised up, and the poor have the gospel preached to them."

"Words from your own gospel book. But if you'd grown up with the poor as I did, you'd have less hope of them."

"You're forgetting again, Father."

I was suddenly very afraid. "You lead me into

dangerous thoughts, Helge. Perhaps the bishop was right about that book."

The day after we returned to Sola I found Arnor in Lemming's smithy, discussing horseshoes with him. I started at finding him there, then regained my voice and asked, "I thought you couldn't look at a smith, to keep the sky from falling. And look—you're wearing shoes now."

"That was before we had the tree," said Arnor.

"Tree?"

"We found a spirit-tree."

I raised my eyebrows. "And what is a spirit-tree?"

Arnor said, "Go ask Asa. She'll show you. I've business to do."

As I left the smithy I noticed that both Thorliv and Fredis were hanging about, near the door but distant from each other. Had Freydis set her eyes on Thorliv's sweetheart? Not a fair contest, that, for all Thorliv's higher birth. Freydis had a way about her, women's skills unsuited to her age.

I walked through the yard to the house by the stable. I found Asa standing on the sunny side of the house, working her loom, which she'd leaned against the wall.

"Arnor says you found a spirit-tree," I said to her. "What in Heaven's name is a spirit-tree?"

She set her beater down and turned to face me, a smile on her delicate face. The pleasure it gave me troubled me. I'd found a woman to love once, and she was another man's wife now, and I'd never looked to care about a woman again. I was a priest, after all.

"I'll show you," said Asa.

She led me north outside the wall to the two ancient burial mounds called Big and Little Melhaug.

"This is an evil place," said I. "There's a dragon sleeps under Big Melhaug. The dragon is an underground-woman, and I've seen her face. She's kept low since Erling's wedding, but I'd not disturb her needlessly."

"Jaeder wasn't always treeless," Asa answered. "There was a time long since when forests covered this land. Trees have ghosts, like men, and trees dedicated to the gods, where sacrifices hung, have mighty spirits. We have found such a god-tree, and it grew once on this mound. A spirit-tree is just as good as a living one for keeping the sky from falling."

"Do you really believe these things?" I asked, shaking my head. "Do you really think there's a tree here that you can't see?"

"Of course. Look up. What do you see?"

I looked up then, and the shock was like a tumble out of bed.

For there, white against the gray clouds, suspended from nothing at all, hung a dead chicken, its neck wrung, its feathers red where it had bled out.

A sacrifice to the gods, upheld by nothing but faith.

CHAPTER III

Summer browned to autumn, and winter passed with snows and rains. Erling chafed, because the winter market he'd started, at Risa Bay up the coast, failed to attract much custom. He instructed the men who collected tolls in Kormt Sound for him to invite (or strongly urge) passing merchants to stop, but those who did didn't stay long and seemed to resent the delay in their voyages.

Preparations for Easter were exhausting, though only part of them were meant for the feasting at Sola. Erling and his family, the bullyboys and I would be with the king at Agvaldsness on Kormt Island. One does not come to a king's feast empty-handed, especially if one is lord in the west, and there were preparations to make.

You never sail any distance in April if you can help it, but Easter with the king is not a thing you can help. So the thralls loaded our supplies in two ships, and we embarked on St. Philip's Day with a foul wind, the men plying their oars and singing. Old Bergthor came to stand beside me as I clutched the rail, clenching my eyes shut to ease the nausea.

We'd just rowed out of Hafrsfjord, bearing west of north.

"If I were a fisherman, I'd say our luck would be bad this trip," he said.

"How so?" I asked, glad for any distraction.

"The seagulls fly to meet us. That means poor weather and bad fishing."

"One expects bad weather this time of year. And I doubt any of us will do much fishing."

"You're a fisher of men, aren't you, priest? Isn't that what you said in church?"

"That kind of fishing can be done in any weather."

"Not if a gale blows us onto a reef and we sink to Aegir's hall."

"Perhaps you ought to go cheer the women, my son," said I. He hated it when I called him "son," so he lumbered off, muttering, no more or less surefooted on the pitching deck than in the yard at home.

The sky went gray and a gravelly snow began to pelt us, but despite Bergthor's augurings we reached the relative shelter of the Kings' Way, the sound between Kormt and the mainland, without mishap. Long and long the men who had controlled that sound had exacted ship-tolls and generally called the dance for a large swath of the west, so naturally one of Harald Finehair's first acts after Hafrsfjord had been to take possession of the king's farm at Agvaldsness. He'd died there, as a matter of fact (in bed, if you can believe it).

We rowed into Bo Harbor, north of the farm, fighting the currents all the way, and tied up at the jetty. We were met by men of the king's guard, and the king's mother, who greeted her daughter with a kiss and offered Erling a horn of ale in welcome.

All together we marched up the hill to the farmstead. Kormt Island is as treeless as Jaeder, but somewhat more rugged. Just outside the walled-in meadow we passed the church, which gave me a heartbeat's pause. It was a steep-roofed wooden house with carved dragons at the gables, much like pagan temples I'd seen. Apparently the king had chosen to simply cleanse and reconsecrate it, rather than razing the abomination and building a proper church. Two tall gray, needlelike standing stones stood just north of it, a little distance from one another, tilting slightly and clearly very old. Pagan monuments without question, but the Norse respect old things. Now that I think of it, so do the Irish.

We entered the yard, and there with his bullyboys was the king, Olaf Trygvesson, tall and fair and strong. He crushed his brother-in-law in a bone-squeaking hug.

"Greetings and joy of the season, Erling!" he shouted. His face was red with drink. "Welcome to my house, you and all who come with you! If any man lacks any thing in keeping with the fast, and tells me of it, and I cannot fill the need, I'll pay him a mark of silver and give him a new sword to boot!"

Everyone raised a cheer for the king's hospitality, and we turned to go inside. But Olaf checked himself, and stopped to stare at something a little way off. We all stopped too and looked where he looked.

There, crouching in the shadow of the wall of a storehouse, was a rag-clad man.

Olaf strode over to the wretch, who tried to run but made bad time, dragging one leg. When the king caught him up he seemed to sag, boneless.

"What are you doing here?" he demanded.

"Forgive me, my lord, I mean not to intrude," the man piped. Up close he was thin and old-looking, though I think less old than he appeared. "I'm a poor fisherman, who cannot work since I was elf-struck and lost the use of my right side. I thought—I thought there might be scraps from the kitchen—"

Olaf put his fists on his hips. "Do you realize the offense you have done your king?" he shouted.

"I meant no offense!" cried the man, eyes wide.

"Then why do you crouch out here, starving, when I dine inside! I am a Christian king! Do you think me less generous than one of your pagan princelings? This is the season of the death and resurrection of the Lord Christ! No man shall leave this place starving, even in the fast!"

The man stared, trying to choke words out.

"As penance for your offense," Olaf went on, "you must humble yourself to receive even more than you ask for!" He drew a twined gold ring off his upper arm and down over his hand. "Take this ring, and get food and clothing, and call your family and friends together to feast Easter morning. Drink the health of your king, and do not neglect to come to church Sunday."

The man took the ring in trembling hands, which sank under its weight. And Olaf grasped him by the arms and lifted him to his feet. The man stood straight.

"I think—" he said, "I think I can walk! I think I can walk again!" And he set out taking a step, then two, then running about in a circle, whooping.

We all shouted then, and the men clashed their weapons on their shields shouting, "Olaf! Olaf!"

It might have been staged, of course. Olaf could have bought a man to play the part of a cripple, to impress Erling and the other guests.

But I think not. Olaf had his sins, stacks of them, but he was never serpent-minded. It might have paid him better had he been. He was a rusher-in, doing what he thought best and saying what he thought right, and the devil with what men thought.

He was also a king. Kings have the healing touch, as all men know. And years later, when some were calling to make a saint of him, they told the story of this healing to vouch for his holiness. It never came to aught, of course.

We entered the hall, larger and grander than Erling's but not much, and took our seats to catch up with the drinking. Erling's people joined other guests at the table on the bench across from the king's men, on the south side (Erling having the seat of honor across from King Olaf), but churchmen were expected to sit together on the king's right, and I found myself there, very nearly across the table from the bishop. Up close his aspect shocked me. Never fleshy, his long-jawed face had wasted to a skull, and his sick man's eyes had grown fearsome—coals in pits. *What ravagement have you done yourself, Father?* I asked silently. This was a good man, as good as any I'd known, but he'd set himself to work that wore him, like a silver spoon spading.

"I don't see Father Thangbrand about," I said to him. I'd been looking for Thangbrand with some unease.

"He's sent to Iceland on a mission," the bishop replied. "He was badly suited at Moster."

I breathed a thankful sigh.

"I understand you have somewhat that belonged to him, my son," he said, too casually.

"I don't know what that could be." In fact I did know.

"A family of heathens, fled from the king's law. It's said you've given them sanctuary. The tale has come from more than one quarter, so I know not how I can doubt it."

"'Tis the truth. They are free folk, and no outlaws as far as I know, and may move about as they please."

"Not when they've defied the king's command to be baptized. Have you baptized them yourself, that you act so freely?"

"I've good hopes of baptizing them in time. I'm an old-fashioned man—I try to spread the gospel through word and kindness."

"Behind the times you are then, Father," said a voice. I turned to face a young man in robe and tonsure who spoke with an English-Norse accent and looked at me out of clear gray eyes. "God's servant must always adapt the gospel to the times he lives in. Turning the other cheek means nothing to these Norse. They respect only strength. So we show ourselves stronger even than they, and earn their respect, and win them."

"Permit me to introduce Deacon Ketil, from York," said the bishop. "He's newly arrived in Norway, and the king sets store by his counsel."

"A long head on young shoulders," said I. "You're a fortunate young man."

"I have a gift. It is from God. I take no credit for it."

"The deacon is a seer," said the bishop.

"A seer? And a deacon?"

"This is a time for seers," said Ketil, "as the Millennium approaches. Great powers are at work in our world, and those with the Sight are needed to winnow good from evil, truth from falsehood."

I faced the bishop. "Have you turned to soothsaying in the king's hall now?"

"What's this?" he answered, with a sad smile. "An Irishman with no faith in signs and second sight?"

"Oh, I believe in them. But I've never seen good come of them."

"Too many scruples, Father," said Ketil, still looking at me with that disquieting calm gaze. "You'll have no scourging and you'll have no scrying. What are you doing in Norway?"

"You've a good heart, Aillil," said the bishop, "and it does you credit. But you've not read the signs of the times. The space is short and there's so much to do."

He coughed into an embroidered napkin for a minute. "Just a year until the Millennium, and so many heathens yet who've never been baptized. There's no time, you see, for persuasion. The work must be done by force or not at all. Catch them, baptize them, and trust God to work faith in their hearts. If I don't do all I can any way I can to convert them, how will I face my Lord a year hence, when He demands an account of my stewardship?"

You'll have marked that I'm a man who likes to talk, and who often as not sets his mouth to work before taking counsel with his brain. But on that occasion I said nothing, could think of no reply, God help me. What might have followed had I found the right words to answer him? I know not. Probably nothing would have changed—he'd welded his mind to his plan. But I didn't even try, and I can't help feeling some fault for the disasters that followed. All I could think was that I was looking at a man who would be face-to-face with the Lord within a year whether the Kingdom came or not.

Our conversation was mercifully shortened by a general call for silence as an Icelander named Hallfred, one of the king's *skalds*, stood before us all and let loose with a new poem in praise of the king. Never had I appreciated the exquisite beauty of Norse poetry before that day. On and on he rambled, about the burden of the tree of the battle and the hater of the burden of the tree of the battle and the lightning of the hater of the burden of the tree of the battle and I hadn't the vaguest idea what he was singing about, but I blessed the thickets of his imagery and the length of his wind.

And when he sat down at last, with a new ring from the king on his arm, the bishop was in deep conversation with Olaf.

So the fast-time feast went on, and I managed to shift my seat back to Erling's table, and we enjoyed countless more unintelligible poems.

I had a chance to talk to Erling's cousin, Aslak

Askelsson, husband to my sweet Halla. Askel had grown much in the year and months since I'd seen him last (his red beard had come in thicker, and he'd put on muscle), but I found it hard to draw him out, and he gave no reason why Halla had not come along to the feast.

Erling introduced me to a woman named Thorbjorg Lambisdatter, a young widow who, he said, owned three ships and plied trade to Dublin, Frankia and the Baltic.

"I always leaned to the business more than my husband, God rest him," said Thorbjorg with a smile. "When he died, I chose to keep my part of the property and build the trade. It's harder for a woman of course, but I've a crew of men I've learned I can trust, and they look after me. There's one or two'd marry me if they could, I think, but none of them could do the job better than I, so why trouble?"

She was a tall woman, this Thorbjorg, with curling auburn hair, a straight nose, and a jaw any man might be proud of. She could almost have been described as manly, except that her hands were long and slender, her voice musical, and she moved with the grace of a maid. Erling spent a lot of time talking to her during the drinking bouts, and I noticed that Astrid marked it. But of course she had no cause for concern. Erling was trying to raise business for his winter market.

We celebrated Easter and bid good welcome to hams and cheeses and eggs, and one night, as we slept on the benches, I woke with the need to go out to the jakes.

After I'd done my business and felt better, I was stumbling back down the well-worn path to the hall when I bumped into something solid and fell sprawling. I heard a curse above me, and looked up to tell him to watch where he went. But there was no one there. It was nighttime, but there was enough light from the moon and stars to show me anyone who might have been around to see.

Again I heard muffled voices. My chest constricted. No man wants to meet unbodied spirits at night in a land still mostly heathen.

In my fear I grasped my talisman, Enda's blessed crucifix. And once again it did its unearthly work to show things truly. My sight cleared, and I saw men in arms, wrapped in cloaks and watching me with bright eyes.

That vision could have been my bane had I not kept some part of my wits. These were men invisible, and they were invisible for a purpose, and if they knew I'd seen them they'd have killed me in a second. So I looked past them, scrambled up muttering, pretending to be drunker than I was, and walked straight down the path, lurching close to one of them so he had to pull back to avoid me. They let me pass and I made for the hall, not too fast, but feeling their cat-eyes boring holes in my back as I went.

Inside I hurried down the hearth-way to the box-bed where the bishop lay. I tapped on the door, afraid to knock too loudly. Clutching the crucifix, I looked around in the shadows, fearful that one of the unseen men might have followed me in, but we were safe so far.

The bishop was a light sleeper it seemed, or perhaps he never slept at all those days. He opened his box-bed door to me straightaway.

"What is it, my son?" he asked.

"Forgive my waking you, Father," I whispered, "and forgive my coming with a mad tale, but what I say is true, by St. Bridget. I've a crucifix here—'tis a kind of a holy relic, and has shown its power to winnow truth from seeming before now. As I was out in the night I touched the cross, and I saw armed men all about the hall whom I could not see before. I fear we're in mortal danger, whether to our bodies or spirits I cannot say. But we must gather the priests and pray now."

He looked at me a moment. "Prayer is always in order, whatever the danger," he said. He pulled his robe on and came out in bare feet, and we waked the priests. "Pray!" he said. "Pray that evil will be restrained, and shown in its true light, and pray that we may be protected by the angels of the Lord."

There was quiet grumbling, but the bishop was not a man to deny, and they were soon with me on their knees. We prayed in Latin, the bishop leading us, and he set a censer burning.

And in a moment a horn was heard without, and there was a shouting and clash of arms, and a man came rushing in to beat on the door of the king's bed.

"My lord!" he said, when Olaf opened to him. "We've caught and taken twenty armed men. We stopped them in the yard."

"In the yard!" said the king. "Were the wardens sleeping, that an armed party came so near?"

"The wardens saw them not," said the bishop, stepping forward. "Father Aillil came but a moment ago to say there were men in the yard who could not be seen. He called us to prayer, and I doubt not it was that that broke their spell and rendered them visible again."

"If this be true we owe you a debt, Father Aillil," said Olaf. "Bring these men in, that we may see their faces and know how to judge them." He closed his door and reappeared a few moments later in shirt and trousers, and set his feet on the step for his boy to lace his shoes on. Then he wrapped his cloak around him and strode to his high seat. A thrall girl, wide-eyed, poked her head out of the king's bed, then pulled it back and closed the door except for a crack through which, no doubt, she watched.

They brought in the attackers. I thought at first

they were drunken as they stumbled and wagged their heads—then I realized they were blind.

"God has turned their darkness back on them," said the bishop.

One, though, was not blind. Last of all the wardens brought in Eyvind, tall and white, and he held his head high and looked me in the eye with contempt, before turning the same look on the king.

"Eyvind!" the king cried. "I should have known it was you. I'd heard rumors you were yet above ground."

"No thanks to you, Olaf Trygvesson. You called me and my fellows to a feast, made us drunk and burned the hall down around us, liar and breaker of hospitality that you are.

"But such a man as I cannot be killed by fire. I live, and shall go on living, to see you cast down and trodden under the feet of your enemies."

"Why should I fear you, Eyvind?" asked the king. "You've seen the power of my God. Against Him your tricks are as a child's skill and a crone's strength."

"Your God has naught to do with it," said Eyvind. "You have a man among you who knows a little of truth." His eyes met mine for a moment. "I should have killed him when I had the chance. Of that sin of omission I do repent."

The bishop stepped forward. "You men have two choices, by God's mercy and the king's. You may be baptized and turned from the evil of your ways, and be granted a quick death. Or, if you will not cast off the shackles of sin, you will be put out of the world with torment and shame."

Eyvind shouted quickly, "None of mine will bow to Christ, now or ever!" His men looked fuddled and fearful, but they said they would follow Eyvind.

"I've seen I cannot kill you with fire," said Olaf then, "so I suppose it must be water. Who knows the tides hereabouts?"

"I do," said a man.

"When is high tide next?"

"A little before dawn."

"Good enough. Is there a skerry somewhere near where we can bind these men, that they may drown slowly?"

"I know of such a place, on the windward side of the island."

"Then let it be done." And the king went back to bed. They took chains and ropes and torches, and marched the wretched prisoners off, and I followed.

Why did I follow? I could have put them out of my mind and rolled back into my bed like the king.

I'd not have slept, though.

I had no reason to love Eyvind and his men. They'd have cut all our throats if they could, or burned us in the hall. But this holy cruelty stuck in my throat like a fishbone.

"Troubled in conscience again, Aillil?" asked a voice, and I found Bishop Sigurd walking beside me on the path.

"You know what I think, Father."

The bishop sighed. "Perhaps you're right, my son. Perhaps we've spoiled all with too much zeal. But what am I to do, with the Lord set to return so soon?"

"Forgive me, Father, but are you so very sure? Is it not written in Scripture that no man can know the day or the hour? What will you say to the Lord if He asks you why you set aside His plain command for the sake of a man's idea, however charming?"

"The Church declared long since that forced conversion can be valid, for salvation is not by man's choice but God's grace."

"Then the Church is wrong in that, for it flies against Christ's plain words as to how we should handle our enemies."

"You speak boldly for a man of questionable ordination."

"I've had the chance to read Helge of Klepp's gospel book," said I.

"We've got to get that book tied down. 'Tis a dangerous thing in untrained hands."

"Why do we fear so to just obey? Do we really think the Lord knew not His own business?"

"Times change. We must change with the times. What use to obey Him in this or that point if we fail to win the world for Him?"

"And what shall it profit if we gain the world and lose our own souls?"

The bishop's voice grew quieter. "I am prepared to sacrifice my soul, if only I can win Norway."

"Father! If I'm certain of aught, it's that the Lord asks no such sacrifice of you!"

"How sweet it would be to be a common priest again, and so sure of God's ways!"

We walked in silence for a time, stumbling on the stony path.

"So what do you intend tonight?" Bishop Sigurd asked finally.

"To watch over these men's deaths, and pray for them."

"No more?"

"No more."

The roar of the waves and the salt in our faces told us we were nearing the west side of the island (Kormt is far longer than broad). The guide led the warriors wading out to a skerry—that's a small, rock island—in an inlet there. Odd that the Norse word "skerry" is so like the Irish "skellig." Since both have to do with rocks in water, I can only reckon that the word goes all the way back to Babel, and that the Norse remember it wrong.

Eyvind and his wretches were bound in chains, tied with ropes and secured to the rocks. The warriors made a fire on the shore nearby and sat down to wait, and the bishop and I joined them.

There was little talk among us, for it was a nasty business we were about, but there was noise from the skerry—shouting and cursing, and weeping and the singing of spells.

And as time passed and the surf swelled, the voices began to scream, and their screams were loud and long and terrible.

The screams rose as the waters rose, and the shrieks of the drowning men became one with the roar of the sea, and it seems to me still, whenever I hear waves crash, that I hear the voices of those lost souls sinking into Hell.

But the screams grew less at last, as one and another heads were covered, and at last there was but one voice, and it was Eyvind Kellda's, and his shouts were curses, on the king and the bishop and Norway and me.

Then only the waves.

After many minutes, one of the warriors said, "There's nothing more to do here. Let's leave the corpses to the crabs."

So they went back to the hall, and the bishop went with them, and I was left alone with the sea and the dead.

I don't know why I went down to the water. No, that's not true. I have an idea, I just don't like to believe it.

I was wearing a robe for the festival, so it was no trouble to kilt it up in my belt, pull off my shoes, and wade into the surf (bone-chilling cold it was, too—shocking as a cane across the shins). The men lay under the water, floating boneless like dead fish on a stringer. I waded over to Eyvind Kellda's pale form and said, "What manner of man were you?"

And his eyes opened.

I could not help myself. I'd seen enough of this kind of thing. I pulled my eating knife from my belt and sawed at the ropes that bound his hands.

When they were free, the hands came up and fastened about my neck.

When I came to my senses I was rocking in the wet bottom of a boat, bound hand and foot. I thought for a confused moment that I was back in the slave ship with Maeve. I lay close beside something wrapped in a piece of woolen sailcloth that felt very like a stiffening body.

I looked up to see Eyvind Kellda at the oars. When he noticed I was awake he gave me a kick in the head that sent me under again.

I woke with a headache right out of Lemming's forge, in darkness slashed by a single, large light that turned, on scrutiny, into a fairly large campfire. My wrists and ankles ached and my hands and feet were numb, bound behind me.

There was a whimpering nearby, and I twisted to see a young woman—a thrall judging by her whitish garment and short-cropped hair—lying bound close by.

Footsteps approached, and Eyvind Kellda towered over me.

He squatted next to me and regarded me as one might a hog marked for slaughter.

"Where are we?" I asked.

"An island. One of hundreds. Nobody's about, so yell all you like."

"What are you going to do to us?"

"Do you see that boat over yonder?" he asked. I twisted my head and made out a boat shape in the shadows, sitting atop a pile of something or other.

"In that boat lies the body of my friend Bjorn. He was the best friend I've had in a long, long life, and your king drowned him on the skerry. I shall give him a Norse funeral of the old kind—I'll burn him in the boat. You will be sacrificed in his honor."

"And the girl?"

" 'Twould be a shame to send him to Valhalla without a woman."

"Has she no say?"

"Of course not, no more than form. She's a woman, and less than that, a thrall. You know, one of the things that makes your religion move so slowly among men in this land is the way you dignify women. Your god's mother, and the one-wife rule, and a single heaven for men and women alike—these are slaps in the face to men with blood in them.

"I've seen a land where wives are burned alive on their husbands' funeral pyres. I thought of doing that for Bjorn, but I felt he'd prefer the old ways of this land. So I'll strangle the girl first. Am I not merciful?"

Tears came up in my eyes. "If I had salvation to offer you, Eyvind Kellda, I'd let you drop into Hell. I cut your bonds. I freed you from the rocks. And you repay me with murder. This girl, who never did you any harm, you'd murder too."

Eyvind laughed then, deep and hearty. "You are so blind, Christian man. You know nothing of the way of god."

"Returning evil for good is not the way of God."

"Those words! Evil and good! What do they mean? Is it good to take care of your parents? What if you steal to do it? Is it evil to break a promise? What if you promised to kill someone? The more you think about good and evil, the less you know. It's like a song that has meaning in a dream but is known for babble when you wake."

"What kind of god do you believe in who cares nothing for good or evil?"

"The more you speak the more you show your blindness. There is no god. Not in the way you think."

"No god? You say this world doesn't exist, that there's only spirit. Now you tell me there's no god. How can there be a spirit world if there's no god?"

"How do you explain light to the blind? How do you explain coupling to children? It would take a very long time, and—I'm sorry—you don't have much time."

"Then I'll tell you. Good and evil exist. They exist because they match the character of God. At the last day He will judge each man according to His law, which He has placed in each of our hearts. And on that day He will send murderous coxcombs like you to the hottest fires of Hell."

Eyvind laughed merrily and struck me backhand. "Talking to you is like talking to a child who believes the world ends at the home-field fence. Killing you will be like killing a child. It ought to be fun."

"At Erling's hall you said each soul is reborn in a higher or lower form. How do they judge what you've deserved if there's no good or evil? And who judges, if there's no god?"

"'Tis not a question of good and evil. 'Tis a question of enlightenment," said Eyvind, as a man speaks to an idiot.

"Why is a man higher than an ape or a horse?" he went on. "Not because he's kinder. A man is crueler than any beast. He is higher because he's cannier. He knows more. He has wisdom those beasts cannot match.

"I am higher than you because I see clearly. A man like you looks within himself and is appalled at what he sees. Because he cannot accept what he is, he looks for some soap to make him clean, like the blood of your Christ. But if you had true wisdom, which may happen in the life to which I now send you, you would accept what you are. This acceptance brings power. This acceptance brings godhood."

"You look to become a god?"

"I am a god. All that is, and all I do, is. It is not good, it is not evil, it simply is. Good and evil are but the fancies of minds uncontent."

"If I had you bound, and were ready to kill you, I wager you'd sing differently."

He cuffed me again. "It is very offensive to me that you keep judging me by these rules of yours.

"There is no injustice in the world. If you suffer pain, it is because in some earlier life you acted in unenlightened ways. It is not my fault if I am the cosmos' tool for working out the balance of your rebirth ring.

"Until you understand this, you will never be released from the ring. That's why all these things you do at Sola—freeing thralls, helping the poor—these are the closest things I know to what you call evil. They prevent the blind ones from working out their earlier lives' darkness."

"If I do it, am I not fated to do it, by your rules?"

He cuffed me again. "Don't talk back on matters you don't understand." I could feel my right eye swelling up. "If you had the misfortune to be born in an unenlightened land, you at least ought to have the decency to listen while your betters explain the facts of life."

"I don't believe in this enlightened land you talk of," I said, tasting blood in my mouth. "I don't believe there's anyplace in the world where they don't know about right and wrong. There is such a thing as natural law. Without it we'd sink to mere beasts."

Eyvind sighed. "Your ignorance wearies me. Of course the land I visited had morality. It had morality because most of its people were young souls, as they are in every land. But I found, as I have found everywhere, that those who have earned higher rebirth—the rich and the powerful—care less for rules than the lowborn. And that is simply one more proof that right and wrong are illusions belonging to the ignorant."

He got up and walked to a small keg near the fire. He broached it with a hand axe, dipped out a beaker of ale, and walked to the thrall girl.

He hunkered down near her head and said, "My dearest friend lies dead in that boat over there. What do you say to that?"

"I-I'm very sorry, I'm sure," the girl stammered.

"I don't think you're sorry. I don't think you care at all."

"No, my lord! I care very much. I'm sorry for your loss."

"Are you? How do I know you care? What will you do to prove it?"

"I don't know—anything you say, sir."

"Anything?"

"Of course. Anything!"

"Good. I have it from your own mouth that you will do anything to honor my friend Bjorn. Let it be known that you have willingly agreed to journey with him into Valhalla."

"No—" she cried, "I didn't—" But Eyvind pressed the beaker to her mouth and forced its contents down her throat, then walked away, leaving her coughing and weeping.

Eyvind crouched beside his friend's pyre and began singing a tuneless song whose words I could not make out.

I took that chance to do a priest's work. "What is your name, child?" I asked the girl.

"Gunn, my lord," she sobbed.

"My name is Aillil. I'm a Christian priest."

"Yes, I heard."

"I'm very sorry, but it looks as if we'll both be in the next world ere long. I have the duty—and the honor—of telling you that the Lord Jesus Christ will welcome you to His Heaven if you wish."

"Yes sir, that's very kind of you, sir."

So I told her the story, how God had come to earth as a man and died to save her from her sins.

"No, sir," the girl said. "Now you say too much. I'm sure He did what you say, but it wasn't for me.

'Twas for great folk—kings and jarls and hersirs and free men. If He's good enough to let the rest of us in with them, I'm most grateful. But don't tell me 'twas for me."

I said, "He told a story once about a shepherd. The shepherd had a hundred sheep. Nine-and-ninety of them stayed safe at home, but one wandered off. And the shepherd left the nine-and-ninety and went to look for the lone renegade. Do you know what this means?"

"No, sir."

"It means that even if you had been the only lost one in this world, He would have gone to the cross for you. There are no small ones in His sight."

"You swear this is true?"

"I'm not the best priest, but I've had a glimpse of His face. I know it's true.

"I've a crucifix—a carving of the Lord Christ on the cross. 'Twas made by a friend—a young man, a thrall like you. He stole a knife to carve it, and they hanged him for it, but he died in faith. The crucifix helped me rescue a girl from the folk inside the mountain, and perhaps my own soul as well—"

"You've been inside the mountain?"

"Aye. And I got out with the girl I went to rescue, and neither of us the worse for it. You see, the crucifix helped me remember that the Lord dwells in the place where death and danger are. When we're afraid—when we're facing death—if we remember to look for Him, He's with us. Especially in those places."

She wept then. "I'd decided to believe in your God already, because that man there by the fire despises Him, and anything he despises must be good. But this—I wish I'd known this before. I would have lived much otherwise than I did."

I took her confession then and prayed with her. There was no way to baptize her, so I troubled her no more with that requirement than the Lord did the repentant thief on the next cross.

Then Eyvind was standing over me, and I was not sure how long he'd stood there, or how much he'd heard.

"I've often wondered how you Christians condemn idolatry, yet treasure your holy bones and statues and bits of wood, and bow down to them, and pray to them. Was there ever such a mass of hypocrisy in one place as in the Christian church?"

He leaned down and probed cold fingers under my collar, pulling out Enda's crucifix on its leather thong. He snapped the thong with a jerk and straightened, examining my relic in the firelight. "Not very good work," he said, "and it's not even finished." With a flip of his hand he tossed it into the fire, not so much as looking to see whether it landed where he'd sent it. It did.

I screamed then, but that scream was as nothing to my cries as he dragged poor Gunn up near the boat and raped her, shouting, "Tell your master when you come to him in Valhalla that I did this in his honor!" And then he took a leather thong he'd secured to a peg in the earth, and choked the life out of her while he stabbed her to the heart with a knife.

'Twas like the rape of Maeve, when the Vikings took us, except that Maeve at least kept her life and what little hope goes with it. Gunn was soon a slack sack of bones which Eyvind swung into the boat at his friend's feet.

Then he turned back to face me.

"I'm waiting," he said.

I didn't dignify him with an answer.

"I'm waiting for you to preach at me, and tell me what an evil thing I've done, and what an evil man I am, and how I'll burn in Hell."

I croaked out of my swollen throat, "No, I don't think I'll do that. If I did, there'd be just the slightest chance that you'd repent and be saved. I don't think I want that to happen."

Eyvind laughed then, and as he laughed he walked toward me, his cord and peg swinging from one hand and his knife in the other.

Then I heard a horn, and I thought it was the angel of death coming for me, and there was shouting, and suddenly men were all around, running and yelling and waving their weapons, but after a few minutes all grew quiet, for there was nobody to fight, only a trussed-up priest and two bodies in a boat.

And there was Olaf Trygvesson, in a gilded helmet with eyeguards and a fine knee-length brynje, shouting, "Where the Hell is Eyvind?"

And there was Erling Skjalgsson, kneeling with a knife to cut my bonds.

And I croaked, as I rubbed my wrists and stabs of pain skewered my hands and feet, "Eyvind was here a minute ago. How did you find me?"

As if in answer, Deacon Ketil of York came to look down at me. "You despised my Sight, Father, but it saved your life this night."

"I could wish you'd come a few minutes earlier," said I.

"Why?"

"Because of the girl Eyvind slew."

"Girl?" He looked around a moment as if he didn't know the word. "Oh," he said then, "you mean the thrall."

He spoke as if thralls were beneath a deacon's notice. I was suddenly whelmed with a desire to throttle this man who'd saved my life. I made to get up, but lances of pain in hands and feet brought me down and curled me up on my side.

I heard Olaf's voice shouting, "He's slipped the net! Dump those bodies in the sea and let's be gone."

I screamed at the top of my voice, "THE GIRL DIED IN FAITH! SHE GOES INTO HOLY GROUND!"

CHAPTER IV

She couldn't lie in holy ground, of course, all unchristened as she was. But the bishop had a heart. He put her just outside the churchyard wall at Agvaldsness. It's a king's church. I think it'll grow. Someday they'll have to move the wall out.

It was back to Sola for us then, with a fair wind, and far from the worst seasickness I've known.

Then followed a busy time, as we set the thralls to the spring spading (both in Erling's fields and the parcels he'd assigned most of them, to earn their freedom on).

I was sleeping raggedly. I missed the slight weight of Enda's crucifix, and it offended my soul that Heaven had permitted Eyvind to destroy it without a fight.

Stripped of my soul's anchor, I was beginning to doubt my eyes and my ears, and the very earth under my feet. Nothing seemed fully real to me. I kept wondering, What's truly here? Are my senses making game of me?

Gradually the world faded, as it were, before my eyes. Things that had seemed sharp and solid—houses for instance, and the mountains to the east—began to blanch, and the mountains disappeared altogether. I was too frightened to tell anyone about it, until I overheard people talking about the fog that had rolled in and wouldn't go away. I noticed then that the air was uncommonly calm—Jaeder is usually a windy place. The fog had come and there'd been nothing to blow it away.

I walked the path down to the church one night for mass, and found myself inside without a memory of using the door. I had a panicked moment, afraid I'd passed through a wall unawares. I said the mass with a mind uncentered, and I thought some of the household looked at me strangely.

Afterwards, when all were gone and I was snuffing the candles, a voice called from without. I went to the door. I unlatched it. I didn't remember putting the latch on.

"Father, can you help me?" The voice was Asa's.

"What's the matter?" I asked, shaking my head to clear it. "Come inside."

"I won't enter your holy place," she said. "I fear your God."

"Why?"

"Your Jesus is a fearsome god. Thor asks us to sacrifice, and to be just to one another. Beyond that he lets us alone. There's no guessing what your Jesus will ask for."

"You should really convert," I said, looking at her through the doorway. "You have a future as a theologian."

Her mouth opened. "I don't understand," she said. I apologized for making a joke over her head and went out where she was.

"Ulf is gone," she said. "I've looked everywhere I can think of except down on the strand, and I'm frightened to go all that way alone in this murk."

I told her I'd be glad to go down to the shore with

her. I lit a fish-oil lamp to give us some light. Little chance of it being blown out with the air as still as a casket of lead.

We took the path together, side by side, talking idly of how the fog had strangled all shipping and fishing. I enjoyed being with her—I hadn't felt so at ease with a woman since . . .

Halla.

Ye saints and holy prophets, have pity on me. I'd as soon not go through that again.

We found Ulf at the water's edge, paddling happily in the surf like a child and singing a tune over and over—I recognized it presently as a snatch of the mass, badly garbled. He smiled up at us, took our hands and came along. Back at their house Asa took his wet clothes off him and put him in bed wrapped in a *wadmal* blanket (that's Iceland wool—gray and shaggy and quite soft).

We stood side by side, watching him sleep on the bench.

"He looks like a baby," she said.

"A remarkably ugly baby," said I.

I don't know how it happened, I swear, but I found my hand had snaked its way around her waist. Before I had time to be shocked and pull it away, she'd turned to me and brought her face up to be kissed. I didn't disappoint her.

"I'll convert," she said when we were done.

"You'd do that for me?" I asked.

"Everything's less frightening when you've a husband."

I pulled away. "It cannot be. I shouldn't have kissed you."

"Why?"

"I'm a priest."

"What of it? Priests marry."

"They shouldn't."

"I don't understand. Thangbrand had a woman.

The bishop has none that I know of, but he says nothing against those who do."

"Bishop Sigurd is an Englishman. Thangbrand is a Saxon. They've a faulty view of a priest's duties. We order things differently in Ireland."

"But you're not in Ireland."

" 'Tis the same God."

She shivered. "Your god—everywhere, always watching, keeping a tally of wrongs—"

"Is that worse than believing in a world packed with gods and spirits whom you might offend by mischance at any moment? The High King of Heaven at least has His commandments out in the open. He doesn't ambush us with unexpected trespasses."

"Do you really think that?" she asked, looking in my eyes. "Have you found him so just and easy to please?"

I was spared answering by the sound of shouting without, and a horn blowing, a noise I didn't recognize at first, until Asa said, "Wolves!"

Why does that word strike such terror in our souls? No doubt you've seen plenty of wolves in your time, as I have, but have you actually seen one attack a man (other than one dying on a battlefield)? They're cowards when it comes to it, but all those stories we heard from our grandmothers to keep us in bed at night stay with us, in our bones, roused the moment we hear that wasteland howling.

"We must bar the door," I said, but even as I spoke I heard a pounding outside, and a human voice crying, "*Let me in! For love of the gods!*"

I opened to the wretch, but what bolted at me was no man. It was a great, gray, hunch-shouldered, slavering wolf, tall as a man's chest, with eyes of yellow fire.

I jerked to close the door, but he got his head inside, twisting it and snapping at me as I beat at his ears (keeping my hand as well as might be away from the fangs) to drive him back out. Asa screamed and grabbed an iron ladle, using it also on the wolf.

He was as strong as three men, this wolf—it came to me that this was no natural beast. Gradually, in spite of our blows, he was working his shoulders inside. I drew my eating knife and began stabbing at him, but although I drew blood it seemed only to anger him.

We'd not have made it, I think, without help. Of a sudden the wolf stiffened and his eyes went wide, then he slumped and the light went out of them. I took my weight from the door to let him drop, and looking out through the open space I saw Erling Skjalgsson with sword and shield, torchlight dancing on his helmet and brynje. Men of the bodyguard were circling him, faced outward, as a shield.

"Werewolves!" he said to me, and his eyes glowed like the beast's. He reached down and took it by the scruff of its neck and jerked upward. The whole skin came off in a piece, and there on my threshold lay a skinny, naked man, hairy and filthy. "They wear these shape-changers' cloaks, and they die harder than rats. This is sorcery, Father, and I've come to bring you to the hall to lead our prayers. I smell more than this filthy shape-changer here. I smell Eyvind Kellda."

I took Asa by the hand and we went—we ran—toward the hall, the bullyboys still keeping their shield wall around us. But we'd gone no farther than a few yards before the main force was on us, and the men had to stand and fight.

Erling joined his men in the shield wall then, leaving only Asa and me, all unarmed, in the center. They were seasoned warriors all, able to split a man to the groin with a single blow, or drop a swallow in flight with a spear-cast, but there were too many wolves. It was hack and fend with weapon and shield, but the wolves were hard to drop, and when one did drop, three more came. Even when they didn't drop, three more came. I've never seen so many wolves, or so large. The noise of their howling and our screaming would have given Azazel nightmares.

One of the bullyboys fell at last, with a wolf bigger than himself at his throat, and then the wall fell apart. I took Asa's hand and ran in no particular direction. Amazingly we got free. We came to the wall that separated the steading from the meadow. Since the wolves we'd seen were within the walls I thought it could do no harm to be on the other side, so I lifted Asa over. We ran and we ran, in the dark, then I fetched up hard against something I could not see.

"The god-tree!" cried Asa. "This is Big Melhaug and my god-tree!"

Even in my fear I shivered to know I had stepped on the mound and touched the unholy tree.

"Come! Let's go up!" cried Asa.

"What?"

"We can climb the tree! We'll be safe from the wolves!"

"Never!" I said, but then I heard a howling, and saw seven great gray shapes with yellow eyes loping up at me, and before I could think about the thing I was clambering up a tree I could not see.

I found the limbs by feeling alone, climbing blind. Then suddenly, as if the fog had cleared, I saw branches around me. I looked down, and something strange in what I saw fuddled me and took my balance away. I fell with a cry, and landed on grass as soft as an eider cushion. I blinked and looked around. The world was wrong.

This was not Sola, and it was not night, and there was no fog. This was no part of Norway I'd seen before. The only familiar object was Asa, standing nearby and looking away.

You must have seen a day when a storm is looming up, and the skies go all over gray, like iron, but the sun still shines from some clear patch of sky so that everything green or bright glows bravely against all that threat of heaven. I've never seen a day like that but I felt bolder and yeastier and nearer to God, and I'll never see one again without thinking of the land we came to that night, Asa and I.

We stood at the foot of a mighty, wide-branching ash tree, on a broad plain, ringed all round by mountains. The mountains glowed gold and orange and pink in the light of the widest, brightest rainbow I'd ever seen. It spanned the sky above us and served this place, as far as I could tell, as its only source of light. Have you ever seen a rainbow that cast shadows? This one did. The only sounds were a kind of chittering in the grass, like insects or frogs, and a ringing in the sky, like the echo of brass, hammer-struck.

I looked up at Asa, who yet stood staring into the distance. "Where are we?" I asked. "What are you looking at?"

"'Tis Thorstein," she said quietly. "My husband."

I wanted to say, "Your husband is dead," but I looked and there he was. Actually I took her word that it was he. I'd seen his corpse, but it's easier to know a dead man from seeing him alive than a living one from seeing him dead. That's been my experience anyway, and I think few will gainsay me.

He'd been a handsome enough man, this Thorstein, somehow managing to look kin to his brother Ulf without sharing his ugliness. He was tall and brown haired. He carried full arms, helmet and shield and brynje, and a sword at his hip.

They flew into each other's arms, the departed and his widow, like doomed lovers in a song. They sighed and whispered endearments and covered one another with kisses, while I, uneasy, moved behind the tree and, to divert my mind, looked in the grass for the source of that chirping I kept hearing.

At first I thought I'd judged it rightly for the squeak of insects, for I soon saw that the grass at foot level was alive with tiny creatures that bounced to and fro in constant activity. *Fleas!* I thought for a moment. *We'll be infested with fleas here!*

But they weren't fleas. A closer look proved them to be wondrous small animals of peculiar shape. In color they were all green or brown, to blend in, and it seemed to me they sometimes changed, or exchanged, colors among themselves. Some were long in the body, with small heads from which tendrils sprouted, and short arms and legs; others had small, roundish bodies. But they all had grabby little hands on all their limbs, and they were forever reaching and catching one another, and wriggling about in chains until one or another beast got himself loose, at which point he would straightway reach out to grab another beast, forming a new chain or connecting one chain to another. It was a constant chaos, a flux that shaped and unshaped itself moment by moment. The creatures seemed to live for nothing but this grasping. I saw no eating or mating among them, and they certainly never tried to bite me. There's not much more to tell of them, but after watching awhile I grew fascinated with the ever-changing combinations, as a man can lose himself watching a hearthfire, or ants at their harvesting.

They seemed oddly familiar, and then I knew them. I'd seen them often, carved on a hundred objects in Norway—bowls and house pillars and axe handles and ships' prows, and cast into sword hilts and cauldrons and the furniture of drinking horns. Where we Irish love to carve sweet, Christian knotwork, the Norse carve these lawless, greedy little beasties wherever they can find a plain space. Now I knew where they'd come from, if only I could learn where I was.

I was so taken with the beasties that I did not hear Thorstein and Asa approach me until he stood over me. They formed a strange picture, both towering over me where I sat in the grass, him with his sword drawn and she with a hand on his arm.

" 'Tis not what you think, Thorstein!" she said.

"And is it this fool you've been keeping company with since I've been underground, and hardly cold yet?" he cried.

In no position to defend myself, and all unarmed, I blathered at him, fumbling for words.

"He's a Christian priest!" she said. "He touches no woman!"

"Then he's a strange kind of Christian priest," said Thorstein. "Where I've been the priests marry, and those who don't are worse than those who do, keeping the women around them as a stallion keeps his mares, and giving each her turn!"

"He's a good man! He rescued us from Olaf's law, and he's done me no insult!"

A strong hand reached down to grasp my shirtfront and pull me to my feet one-handed. Looking me in the face, he cried, "Aye, a fair ruse to get a woman in your bed! Gain her trust first; make her think your spout is but for draining your bladder, take advantage of her innocence—"

"You're dead, Thorstein," said I. "If all this were true, it would count for nothing. Asa's a lawful widow."

(*Why do I say these things? Am I mad?*)

He set me loose and leaped back to give himself sword-room, holding his shield in the guard position. "No man calls me dead and lives! Defend yourself, god-man!"

"Oh for Heaven's sake," I replied. "I'm unarmed. You can murder me if you like—I can't offer you better sport."

And God help me, he did. Or rather, he swung his sword, and I lifted my arm to protect my head, but I felt no blow—

The next thing I knew, we all sat on the ground, and I vaguely remembered noise and light, and there was a hot smell that said to me "lightning."

And towering above us we saw a looming, mountainous figure whom I recognized from a dozen images I'd seen in heathen shrines or blazing on Olaf's pyres. There was no mistaking him. This was Thor himself.

Thor, the lightning wielder. Thor, dispenser of justice. I'll tell you this freely—I am a Christian, and would lay down my life for Christ the Beloved, but I was tempted that moment to worship Thor.

He was a giant all aglow, shining and sparking from every part. His hair and beard were red as steel out of the forge, and seemed to curl and twine of their own volitions. His eyes blazed white-hot under spiky red brows. His bare arms and face seemed as hard and smooth as wood rubbed with oil, and on his right hand he wore an iron glove, and with the glove he grasped his great hammer, larger than his head, with the handle somewhat short for its size. The hammer glowed yellow and shot sparks of its own.

He stood in a fiery brazen chariot pulled by two great black goats with ivory horns and glowing, gold demon eyes.

"WHAT GOES ON HERE?" the god roared, and the earth shook, and the tree shed leaves in a whirlwind.

We all stood mute as scolded children a moment, but Thorstein, who was still angry despite the uproar, squeaked (it seemed a squeak after Thor's voice), "This Christian priest has been groping my wife, and I drew steel to defend what's mine!"

"Sword and shield against a man unarmed?" cried Thor. "Is this how you act in my land?"

Thorstein bowed his head.

"And what do you mean by 'Christian priest'? How did a Christian priest come here?" Thor glared at me with eyes like red-hot skewers. "No, more than a Christian priest! A living man! And a living woman! How came you here, outlanders?"

Asa and I exchanged a glance. I felt guilty, like a boy caught in his neighbor's orchard.

"We climbed the tree," said I. "We'd no inkling where it would lead." I tried to meet his eyes, slid my gaze away and found his image burned into them.

"You need not trouble over that," said Thor. "This is my country, where justice is done. No one is punished here for sins unintended. Mine is not like the world your god made. Here all is just. No evil falls on the innocent. All wrong is forestalled, or if not forestalled, undone."

"You've made your own world?" I asked.

"This is Thrudheim, land of might, the home of Thor. Here come my worshipers when they die, to live with me and enjoy my bounty till the day of Ragnarok, the end of the world."

"Then all men and gods will stand before the great God Jehovah," said I. (There I went again.)

"Yes!" cried Thor. "So we will! And when that day comes I will tell your Jehovah to His face that I have made a better world than his, and so should be judging him!

"Your Jehovah made a world a good man can't even live in. Your Christ admitted as much. He said that anyone who wanted to follow him must go with him to the gallows-place.

"I'll say to your Jehovah, 'I have made a good world for my followers, a decent world where there is no pain undeserved.' And let him do what he will to me, he'll know I spoke truth!"

"Then judge for us, great Thor!" cried Thorstein. "This Christian priest has trifled with my wife while I've been underground. Has not a husband the right to take vengeance for his wife's honor?"

Asa said, "You mistake us, Thorstein." She addressed herself to the god. "My husband takes offense that Father Aillil has shown me kindness since his death. I mean no disrespect to Thorstein, but he's dead and

I yet live, and he will not see the distinction. He tried to kill Father Aillil."

"You need not fear for that," rumbled Thor. "No violence is done in my land without my consent. Did Thorstein strike the priest?"

"Yes, he did."

"But the priest took no injury?"

Asa looked at me and I said, "No—none that I can tell."

"Nor will he," said Thor. "In my land there is no undeserved harm. Fall on a rock, or let the rock fall on you, and it becomes soft as a mushroom. Strike with a sword, and the sword does no more harm than a sausage would. In this way I show myself greater than Jehovah, who left all his creatures in danger from the world itself, and from each other."

"But this priest richly deserves keen steel!" cried Thorstein. "Surely you see that, mighty Thor!"

"That's the thing I must consider," said Thor. "Perfect justice must be meted out, and I make justice for all my children. Now let me think." He furrowed his sloped brow and set his chin on his fist.

"AILLIL THE PRIEST!" cried a voice, and I turned to see, looking hale as ever in life, Soti the smith, my great enemy. Broad of shoulder, naked of skull, small of eyes, with even the burn scar still running down one side of his face where lightning had struck him. He carried an axe and a shield.

"Aillil the priest!" cried Soti. "Great Thor, I cry your judgment on this Christian monster whom the Norns have placed in my power once again! This man schemed to put away your worship at Sola, and connived with Erling Skjalgsson to cheat me of my rights in the iron-ordeal, and helped to torture me, a thing unlawful under our laws, and paid a thrall to burn me to death! Never was such an evildoer seen in the northland from old times to today, and I must have my rights of him!"

"Wait your turn, man," cried Thorstein. "I've a case of my own against this priest, and Thor ponders it now."

"And who are you—a small bonder of little wealth or honor—to tell a man such as me to wait?" cried Soti.

"And who are you? A devil-smith with Lapp blood, little better than a thrall! Give place to your betters, man!"

"I'll give place to one when I see him!" cried Soti, raising his axe and shield, and then they went at it hammer and tongs. Only their weapons bit not at all, and made no more sound than if they'd been slapping one another with wet washing.

"I needs must let them do this," said Thor, sighing. "I blunt their weapons, so they do each other no harm, but that just makes them angrier, so they usually go at it until they're both winded. It drains off their energy at least. But it's so distracting while I'm trying to judge a matter. And things have piled up so—so many cases in the backlog, from this world and yours."

"You're trying to give justice for every evil ever done?" I asked.

"Those brought to me, yes," said Thor.

"How many have you settled?"

"Well, not any, actually. It's all so complicated—the more you learn the more you understand, and the more tangled it gets—I've been trying to make peace between the Volsungs and the Niblungs for hundreds of years now for instance, but I can't find a settlement that'll satisfy them—they keep demanding burning for burning and blood-eagles and all that nonsense, but for the life of me I can't figure out who deserves to kill and who deserves to be killed, and I can't decide until I'm sure—absolutely sure, you see—and I never get to the end of the evidence. Because if I'm not absolutely sure I can't throw it in Jehovah's face at the last judgment.

The Ghost of the God-Tree

"I mean—you take a simple case, like murdering a child. Cut and dried, you'd say. But then the murderer comes up and says, 'Wait, I only did the deed because somebody did some evil to me when I was a child, and I got my soul all twisted and scarred before I had any real choice,' so you have to go back and look at his childhood, and the ones who hurt him have hurts of their own, and pretty soon you're doing a genealogy, and you know how genealogies are. They branch like Yggrdrasil, and never end.

"The further back you go, the more you see that all the crimes are connected—it's all one great crime, and each of you humans shares in it more or less. You're all accomplices. How do you judge between a thousand thousands of accomplices?

"But I'll do it! I am Thor, the trusty god, and I will make justice, and I'll rub your god's face in it when the day comes...."

"Justice!" cried Thorstein, and he turned away from his fight with Soti. Soti bounced his axe off his head when he did it, but so what?

"Justice!" Thorstein cried. "You call this justice? Cases backed up a thousand years, no killing allowed—we can fight each other all we want, but we can't do any damage—I'm going mad in this place!"

"What do you want?" roared Thor. "Your old world, where the innocent suffer and no one can get his rights?"

"At least we could try in the old world! In this world all there is is rage and more rage, until we just go mad and you—"

Thor roared so the whole world shook. "I AM SO SICK OF YOU PEOPLE! I give you a world without pain, and you still won't bridle your anger!"

"That's because you don't give us the one thing we really want!"

"And what is it you really want?"

"*Our way*, of course!"

Thor swung his hammer in a wide arc and made red fire in the air. "YOU CAN'T *ALL* HAVE YOUR WAY! SOMEONE MUST YIELD PLACE!"

"In a world without pain, why should we ever yield place?"

Thor roared again, and Thorstein disappeared, and Soti with him.

"What happened to them?" Asa asked.

"I changed them into grippers," said Thor.

"Grippers? Those little beasties on the ground?" I asked.

"Yes. After they've bounced about as grippers for a time, they calm down at last."

"There's a lot of grippers about," said I.

"Well, there's a lot of anger at this stage of my plan," said Thor. "But once I get my caseload under control, it will be better, I'm certain."

"You're trying to change the world without changing men's hearts," said I (Aillil, counselor to the gods). "It won't do, you know."

"WHO ARE YOU TO SAY WHAT WILL DO IN MY LAND?" came the predictable answer. And the grass suddenly grew to the height of my ears, only it wasn't the grass that had grown, it was me who'd fallen on my back, and the earth was shaking like a merry glutton's belly. "DO NOT THINK THAT I CANNOT KILL IN MY OWN LAND! YOU ARE NOT DEAD, YOU LIVE—THEREFORE YOU CAN DIE!"

And I saw him swing that great glowing hammer, and I saw him cast the thing, and I thought, *Now I'm finished for certain, and do you suppose there's a road to Heaven from this place?*

But the hammer flew over our heads, and I turned to see where he'd flung it, and there in the distance was the greatest bear I'd ever seen, big and white and blue as an iceberg, with glowing blue eyes.

And the bear gaped his mouth, showing teeth the size of trees, and he spoke in a voice like the crashing of waves, and he said, "LIVING MAN AND WOMAN, COME TO ME IF YOU WOULD LIVE ON!"

I hesitated for one moment, glanced back at Thor, who was catching his hammer again (as I understand it, the weapon always returns to his hand when thrown), and I grabbed Asa's hand and started to run.

She resisted. I looked and saw in her eyes that she feared Thor less than the bear.

"Trust me," said I. "I've learned that the only safety lies in running toward what you fear most."

Her eyes widened, but she came with me.

We ran together. We ran toward blazing blue eyes and a cavelike red mouth and razor-sharp fangs and a mountain of white fur blazing like snow blindness.

Then the mountain of fur became a mountain pure and simple, and before it stood a man I knew—the dark Wanderer I'd met on the road to Klepp.

"Are you ready to go home?" he asked.

"I think so," said I. I looked at Asa. "Will you go or stay?" I asked her.

"This place is no good," she said. "I'm not ready to join the dead."

"This you should know," said the Wanderer. "Thor spoke truth in saying this is no place for living men and women. To come here once by mischance may be forgiven. But if you ever return it will be by your choice, and then you must stay here till Judgment."

"I'll come here someday, I hope," said Asa. "But in the usual way."

"Take us home then," I said to the Wanderer.

He smiled. "Would you go back to the very time and place you left?"

I rubbed my chin. "Things were rather lively at Sola then. Can you help? That bear would be useful."

The traveler said, "Your trouble at Sola is only that the light can't shine in. You can change that with a word."

"A word? What word?"

"Go back to the beginning."

"What's that supposed to mean?" I asked, and then we were at Sola, in the fog, and all around were shouts and howlings.

We could just make out Erling and his men. They'd reformed their ring, and the werewolves (who didn't seem very well organized) had moved off for a moment. We rushed toward them and they opened a gap to admit us.

"Where'd you get to, Father?" Erling cried. "I thought we'd lost you this time."

"You'd not believe me," said I.

Then the wolves found us again, and Asa and I crouched to avoid being struck by the backswings of the men's weapons. The warriors yelled and the wolves howled, and it was like feeding time in Hell.

Asa shouted to me over the din, "Why don't you stop it?"

"How?"

"With what that man told you!"

"'Twas a riddle! I'll probably figure it out after the danger's over, if we live so long."

"He said we needed to let the light shine in!"

"It's nighttime."

"He said you could change it with a word—he said to go back to the beginning."

"The beginning of what?"

"What were the first words spoken?"

"Spoken when?"

"Ever!"

"How would I know? I know the first words God spoke over the world, but He was around long before then."

"Well what did He say then?"

"He said *'Fiat lux.'*"
"What?"
"*Fiat lux*. It's Latin."
"What does it mean in human speech?"
" 'Let there be light.' "

All the men turned to look at me.

That was when I noticed that things had grown quieter. They wouldn't have heard me a short time earlier. But the wolves had hushed and begun to slink back. I could see this because the fog was clearing. A breeze had blown in out of the north and shreds of mist were flying before it, peeling great rents in the gloom. As the sky uncovered, you could see that the moon was full and large as a cathedral, and the stars, as if they'd been hoarding their strength, blazed on us like long lightning.

And with the fog went the wolves. As we watched them flee, they became skinny men in fur cloaks, jogging on two feet.

"Hunt them down and kill them, all you can find," said Erling. "No, wait—bring one back to me. I want to know who sent them, though I have a guess."

They brought one back at last, when we'd withdrawn to the hall to look to our wounds and restore ourselves with ale. He looked like a man who'd been through a famine, and he quivered in every limb. I remember he was quite bald, and he had a birthmark on one cheek.

"Who sent you, shape-changer?" Erling asked.

The wretch flung himself at Erling's feet. "I cannot say—he'd fry the brain in my skull with a thought. He's a mighty magician."

"My priest blew your master's spell away with a word. I'd have a care if I were you. There's magic and magic."

The man shivered yet more violently (werewolves as a class, I've noticed, are not very brave), and darted his eyes back and forth between Erling and me. At last he crumpled onto the floor, curled up with his knees in his face, and whispered, "Eyvind Kellda."

"For that word, I give you your life," said Erling.

The man leaped to grasp Erling's knees. "No!" he cried. "If Eyvind learns I betrayed him, he'll put a serpent in my belly. If you have mercy, slay me now!"

Erling said the word and the bullyboys dragged him out. I followed, thinking to offer him baptism this side of the River, but Erling's men did not linger over their work.

CHAPTER V

Here begins the saga of Hoskuld the Coal-chewer, such as it is:

Now there was a man named Hoskuld, son of Kolli, son of Hnaki, son of Thorstein . . .

And so on.

Hoskuld was not such a man as skalds love to praise, who does his first murder at the age of six, gets outlawed a couple of times in his teens and is burned to death in his house with his friends and family by twenty-seven. Hoskuld was what they call a "coal-chewer"—a wretch who'd rather loaf in the house by the warm hearth than be out in God's nature slaughtering beasts and avenging blood-guilt.

Hoskuld came to Erling Skjalgsson one day in the summer of the year 998. Erling was with Arnor the horse boy that afternoon, and they were arguing. He'd just come back from Nidaros and what was supposed to have been the king's wedding (the bride had tried to stab the groom on their bridal night, as you've doubtless heard) and he was out of sorts. He'd wanted to go raiding in Scotland that summer, but had stayed for the wedding, and now he was home with time on his hands and he chafed. So he was talking about selling off some of the horses, and Arnor pointed out that he needed a varied stock at this stage. Erling gave him a fair hearing, but you could tell he didn't like being naysaid. He answered Hoskuld a tad shortly when he came begging a favor.

"I want you to take over my lawsuit against Thorarin Hranisson," Hoskuld said, humbly. Hoskuld did everything humbly. He was the sort of man there's no proper place for in a pagan land. In Ireland he'd have made a monk, and possibly a good one, and doubtless happier. He was skinny, of middling height, with a large forehead and nose, lank brown hair and a sparse beard. He was prone to pick his nose when nervous, and he was nervous now.

We all knew about his lawsuit of course. Thorarin was Hoskuld's neighbor, and their two farms had shared meadowland since time immemorial. Hoskuld's thralls had seen Thorarin's thralls drive Hoskuld's sheep off the common land and into a bog where they had the devil of a time getting them out again, and this had happened more than once. When Hoskuld sent a thrall to complain to Thorarin, Thorarin had killed the thrall. So Hoskuld went to law.

"Why should I take over your lawsuit?" Erling asked.

"Because I haven't the friends or the strength to win it myself," Hoskuld answered. "Thorarin has lodged a suit of his own now, since I struck him at the Thing, and I know he'll take my farm. He has richer kin than I, and men respect him. As I see it, my farm is lost whatever I do. I'd rather you took the farm and made me your tenant than yield it to Thorarin and have no home at all."

It had the kind of logic Norse lawsuits abound in, but Erling was in a cross-grained mood. "I've land enough," he said. "I've no wish to make free men tenants. I like having freeholders about me—they make for a strong commonwealth. I'll take your lawsuit over and give the land back when all's done."

"No!" cried Hoskuld. Actually it was more like a squeak, but there was real feeling in it, and his eyes goggled. "I'm not a thrall who comes to beg land from you! I have some pride! I take charity from no man! If you'll not take my farm, I'll go elsewhere for help!"

"And whom will you get to help you?" Erling asked.

"I'll send for my brother Baug."

Erling hadn't given Hoskuld his full attention until now, but he turned and fixed his eyes on the man. "Baug is outlawed," he said.

"His outlawry ends this summer."

"As much as I like having freeholders about me, that much I dislike having berserkers."

"He's my kin. If I can't keep my inheritance, and if you won't take it, I'd as soon it stayed in the family."

"As I recall, you've no reason to love your brother."

"Yet he is my blood."

"And your blood is what you're like to see if you bring him back," said Erling.

As Hoskuld slouched away, I moved in and said, "I've heard of berserkers, but what are they really?"

"They're like werewolves," said Erling, grumping, "except they don't change their shapes. They lose their minds, they go into black rages, and they fight with a madman's strength. They're wonderful shock troops if you can control them. I've never gone in for them."

"What sets them off? Drink? Some drug?"

"They don't need drink or drugs. All a berserker needs is permission. Thorliv! Don't you have something useful to do this time of day?"

Erling's sister Thorliv, the older one, had found some excuse to come near and engage Arnor in talk. I'd never marked her as a horse fancier before, but lately she'd taken to hanging about the pens. She gave a start and ran off, giggling.

"I've spoiled those girls," said Erling.

That night was the first the Night-mare appeared.

We menfolk were all drinking and yarning ourselves sleepy—the usual after-supper entertainment—when Ragna came in and stepped up to Erling's seat and spoke in his ear. I heard what she said, my seat being next to his.

"Thorliv is nowhere to be found," she said. "I went to Asa's house, and Arnor is missing as well."

Erling sighed and braced himself to get up. "It was bound to happen," he said. "Shall I have the men search?"

"Naught may have happened yet. There's no use dishonoring the girl. You and I will go, and Father Aillil, to put the fear of God in them. But let's not tarry."

So Erling bid me come along, and we went out searching. It would be no great problem to find two young people in the steading.

It wasn't yet dark, being high summer, but the skies were cloud-cloaked, and a light rain fell. This would have made it harder to search, except that we could expect to find them under a roof somewhere. I was glad of the gloom because I feared I was blushing. I felt the hypocrisy fathers feel, I suppose, when they're warding their daughters' honor, remembering their own youths. . . .

The scream brought us all up short.

It was like a bird's screech—an eagle's or a gull's perhaps, except that it stretched on and on, as if whatever was making it had no need of breath. It reminded me of something, I couldn't say what.

Erling was looking at me, saying something, but I couldn't hear him. My ears ached. I put my hands over them.

I recalled then what the screaming put me in mind of. I'd heard a pony once, caught in a mire, being sucked under and screeching its terror as it struggled. That sound had been like this, except that this was louder, and there was no fear in it.

Soon there were people all around us. Everyone had come out of the houses, roused from sleep or near sleep by that brain-ripping sound.

And there with us were Thorliv and Arnor. I peered at them, but couldn't spy any embarrassment in their faces, though Thorliv had a couple straws caught in her hair.

Arnor, with the sharp eyes of youth, began to point, and to shout something we could not hear. We looked where he pointed and beheld a light coming from the south, across the flat land. The light was blue and white, and it grew as it approached. And ever as it came, that screaming grew louder and louder, loud enough to drive a man to jam an awl into his ears, just to stop it.

The light became a shape, and the shape became a horse. Such a horse was scarce seen in Norway, and never, I think, anywhere else. I had seen it once, but only once.

It was a horse two men tall, and it had no head. It was the gray horse of the king of the underground folk, come back to torment his displacers.

I reached instinctively for Enda's crucifix, and cursed, not for the first time, to find it missing. With its help I might have had at least a little power in the case; I'd have been able to say, "My lord, this is but a seeming, a trick of the devil."

Or not.

Then Arnor was running toward the horse pens, and I saw what he went for, for Erling's horses were going mad, galloping and rearing and biting one another, and hurting themselves against the stone walls.

I ran with him, and Erling came too, with many of the men, but there was nothing to do. The horses were clean mad, dangerous as wildfire to approach. We could only stand helpless and watch them, screaming, rearing and wide-eyed, expecting to see them kill one another or break loose and be lost.

Then suddenly they went still, each with its ears back and its ribs heaving.

And there among them was the Night-mare.

And the screaming went silent, and there was no sound but the wheezing of the herd.

And the Night-mare stood on its hinders, and reached out its forelegs as a man would, and clutched black Ravn in an embrace, and of a sudden its blue light went dark and there was the sound of hooves galloping away, but naught to see. Only proud, shy Ravn, Erling's treasure horse, was gone as if he had never been. And for a minute the wind whipped around us, blowing the rain in our eyes like a storm. Then it fell back to its wonted nightly peace.

We stood silent, all of us, and the first to speak was Arnor. "It's the great horse of the world," he said. "It's the horse over all horses. If a man could ride that horse, he'd become a god."

"Hush such heathenish talk," said Erling. "You get to your bed, Arnor. Tomorrow morning we search for Ravn."

Instead Arnor went into the pen to check over the animals without even a glance back at Thorliv, who followed him with her eyes.

Sigrid joined her sister, and I tagged behind as they walked to the women's house. I was spying, but for their own good.

"Don't stub your heart on that horse boy," Sigrid said. "He'll always value livestock too much and you too little. Besides which he's poor."

"You loved Halvard Thorfinsson. He wasn't rich."

"The more fool I. I'll not make that mistake again."

"Kind hearts are more than dragon ships, and simple faith than Yngling blood."

"Who said that?"
"Some skald."
"Well, you can tell him from me he's an idiot. I've learned my lesson. I shall marry a man with chests of silver and leagues of land and many thralls. He'll give me everything I want, and I'll rule the estate when he's gone a-viking, and he'll love me to distraction. There's not much time until the end of the world, and I don't want to miss my chance."

Ravn was not to be found, though Erling and Arnor and many of the bodyguard and thralls searched every yard of the neighborhood. The business put Erling yet more out of sorts, and we all watched our step with him for a couple of weeks.

One evening, while we were at table, a visitor was announced. We turned in our seats to see a tall, broad man dressed in filthy clothing. We could smell him as he approached the high seat. From one hand he swung what looked like a hairy sack with a ball in it, but closer up it proved to be a man's head, dangled by the hair.

"I am Baug Kollasson," the man said. "I come to declare that I have taken over my brother Hoskuld's lawsuit against Thorarin Hranisson, and ended it as well." He let the head go, and it rolled among the rushes on the floor.

"Thorarin?" Erling asked, gesturing at the head.
"Yes."

"Killings don't end lawsuits," said Erling. "Killings only turn them into blood-feuds."

"I'm content with that. Let any who wish to avenge Thorarin come to me."

"Then you've taken over Hoskuld's farm as well?"
"I have."

"You are under my law then, as I am under the king's. Know this, Baug Kollasson—I keep the king's peace, and I do not suffer troublemakers. I also do not like berserkers."

Baug laughed shortly. "I've seen the world and sown my oats," he said. "I've paid my debts. Now I wish to be a bonder like my father, and live my days in peace."

"This head in my hall says otherwise."

"There's no peace under the heavens without a few heads knocked off."

"You turned a lawsuit to manslaughter, Baug. There's no need for that. I know your ilk, and I'll keep my eye on you."

"I am honored by the attention of so great a man as the hersir of Rogaland," said Baug with a courtly bow. Then he turned and walked out, laughing.

That was the summer Erling began the road to Opprostad. I was pleased with the plan, as roads permit more people to come to church, and the priest to visit his flock more easily. Also it would speed my visits to my friend Helge at Klepp. Erling had those things at heart of course, but he was concerned too with the defense of the land. He wanted closer ties with Opprostad.

Road-building in Norway (as in Ireland, come to think of it) consists chiefly in laying causeways over boggy stretches and streams. There were already a lot of pathways along the seacoast, but they were disconnected and in varying repair, depending on the care of the bonders. Erling used stone, a material richly to be had, and he set thralls to the work, following his usual pattern of paying them for any work beyond a set day's goal. This proved easier said than done in the case of road-building, as each day's work was farther from home than the last. It offered an interesting challenge for the man in charge of the freedom-purchase scheme (that would be me), but at length I worked out a plan that all could live with, and told the thralls I'd take volunteers for a special work crew to toil their way south for a set rate of pay.

The first to volunteer was a thrall called Patrick, born in Norway of Irish stock (or rather his mother was Irish—the father was problematical). I'd wed Patrick to another thrall not many months before, and they were to be parents now. He saw Erling's road as his shortcut to freedom.

"I've no cause to go to Ireland," he told me cheerfully. "I'm Norse-born and Deirdre barely remembers her birthplace. If we can get a bit of land and live as freemen, and raise our children free, what better could we look for?"

I looked over at Deirdre, watching us from the other side of the churchyard. A sturdy, red-cheeked yellow-haired girl she was, born to be a mother and a man's better angel.

I blessed them, well pleased. Those were the moments I loved, when I saw my work bear fruit in human hope.

The labor began the following Monday, and eased south under an overseer, who kept records carved on sticks.

A southbound ship sailed in from Hordaland one day, and a messenger brought news for Erling and Astrid. I was not there to hear it delivered, but afterwards Erling took his best remaining horse without a word and rode south to see how his road was coming. A thrall came to me as I sat outside my house, tallying freedom-silver on a scrap of parchment, and said that Astrid bid me attend her.

A summons from Astrid was a rare thing for me. I changed into my best shirt and went to the hall and up the outside stairway to the loft. I found her on the balcony, doing needlework with Sigrid and Freydis. She sent the girls down.

"Let's go inside," she said to me, and we went in, leaving the door open for light. She sat and bade me do the same.

"You're not overfond of me, are you, Father?" she

asked, looking me plain in the eye. She had a formidable gaze—there was much shrewdness in those wide-set blue eyes under the white wife's headcloth.

I sat straighter. "You are one of my parishioners. I love all my flock."

"But you think me cruel."

What use to lie? "Yes, I think you unnatural cruel."

"They say you thought otherwise of Halla Asmundsdatter."

"I admire Halla. She's brave and gentle, and she never hurt a soul."

"Unlike me. Would you think it strange if I were jealous of such a woman in my husband's past?"

"I see no reason why you should begrudge to another what you yourself despise. But Erling always set you above Halla. Speaking plain, I think he was a fool in that."

Astrid smiled a wry smile. "There are even rumors," she said, "that you yourself harbored feelings for Halla beyond the love a priest owes a parishioner."

I went all over sanctimonious then. "If that were so, I can yet say in truth that I never betrayed Erling by doing aught about it."

"That is why I asked you here, Father, that you might hear it from me, under four eyes. Halla is dead."

At those words as it were a shroud fell over me, and I neither heard nor saw for a moment. When I came to myself, Astrid was shaking me.

Dead? Halla dead? Halla of the bright eyes, the liquid laugh, the long-legged girl's grace? Halla, whom I'd held in my arms (to save her life only) in this very loft room? It was not right. Oh God, it could not be—

"Are you well, Father?" Astrid asked. She stood fanning me with her apron.

"She's dead?" I asked. "How came it to be?"

"She was with child. They'd feared she was barren, but she quickened at last. The carrying went ill, though. The child tried to come beforetime; there was a lot of bleeding, they say. The child is dead also."

"Saints have mercy. I must say a mass for them."

"A messenger came from Aslak. He said Halla's last word was 'Erling.' Aslak had bid him most particularly to say this last in my presence."

I pondered that. This looked like bad blood between kinsmen.

"I must go," I said, and turned to the door. "I thank you for your kindness."

"You're weeping, Father."

"Weeping? I?" I put my hand to my face and found it wet. *How odd*, I thought. *I never weep. Not for less than rape and murder before my eyes.*

Astrid put a slim hand on my arm. "I am not hateful, Father, and I bear no grudge against poor Halla. If you can believe it, I neither hate nor despise Erling either. A woman must keep her vows, as a man must. And vows to oneself are second only to vows to God. When you think of me, think of me as you did of Erling, when he kept his word to Halla at the Gula Thing, all against his heart."

I gave her a clumsy blessing and fled. I entered the old hall and went to Halla's tapestry of David and Goliath, on the wall near the high seat. I put a hand on it and stood there long.

CHAPTER VI

Lemming stood by the forge, shirtless in spite of the late autumn weather, his corded body glowing in the smithy's gloom from the forge light, his eyes gleaming in reflection under the shaggy brows and the sweat-rag he'd tied around his head. With wide-mouthed tongs he held a short bundle of rods—some iron, some steel—heated yellow in the forge.

He set one end of the rods into the vise, two jaws in a V-shape, banded upright to the side of a wide wooden block set in the ground. His helper leaned down and jammed in a wedge at the bottom with practiced hammer blows, to tighten it.

He began to twist the bundle into a single, striped rod, spiraled like a narwhal's horn. It seemed to twine as easily as wax, but the writhing muscles of his arms and the sweat that runneled down his skin bespoke the force he was spending. When the bundle was all of a piece he grunted and the boy knocked the wedge out. Lemming spun around and laid the thing on an anvil, then went at it with a hammer. He struck with practiced rhythm, alternating rings on the anvil with blows to the rod—ring-clash, ring-clash. As if by wizardry, the spearhead began to take shape under his harnessed violence. Sparks flew in a fountain and sprayed his leather apron. The air smelled like a dragon's belch.

Most folk think a smith some kind of unnatural being, and it's easy to believe it when you watch a good one at work. Lemming did nothing to dispel the mystery, not because he cared to be an object of superstition, but because it was his nature to hoard words as a landlord hoards silver.

He was using the centuries-old twist-forging method. They once made swords in this manner (swords such as Smith's-Bane, which he himself carried), and I suppose they still do in some places, but imported Frankish swords, better in quality, have crowded them out. There's still a market for fine, forged spearheads though, and Lemming hoped to sell a number of them at the Risa market come winter. A good two dozen completed heads rested in a box in the corner. They were fine ones, not only well-forged but engraved and silver-inlaid.

I went out of the forge, blinking in the daylight. A man called my name as he trotted up to me. I recognized him as a tenant farmer of Erling's. He carried a coil of fishing lines.

"Will you bless my tackle, Father?" he panted.

"Of course," said I. "What's your hurry?"

"The herring are running, Father! 'Tis the biggest run in years! There'll be plenty of fish to smoke for the winter—no one need go hungry! I'd ask you to bless my boat, but I keep it up at Tananger, and it's a bit of a walk."

I hurried to say some words over the stuff, and the fellow went on his way happy. Everywhere I could hear voices raised, as men set out for their berths. Nobody keeps boats in Sola Bay, because of the surf, but many have ancient rights to keep boathouses up at Risa or Tananger or in the Hafrsfjord. Those who had no boats could hire on as crew, for a share of the catch.

I saw Arnor heading north with the crowd, carrying his own lines. I hailed him. "A fisherman as well as a horseman?" I asked. "You're a lad of many parts."

"I own a boat after all," he said cheerfully. "It's berthed at Somme, so I'll have a bit of a pull northward in the fjord until the afternoon breeze comes up. But I hope for a fair wind for my sail, and there's fish for the taking, they say."

"That boat of yours is large for one man. Are you going by yourself?"

"A man with a boat can always get help when the herring run," said Arnor.

I let him go then, and went back to the church to say a mass for the safety of the fishermen, and for a good catch.

But when I came out into the sunlight again a bank of storm clouds loomed in the west, above a leaden sea. The wind was rising, from the southwest as Arnor had hoped, but I feared this wind would be no friend to him.

I went back inside to pray some more.

The storm struck that evening, just before the early sunset, while the fishermen were trying to pull home, against the wind. Some had been prudent and given it up early, but there are always reckless or desperate men who'll try for a little more time. It would be their bodies washed up along the shores from Agder to the Sognefjord over the next few days. Fisherman in Rogaland tattoo their hands, a different mark for each farm, so that if kindly folk find their bodies and give them burial, word can be sent of it. Because of this we were able to account for many of the dead, but some vanished as if snatched by Aegir's daughters.

We sat all together in Erling's hall that night, listening as the wind leaned on the walls, making the rafters groan and setting the hams and fish that smoked in them to swinging above us. Asa sat miserably among the women at the east end. Arnor was one of those missing on the sea.

Among us men Lemming could not be found. I did not fear for him (or not much) for I knew what he was about. He was tramping along the strand in silent agony, wet to the bone, daring Thor to strike him, for Freydis was missing also.

No one seemed to know what had become of her. All we could think was that she must have joined the fishing, odd as that was for a young girl. Not that she wasn't strong, but she didn't know the work and there were certainly enough men eager to help. There would have been no need to bring Freydis.

I could think of one fisherman who'd have taken her along though.

When we were done feasting, the trestle tables were taken down and set against the walls and we all sat in miserable fellowship on the benches, men and women alike. We knew there'd be no sleep.

Asa came and sat by me. "Have you seen Thorliv's face?" she whispered. "I know she thinks Freydis must be with Arnor, and she's broiling."

"It's a reasonable enough guess," said I.

"He likes the girls, and they like him. Is that so great a crime? That's how it is with proper men, the kind who make mothers—and aunts—proud."

"It's harder on the girls," I murmured.

"Girls should know better. I liked boys too at her age, but I never ran off alone with them. I waited for my parents' choice of a husband, and I did my duty. Nor did I ever regret it."

"'Tis the times. Young people today have no sense of decency."

We were silent a moment. Asa said, "You've never answered my offer to convert and be your wife. Since the news of that woman's death—Erling's leman that was—you've stood off from me."

How could I tell it without sounding unmanly?

How could I explain how deeply I'd cared for Halla, and how I'd always felt the wreck of her dreams was somehow my doing? Now she was dead—*how could the name Halla and the word dead abide in the same sentence?*—and was that somehow also my fault? I'd bungled everything in my dealings with her. It all boiled down to one conviction, there in my heart like a stake—a priest should not seek to marry.

"You remember how you and Arnor went barefoot, and never looked at the smith, and all the rest, when you first came? Because it might displease the gods and bring disaster?"

"Yes, of course."

"My unmarriage is like that. It's something I offer my God. When I've broken the rule in the past, only tragedy has come to the women I cared for. I'd not have the same happen to you."

"Then you do care for me?"

I made no reply to that. "I'll gladly baptize you whenever you like, though," I said.

The storm blew itself out around dawn. We went out into the cold, pale-skyed, blasted landscape, and walked the shores among the trash of seaweed, dead fish, birds and driftwood to seek out the smashed boats and the stiffening men with skin like cods' bellies. Boys were sent running to tell the names of the dead and where they could be found, and the cries of women went up in their wake.

Among them all there was no sign of Arnor, nor of Freydis. I saw Lemming from time to time, a shadow against the sky on some high place, scanning the sea.

As that second day drew toward evening, I sat at last on a clump of heather, weary and boneless as an oyster, when I heard Asa's voice raised. At first I thought she was weeping, but then I knew it for laughter. I scrambled to my feet and ran toward the sound.

And there was Arnor, coming down the path from Somme, ice in his hair, bearing Freydis in his arms.

"I rode it out," he said. "'Twas hard work, but I made it. I . . . I found Freydis on my way back."

But there were blisters on her hands, as if from hard rowing.

And then it was Jul again, with all the bother and delight that helps Christian folk forget the dark and the cold of the murderous months.

It was the custom at Sola, as it was and is everywhere in Norway, for all, high and low, to sleep on straw in the great hall on Christmas Eve. Even Erling and Astrid forsook their loft (which they might have kept to without offense) and joined the rest of the household on the benches.

But there were some for whom this yearly fellowship was not so much a matter of delight as of refuge. The remaining heathen, Asa among them, believed that Jul eve was the time when angry spirits rode across the sky, on the lookout for hapless wanderers caught out-of-doors, whom they might snatch off and carry away to unspeakable fates. For them it was also the night when the dead of the past year came back to their old hearths, for a tender or bitter farewell as the case might be.

Only two human souls at Sola slept alone that night. One was Lemming, who did not care much for people close about him and who, if he believed in spirits, thought himself a match for any of them. The other was myself. I had to work hard at my celibacy, and there was too much groaning and panting in dark corners on such a night for me to endure, even after heavy drinking. Perhaps especially after heavy drinking.

"But you cannot go out to your house alone!" said Asa to me as I left. I think perhaps she'd hoped to lie beside me and trust to nature. "The spirits will take you! Or if not that, the dead are about!"

"And may God save all the dead, and the spirits too, if possible. I've no cause to fear them."

I pried her hand gently from my arm, and went outside into a night filled with mist. No Bethlehem star to guide my way tonight, I thought. But I knew the path well enough, steering by landmarks like a sailor under overcast.

It was near the women's house that I saw her. Queen of the year's harvest, she had come back to the place she had most loved.

"Hello, Halla," said I.

She looked as I remembered her, her honey-colored hair uncovered, her eyes bright enough to make good the lack of stars. But she bore in her arms a babe. A stranger might have thought her the Blessed Virgin herself.

She spoke no word, but smiled at me.

Death had not withered Halla. For me rather, she withered death.

"A blessed Christmas, fair one," I whispered.

CHAPTER VII

The market at Risa was, in fact, not a new thing. The farmers north of Hafrsfjord had gathered on the level ground by the harbor for generations to sell and trade for their surplus grain. But Erling's dreams for it went far beyond such. He wanted a place where merchants would come and spend weeks or the whole winter. Eventually, I knew, he wanted a town, like Visby on Gotland, something that did not exist in Norway at the time, though Olaf was trying the same plan up at Nidaros. And why not? The world was changing fast.

To help him in this undertaking came Thorbjorg Lambisdatter. She in fact rarely sailed with her three *knarrs*, she said, but she could direct the business as well from Risa as from her home up north. Erling gave her trade favors, but I suspected those were not her chief reason for coming. I misliked her motives. I did not mislike *her*—she was a good, honest capable woman, no more nor less prone to temptation than the rest of us—but I feared her hopes.

I saw them in close conversation one night after supper, at the doorway to the entrance room (we'd taken over the hall at Risa farm). She put her hand on his arm and he smiled and lifted it off. She went out to her bed alone.

I've seen Erling swing his sword over scores of dead foemen, but I was never prouder of him than I was that night. You don't generally expect fidelity in marriage from Norsemen (or Irishmen, if it comes to that), but Erling had grasped—God knows how— that a vow to a wife was as weighty as a vow to another landed man.

I took one of my seaside walks that evening (which of course was as dark as midnight that time of year, except for the light of an almost full moon). I was going along the shore of the harbor when the moonlight caught what looked like a man standing in the water. This was no time of year for sea bathing. I went nearer and saw that it was Erling, trouserless in the shallows. The very thought made me shiver and pull my cloak tighter about me.

I said, " 'Tis a sin of presumption to choose your own penance before you've even confessed."

"I thought you'd be overkind with me," said Erling.

"I knew monks in Ireland who used to do penance this way. As I recall, when they got older they tended to stiffness of the joints. I'd think a man of war wouldn't care for that."

"It's less a penance than a shield."

"Come out of the water and tell me about it."

He came ashore, rubbed his legs down with his cloak, pulled on his trousers and told me. I can't tell you what he confessed. It was about what you'd expect if you're charitable; less than you'd expect if you're filthy-minded.

I pronounced absolution and told him his cold bath would do for penance.

"Sometimes it's frightening to be strong," he told me. "Sometimes I'm afraid of what I could do."

"I think your faith is strong too," said I.

"Is it? I'm not sure I even know what faith is. Give me words, Father. That's your gift."

"What is faith?" I mused. "I suppose I understand it no more than other men. But on the rare occasions when I've possessed it it's been as if I was riding atop a ship's mast, keeping watch, sitting on the sailyard. You've done that, haven't you?"

"Aye, many times."

"Then you know how it feels. The mast top sways all about—you feel every motion of the sea ten times more than you would on deck, and you sway out over open water, first to one side, then the other. Your head tells you the yard will hold you up, but your belly keeps saying you're going to fall.

"But unless you're a coward, you believe your head and ignore your belly. That's what faith feels like."

"Thinking over feeling? I thought faith was all about feeling."

"Feeling comes with it, just as you feel every pitch of the ship more strongly on the mast top than down below. But feelings are quicksilver. You can't grasp them, and they poison you if you try to live on them. Faith is trusting God and telling your feelings to sit down and shut up."

We went to our lonely beds then.

And so the people came, the free and the unfree, in sleighs or on skis (we had a good snow blanket that year—a thing that doesn't always happen) or on foot, carrying their wares, and the craftsmen paid Erling for the right to set up booths (the thralls took it out of their freedom-silver—I tallied it). There wasn't much order to the booths—people set them up higgledy-piggledy—but as time went on winding paths appeared among them, and we became a kind of community, like a strange, secular cloister. We could tell visitors, "You'll find Egil the comb-maker down that path—turn right at the woolen merchant's and left at the midden."

Thorbjorg had done well by Erling. She knew every merchant and craftsman from Lofoten to Lindesness, and she knew who wanted a change, and she'd steered such to Erling. "We're hard by the sea lane here," said Erling, "and one of the few good harbors on this coast. And if only for the grain we have to sell, they'll come. Grain is gold in Norway." Erling held most of the grain himself, having bought it from his thralls for freedom-silver or received it in rents from his tenants. I suppose you could argue that he should have let the thralls sell their own grain and get their own best price, but they were more likely to get skinned in that case, and they couldn't afford it.

Thorbjorg stayed in the women's house. Astrid had chosen not to come along. Whether that bespoke trust or contempt, who could say?

One icy morning I was arguing with a thrall over the value of his oats (they often tried to sharp me, and who can blame them?) when I heard a horn blow. I knew the call. It was the summons to arms.

I ran to Thorbjorg's booth, where Erling was most often to be found. Erling was opening a chest brought by his shoe-boy, pulling out iron arrows which he distributed to several men.

I edged close to Steinulf and asked, "What goes on?"

"Our balefire northward on Fjol Island has been lit," he said. "you can see the smoke yourself. Some force must be coming by sea. This market would make a sweet prize for Vikings."

Over the next hour or so men streamed in from the nearby farms, summoned by the war-arrows and the horns. Erling had men working aboard the two warships he'd brought, getting them ready to launch when he knew more of his enemy.

A runner on skis came at last. "Two ships," he said to Erling. "Big ones, and heavily armed. They're sailing fast."

"You're certain it's only two?"

"They're hull up and no more sails to be seen."

"Good!" said Erling, smacking his palm with a fist. "We'll handle them and make a profit in armor today."

He began getting his armed men on board, along with the merchants (who are a warlike lot when their goods are threatened) and bonders who'd come in response to the horns.

They were ready to embark when a second ski-runner came in, winded with exertion, and was brought to Erling.

"There are five ships," he coughed.

"Five!" Erling cried. "I thought there were but two!" He turned a glare at the first messenger.

"It seemed so," said the new messenger. "I saw it myself—two ships and no more to the horizon. But three more appeared. I can't say how. It must be witchcraft."

As I listened to this exchange I thought there was a change in the light, as if in an eclipse, and I noticed that the messenger who spoke wore a purse on his belt, with rings and bits of hack-silver, along with a slice of cheese, inside it. The purse hung on the other side of his body from me.

For just a moment I seemed to see through all things. I could see the bones in men's bodies. I could see the fish swimming under the ship's belly. Then my sight cleared (dulled?) and all was as before.

"Eyvind Kellda is in this," I muttered, but nobody heard me.

"This isn't a raid, it's an invasion," said Erling. He turned to his lieutenants. "Can we handle five ships with two?"

Steinulf and Eystein looked at one another. "We could try," said Eystein after a moment. "But I wouldn't wager much on our chances."

"We must make a land-defense then. Not here by

the harbor. Somewhere up on the heights." He pointed toward the eastward hills.

"What of our goods?" a merchant cried.

"Take what you can carry. The rest isn't worth your lives."

"I've been trading for twenty years and never saw such an attack from countrymen. You promised us the king's peace, Erling Skjalgsson!"

"If you've claims against me, bring suit at the Thing," Erling snapped. "Right now our concern is to live the day out." We disembarked and went to work.

There was a thrall woman—a widow—who'd nearly purchased her freedom. Her hope for the balance was the knitting she'd done and brought to market. I went first to her and helped her carry her stock of mittens and mufflers (bulky but not heavy) up to the hilltop Erling had chosen for a stronghold. Then I found another thrall to help. I let the merchants worry about themselves. The rich have many friends; the poor have only one in this world, and I was His agent.

At last we stood on the hilltop, armed men in a battle line. The women, children and old people hurried on to a higher hill beyond us. I was one of the armed men (and don't tell me churchmen shouldn't bear arms—I won't stand by and watch people killed when I can help defend them, and I'll gladly answer to God for it).

We watched as they tied their ships at the pier or simply beached them, and as they tore screaming into the market and began looting. Their leaders had a job of it to get them to drop the plunder and reform as an army. This gave us time to estimate their numbers and compare them to our own.

It did not look good.

We had the merchants and bonders in addition to Erling's two ship's crews. But even so they outnumbered us about two to one.

"Take heart," said Erling, standing surrounded by his bodyguard under his twin-eagle banner, which Steinulf carried. "We have the high ground."

It's always good to have the high ground. But it's not everything, as we soon learned.

Three men climbed up near our position under a white shield of truce. A powerful-looking man of middle height with graying golden hair shouted, "Erling Skjalgsson of Sola! I would have you know the name of your destroyer!"

"Pray tell me your name," Erling shouted back. "I'll need to know where to send the body!"

"I am the hersir Brusi Arnfinsson of More! You hanged my son!"

"I've no shame in that," said Erling, "though I took no pleasure in the thing. He broke the king's peace. He plundered, killed and kidnapped in my country. But this I'll say to you—your son died well."

"See that you die well yourself, Erling Skjalgsson! For if I find you alive when we've overrun you, I vow I'll hang you as you hanged him!"

He cast a spear over our heads, shouting, "I give you to God!" and went back to his army.

As their battle line drew up, we saw that theirs was longer than ours, and deeper. They were using the "swine formation"—a wedge of men in which each line is two men wider than the one before it. We thinned our line to spread it, and Erling called, "Archers and spearmen! Remember to aim low—it's tricky to hit a mark downhill. We'll need to make the most of our position."

When the More-men came into bowshot our archers let loose at them. Despite Erling's warning a lot of arrows went over their heads. Others wasted themselves in shields, but a fair number dropped men.

Meanwhile they were loosing arrows as well, and theirs tended to come low. A lot of them buried themselves in the turf before us, and several of our men got them in their legs. All in all our shooting was probably better, but not enough to even the odds.

The high ground told more when they came in the range of our casting spears. Our spearmen were more careful than our archers, and the enemy, wearied with their climb, had trouble keeping their shields high enough to cover themselves properly. Their spear casts in reply seemed somewhat feeble to me, and I don't recall that they did much damage.

We stood on a sort of rim, the ground falling away sharply before us. That gave us good vantage as they came on from below, especially when they got in range of the thrusting spears. We did real slaughter then. It was nearly a matter of simply poking your weapon in, over the shields, until you found something solid, and pushing. It was there we stopped them, and their wedge went to pieces, and they drew back in disarray.

We stood and watched them, panting and feeling our nerves sing. Before us lay the enemy wounded and dead, quiet or writhing in pain and screaming, and I felt strong and intensely alive, unconquerable and without pity.

But Brusi Arnfinsson felt unconquerable and without pity as well, and he soon had his men reformed and ready for another attack.

We beat them back once again, but it was harder and took longer, and we were more weary when it was done. We lost a few men too.

There's a sort of reckoning you do in your head during a battle, when it's small enough for you to see most of it, and it began to dawn on me (I think I wasn't alone) that we could not keep this up. They would bear us down by weight of numbers, if not now then soon.

The confidence I'd felt became weakness and a foggy foreboding. I would die here—I'd be struck down and my throat would be cut by those who stripped the dead, and the ravens would pick at my flesh.

I knew as I watched them close with us that this would be the end. This time they would run over our line and cut us to pieces. The great saga of Erling, and the little saga of each of us who followed him, would end here, in a narrow place fighting deadly odds.

They came on like winter, they came on like old age, they came on like the end of the world.

Their faces as they approached were not the faces of men. They were the faces of the dead, the faces of the overwhelming force of the fathers and grandfathers and great-grandfathers of all of us, who had gone before and fallen, hard or easy, beneath the great Reaper's sickle edge.

It was with something like relief that I watched them come. *Soon the fever will break. Soon the fit will end. Soon the yearning and the fear and the regret will be done.*

Then there was a screaming, as if from a herd of wild pigs, and a force of men, hairy and unarmored, swinging axes and clubs and swords and stinking like corpses, came up from our left flank and smote Brusi's force as with a smith's hammer. "Baug Kollasson!" someone cried. The berserker had come from the south with a few of his friends.

That charge saved our lives, but I watched it with horror and have never since been able to think otherwise about it. Filthy, ragged men, wide-eyed, howling and gnashing teeth, they fell on Brusi's force like wolves on sheep. Brusi's men far outnumbered them, but the sheer shock of their onset, along with the confusion of a flank attack, knocked them sideover.

They never had a chance. My heart was wholly with Brusi's warriors at that moment, as whose wouldn't be, seeing his fellow men slaughtered by wild beasts? Better to die, I thought, than be saved thus.

Something deeply wrong, wrong at the very roots, was here. For thousands of years we've struggled to keep ourselves above the level of beasts. These berserkers cared nothing for that; less than despising it they paid it no more notice than a cast-off pair of shoes. Their mind seemed to be, *Why bother yourself with humanity? It's overprized. Drink the wine we drink, and set aside your burden of custom and decency. Admit you are but a beast as we are, and all your sorrows will be gone, and you'll wonder how you ever troubled at them.*

When our foes were utterly confused and disorganized we charged them from the front and shooed them away like flies from dinner.

At last the only More-men not fled or slain were Brusi Arnfinsson and some of his bodyguard. There was no cry for quarter; Brusi had chosen to die with honor.

He would have too, had not the berserkers spent their wind. I suppose there'd never be survivors of any battle involving berserkers if they could carry on for hours as they start, but that kind of work wears you down, and Baug's men had run a long way. While sane men carried on the fighting, the berserkers faded and fell and lay themselves down in the snow for a nice snoggy nap, or slouched off to find a more sheltered bed.

That gave Erling the chance to call his men off and speak to Brusi.

"You've done all as a father should," he called. " 'Tis but proper you should seek mansbot for your child. You've failed to take it with an army, but I owe you the chance to take it in person. I'll fight you in single combat, if you wish it."

Voices were raised among Brusi's men, but he cut them off and stepped out from among them bearing sword and shield.

"You do me honor, Erling Skjalgsson," he said.

"Almost I think we could be friends if you'd not spilled blood of mine. You're a more proper ally than that milk-faced warlock."

"Milk-faced warlock? Eyvind Kellda?"

"Aye. He cloaked three of my ships with his magic. We'd hoped you'd sail to meet us with a smaller force, or failing that at least underreckon us. It almost worked."

"You made a deal with the devil."

"I see that now. But the lad was my son after all. Blood cries out."

"A son is a son, but he's also his own man in the world. He must account for his deeds."

"He'd not have been on his own, perhaps, had I done handsomer by him."

"I've no doubt you did all you could for a younger son. Whatever bitterness he bore, whatever choices he made, were no fault of yours."

"Thanks for that word, Rogalander. Shall we get to business?"

They faced off against each other and began swinging.

Brusi gave the first blow, as was his right. Erling caught it on his shield and struck back with a swing that Brusi fended.

It went on like that for some time. It went on, in fact, longer than it should have, considering Erling's youth and greater reach. I'd not have reckoned that Brusi's experience would have counted for as much as it seemed to. I'd seen Erling kill bigger and cannier men in less time.

I suppose he could have let Brusi fight until he dropped from weariness, but that would have been to shame him, a thing far worse than killing.

At last Brusi tried a feint, a swing of his shield followed by a back-handed sword blow, which Erling stopped by catching the blade on his sword guard, bringing his iron shield rim down in Brusi's face, and swinging his sword down and behind to slice Brusi's hamstring, just back of the knee. The old man fell hard and lay face up, his chest heaving. He must have known, as we all did, that Erling had spared his life, but his honor was left to him.

"You've finished me as a warrior, Rogalander," he said.

"You've earned a rest," said Erling.

"This means the straw-death for me."

" 'Tis no shame for Christian men to die in their beds. But live long, Brusi Arnfinsson. Live long and be a good lord. And come to me if you need a friend. I owe you that."

His bodyguard carried him back to their ship on a shield.

Only three ships sailed back northward; the other two were profit for us. They helped to make good the merchants' losses. Erling was generous, as he wanted them back the next year.

"But not here at Risa," he said to Thorbjorg as they surveyed the littered battleground. "This place is too much exposed. I need a marketplace easier to defend."

"I owe you thanks, Baug Kollasson," said Erling that evening in the hall at Risa. "You came just at the time you were needed."

Baug stood before him by the long fire in an idle pose, a grin on his greasy face, his long-hafted axe over his shoulder. "It was no more than an honest bonder owes his hersir," he answered.

"I wonder to see you bring so many of your own kind. How many do you have? Twenty or so? That's a great household for an honest bonder. I told you I dislike berserkers in my lands."

"And now you see how squint-sighted that was. There are kings who'd pay much to have a force like my household at their beck."

"Only very desperate ones, Baug. But it would be

ungracious to complain of it now. Here's a gold ring for your services, and there'll be silver for your men. But know this—I'll hold you to account for their conduct."

"Once again you do me honor, lord." Baug's teeth shone in the firelight.

"I've found the place," said Thorbjorg Lambisdatter the next day, while everyone was salvaging what they could of their goods and dividing up the captured weapons and armor. "While you were hanging rings on berserkers' arms I was with the women, talking of where a market should be."

"Exactly what I was wondering," said Erling. "I've had some ideas—"

"Forget them. Listen to me. I talked to the women. The women know. 'Tis they who run the farms and do the trading in summer, while you men are away spoiling foreigners. They sell off the unneeded stock in autumn too as often as not. And they care about safety without thinking it shameful. Almost all agree that there's but one place, better in a hundred ways than Risa."

"And what place is that?"

"To the east of here, across the peninsula. A sheltered harbor that's not a far ride for you, and easy of access for all the people of the inner fjords as well. Easy to defend.

"A place called Stavanger."

CHAPTER VIII

Olaf Trygvesson had spent the winter cracking heads in the far north. When he'd bullied and held feet to fires (literally) and forced the lords to pretend to believe what they didn't, he baptized them all and took hostages so they'd remember to keep pretending. He kept most of the hostages around himself (no fool he); but two of them—two boys from Halogaland named Thorir and Sigurd Thorisson—he sent to Erling.

They came with Sigurd Eriksson on his way south to Opprostad. Sigurd would have stopped to feast with Erling anyway (anybody who was anybody did). I was there with the greeting party when they disembarked at Somme. The two hostages, fifteen and sixteen years old, were handsome lads with upturned noses, red-gold hair and freckles. The three girls, Thorliv and Sigrid and Freydis, who never missed a landing, broke into muffled giggles and chatter when they saw them.

They also giggled when they saw the master of the second ship that came with Sigurd's. This was not a warship but a knarr, well tarred and bright-painted and outfitted with a brand-new diamond-patterned sail. This master was a young man, tall and broad-shouldered, with red hair. He looked very grave, as if he were on an unwelcome errand, but he gave the girls a long, appraising look. He and his men were well-dressed and flashed gold and silver.

We took them all to Sola and Erling met them in the yard. Sigurd introduced the hostages, then put a hand on the redhead's shoulder.

"This is a most important guest," he said.

"From the new sword he bears, I'd say he has Olaf's favor," said Erling.

"This is Leif, son of Erik Thorvaldsson of Brattahlid in Greenland."

"I know of your father," said Erling, offering his hand.

Leif looked at the hand and made no move to take it.

Erling paused, then said, "Well, let's go inside. We've much to talk of, and talking is dry work."

We adjourned to the new hall for drinking and feasting. Erling set Sigurd Eriksson, of course, in the guest's high seat across the hall from him, Leif Eriksson at his right, but he honored the hostage boys by seating them directly on his own left. They looked sullen, as who wouldn't in their place? We were not a cheerful company.

We drank, and then we ate, and then we drank some more and there was poetry, music and dancing, and at last the time came to talk business.

"Well, Leif Eriksson, let's hear your case against me," Erling said, after he'd called for southland wine and had the thralls set glass beakers of it before Sigurd and the Greenlander.

"I did not say I had a case against you," said Leif, leaving the red drink untouched.

"I'm not a fool," Erling replied, "and I've no use for feuds. I'm a man of property and business. I'm sure I have something that would buy peace with you, and I want peace."

"I live in Greenland, on the edge of the world," said Leif drily. "Why should you care whether you're at peace with me?"

"Now you're gaming with me, Leif Eriksson. Speak plainly in my house. This is not Nidaros. I am not Olaf."

The young man paused for a long moment before speaking. "Your father Skjalg picked a fight with Thorvald my grandfather. It mattered nothing what my grandfather had done—it mattered nothing where the right was in the case—he was only a counter in the great game your father played with our kinsman, Erik of Opprostad. Erik managed to save Grandfather's life by brokering a settlement that gave Skjalg our farm and outlawed him. And so we went to Iceland—latecomers forced to take what scrawny land was still available. In the end we found Greenland and made a life there, but that is only because my father is a man of daring and dreams. My grandfather died in Iceland, a broken man."

"I make no excuses for my father," said Erling. "He was a hard man who did what was right in his own eyes. But cases have changed. You have the upper hand now. So you must name your terms to make peace."

Leif's face went red. "You jest," he said.

Erling raised a hand. "Not at all. You're a friend of the king, and kin to his chief counselor. No doubt you need grain in Greenland, but you can always get it from them. I can bargain and offer you terms, but there's no reason you'd want to do business with me.

"This is truth—you have much that I want in Greenland. You have walrus hide for ship's ropes, and narwhal and walrus tusks for ivory, and white falcons, and white bears, and rich furs, and other things that can be got nowhere else in the world. I want to build a market town. I want to handle trade—not only with Norwegians but with all the world. I want a share of the Greenland traffic. What will it take to get it from you? Do you want your ancestral farm, Oksnevad, back? It's yours if you wish it."

"I am the son of the chief man in Greenland," said Leif. "In my way I'm a prince. Why would I come back to Norway and be a bonder?"

"Greenland is a remote place. It costs to carry things there. You must have needs."

Leif allowed a small smile to raise one corner of his mouth. "I suppose I could do what you did with Olaf, when you were in a like case. I could ask for the hand of one of your sisters." There was giggling from the women's end.

Erling didn't turn a hair. "I'd give it strong thought."

Leif allowed himself a sip of wine. "My marriage is already arranged. Charming as your sisters are." He looked at the women's table and hysterics followed.

"What then?" asked Erling with a smile.

"Freedom from all docking tolls and taxes here."

"The king expects the taxes paid."

"Pay them yourself. Half of them go to you in any case."

"I'll meet you halfway."

"Done." Leif grinned and drank his wine down, then stretched his hand out for more.

The second night of the feast Sigurd sat silent for a long time, which was not his habit. Erling asked him about it at last.

"I've a message from my kinfolk," said Sigurd, shaking his big, handsome head and twisting one of the rings on his left arm.

"Have I offended you in some way?"

"No. No. The other side of the house altogether. You've been a good kinsman and neighbor, and brought us all profit. We want to give you somewhat in return."

"Indeed?"

"You refused to be made a jarl, at our bidding, as a favor to us. We've talked the matter over, and this is our thought—you should be a jarl. You are a jarl in all but name. We take back our objection. Be a jarl, Erling Skjalgsson."

Erling took a long pull from his best blue Frankish glass beaker.

"This was Olaf's idea, wasn't it?" he said at last.

"He . . . may have brought it up, yes."

"I thought so."

"What of it?"

"*Hersir* Erling. I've come to like the sound of it. Jarl Erling sounds less good to my ear. I think I'll keep the name I have."

Sigurd frowned. "You know the story of the death of King Haakon the Good, don't you?"

"Of course. At Fitjar. Haakon was of my kin after all."

"And mine. We've that in common. Eyvind Finnsson took a hat and set it on top of Haakon's helmet, because it was such a rich, gilded thing that everyone could pick him out by it."

"It wasn't enough though."

"No, Haakon died that day in any case. Because it's always dangerous to outshine the men around you."

After the feasting was done, I leaned near to Erling and asked him, "What was all this about jarldoms and Haakon the Good?"

Erling smiled and spoke low to me. "All these killings and burnings Olaf is doing up north—'tis not about Christianity, you know."

"Of course not," said I. " 'Tis about power."

"Exactly. How much power the king will have. I've seen a bit of the world, and I know that Christian lands don't really have to have mighty high kings who tell everyone where they may sleep and what they may eat and where to relieve themselves. It's not like that in Ireland. It's not like that in England. But for Olaf it's not enough to be a king that way. He wants to be a king like his friend Valdemar in Russia, or Charlemagne in Frankland while he lived."

"But I thought you wanted to be a jarl."

"I wanted it once. I thought it the only way to hold my rights under a king. But I got the power without the name. And what do you think? I like this better. My title is my own. It's mine by birthright. It's not the king's gift. I'll wager that makes Olaf nervous."

"I see. I heard a story once of a king who went through the fields, snicking off the tops of the tallest grain stalks with a stick. He meant it as a lesson in politics. Get rid of great men if you want to keep power. Olaf has gone to his school," I said.

"Haakon the Good was a different kind of king from his father Harald Finehair. Harald wanted to make thralls of every man in the land. Haakon worked along with the lords. He respected their rights. He let them steer their lands, and he himself looked to the good of the whole commonwealth."

"And he compromised his faith. He sacrificed to the old gods."

"Yes. He payed for that too. But it won't come to that for Olaf. Times have changed. My dream is to make a bargain with Olaf that will let me work with him as my father worked with Haakon."

"You want to force Olaf Trygvesson to king it on your terms? You've a bold mind."

"It's for Olaf's good as much as mine. If Olaf tries to be the king he wants to be, and fails, it will be a sad fate. If he succeeds, it might be worse."

On the morning when Sigurd and Leif set out, we gathered at the pier and old Bergthor came stumping over to Erling (he was getting quite slow by now) and said, "Do you know what that crazy Greenland lad wants to do?"

"I gather he plans to sail home."

"I tried to give him good advice on sailing directions to the Faeroes, and do you know what he said?"

"No."

"He says he plans to sail over open sea all the way! No stop in the Faeroes, no stop in Iceland! He says he can sail north to Hernar, then shoot straight west and come to Greenland! Days and weeks, maybe months without clear sight of land, trusting the stars to keep him on course! He's mad!"

"He's bold, I'll give him that," said Erling. "It was bound to be tried sooner or later. I wish it had been me."

"The sea is not a pond for children to game in!"

"No, but the world belongs to bold men. You know that, Bergthor. You told me as much once."

"I didn't mean madness. Those Oksnevad men were always mad. I knew Leif's father Erik the Red—rash-bold he was. A great warrior, though. This boy will never make a name as he did."

Loud laughter came from behind us. It was Freydis Sotisdatter, looking at Bergthor and hugging herself in mirth.

Sigurd was heading home to attend the Quarter Thing, held at Klepp. I've told you about the Thing at Sola, where I went through the iron-ordeal. That was a Quarter Thing too, but at that time our Quarter had had two Thingsteads. This wasn't the time-honored way of doing things, but Thorolf Skjalg had set up his own thingstead some time before, due to his unfriendship with Erik Bjodaskalle. All that was past now, and we gathered in early spring all together at Klepp, as in ancient times.

We used Erling's new road, as far as it went. Those of us who rated a horse rode, and others walked, and we carried goods in carts for trade and gifts.

Once we'd passed the limit of the road-building

there was a lot of wrestling with carts mired in muddy places, and once or twice a stop to fix a stone-broken wheel. We had to keep our pace down to match the slowest among us, and in bad weather we all huddled under the tent awnings we'd brought for the booths.

But the weather wasn't foul all the time, and one morning Thorliv moved up beside me on her horse, and with the ease of a master horsewoman maneuvered me a little away from the rest, behind the last rider and before the first walker.

"Father, would you marry a man and a woman without their parents' consent?"

I looked at her twice, because I'd had this conversation once before, with her sister. I told her as much.

"I don't think it's right, to tell people whom they can marry," she said when I was done. "People should marry whomever they wish."

"And whom do you want to marry?"

"Arnor."

"Arnor? Isn't he . . . friends with Freydis?"

"Oh, that's just Freydis. She leads on all the boys, but it's never serious. No, Arnor is mine."

"Arnor's a good boy, daughter, but he's beneath your rank. You know your brother and mother would never stand for it."

"Arnor's free, and he has a trade."

"Your brother is as good as a king. He'll wed you to someone with land and ships."

"Whether I like him or not?"

"You know he'll never force you. But he won't let you throw yourself away either."

"Yes, God forbid anyone should ever do anything just to be happy. God forbid anything should happen that doesn't profit Erling."

"Erling has your good at heart, and the good of everyone in the west, down to the thralls themselves. You know this."

"Does he really? Are you so sure?"

"Why would you doubt it?"

"Think of all the good Erling does. He is brave. He keeps his word. Those things earn him honor among men whose support he needs. He gives generous gifts. That binds men to him with ties of obligation. He helps the thralls free themselves. That earns him gratitude, and a profit, and gets him new tenants to pay him rent. Everything he does makes him stronger and richer."

"Well that's always the puzzle, isn't it? You can ask that question about every good man and every good deed ever done. You never know until the test comes."

"What test?"

"The test that falls on each man soon or late. The day when doing right costs. Does he still do right then? Or not? That's when we know for sure."

"It would cost him to give me to Arnor."

"It might cost you as well, daughter."

We came at last to the Thinghaug at Klepp, and set up our booth in Erling's traditional spot.

We'd expected a lively Thing, for there were many lawsuits that year, mostly involving Baug Kollasson, who seemed to have a bent for putting a toe over his neighbors' fence lines.

But about half the lawsuits had been dropped. Another few had been voided by the deaths of the plaintiffs. And the rest came to Erling Skjalgsson's booth.

One after another the men came, shoulders slumped, still bearing their swords or axes but somehow disarmed.

"I'll be gaining a lot of new land off this," said Erling to me after the first afternoon. "Free bonders become my tenants in return for my taking up their suits against Baug. What can I do?"

"Isn't there some other way they can repay you?"

"Some can. Others have nothing else to give. I'll try to help them buy their land back. If I can do it for the thralls, I'll do it for the bonders. But I can't make them think I'm not giving them charity."

Erling won every suit. It went without saying. Nobody could challenge him for power except perhaps Sigurd Eriksson "Karl's-head" of Opprostad, and why would he want to? Baug paid the fines assessed against him without visible grudge, sending his brother Hoskuld to fetch a chest of silver. Everyone wondered where Baug had gotten such wealth.

Afterwards Hoskuld Coal-chewer swaggered over to the place where Erling, Steinulf, Eystein and I were standing.

"Not too high and mighty to take up another man's lawsuit now, are you Erling Skjalgsson?" he sneered.

"I treat none of them otherwise than I treated you, Hoskuld," Erling replied. "I'd have stood your friend if you'd not been so proud."

"Well, it's good I didn't. Because it brought Baug home, and now we have power and honor. Our kin are great in the world today."

"And you'd rather be Baug's thrall than my debtor?"

"I'm no thrall!" Hoskuld's face went black with anger.

Erling wasted no more words on the wretch, but turned his back. This enraged Hoskuld, who rushed at him with fists raised. Erling heard him coming and turned back almost casually, flicking his arm and sending Hoskuld flying onto his back on the grass.

"Beware Erling Skjalgsson! You're not so great as you think!" Hoskuld screamed.

Helge of Klepp was the Lawspeaker for the Jaeder Quarter. This gave him many social obligations and made it hard for me to spend time with him (though he kindly lent me his gospel book for the length of my stay).

But I found him one evening after supper, sitting alone with Freydis on a stone wall in the red sunset light.

"Here's Father Aillil," she said to him.

"Ah, Father! Freydis is showing me her dolls."

"He can't really see them, but I'm telling him about them," said the girl.

"And what are their names?" I asked, sitting on her other side.

"Freydis, Thorliv, Sigrid, Arnor, Thorir and Sigurd."

They were cunning little images, cleverly carved, clothed with scraps of wool and topped with hair in the proper colors. Somehow she'd managed to limn the character of each so that I could have named them without being told.

"Tell him whom they love," said Helge.

"Thorliv loves Arnor. Sigrid loves Thorir. Both the boys love Sigrid."

"Interesting.

"But these things will change."

"How do you know?"

"Because all the boys belong to Freydis. They don't know it, but they do."

I felt very serious of a sudden. "How do you know this?"

"I have ways."

"No magic, Freydis," I said, standing and taking hold of both her arms. "Listen to me. If the king's priests found you doing magic, they'd kill you. No matter that you're young. They'd kill you, and they'd do it very painfully."

"Don't be silly," said Freydis, shaking loose and skipping off. "The king has a deacon who divines for him. He has no quarrel with magic."

I sat beside Helge and watched her go. "Sometimes I feel the world has ended already, and I'm in some other place," I said.

❖   ❖   ❖

One of the many pleasures of the Thing was that there the freedoms of thralls were announced. It put the stamp of the law on their status, and made them less likely to be taken for runaways.

One of the thralls being cried that year was a black Irishman named Ciaran, whom I'd always thought one of the best. He was big and strong, and he worked hard in the evenings on the piece of land Erling had set him to. He'd never taken a wife, preferring to concentrate on becoming a freeman before he took on gentler burdens.

Erling gave Ciaran a horn of mead in the booth that night. "What do you wish to do now?" he asked him. "Do you want land? You'll make a good farmer."

" 'Tis not what I'd choose first."

"Do you want a herring boat?"

"No, I'm no fisherman."

"Do you have some skill I don't know of?"

"Yes, one."

"And that is?"

"I was bred to be a warrior."

Erling sat silent a moment. "You came to Norway young, as a captive. You can't have much training."

"Nevertheless, my father was a warrior, and his father before him. I learn fast."

"So you wish to go back to Ireland?"

"No. I wish to fight for you."

A murmur went around the men gathered in the booth.

"It's not done, Ciaran," said Erling. " 'Tis true we arm thralls for defense now, but the men of the bodyguard would not stand for a freedman in their company."

"I know that," said Ciaran. "I don't ask to join the bodyguard. I wish to start a new company of warriors. Irishmen or freedmen all. Give an Irishman an axe, and he'll defend his lord as long as he has legs under him."

Erling rubbed his chin. "I know that to be true," he said. "But a one-man guard is of little use."

"There'll be others in time."

"You still need training."

"Give me Lemming. Make him captain. You've never been able to use him as he deserves."

"He's not a trained warrior either."

"And what a loss that is! Steinulf will train us, won't he? Or Eystein?"

"Perhaps . . ."

"Not I," said Steinulf. "I've seen enough of thralls putting on airs."

"I'll do it," said Eystein, almost invisible in the shadows. "You can never have too many fighting men."

"But you can't let them live as the guard does, training and protecting you and running errands for you. The men would never stomach it," said Steinulf.

"I'll work as I have, with the thralls," said Ciaran. "Pay me and feed me. Just let me get my training and form the company. You'll not regret it."

Erling stood. "You've a long head, Ciaran. We'll give it a try."

"These freedmen will not dine in the hall with us!" cried Steinulf.

"No, we can't have that. They'll eat in a separate house, and in the old hall when we feast."

CHAPTER IX

"What am I to do with you boys?" Erling asked the two hostages. "You went into the storehouse, which is forbidden, and opened the chests, which is twice forbidden, and scattered the seed grain, which is murder, and left the door open behind you so the rats and birds could go in, which is treason." We were all in Erling's hall, seated on the benches on both sides, and Thorir and Sigurd stood pale-faced before the long-fire facing the seat of judgment. Their freckles showed clearly against their bloodless faces, though they held their heads up.

Thorir, the younger and bolder of the two, stepped a little forward and said, "We are men of Halogaland. We do not stoop to planting seeds and grains and digging in the dirt. We live by hunting and fishing, whale-taking and the Lapp trade, occupations worthy of free men."

Erling sat still a moment before answering. "I suppose you do eat bread up in Halogaland, don't you? I mean, you don't just smear butter on dried codfish like the Iceland thralls?"

"Of course we eat bread. We eat the best barley

and wheaten bread. Our foster father's is a landed man's table."

"And where do you think the bread comes from?"

Thorir looked puzzled, as if this were a new thought.

"I'll tell you where the bread comes from," said Erling. "It comes from me. It comes from grain and meal that I sell your foster father every year when he sends his knarr south to trade. If it weren't for my dirt digging, you'd be feasting on buttered codfish, free men or not."

This seemed to subdue Thorir, and he hung his head. But he yet looked sullen and gave no sign of bending.

"Because of what you've done, when your foster father sends his ships this autumn there'll be less for him to buy, and what there is will cost him more. So you've robbed him, just as if you'd broken into his treasure chests.

"Now all that remains is your punishment."

The boys shuddered visibly.

"Eystein!" called Erling. "Carry out the punishment."

Big dark Eystein came down the hearth-way with a hazel-wand in his hand. He gave each of the boys two sharp whacks across the buttocks. They gasped but did not cry out.

"Now watch your steps in future," said Erling, "and we'll say no more about it."

"That's—that's all?" asked Sigurd, rubbing his backside, his eyes wide.

"Of course. What more did you expect?"

"We—we thought you'd kill us."

"Kill you? What gave you that idea?"

"It's well known that Christians kill and torture men for the least wrongdoing."

Erling shifted in his seat. "I don't think even King Olaf would kill boys for a prank. But let me speak clearly so there'll be no misunderstanding.

"You came to Sola as hostages, surety for your foster father's submission to Olaf and the Christian faith. But I told you when you came, and I tell you now, that I rank you foster sons, not hostages. You will be treated and trained as I would sons of my own, and held to the same rule. You may not think so now, but I expect we'll be good friends before you go home."

The boys looked confused, but they knew their manners. "You do us honor, Lord Erling," said Sigurd.

"Not for the last time, I hope. Now go and play."

They do not plow in Jaeder, due to the particular rockiness of the soil. This seems no hardship to Norsemen, who turn the earth with iron-shod wooden spades (or send their thralls to do it) and will tell you smugly that "stones feed the ground."

The boys' transgression notwithstanding, there was plenty of seed for home and export purposes, God granting a decent summer.

So the thralls went out, spades on shoulders, and the air grew sweet with the breath of the mould, and the seagulls flew in to feast on bugs and worms they turned up. And in the evenings, you could watch Lemming and Ciaran and the company of freedmen drilling and practicing weapons' play with sticks and basket-woven shields. The company had a full three men for a start, but as the nights went on it grew to more than twenty-five. The bullyboys laughed at them, but not before Eystein.

The road-builders went out again too, Patrick the thrall and his friends, to make high the low places and make low the high places and make straight the way for Erling Skjalgsson and Sigurd Eriksson. They set out on a drizzly, gray morning. Patrick the thrall kissed his Dierdre good-bye, and started the others in a song as they tramped south along the highway.

'Twas the next day they came back, all of them save

one, walking fast but weary, and casting many a glance over their shoulders.

"It was the berserkers," said one of them to Erling, who had rushed up from the fields to meet them. "Baug's men from Harvaland farm. They came to mock us at our work—well, you expect that, especially from berserkers. But they wouldn't quit. Njal the overseer tried to tell them to bugger off, but they started pushing, and then there were words and things got out of hand."

"Was anyone badly hurt?" Erling asked.

"Patrick is dead."

My heart sank.

"No more? They just came to their senses?"

"Berserkers? Not likely. No, it was the bear that saved us."

"Bear? You mean a man named Bjorn?"

"No—a real bear. A beast. A great white bear with blue eyes. It appeared suddenly and came between us and Baug's men. If we'd not been ready to run from them, we'd have run from the bear in any case. We ran as long as we could, but neither they nor it followed us. I hope the bear ate them all."

"I'll take some men and see to Baug Kollasson," said Erling. "And this bear must be looked to also."

More and more people, mostly thralls, were running toward us, and I looked around to see Deirdre coming. I rushed to meet her, but some busybody beat me with the news.

Her screams started the seagulls from the fields.

"This bear they tell of, was it a thing of this world?" Deirdre asked later that day.

We sat on a bench in one of the thrall's houses, where she and Patrick had lived. No one else was there except Asa, who had come along unasked, as if her place were at my side, my work hers to share. It felt strange, but it felt good also. Deirdre had wrapped herself in a blanket and her head glowed faintly against the gloom in the light from the smoke holes in the gables. She shivered from time to time and rocked her baby.

"There are white bears in Greenland, so I'm told. But never in Norway. No, that was no earthly beast."

"Was it of the devil then? One of the old gods in disguise?"

"I think not. I saw such a bear once before, in another world, and I believe it to be from God Jehovah."

"It was a bear from God," she said, so softly I could hardly hear.

"I believe so."

"And it saved those men."

"Yes."

"All but my Patrick."

I sighed. "Yes."

"A miracle. A miracle for all of them. All but Patrick and me."

"I've no explanation—"

"Oh, I know the explanation. God hates me. He's always hated me."

"No. You mustn't think that. I know it seems hard and cruel, but you have to believe—"

"I have to believe what I've seen. I have to believe what God has done in my life. He let me be taken from my home and made a slave in a strange land. He let a man of the bodyguard, all hairy and boozey, take my maidenhead when I was fourteen, and he let the same man set my baby out for the wolves because he didn't want to feed it. He gave me one moment of joy in my life—my time with Patrick—then He took that away, along with all our future and our hopes. Tell me how God loves me, Father. Tell me how He loves my child. Tell me about His tender care."

"He does care, daughter—"

"What did the Lord say? 'By their fruits you shall know them.' You told us that in church. What shall

I know by God's fruits? How has He shown His love for me?"

"You're in pain, daughter. I don't think God blames you for suffering. There's nothing I can tell you to change your mind, but I'll pray that He comforts you."

Asa said, "Go away, Aillil. Stop talking of things you don't understand. I'll see to this." She crawled over to Deirdre and took her in her arms, rocking her as she rocked the baby and cooed.

I left them there.

We led the ninety bullyboys southward along the road the next morning. Erling and I, Steinulf and Eystein rode horses; the rest marched. We were armed and we were angry. A light spume blew in from seaward.

"Do you think we can handle the berserkers?" I asked Erling as we rode.

"As far as I know there's not above twenty. I think twice double their number ought to serve."

About midmorning we met two horsemen coming northward. They thickened out of the mist like wraiths. It was Baug Kollasson, along with his brother Hoskuld.

"Erling Skjalgsson!" Baug called. "Well met!"

"I come on no neighborly errand," Erling called back.

"This I foresaw," said Baug. "My men broke the peace and did you offense. I come to make amends."

"What amends do you offer?"

"This," said Baug. He waved a hand at Hoskuld, who hopped down from his horse and came trotting up to us with a woolen sack in hand. I took the thing and he let go as though there were serpents inside.

"The heads of two of my berserkers," said Baug.

I dropped the sack (I meant no disrespect to the dead, but it was a shock).

"Two free men for one thrall," said Baug. "I call that handsome mansbot."

"I cannot gainsay that," said Erling with a frown.

"Then we are at peace?"

"For the moment."

Baug grinned and reined his horse around. He galloped away, Hoskuld following. Their figures faded as their hoofbeats muffled.

"Two of his own men," I whispered, as one of the warriors moved up to retrieve the sack. "He's a cold one."

"That's the trouble with this bargain," said Erling. "Two warriors mean less to Baug than one thrall to me. But I could hardly say so."

The wind out of the west strengthened as we returned, and brought rain to soak our woolens. When we got back to Sola, one of the thrall women trudged through the mud to me as I dismounted and told me, "You'd better see to Deirdre. She tried to hang herself in the old storehouse."

Erling and I went to the house where she lay under a blanket on a bench. She'd an ugly welt on her throat but had taken no lasting harm. The mischief of Sigurd and Thorir had profited for once. They'd found her in their exploring and cut her down.

She was thrashing about, held down by some of her friends. She cried, "No! No! I want to die! Let me die!" No need to shrive her, so I gave her a blessing, and Erling and I went out in the rain.

"Her man died in my service," said Erling. "I'll do what I can to make it good. It will fetch her freedom."

"Thank you," said I. "You'd better see the boys and give them some reward. This will be a chance to make friends."

"My very plan. Do you think the woman will be well?"

" 'Tis hard to say. It's not easy to keep someone in life if they truly wish to go west. But if we keep her under watch for a while, we might hope to have her come right."

"I'll see to it. She's no profit to me dead, and she seems a good enough woman."

The next day was fair and Erling rewarded Thorir and Sigurd by letting them practice weaponry with the bodyguard. This was a particular honor as they were playing the Baldur-game, too dangerous for children.

The Baldur-game went this way: The men were told off in two companies, each of which took turns casting blunt wooden spears and shooting blunt wooden arrows at the other, giving each side shield practice. Blunt weapons or not, such capers can put an eye out, and I watched with concern.

But the boys were quick and deft, and used their shields to good effect. No harm came to them, or indeed to any man else that day. It rattled on for some time, till both sides were well winded.

Then Erling stepped forward in his bright helmet and brynje, sword and shield in hand, and announced that he would play the *true* Baldur-game. A hush fell on the company, and the men eyed one another aslant.

I'd heard of the "true" game, but hadn't seen it since I'd been at Sola. I wasn't keen to see it now.

The legend of Baldur tells how the gods threw deadly weapons at him to honor him, for all things on earth had sworn an oath to spare him. But through the cunning of the demon Loki, a mistletoe plant had been overlooked in the oath-taking, and being cast at Baldur gave him his death-wound.

Erling was the only man in Norway (or anywhere) I ever heard of playing the "true" Baldur-game. When he played, the spears and arrows were steel-headed, and deadly sharp.

As I watched him set himself in his place in the meadow, the reluctant bodyguard massed a bowshot away, I found my fists clenching so that I must relax them lest the nails draw blood. Erling's face showed no emotion, except that his blue eyes blazed.

"Now!" he cried, and the archers let fly.

They did not spare him, for they knew his command and his temper. The arrow-storm they unleashed was just what they'd have loosed at Svein of Denmark, had he been there. And when the archers were done the spearmen ran closer and let go.

Erling was a marvel. I'd never seen anything like it, and I'd seen him fight before. Surely no man of flesh could move so quickly, pivot his shield so deftly, cut missiles from the very air with his sword so lightly. He seemed a blur in the light, as if he'd lost bodily presence and become a spirit without flesh to wound. The thing did not last long, but when it was done he called for a second volley, and a third.

When it was over, and it seemed hours to me, his men opened their throats and shouted, and banged their swords on their shields. *"Erling!" "Erling!"* He was the greatest warrior in the world (tell it not in Nidaros!), and he was their lord. I shouted too, and looked at my hands to see them smeared with blood.

Thorir and Sigurd were with the men, and they shouted as loud as any. So I understood why Erling had done this madness. He'd gotten himself two lifelong worshipers.

I took one of my seaside walks that evening, stopping a few minutes to watch the freedmen drilling in the meadow. I didn't know how they'd do as warriors, but it always warmed me to watch them. A few leagues southward along the shore I found Freydis Sotisdatter, wandering loose on her own like the wild creature she was. She stared southeastward over the wide crescent plain that faced the bay.

I walked up and asked, "What do you see?"

She started and turned to me. "Father! I was just—thinking."

"What do you see, child?"

"How do you know I see something?"

"I know the look. Tell me what you see."

"I've seen it before. Just there. Only there. Never anywhere else. At the north end of the crescent. A bird."

"What kind of bird?"

"Not a true bird. An image of a bird. 'Tis plainly made of metal—silver, perhaps. It comes circling down to the ground there, and soars in to land. It doesn't flap its wings or such—it's just a flying image. And a door—I know it sounds mad—a door opens in its side, and a stairway comes down, and—and people come out."

"Out the door?"

"Aye."

"Are they frightened?"

"No. Not at all. They laugh. They talk with one another idly, as if they were all doing something natural."

"That's a queer vision."

"What does it mean, Father?"

"I've no idea."

"Is it from God?"

"Who can say?"

She sputtered at me. "You're supposed to know these things! What use is it to have a god-man if he can't tell you about the mysteries?"

I don't know how I'd have answered if the sound of hoofbeats hadn't startled us. The sound came from the south and approached along the beach, and as it came we heard that death-screaming we both knew, and blue light began to cast shadows at our feet. I seized Freydis, clutched her to me and rolled into the weeds.

The Ghost of the God-Tree

The great, gray headless horse galloped in view and crowded the sea out of sight, and we pasted our hands over our ears lest they burst with its screams. And when it was gone, and the screaming ended, we took our hands away and heard Arnor in the distance, crying, "'Tis the horse! The horse!"

The next day I watched as Astrid went out hawking with two of her ladies and two of Erling's men to watch them. She was a fierce huntswoman and a headlong rider. She rode a taller horse than any of the others, and they were going hard to keep up, but falling back nonetheless as they headed south on the paths between the fields.

I heard the two boys' voices then, Thorir's and Sigurd's, raised in excitement. I hoped they weren't getting into new trouble that would spoil their peace with Erling, so I went to see. I found them on the back side of the brewing house, on their knees and playing at dice.

"You're young to be learning the vice of gaming," I said to them.

Sigurd looked up at me, dice in hand. "Vice?" he cried. "Gaming a vice? Aren't you the one who tells us every week in church that God wants us to take risks?"

"Risks, yes," I said. "Laying down your life. Doing right when it costs you. Making the choices that set your soul bare to the world's cruelty for the Beloved's sake. But this—this is none of God's risks. This is just a way to fool yourself into thinking you can live without working; make your hoard and never take a risk again. I'd have you learn better lessons while you're here."

"Be easy, Father, we're not playing for silver," said Thorir. "We're playing for the girls."

"The girls?"

"Thorliv and Sigrid. We've decided to ally ourselves to Erling by marriage, but we both like Sigrid better. So we're playing for her."

"She's not a horse. And what's wrong with Thorliv? She's a sweet girl, and there's not a hair to choose between them for beauty."

"Nothing against Thorliv," said Sigurd. "But Sigrid has more fire. She'll make a true Viking's wife. Anyway, Thorliv is mad for that horse boy."

"And what about me?" came a voice, and we looked up to see Freydis, who'd been lurking behind the house corner. "Am I not fit to be a Viking's wife?"

"You're a passable enough girl, but you're lowborn," said Thorir. "And anyway, anyone can have you."

I had to grab her as she ran by, lest she tear their eyes out with her fingernails. She screamed and Lemming soon appeared, all teeth and fists, and the two boys started like quail.

It was quite a show while it lasted. The boys were quick and agile enough not to be caught, but they couldn't avoid a few boxed ears and boots where it would do the most good. They covered all of the yard and most of the meadow before Lemming finally cooled and was content to spit at them and walk away. The boys laughed watching him go, but their freckled faces were white.

"Boys and girls, girls and boys. The dance goes on forever," said Ragna, who'd walked up beside me.

"Sad times these are," said I, smiling. "Young people have no sense of what's proper. I'm sure it was far different in your day."

Ragna turned and looked at me from crystal-blue eyes. "Are you making game of me?" she asked.

I dropped my smile. "No indeed," I said. "Or only in a friendly way."

"But you've heard about Thorolf and Lodin?"

"Lodin? Who's Lodin?"

She smiled a thin smile. "You've never heard the story of Thorolf and Lodin. People here are more close-mouthed than I'd thought. Or is it possible everyone's forgotten?"

The Ghost of the God-Tree

"Steinulf told me about your father, and how Thorolf courted you."

"This came later. Steinulf may be the cause of the silence—he used to flatten the nose of anybody who brought the story up. We'd best walk, and I'll tell you it. Better from me than another, and you're bound to hear it in time. Haven't you even heard this from the thralls? About Ragnvald and the uprising?"

"Someone mentioned an uprising, I think. But it seemed a sore subject and I didn't push it on."

We took the path to the sea. The day was cloudy, but dry so far. The sea roiled gray in the distance, like molten lead.

"I loved Thorolf, and I miss him like youth itself," she said as we went. "But he was not the blameless husband. He had an eye for the women, and took many lemans."

"A common enough thing."

"But he broke the Commandment. We didn't know it was a commandment in those days, but we knew it was wrong even so. He coveted his neighbor's wife."

I mumbled something.

"To make all worse," she continued, "the neighbor I speak of was his oldest friend—a man named Lodin, a freedman's son who'd grown up with him here at Sola. They'd been like brothers all their lives.

"Lodin took a wife. Thorolf had given him a gold ring as a gift—he was always generous, was Thorolf—and with it Lodin bought himself a thrall wife. She was a prize. She was Jaeder-born, but her mother had been captured in Greekland. She had black eyes, and hair like a raven's wing, and skin the color of mead. She was tall and lovely as an underground-woman. Truth to tell, Lodin was a fool to think he could hold onto such as she.

"From the moment Thorolf saw her, he lost his senses. He paid less and less attention to his lands, to his duties as hersir . . . to me. He sat in the hall, or walked in circles in the snow, and I knew he was wrestling himself. The baser man won."

"That must have hurt you much."

"Yes, and as much to see what was becoming of him as for the insult. I tried to touch him, but he was like a man snatched into the mountain.

"At last he hosted a Jul feast here at Sola, and invited Lodin with many others. And in the course of things he challenged Lodin to a wrestling match. It was no contest. Lodin was never a fighting man. As they wrestled, Thorolf snapped Lodin's back."

"Dear saints."

"After a seemly time he took the girl for his own. As Lodin had been a freed man of the family's, all his property fell to Thorolf. Everyone knew what he'd done. Gyda—that was the girl's name—knew what he'd done. And she hated him with all the fire of her southland blood.

"Thorolf made it worse. Gyda had a child, Lodin's son. Thorolf made him a thrall. But the boy was much with his mother, and he learned from her for what purpose he'd been born.

"It happened at another Jul feast, exactly fifteen years after Lodin's death. The boy—he was called Ragnvald—had gathered his thrall kinsmen, and other thralls from Sola and many farms hereabout. They fired the hall."

"A nightmare."

"It was. Some died in the hall, smothered with smoke, but Thorolf made a breach in the wall and brought many of us out. He and his bodyguard came forth armed and angry. The thralls were no warriors. Thorolf and his men slaughtered them like rabbits, except for young Ragnvald, whom they captured alive. You can fancy what happened to him."

"I fear I can. And what of Gyda?"

"When she saw Thorolf alive and her son taken,

she walked into the burning hall of her own will, and came out no more."

"I've heard them say, 'As wrathful as Gyda.' I see now what that meant."

"'Twas because of all this that we kept thralls out of arms in Jaeder so long. When it was done, and the rebellion crushed, Thorolf regained his senses. He never took another leman. But he bore a burn scar on his face to his grave. And sometimes, when he slept, I heard him say her name."

"Erling saw all this?"

"Yes. He was but a little older than young Ragnvald."

"And he still bethought himself to be a good master to his thralls."

"I think he felt for Ragnvald more than ever he let on. They had never been friends, but I doubt not Erling pitied him."

There are sides to life at Sola I've spoken little about. One of them is how people slept. You know that the bullyboys for the most part lay on straw on the hall benches, each in his bedroll, ready to spring to Erling's defense in a moment (though that's less fine a gesture when you remember they mostly lay down dead drunk). It was the same sort of arrangement you find in Ireland or England or anywhere else. And, as in better places, you couldn't really expect them to lie alone.

This was one reason I'd slept in my own house, cold as that could be, from my first night in Norway. You can't wink at fornication, yet I'd never found a formula for telling strong men not vowed to chastity that they must wait for marriage. Especially since bodyguard men marry late or not at all. Either they die young, or they wait until they've begun to dull, like axes too often sharpened. And sometimes they never wed at all—they choose the warrior's pension, which is death in battle, when strength and speed have gone.

One of the necessaries provided the bullyboys, just like food and drink and clothing and new weapons, was thrall women for the night. They expected it, as did the women. A woman who pleased a man might get gifts, which served as well as any other wealth to help buy freedom.

There were rules though, understood by all. I'd have insisted on them myself except that I'd found them in place when I came. No woman ought to be forced against her will, and married women were off limits (at least before men's eyes).

And of course it all went on before men's eyes—another reason for me to stay well away. They all shared a bedroom (though thank God for darkness), and Norsemen are not shy about making noise at their sport.

A priest is a meddler by nature, though. There were certain thrall women I kept a watch over, for this coupling without promises is a dangerous game and thralls make away with themselves too readily.

Dierdre, Patrick's widow, was one I watched. She shouldered away all offers for some time, and of course her child helped. Most men judge a squalling suckling a poor addition to night games.

But one day I came into the hall for breakfast and saw her rolling up Eystein's bedroll for him, the babe lying to one side.

I thought I'd just have a word with Eystein about that.

CHAPTER X

Erling sailed to Scotland to raid that summer. He told me he'd pass by Ireland thereafter, out of respect for me.

"I care not if you raid in Ireland," I said, "as long as you let Connaught alone. As a matter of fact, I can give you a list of places I'd be pleased for you to harry."

"The word is, it's a good year for Scotland."

"As you wish. Will you take thralls?"

"I've little stomach for slave-taking anymore. I'll snatch some hostages to ransom, no more than that. I can buy thralls in the markets."

It always made me nervous to see Erling call up a levy and sail off with his ships full of fighting men. I remembered too well how enemies had taken advantage of his absence before. And with Eyvind Kellda alive and about somewhere, I found reason to spend much time on my knees.

But no harm came that summer. It was no small thing to challenge Erling Skjalgsson, even with his back turned, and his name alone was worth a hundred armed men.

Things were dull with so many gone. The bored skeleton force that stayed behind under Eystein mostly talked, of an evening, about the fun and plunder they were missing. I took to going for walks after supper, and the walks started ever earlier as time went on.

One evening I was just coming out into the watery midsummer glow when I heard a voice in song. I followed it and it led me to the god-tree's place. There I found Freydis Sotisdatter. She sang:

"Your weakness makes me stronger.
Your hunger is my food.
I stand because you've fallen;
My life is in your blood.

You love because I hate you.
You give that I may take.
Your birth-day came to serve me;
Your death is for my sake."

In the twilight I could clearly see what she was about. She had her dolls there—Arnor, Thorir and Sigurd, Thorliv, Sigrid and herself. She'd taken three of them into her hands, and was binding them together—two male dolls bracing a female one.

"What are you doing, child?" I asked.

"I'm binding Arnor and Thorir to myself," she said.

"What are you binding them with?"

"The guts of a cat."

"You killed a cat?"

"One of the thralls drowned some kittens."

"Why do you do this?"

"So that Arnor and Thorir will fall in love with me."

"Do you mean to marry them both?"

"I mean to spurn them both."

I sat down on Big Melhaug beside her. "Daughter, daughter. Setting to one side the sin of sorcery, why would you wish to hurt people? As much as this spell-binding troubles me, it troubles me more that you'd rather cause pain to others than joy to yourself."

"There is no joy for me."

"Not so! Or rather it's only true if you choose it."

"I've no choice. I've never had a choice. I had a purpose once. I was the gods' gift. But you took my purpose away."

"I saved you from abuse and perdition. Your life after that is what you let God make it."

"To have a choice I would have to have power. The only powers left to me are the power of the old magic in my blood—my birthright from my mother—and the power of the thing between my legs."

I took her by the shoulders. "Is that all you think you are? Is that all your uncle's love means to you? Is that all you've learned in church? You were made by God! You're not an ill wind, and you're not a breeding cow! Why must you act as if you are?"

Her pale eyes staring back at me seemed empty as a cat's. "My mother and Soti taught me what I was long before you and Lemming took them from me. I let you christen me, and I let you tell me your tales. But I don't believe them. Perhaps someday I'll find a new purpose. Until then I will amuse myself."

'Twas like arguing with a stone wall, or an Englishman. I let her go and walked away from her backwards, crossing myself with my right hand and crossing my fingers against the Evil Eye with the other.

I turned about when I was out of sight of her, and felt dizzy. The whole sky seemed to shrink to the size of a calfskin above me, and once again it seemed to curl and crack like a piece of parchment grown old. I sank to my knees in the heather. The whole creation, I thought, was wearing away before my eyes. 'Twas then I felt a hand on my shoulder and looked up to see the dark Wanderer from Eastland. Had I not been so soul-sick I'd have wondered where he'd come from.

"Did you ever hear the tale of the thirteenth apostle?" he asked me, sitting on a mound.

"Who? Matthias?"

"No, Matthias was the one who took Judas' seat after the Resurrection. This was Thaddeus."

"But Thaddeus was the same as Jude the Less. I think."

"No, that's a mistake. They weren't the same man. The fact is, the reason the lists of apostles in the gospels differ a bit is that the group wasn't iron-bound. Some came, some went; some grew and stayed on while others lost their nerve and ran away. Thaddeus was a stayer—he did not give up easily, but he kept to the edge. He had trouble opening his heart to the others. He saved some part of himself . . . apart.

"When his Lord was crucified, Thaddeus did no better and no worse than the others. He ran. He found a place to hide. He stayed there, not sure whether the Romans or the temple police might not be after him next.

"By late on the second day, most of the men had gathered in a friend's house. Thaddeus was not one of them. No one knew where to find him. So the next morning, when the women came with the news of the Resurrection, he wasn't there. He didn't hear the tale of how Peter and John ran to the tomb and found it empty. He didn't hear the story of the two disciples on the way to Emmaus, who met the Beloved on the road.

"It wasn't until a couple days later that Bartholemew found him and told him, 'We've seen the Lord! He's risen from the dead, just as He said!'

"What do you think Thaddeus said?"

"I don't know."

"He said, 'That's very nice for you, Bart. I'm sure

you sincerely think that what you say is true. But let's look at it realistically. We've all had a big disappointment. We wanted badly to believe that the Lord would come back. So you've worked yourselves into a state where you actually believe that He has. I'm happy for you, but it doesn't work for me.'

"Bartholemew said, 'No, it's true! We saw Him! We touched Him! He ate a piece of fish in our sight.'

"Thaddeus shook his head. 'It won't do, you know,' he said. 'People are too shrewd to believe a story like this. Even if it were true, it wouldn't really matter. It would be just a thing about this world—this low and miserable world.

"'I've thought much about our Lord's teachings, and I have seen the true meaning at last. This world is nothing. Anything that happens here, even a resurrection, means nothing. Our Lord was too good for this world, so He died. He's in a better place now, and He wants us to understand that the true meaning of His promise of resurrection is that His moral teaching lives on. We must do good in this world, and not look for any other world.'

"Bartholemew went away in sorrow. Thaddeus closed the door and turned back inside. To his amazement, he saw the Lord standing there before him.

"'Do you think I am only a seeming?' the Lord asked.

"'Yes,' said Thaddeus.

"'What if I were to touch you?'

"''Twould prove nothing.'

"'There's naught I can do that would make you believe?'

"'There is naught,' said Thaddeus, 'that would persuade me to set myself in a place to be betrayed again as You betrayed me. I will believe the truths You spoke, and forget about Your false promises.'

"So the Lord left him alone, and Thaddeus went on to begin his own church, where he taught a very spiritual doctrine. He told everyone that his church was bound to outlive the other apostles' church, because his was founded on hard-headed facts, not wild stories. But in truth it never went anywhere. When the persecutions came, all his followers renounced the Name, and Thaddeus ended up selling fish in Joppa."

Another matter I've spoken little about is bathing. The Norse are cousins to the English, but are like the Irish in at least one respect—they prize a clean body.

They get clean, however, in a peculiar, barbaric fashion. There is on each farm a house, small or large after the size of the household, with a stone oven in it. Unlike their other houses, this one has no gable-peak holes for ventilation. On Saturday nights (their word for Saturday is "washing day") they fire up that stove with birch wood until the stones shimmer like water and the house fills with smoke, and they go inside and throw water on the stones, making the place a steaming, choking, blinding, flesh-searing purgatory. Then they sit naked on two or three levels of benches around the walls and tell each other dirty stories.

In time someone with enough reputation not to fear being called a coward suggests that they all go out and cool off. Such houses are built near rivers or ponds, so everyone goes out of the hot house and jumps straightway into the cold water (in winter they just roll in the snow).

Then they all go back inside and repeat the liturgy again and again, until either the next group demands its turn or the Chief Rooster decides they've had enough. Even so, men of honor take pains to be the last to leave.

Then they chase each other around naked for a while, flogging one another with scrub branches.

I'm not making this up.

Such rituals are a sort of test of manhood. The time you take before suggesting a cool dip (if you're Chief Rooster), and the level of bench you sit on, are matters of status. So is your willingness to throw water on the stones and send up yet another smothering cloud of steam.

The first time I took such a bath (in Visby, if you recall), I went through the standard newcomer's initiation. The men in the house with me (Eystein was one of them, as a matter of fact) told me seriously that there were two ways to control the heat of the steam. "Hot water on the stones makes the house hotter," they said, "and cold water makes it cooler."

Think about it for a while. They had a good laugh at me over that.

Of all the bullyboys, no man had higher bathhouse honors than Eystein. He sat on the upper bench always, and called for more steam whenever anyone was in danger of getting his sight back. I did not ordinarily bathe with Eystein.

But I'd been meaning to talk to him, and I wanted to do it alone. I realized with dismay that, busy as he was with many things, the only time I was likely to catch him by himself was at the end of a bath.

I've run into Irish priests, now and again, who've told me that my years in Norway, under English bishops, has made me lax in my penances and fasts.

Such men have never sat in a Norse bathhouse with Eystein.

There were some surprised looks when I joined Eystein's bath party that particular Saturday evening.

"Trying to impress your heathen woman with your manhood?" someone asked me, laughing.

I made no reply. I couldn't have if I'd tried. I was climbing, on sheer will power, up to Eystein's bench. I suppose I must have breathed, because I did not die, but I don't remember doing it. I sat, leaning my back against the sooty wall, and tried to be very still.

The party went on. The air burned my nostrils with every breath. The men laughed and made new steam.

We went outside and cooled down. It's hard to imagine a state where a leap into a frigid pond is pleasant, but I swear it feels like silk sheets after the steam.

We went back in. We boiled ourselves.

We went back out.

It was the longest evening in the history of the world. The hours Joshua took when he made the sun stand still were repaid then, with usury.

At last Eystein said, rather quietly, "I think this is probably enough for tonight, lads."

We could have recited the 119th Psalm, I think, in the time it took before somebody on the lowest bench said, "I suppose so. I've got a woman waiting for me," and headed for the door. One by one, with all the breakneck speed of cold pitch, the rest followed him out.

At length—at long, long length—only Eystein and I remained. It would have been sooner, but some other fellows coveted the honor of staying as long as Eystein, and I had to wait them out. Why I wasn't carried out I'll never know.

But I realized at last that it was only he and I in the house. I opened my mouth to speak, but could only cough for some time.

"What's on your mind, Father?" Eystein asked.

I pretended not to know what he meant.

"You wouldn't be here still if there wasn't something on your mind. You've done very well, you know. The house was specially warm tonight. I think you'll find the men respect you more tomorrow."

"'Tis Deirdre," I said.

"And what of her?"

"She's been through a hard patch. She tried to

make away with herself once. I can't tell you to stay clear of her, but for God's sake, don't break her heart. She's like a bird's egg since she lost Patrick."

"And you think I mean to break her heart?"

"Sometimes you men forget that thralls are full as human as you, and your even Christians to boot."

"You don't know me well, do you, Father?"

"We've never been boon companions, I suppose."

"Do you know my mother had thrall blood?"

"Do you say so?"

"Aye. Her mother was a Cornishwoman, taken by Erling's grandfather. I knew her when I was young. I get my dark hair from her. She sang like a bird."

"Then I take it you've no plan to wed Deirdre. You'd not want more thrall blood in the family."

"That's what I would have said a few weeks since. But there's a thing that can alter such reasonings."

"And what's that?"

"Falling in love with the woman."

Just when you think you've seen everything under the sun, I thought to myself.

CHAPTER XI

Erling came back from Scotland with few men lost and good profit. I almost wished I'd gone along. Thorir the hostage bore a new scar on his arm, of which he was exceeding proud.

But in the midst of the feasting, while the ale flowed and the skalds sang, I felt something like a wet turf laid over the fire of my soul. I saw before my eyes (somewhat fuzzy with drink, I'll grant you) the faces of farmers whose living was gone and winter yet to endure; and their wives and their children. I saw houses burned and horses run off. Perhaps the farmers were little souls, with little dreams—men whose deeds would never be sung in a hall. But the dreams were their own, and as precious to them as mine to me. And their hunger would pinch no less than anyone's, Norse or Irish.

The dimness of the hall seemed of a sudden gloomy to me; the smoke thick and stinging in my eye-corners. I went out again to seek comfort in the fresh air and the twilight.

My wavering steps took me at last on the path to Big Melhaug, and there I came on Asa, kneeling before her god-tree. The chickens hanging in space did not stir in the still air. She sang a song to Thor, holding a horn of ale over her head. When the song was done, she poured the ale out where the tree roots should be.

She stood and turned then, and saw me watching her.

"Perhaps you should convert to my faith," she said. "We could pray together, and there'd be nothing to keep us from wedding."

"Do you really think you're keeping the sky up with these things?" I asked.

"If the gods can keep my offerings hanging in the air, they can surely keep the sky up too. And I have my own sky, you know—inside my heart. If the offerings but keep that one from falling, 'tis enough."

"The Lord Christ could do that for you as well. Better."

"Thor gave me this tree, and he showed me his face. Gifts from a lord are not to be despised."

We said nothing for a few breaths.

"Thormod Hrolfsson has asked me to be his wife," she said at last. Thormod was one of the bodyguard.

My throat felt tight. Apparently matrimony was going around like the croup. "That's a good man. And you're too young and fair to be alone."

"But he's a Christian, too. I'm not sure I care enough for him to be baptized for his sake. If I'm to take the Christ-bath, it must be for someone I care for deeply."

I turned my back on her, shuddering, then came around again. "The best thing of all is to be baptized for Christ's sake, His alone."

"And how often does that happen?"

I hugged my stomach and sank to my knees, too shaken to stand. All the folly of this work in the North seemed to drop upon my shoulders like a brynje of leaden links. What were we doing, baptizing people out of fear, or the promise of gifts, or the king's friendship? What had any of it to do with the things I knew, deepest in my soul, to be true?

Asa came and knelt by me, putting her arms around my shoulders and leaning her head against mine.

"Please don't," I said. "I haven't the strength to fight you, but I beg you."

"I won't lead you to bed," she whispered. "You'd only hate me for it tomorrow."

"Why do you cling so tightly to the old ways?" I asked. "You know they'll never come back. Thor is passing, whatever gifts he's given you."

"Gifts from a lord are chains of loyalty. So are gifts to a lord."

"I don't follow."

"I had a child once. In her first year the lot fell on her, and she was given to Thor at the Summer Sacrifice."

"Sweet Mother of God . . . 'Tis plain then. If you were baptized—'twould make your child's death meaningless, wouldn't it?"

"She was a sweet babe. She had her father's eyes."

Asa went to her house, and I stood and looked about me. I needed sleep, but was too troubled to seek my bed. I looked westward, toward the sea, and clouds were roiling there, blocking the stars and glowing now and then with lightning like a flame in an eggshell.

I wanted to meet this storm. I wanted to stand in Thor's path and say, "Thus far shalt thou come, and no farther!" I set out on the path to the bay.

As I came to the stone-walled lane, I met a hulking shape. I thought for one muddled moment it was indeed Thor. But 'twas only Ulf, gentle Ulf who'd been party to the greatest outrage ever done to me.

I tried to ignore him, as usual, but he put himself in my way and blocked me. He held something out in his hand. I thought it at first some kind of knife.

"For you," he said.

What he offered stopped my breath. It was a wooden crucifix, as like to the one over the altar in the church as one shamrock to another, only smaller. It was excellently done, and strung with a leather thong. I stared at it. I'd never guessed he had such skill.

"Take," he said.

I wanted nothing in the world from Ulf, but somehow I could not refuse this thing. It put me so in mind of poor Enda, and I'd missed his crucifix so much....

I took it from his hand. Even in the darkness I could see the ugly man's wide grin.

"Jesus water?" he asked for the umpteenth time.

"Perhaps," I said distractedly, and went on my way to the sea, cross in hand. Almost without knowing what I did, I hung it around my neck.

And as I came to the storm, the storm came to me, welcoming as a kinsman. The surf threw down and spat, and the wind braced a big hand against my chest, and my hair drove straight back from my head and stiffened there with salt. Soon I was wet to the skin and shivering. It felt grateful to my soul.

I stood on the dune above the sand and shouted, "What am I doing here, O God? Your enemies offer me gifts—is it treason to take them? What is the greater sin? To serve You with the devil's tools, fire and iron, or to receive simple kindness from Your foes? You who feasted with publicans and sinners, tell me what it means to do Your work!"

I was answered with a vision.

The storm let its guard down for the time it takes to sigh, and the moon peeked through the clouds. Out of the wind and water that blew in my eyes, the face of a dragon appeared. It broke from the weather a couple of spear-casts offshore so suddenly that it stopped my breath and froze my blood.

Then I heard the screaming and knew it for naught but a ship with a dragon's head, a knarr in fact, running before the wind and set to smash itself on the reef. There came a screeching and crunching as the keel plowed into the rock and the ship came to a sickening check, springing and snapping its strakes and sending the naked mast toppling forward.

I rushed out into the surf, struggling to keep my feet and getting buffeted under twice by waves that fell on my head. With cries the people on shipboard began throwing themselves overboard, carrying oars and sea chests and clinging to anything that might bear them up. I waded to each as they drifted in and helped lift them or push them shoreward.

At last every living person had abandoned ship but one. A woman slogged to me, put her hands on my arm and shouted over the blast, "My husband! He's the ship's master and he won't come off!"

"What's his name?" I cried.

"Thorgrim!"

I called, "Thorgrim! Thorgrim Skipper! Speak to me! I am a priest!"

His sodden head appeared above the rail. The ship had listed and lay heaving on her port beam. "Go away!" he called. "I die with my ship!"

"You must live!" I cried. "You've a wife who needs you!"

"This ship is my living! I can no longer feed a family. She's better off widowed!"

" 'Tis sin to speak thus! There is hope if you believe in God!"

"I don't believe in your god, priest! I've seen my own fetch—I know it's my time. I sleep in Aegir's hall tonight!"

Then the ship shuddered and went to pieces, and the man appeared no more, until his body washed up the day after.

I waded shoreward and got overborne from behind

by another great wave, so that the surviving castaways themselves had to drag me out of the surf and up the dune and lay me down in the stiff grass. When I came to myself a tall shadow loomed over me, bent and dripping and peering down in my face.

"Brother Aillil? Is that you? Then praise God, this must be Sola!"

'Twas Thangbrand the priest, back from his mission to Iceland.

We managed to drag ourselves up the path to the farm. Erling, Astrid and Ragna rallied the thralls, and soon everyone was warmly wrapped and drinking ale before a roaring fire in the old hall. Shortly there was hot broth for all.

Everyone wanted to talk—to tell or to learn all that had happened, but weariness overcame us and they put us to bed on the benches. I didn't even bother to crawl to my own house.

We woke to the bustle of the thralls making ready for breakfast. I could have slept longer—much longer—but the tables needed setting up where we lay. We dragged ourselves out, scratched, and did our morning things. I noticed with surprise that Thangbrand, who'd lain by me the night before, was already up and gone, his wheat-colored head nowhere to be seen.

I went to the church to say morning mass, but found the service already begun. Thangbrand, without a by-your-leave, had clothed himself in my vestments and was singing the service (in fine voice, I must admit) to a small gathering which included Erling and his family, Steinulf and the two hostage boys.

When all was done I followed him to my house, where he removed the vestments to reveal a green shirt Erling had lent him, and packed them neatly in my chest.

Before I could reproach him, he reproached me.

"Brother Aillil," he said, in a tone much like my old abbot's, "I must ask you to explain your ways in this parish."

"I explain?" I sputtered. "I explain? How do you explain—"

"I've learned there is a heathen man here who has requested baptism, and you have refused it."

I drew up my dignity. "Brother Thangbrand, I am priest at Sola. I know more about matters here than you do."

"The more shame to you then, to let a sheep run loose."

"This man is no sheep, but a wolf."

"If he repents of his sins—"

"He does not repent of his sins. He has forgotten his sins. He took a knock on the head and became an idiot. I happen to know about this man's sins, and I know he cannot confess them, because he's lost the knowledge."

"Be that as may be. Such matters are for God to decide. Your duty is to give him instruction, such as he can receive, take his confession, such as he can recall, and christen him."

I took a half-step forward and put my face near his chin (he was a big fellow). "It's not for you to tell me how to care for my parish. You are a brother priest, no more!"

"There are priests and priests, Irishman. I am a man of high birth and learning, close to the bishop and the king. You are a peasant with an irregular ordination."

"You are a bladder of gas who was exiled to the end of the world because you'd made Norway too hot for you!"

"I did God's work in Iceland! The only reason I came early back is that those pestilential Icelanders are cursed, and outlawed me!"

"Highborn or low, at least I don't get booted out of every mission I take up!"

"That's because you stand for nothing! I've heard what you've done here! You have heathens right under your nose, allowed to carry on their devilry, and you do naught to hinder them!"

"I do not do naught! I strive to convert them by Christian means!"

"In the last year of the world, when the powers of Satan and God poise for Armageddon, you dawdle along with extra miles and cheek-turning! You must change your ways, and now, or I will report all to the bishop! You can explain to his face the un-Christianity of his ways!"

"Yes, you'd like that, wouldn't you? Cover over your own failure by smearing tar on me!"

"I'm not a failure! I'm next thing to a martyr!"

"You're next thing to a horse's tail!"

"Enough of you, I'm going to see Erling!"

He stalked out and I followed him into the old hall where everyone was having breakfast.

"When are you people here going to begin carrying out the king's will?" Thangbrand demanded of Erling.

Erling put down his knife and said, "Good morning to you too, Father."

"Don't trifle with me, Rogalander. The king has decreed that the people shall be baptized by all necessary means, including the reverent use of force!"

"I think my way is working just as well," said Erling.

"You speak like a peasant—like your priest! I am a man of high blood from Saxony. Do you know how Charlemagne christened Saxony?"

"Oh, aye. Everyone knows that. He fought them, he captured them, he baptized them, and then he slaughtered them by the thousands. Sometimes I am hard put to tell him apart from Christ."

"It worked! Saxony is Christian today! The end is all that matters!"

"God help us if the Church ever comes to believe a thing like that!"

Thangbrand folded his arms. "I will not eat at your board," he said. "I demand immediate passage to Nidaros!"

"Consider it done. Eystein, arrange it."

Thangbrand and Erling went together, in fact, because the king was getting married (again), and Erling and Astrid had to be there. I would have liked to go, but I couldn't stomach spending more time with that ass Thangbrand.

But before he left, Thangbrand baptized Ulf. The half-wit wore his white baptismal gown for weeks, until it grew filthy and Asa took it away.

CHAPTER XII

It looked to be a cold winter, according to those who read such things from their joints or the coats on the beasts. We came to the end of September—or the middle of Harvest-month as the Norse style it—and approached St. Michael's Day.

St. Michael's Day was one I neared with mixed feelings. As the feast day of the chief archangel it suited me fine, but it also marked the day for the Winter Sacrifice among the heathen. I knew they'd be gathering in houses and secret places to feast and shed blood and make their vows. My conscience told me I ought to do something to stop it, but then my conscience also told me to love my enemies—so I told my conscience to go away and come back when it knew what it wanted.

I was polishing the silver candlesticks in the church that afternoon when the light dimmed and I turned to see Lemming in the doorway, blocking it as well as any door. He didn't look much awed by the house of God, but he didn't step over the threshold either. I often wondered what the man believed in. I guessed he was one of those plain men who believe in their own strength and some kind of fate.

He just stood and looked at me. I knew I'd never get him to open the dance, so I went to him and asked, "What's on your mind, my son?"

He jerked his head to bid me come out, and I wrapped my cloak about me and did so. It wasn't bitter cold, but we could see our breath.

Lemming's face strained as he labored to squeeze words out. "Freydis will sacrifice," he said at last, and breathed heavily as if he'd given birth.

"She's not sacrificing herself, surely?" I asked. It might be a real danger with that strange child.

He shook his head. "Tonight," he said. "Asa's house."

"Does it matter to you?" I asked, looking him in the eye. "Do you really care what god she worships?"

He returned my gaze, unreadable as a wolf. Then he turned and walked away.

I stood and thought a moment, and decided that even my fuddled conscience had to agree that it was within my authority to tell a child of my christening not to sacrifice to Thor. So I went to seek Freydis.

I had a time finding her. No one had seen her for some time. I went from one building to another without luck. I'd have worried for her safety had I not known better.

At last I saw her, walking hand-in-hand with Thorir, whose feelings toward her seemed to have changed markedly. They were both flushed, and they had straw in their hair and clothes.

"Freydis, may I speak with you?" I asked. At the same time I gave Thorir a look that wilted him a little. He said he had to find his brother and eased off.

"I sacrifice tonight," she told me. "There's no use trying to talk me out of it."

"You're not an innocent pagan, child. You've been instructed in the Faith. Apostasy is a weighty sin."

"Do you think I do it lightly?"

"I worry for you. Your welfare matters to me."

"Thank you, I'm sure. But tonight will be a great night. The mer-wife is coming."

"The woman in the stories? The witch from the sea with the cow?"

"She comes this night, if she comes at all. The farmers put out sheaves of hay to keep her beast from eating up all their stores. She cannot come if the wind's wrong, but it will be right tonight. I feel it. Great things will happen."

"I fear for your soul, child."

"I'm like the undergrounders, Father. I have no soul. When I die I go to dust, like the beasts."

"Who told you these things?"

"My mother, of course. She speaks to me in the nights."

"You speak to the dead?"

"I do many things that would shock you, Father. I do not say you are wrong. I do not say your Christ is not a god. Perhaps he is, as you say, the Great God. But he is not for me, any more than for the goats or the horses."

" 'Tis a lie, child. And whatever spirit speaks to you is not your mother. 'Tis a devil out of the pit, sent to deceive you."

"What of it? All the world is but a seeming. How can you say truth is other than lies, when all's a lie in the end?"

I stood dumb a moment. "I know your demon's name," I said at last.

" 'Tis my mother. If I want it to be my mother, then that's what it is."

"No. Its name is Eyvind Kellda."

She laughed and walked away, and I went to the church to pray, and stayed there.

Evening was sliding in when I was roused by shouts outside. I went out and walked toward the steading.

There I found a cluster of people ringing a pair of young men fighting. This was no boys' fistfight—they both had knives and they were after blood. One was Thorir the hostage; the other was Arnor the horse boy. Arnor had blood on his left arm.

"What's on here?" I demanded.

Thorliv came and put her hand on my arm. "Stop them, Father! Freydis has bewitched them! She's got them fighting over her!"

"Stop this, boys!" I cried, stepping between them. I nearly got a blade in the ribs for my pains. They weren't in a listening humor.

I stepped back quickly, then sprinted to the smithy, where I found Lemming.

"Your confounded niece has set Arnor and Thorir on one another with knives!" I said. "Help me stop them, or she'll be the cause of a killing!"

Wordless he put down his hammer, threw off his apron and came out to me. We went together to the fight, and between us got them parted and disarmed.

Stymied in their cutting, the boys thrashed in our hold and screamed at one another.

"Peasant!"

"Sod!"

"Horse molester!"

"Mother—"

"Enough!" I shouted. "What's the meaning of this? Arnor—I thought you loved Thorliv! Thorir—I thought you wanted Sigrid!"

"Thorliv's a milksop," said Arnor.

"Sigrid's mad," said Thorir.

"Freydis is a real woman," Arnor went on. "She's destined for me, and this honey-nosed northerner thinks he can buy her away with trinkets!"

"No, Freydis is destined for me!" said Thorir. "This lowborn groom thinks he's fit to put his smelly hands on her fair body!"

"I've put my hands on her body, and more!" shouted Arnor.

"You lie! She's lain only with me!"

I saw Lemming's face go black-red, and it crossed my mind that he could snap both their backs with his bare hands.

So there might have yet been murder, had we not been distracted. We heard the voice of Freydis Sotisdatter, high and sweet, singing a song I'd heard somewhere before, and turned to see her approach from Asa's house, robed in a fur-trimmed black dress I'd seen her mother wear on the same terrible night I'd first heard the song.

"Musk for sporting;
Steel for killing;
Gold for stealing;
Ale to forget.

Lies for friendship;
Oaths for treason;
Blows for the weak and
Truth for the dead."

"She comes! She comes!" cried Freydis. "The woman from the sea—the mother of all life! She comes to feed her cow, and all cattle not under roof will follow them home! I am kin to the mer-wife, and kin to her cow, and therefore I have loosed all the cattle!"

And as she spoke the mooing and bawling began. All around us the cattle and horses milled, mad and round-eyed, running with crashings into and through all things and anything. Then everyone was out of the houses trying to control them, and it was hard work, for it took several strong men to hold a cow, and the bull could not be held at all, even with Lemming's help. One by one we wrestled cows, twisted ropes around their horns to lead them, and dragged them into the byres where they grew quiet. But a dozen or so managed to jump the fences and lope toward the sea.

Some of us tried to follow those cattle. We caught one, but the others went into the waves like lemmings. And there among them I caught sight of a naked woman, green of skin and with hair like seaweed, whose great round eyes glowed yellow. She must have stood nine feet tall, and her giant cow, also green and yellow-eyed, stood beside her. I could clearly see the gills in its neck opening and closing, like those of a beached shark.

I should have exorcised her then and there, but I was forestalled again. The familiar screaming rose in the south, and soon the great gray headless horse was galloping among us.

And I caught one glimpse of Arnor, who shouted and sang as he caught the thing by its mane and swung himself up onto its back. He was on it as it galloped away, and if he was seen again in the world of men, I've not heard of it.

We were a sore and weary lot who gathered in the old hall that night. Thorliv and Asa wept over Arnor. Sigrid turned her back on Thorir and refused to speak to him. Thorir sat trying to be brave about the pain of a newly set leg, which I supppose was the only thing that kept Lemming, who fumed in a dark corner with his arms crossed, from murdering him. And among them all sat Freydis, looking well-pleased with her work.

Ragna stood among us and said, "This has gone far enough. It's time we made some marriages, and put paid to these caperings. Since Freydis seems to have been generous with her gifts, and since Arnor is gone, I suppose we should try to wed her to Thorir. Do you think your foster father would agree to this, Thorir? Or would he think her too lowborn?"

"I will not marry him," Freydis put in.

"What do you say?"

"I will marry no man. Men treat women as playthings. I will treat them in the same wise. I cared nothing for Arnor, and I care nothing for Thorir. Let Sigrid have him. I'm done with him."

"I'd never wed a man who'd touched Freydis," said Sigrid, tossing her hair. "But I'll take Sigurd."

"Sigurd and Sigrid," said Freydis. "How pretty it sounds. But mark what I say—watch out for seals."

I demanded to know what that meant, but she would say no more.

CHAPTER XIII

"What do you do when you've climbed the highest mountain to fetch the magic ring, and you've reached the top, and the ring's not magic at all?" asked Olaf Trygvesson. "'Tis the highest mountain you know of, and cost much blood and weariness to climb, and you know you haven't years enough left to climb another, even if you could find it. What's left then? It's all a cheat. I've given the only lifetime I've got for a cheat. If a throne doesn't feed my soul, what else is there?"

This was a different Olaf from the jolly Viking I'd first seen sailing in the Boknafjord. He wasn't an old man, but he seemed old. He'd put on weight in the wrong places, and sometimes in the mornings or when he was drunk and tired, you could tell the old whip scars from his slave days were giving him pain, and he'd walk a little bent.

I was an unwilling vessel for the king's confidence. We'd come to Agvaldsness again, for Christmas this time, and night came early and the drinking carried on late, and Olaf took pride in being the last to sleep however much he'd tippled. Most of the men were snoring on the benches, blankets around them or not, and he and I were among the few still up in the dim hall. Somewhere in the shadows I could hear Father Thangbrand arguing with someone, but that was a sound as constant as the sea, and as easily ignored. It wasn't my strong head that accounted for my wakefulness; I just hadn't been in the drinking mood. I was drunk, but not sociably. The whole feast had set my teeth on edge. Nobody dared be unsociable though when Olaf Tryggvesson cornered him. He was big and he stuck close, like a goiter.

"You're not the first to feel thus, my lord," I told him. "It's as the Scripture says—what shall it profit a man to gain the world and lose his soul?"

He closed one eye and peered at me with the other (red) over his ale-horn. "Are you saying, Irishman, that I've lost my soul?"

"No, no, no, no," I burbled. "No, no. No. No. Not at all. It's the . . . the principle . . . of the thing. What the Lord meant was that everything in this world—even kinging it . . . will let you down. Only the love of God gives the soul the nood it feeds. Food it needs."

"But I'm doing God's work! I'm His tool to convert the land! Isn't that as good to Him as some capon monk hoeing peas or scratching away in a scrip- scrip- . . . writing room?"

"I guess that depends on what reward you're looking for," said I.

Olaf slumped back on the bench. "You know, I've never thought about that." The hearth-fire and the hanging lamps made shifting shadows on his face.

"Well, what do you truly want?"

"What does anyone want? I want to have my way. I want to be right."

"Begging your pardon, my lord, but that's a thing for the next world. In this one you can have one or the other—not both."

"I want to be king. That's been the mark all my life. What more could there be for a man?"

"If that were the only goal, very few would have a chance of happiness. And to speak truth my lord, I've known monks who owned not a stick of furniture or a pair of shoes who were happier than you seem. There are so many good things to strive for. Mercy. Love. Justice. Continence. Truthfulness."

"Humph. They don't sound a lot of fun."

"There comes a time to grow up, my king. Manhood has its pleasures too. I'll wager when you were a small boy, you had no taste for women. But you matured, and learned a new thing to enjoy."

"Women," said Olaf. "There's another of life's cheats. First I marry Iron-beard's daughter up in Yriar, who tries to stab me on our wedding night—"

"Well, you did kill her father."

"And I call it unwomanly of her to take it so to heart! Vengeance is a son's business. Daughters should be content with the husbands their pin kick them. Kin pick them.

"And now I have my new bride, my Danish princess. What think you of Thyri, priest? Answer honestly."

"She's fair and pious."

"And ambitious. Ambitious as I was not long since. I suppose that's why we got on so, when she showed up at my door. I'd been an exile as she had; we'd both been through adventures and hair's-breadth escapes.

"And I thought, it will truly tweak King Svein Forkbeard's nose in Denmark if I marry his sister without his blessing. Remind him that I'm king here, whatever he may say about overlordship. It seemed a good plan.

"But she's mad. She harps on the lands she claims are coming to her in Wendland. I've pointed out to her a thousand times that the lands were to be her morning-gift from King Burisleif the Pole. Since she naysaid her brother and refused to marry Burisleif, she can hardly expect him to hand over the property."

"What says she to that?"

"She says Burisleif would make an excellent ally, and that I could use one in the Baltic. Which is true enough. She says if we went to Wendland and offered friendship, I could surely get her lands from him as a concession. I don't know why she's so set on Wendish land. I could get her land just as good—handier anyway—here in Norway, but no, Wendland it has to be."

"A voyage to the Baltic strikes me as a chancy act, with the world as it is."

"You're right in that. The Danes guard the doorway, the Swedes control the east, and they're both enemies of mine. And let's not forget that Burisleif's sister is married to Svein. I've heard tales of Erik Haakonsson, Jarl Haakon's whelp, too. They say he's churning the sea in Svein's service, and recruiting men for a stab at me in his father's memory. I'd be sailing into a wolf's mouth."

He chewed cud for a moment, taking a pull at his horn. "But it would be a kingly act, to take the fight to them rather than awaiting it here. . . . The worst thing about gaining a throne is that it makes you cautious. I'm getting so cautious it makes me want to wring my own neck."

His revery was disturbed by Deacon Ketil, who had approached without either of our notice. "Your Majesty, the queen awaits you," he said.

"And the queen must have her way, whatever the cost," said Olaf, moving to get up but having trouble with it. Ketil gave him his hand.

"One might do worse than heed the lady," said Ketil, helping him rise with easy strength.

"Is that your counsel?" asked Olaf. "Is that what your crowbones tell you?"

Ketil glanced at me, and he must have read my face. "I take it you think divining unfit work for a churchman," he said, without rancor. His tone did not ease me. It was as if he judged my opinion beneath his notice.

"'Tis not for me to counsel the ding's keakon. King's deacon."

"The Lord adjured us to recognize the signs of the times. That's all my bones are—they are signs of the times."

I'd have liked to sleep late (as would we all) but the bishop said mass in the morning, and anyone who missed that would be marked. It was a sort of test of manhood in those days (like a steam bath) to see how long you could last on little sleep and much ale. Still is, now I think about it.

Much tenacious feasting got done that day, and toward evening the king began to give gifts. That's one of a king's chief jobs of course—to keep the wealth flowing in ways that will bind grateful men to him. The thralls brought in chests and bundles, and one after another the great men received swords or brynjes or helmets, or gold or silver rings, or necklaces of costly stones, depending on their needs and Olaf's reckoning of their dessert.

As the distribution went on, an unease set in among us Jaederers. One name was missing among the giftees—Erling Skjalgsson. One by one the king's men received their prizes, but there was naught for Erling. Erling himself sat drinking quietly, giving nothing away by his face, but rage swelled among us as rising water presses against a dam.

"This is infamous," whispered Thorir the hostage, who was sitting across the table from me. His brother Sigurd sat by him, and next to him Sigrid Skjalgsdatter. They were newly betrothed, Erling having worked out an agreement with their foster father the day we arrived (it was a season for weddings that year. Eystein and Deirdre were betrothed as well). I knew the boys' nature, especially Thorir's, and put a finger to my lips, praying they'd heed me.

Everyone in the house felt the strain, and things were unwonted quiet below the expected words of thanks. I happened to look over where Aslak Askelsson sat, who'd been Halla's husband. He sat motionless, staring at Erling with a cat's concentration.

At last the gifts were gone, and Erling yet sat empty-handed. King Olaf called for wine and then said, "Erling Skjalgsson, brother-in-law, do you feel aught has been overlooked?"

Erling said, "'Tis for the king to say what gifts are given in his own house."

"Don't go all courtly with me, Erling. I give you no gift because you've made it plain you want no gifts from me."

"When did I say such a thing?"

"I offered you the gift of a jarldom, and you spurned it."

"You know my reasons."

"My kinfolk have withdrawn their objection."

"I am still the great-grandson of Horda-Kari. The title of jarl has never been used in my family."

"Your kin were keen enough to have you made one."

"I prefer to be a hersir. It makes no difference in my service to you."

"So you say. I've spoken much with Sigurd and the Opprostad folk about your family and the history of Westland. In elder times there were no kings or jarls in Hordaland. The chief man was called a hersir. In all ways he was just what a king was, in those days of small kings.

"So this is how I see it—when you, coming of Horder stock, style yourself hersir, you in fact make yourself equal to a king. You rule in your own realm, and carry a title which is yours by birth, not my gift.

"What does this mean? It means that one day you may decide to take the name of king as well as the dignity. It means that, if you mislike my ways, you may try to put me out of the land. It means I must always watch my back with you."

"Who has bruited such things?" asked Erling. "I'll fight him. I've sworn to support you and taken your sister to wife. Who calls me forsworn?"

"Take my gift if you'd have my trust."

"May a man not be faithful in his own way? Must all men cut their feet off to be the height you decide?"

"I've a dream for Norway. 'Tis a dream from God. Do you believe in my dream or not?"

Erling drank from his horn. He wiped his mouth and said, "Let us talk further of this tomorrow."

After supper I took one of my walks. I know I seem to have taken a lot of walks in those days, but sometimes I needed to be quit of these Norse. I wasn't one of them, and I felt it. 'Tis hard to say how a Norse drinking binge differs from an Irish one, but it always seemed to me it did, and it turned me rueful.

The snow lay thin on the ground, pooled in white shadows in the cart ruts and the north lees of the rocks. The wind blew stiff, and helped to revive me.

A dark figure came on at a rapid pace along the path from the harbor. I saw his approach a good way off in that sheep-stripped country. His long form and the way he swung his staff seemed familiar.

He wore an ankle-length gray cloak with a hood, but I knew him when he neared. 'Twas my dark friend, the Wanderer. He grinned when he saw me.

"Well met, Father Aillil," he said.

"Good morning to you, man of the wide world and worlds beyond," I answered. "The joy of the season."

"To you as well. I'm told the king is at home here."

"He's in the hall."

"I suppose you know him well?"

The Ghost of the God-Tree

"He's not one of my bosom mates, but we know one another's names."

"Good. You can introduce me."

"You've business with the king?"

"Oh yes. He doesn't know it, but I do."

"I've never learned your name. Whom shall I say I'm presenting?"

"Tell him I'm a teller of tales, bound by oath not to reveal who I am."

"Just like in the stories. That'll get his attention at least."

"Will you present me?"

I stood quietly a moment. "I'd feel easier if I knew who you were."

He looked in my eyes. His were black, and they shone like beads of jet in water. "You know enough of me," he said.

I looked deeply back. There were things in his eyes I'd never seen before, but felt I remembered, and I wished I'd a century to explore them. "'Tis important you see the king then," I said, kneeling.

"You love him, don't you?"

"The king?"

"Yes."

"In my way. He's more than a king you know—he's a hero. A true hero, like Erling. But he doesn't ken a hero's path—the low gate and the narrow road. He could be the man for Norway, the one who builds a kingdom to last a thousand years. But he can't see the way."

"You guess why I've come then."

"Have pity on him. His heart is good, but he's lived in such a world—such a hard world, pitiless and full of pains. Not just the Norse world—Christian lands are near as bad. Sometimes worse. We do the best we can with the lives we've been handed."

"'Tis not about doing the best you can, Aillil. You know that."

"I had to bow to the death-blow; to die to be reborn. But I'm a peasant, and look for little from myself. If it was so hard for such as me, think how it will be for Olaf!"

"Just bring me inside. Leave the rest to me. I know my work."

"True enough. Come on, then."

I rose and led him through the entranceway and into the great hall. Have you ever heard a house go silent when a great, or a much-feared, man stepped inside? It was thus with my dark friend, though he was unknown to all. As we passed down the hearthway, men hushed their talk. Fully half the house was quiet when we reached the king's high seat. Even Thangbrand shut up.

Olaf didn't mark us at first. He was in loud conversation with the steward of the royal farm. "I can't believe no one knows these things!" he said loudly. "For a king to be great and feared, and to leave landmarks behind him, but then to have all his great deeds forgotten—it should not be! It must not be! Surely someone remembers!"

The steward got up from his bench across the longfire. "I can go and ask some of the old people..." he said, but he didn't look keen.

"Who's this?" Olaf asked, turning to me and my friend.

"This wanderer has taken a vow not to give his name," I said with a bow, "but I've met him before and know him for a man of wide travel and much learning."

Olaf harumphed. "What I need is someone who can tell me about King Agvald, who lived here in olden times, and after whom the ness and the farm are named."

"I can tell you of him," said the Wanderer.

"You? A southlander? Greek, to judge by your face, or perhaps even an Arab."

"No land under the sky is strange to me, O King. I can tell you of Agvald."

"Then say on. If the story's good, I'll set you beside me on the bench and give you a gold ring and ale to drink."

"The king's ear is all the reward I wish," said the wanderer, leaning on his staff. "Hear then the tale of King Agvald.

"Agvald ruled here at Agvaldsness. 'Twas in his time that men first began to set keels on their boats, and learned to use the wind to ply up and down the north-way, buying, stealing, and selling more widely than ever before.

"This Agvald was out in the meadow looking over his herds one day, and he was alone, and he spoke to himself, thinking no one heard. ''Tis a bad year,' he said. 'The rain's been too heavy; the crops are meager, even the sheep and cattle show their ribs. I fear me the bonders will do according to their custom, and sacrifice the king for a better spring next year.'

"Then he heard a voice say to him, 'Would you be the richest king in Westland, and win many battles, and be warded from all wounds and defeats?'

"Agvald looked about him, startled. 'Who speaks?' he cried, for he could see no human about.

"''Tis I, the brindled cow,' the voice answered, and Agvald looked and saw that indeed the cow was speaking to him.

"'Who are you?' Agvald asked.

"'One of the underground folk,' the cow answered. 'A mighty Old One and a great magician. I was set under a curse by the high gods, and so walk in this body.'

"'And what will you have from me, in return for all these gifts you speak of?'

"'You must worship no god but me. You must make sacrifices to me at the festivals.'

"This was surely a demon of Hell," said Father Thangbrand, breaking in.

"No doubt," said the Wanderer. "Such were much about in old times, and can be met with now and again even today.

"'I shall do what you ask,' said King Agvald. 'What good have the high gods ever done me?'

"'Then I shall give you my milk to drink,' said the cow, 'and while you drink it every day you will take no deadly wound, and you will have luck in all you undertake. But see that no other man drinks of my milk, or he too will share in my power and so will be a threat to you.

"'Now listen to what I say. Go down to the shore across from Bukk Island without hesitating. There you will find that which will be your fortune.'

"So he did as the cow said, and down on the shore he found a keeled ship wrecked, and with the wreckage a living man, lying senseless on the rocks. He took the living man home, and fed him and restored him to health. The man proved to be a shipbuilder, who became Agvald's man and built him a swift vessel. With this ship Agvald was able to patrol the sound here, at its narrowest place, and exact tolls from all who passed. And so in time he got more ships, laid all the great men under his power, and became rich beyond his dreams; and when any defied him, Agvald made war on them, and he was always victorious.

"Then one day the men of his bodyguard brought a young man in to him. 'We found him in the Cow's byre,' they said.

"'Take him out and hang him,' said Agvald. 'No man must come near my god.'

"'Think again, O King,' said the young man.

"'What do you mean, rascal?'

"'I drank the milk.'

"Agvald stood up from his seat, and the blood

drained from his face. 'No common man may drink the milk of my cow!' he cried.

"'Yet I have done so.'

"'Then you must die for your sacrilege!'

"'As I said, think again. You say the cow's milk protects you from harm, and gives you victory. What will men say if one who has drunk the milk can be killed?'

"Agvald sat in his high seat, set his chin on his fist, and thought. He thought a long time. Everyone sat quiet in the hall while he thought, and after a while they began to grow nervy, for it was clear the king could see no way out. Anything he did to this young man would be something that—conceivably—could be done to him.

"'What are you called, scoundrel?' he asked at last.

"'Varin,' said the young man.

"'Well, Varin the Lucky,' said Agvald, 'It seems you have me by the short hairs. I can see no other course than to let you go. I thought perhaps I could bind you and set you adrift in a boat, but that would be a defeat for you, and would reflect on me. So instead I shall give you a silver ring and turn you loose, that all may know what luck the milk brings. But let me never see your face again.'

"And Varin went, and told the story of what he'd done, and was taken into the household of a king near Haugesund, and when that king was burned in his house with all his sons, Varin, once again lucky, was away. He was hailed king by the bonders, and he grew in power, and made war on King Agvald.

"He slew Agvald at last, and Agvald is buried in the mound here, which you know. The Cow is buried nearby."

"An odd tale," said Olaf.

"A riddle follows it."

"Give us it."

"Harken," said the Wanderer. "What killed King Agvald?"

"Varin killed him."

"No. Agvald died of cowardice."

"Cowardice? He was a king defending his rule. A king must do that, if only for the land's sake."

"Must he?"

"Of course he must."

"Answer me this, O King—what is the difference between a hero and a coward?"

"A hero stands and fights. A coward runs away."

"No. All men stand and fight at one time or another, and all men who are not fools—even heroes—run from time to time. The difference is something other."

"Explain to me then."

"A hero knows he will die, and makes changes in himself to prepare himself to die with honor. A coward thinks he can live forever, and tries to make changes in others to protect his life."

"But 'tis a king's work to establish law; and what is that but trying to change others?"

"Very true. Which is why 'tis harder for a king to be a hero than for an ox to squeeze through a needle's eye. It takes great wisdom, and skilled counsel."

"That is my place," said Bishop Sigurd.

"Are you a wise man?" the Wanderer asked in return.

"I hope so," said the bishop.

"Then answer me another riddle."

"I shall try."

"Listen—what is the loneliest place in the world?"

"May I think a moment?"

"Think all you like."

The bishop sat for a space, staring into the fire.

At last he sat up. "The loneliest place in the world is Calvary," he said.

"True as far as it goes," said the Wanderer. "At His

last supper with His disciples, the Lord said, 'Where I am going, you cannot follow.' He meant Calvary. Yet only a few moments later He said, 'Where I am going you will follow.' He was speaking of the loneliest place.'"

"And what place is that?"

"The place where a man stands alone, knowing that he must do what is right, and that no one else can help him or stand in his stead. 'Tis the place where the things He believes cost him everything, and he knows all men of sense judge him a fool, and even his friends have turned aside. That is the loneliest place in the world. That is where heroes go. The Son of Man went first, and His disciples followed. In one way or another, every Christian comes to that lonely place."

"Even kings?"

"Oh, aye. And since kings must be canny and prudent, it pinches them more than most. When they come to the Loneliest Place they may lose everything, not only for themselves but for their kin and followers."

"There must be passing few kings in Heaven," said Olaf, his beard sunk on his chest.

"With God all things are possible," said the Wanderer. "But this I can say. Few kings are heroes too. Few wear crowns in the Fair Land. Most have all their reward in this world."

"Perhaps that should be enough."

"For a hero, 'tis never enough."

"Tell me of some heroes," said Olaf, in a quiet voice. "Tell me how 'tis done."

So the Wanderer began a story, and there was another story after that, and another. The daylight went, and the long night began, and still the Wanderer spoke, and still the king listened.

At last Bishop Sigurd came to me, and put his hand on my shoulder, drawing me with him out into the entry room.

"Who is this talewright?" he asked, fixing my eyes with his.

"You know as much as I. But of this I'm sure—he comes from the Beloved."

"Are you certain?"

"Yes. I've no doubt."

The bishop scratched his long shaved chin. "This puts me in an awkward place."

"How so?"

"Deacon Ketil says the Wanderer is of the Devil, and that you are deceived."

"Deacon Ketil reads crowbones and cat guts. I can't believe you put stock in such."

"He's been right so often . . ."

"Right forecasts may come from springs other than God. You know this."

"But this is Norway! It's not the same as in England!"

"The rule against augury is the same."

"I don't know. I've seen so many marvels . . . I've had to change my mind about so much. . . ."

"Too much! Don't lose sight of the center, my lord! That's why I trust the Wanderer—his words remind me of things I know, but so often forget. And he troubles me. That's always a good sign."

"I think it's late," said the bishop. "I think the king should sleep."

"You know best, my lord. But if any were to ask me, I'd say he's chosen the better part and it should not be taken from him."

We went back into the main hall.

"I've heard the saga of Daniel before," Olaf was saying to the Wanderer, who yet stood where we'd left him, leaning on his staff.

"Not this Daniel," said the Wanderer. "You've never heard of this Daniel, because no one remembered him. He lived after the Daniel of whom you've heard; one of the Jews who stayed on in

Persia after most had returned to Israel. Like the other Daniel he was a high official in the king's house. Like him, he fell afoul of his enemies because he would not deny God, and was denounced as a traitor.

"The choice was set before him—bow down and worship the gods of the land, or be thrown into the lion's den, along with his wife and children—this was a sorrow spared to the first Daniel, who had no family.

"The first Daniel was a great and good man, but he never faced the horror of seeing a lovely young wife, and innocent daughters and sons, thrown to be mauled and eaten by starving lions, and to hear their screams as they called to him for help. He went almost eagerly when it was his turn to die."

"What sort of story is this?" Olaf asked. "Such a story would be in no way different if there were no God at all."

"Indeed. Daniel felt much the same as he plunged into the beast-pit."

"So he lost his faith and was damned anyway?" Olaf asked.

"A good question that! The true question of the Loneliest Place! You are near to understanding, O King!

"No, Your Majesty, God did not judge Daniel by his feelings. When he reached the Blessed Land, he was reunited with his wife and children, and repaid a hundredfold for what he'd suffered—for God will be debtor to no man. But he could not have entered into that happiness without first standing alone in the Loneliest Place."

Bishop Sigurd stepped forward and said, "'Tis late, O King. Sleep calls us. There'll be time for more stories in the morning."

"Yes, yes," said Deacon Ketil, rising from his seat. "'Tis very late."

"Yes," said Olaf, making to rise and rubbing his eyes with a big hand. "I feel as if I've been ten days waking."

The Wanderer did not shift his stance. "Have you heard the tale of Honir the god, brother of Odin, Your Majesty?"

"Of how he was sent a hostage to the Vanir?" Olaf asked.

"No. This came later. He was kidnapped by the trolls."

Olaf had been unfolding his big frame. Now he stopped and moved to sit again. "I've not heard of this," he said.

"Your Majesty, you'll want to be up for mass in the morning," said the bishop.

"They put Honir in a cave for a prison," said the Wanderer. "The cave had but one opening—a small crack—where the light could come in, because the trolls care nothing for light, as you know."

"My lord, the hour!" said the bishop.

"Time for trolls tomorrow!" said Deacon Ketil.

Olaf looked at them almost guiltily. "I really must sleep," he said.

"I'll keep you company to your bed," said the Wanderer.

The king rose and went to the far end of the hall, where his great box-bed stood. All the men who slept elsewhere began to move out, while the bodyguard pushed the sitting benches back and began to unroll their sleeping bags.

As he undressed, Olaf asked, "How did the trolls manage to capture a god?"

The Wanderer said, "Honir was never one of the mighty gods. And the trolls created an image of a woman, all of gold, so fair that Honir fell in love with it and lost his senses, so that they could bind and disarm him."

Olaf went inside the bed, where his wife already

slept, but did not close the door. "What did the trolls want of him?"

"They wanted everything," said the Wanderer, sitting on the bed step.

"Honir spent all his time gazing through this crack at the light if it was day, or at the stars if night. And in time the trolls understood that he drew strength from that light. So the king of the trolls came into Honir's cell and said, 'I apologize for my shabby hospitality. All this time there has been a draft in your quarters, and I've done naught about it. I shall send a mason to stop up the hole.'

"And Honir said, 'Spare me the light. I will give you anything if you leave the light to me.'

"The troll king said, 'What have you to offer, brother of Odin? We've taken your weapons and your jewels. All that remains is your body.'

"'I will give you one of my feet,' said Honir.

"The foot of a god is no small treasure, so the troll king agreed. He cut off Honir's foot and left him to look through the crack at the light of the wide world.

"The next day the king came back and made to stop up the hole yet again, and Honir gave him his other foot.

"The next day he made the same threat, and Honir gave him his left hand. The day after it was the right hand; then Honir gave up his legs and arms, and his ears and nose, until finally he was left with only a cropped torso, and two eyes in his head. And one of those eyes he had to yield up as well."

"Odin gave an eye for wisdom," said Olaf.

"But his brother Honir gave all but an eye, so that he could see the only light he had. That is why Odin will die at Ragnarok, while Honir will return afterward to rule in Asgard under the High God. For he found the pearl of great price, and sold all that he had and bought it."

The bishop came now and put his hand on the

bed door. " 'Tis time for sleep, in God's Name!" he said.

"Yes—" said the Wanderer. "Sleep in God's Name, O King."

"Of course," said Olaf faintly, from within. "In God's Name."

"You may lie in one of the outbuildings," said the bishop coldly to the Wanderer.

The Wanderer stood and bowed silently, and strode out.

"One more story?" came the voice from the bed. The bishop closed the door firmly.

I followed the Wanderer out. "Aren't you going to bed?" he asked me when we stood under the cold stars. "The bishop is right. 'Tis very late."

"I'd rather not waste the time I have with you," said I.

He smiled, and his teeth were very white in the darkness. "So be it," he said.

"And yet 'tis true I'm weary. But it's not sleep I need."

"What do you need?"

"Hope, my lord. These great men speak great words and rattle their swords and their crosiers, and what hope have I that my chicken peeps will be heard? What hope have I of turning them from the mad courses they've plotted?"

"It puts me in mind of a story," said the Wanderer.

"Now why am I not surprised?"

"Come, let's sit on these stones and I'll tell you about it. There was a kingdom once, far, far away, and it was ruled by the wisest laws ever seen in this world. Good men had made these laws, and they taught them to their children, and the children learned them well. The foundation of the law of that land was that every man should have his say freely, so that each could ponder all sides of a question, and judge what was best. They believed truth was in itself stronger and more beautiful than falsehood, so that no great harm could come from letting each man speak his piece. If he was wrong, he'd be seen for a fool. In that land there was nothing thought so shameful as to be a fool, or a narrow-minded man."

"I'd dearly love to see such a land as that," said I.

"And of all the wise men in that land, the wisest was the king. But even wise men have their weaknesses, and this king, I'm sorry to say, was somewhat vain. And the older he grew, the vainer he got.

"He was specially vain about his body. Therefore he feared growing old, and sought over the world for physicians and remedies that might keep him young and strong.

"One day a man came to see him, claiming to be a healer from distant lands. He told the king that there was one reliable way to health—to throw off the confining, poisonous garments he wore and go naked at all times. The king was not averse to this idea, as he'd always been proud of his appearance.

"'It may be a little chilly at first,' said the healer, 'but that is only a temporary condition, while your body grows accustomed to the change. Some people will use the word, "naked." Have such people shut up immediately, for "naked" is an ugly, judgmental word, born of ancient traditions and prejudices, and has no place in the thinking of broad-minded men.'

"The next day the king had his governor summon an assembly, and there he announced that the king would display his new, healthful fashion. Some people, he said, might use an ugly word to describe the king's new way, but such people were only showing their ignorance and narrow-mindedness.

"When the speech was finished the king came out and paraded before the crowd. And all the folk were ashamed to be thought narrow-minded fools, so they said nothing against it.

"Only one old woman raised her voice and said,

'I don't care what the rest of you say, I say the king is naked!'"

"The king and the governor shouted, 'That woman is a narrow-minded fool! Stone her!' And the people did so.

"So the king caught a chill and died of a fever, and in the disorder that followed the enemies of the land attacked and conquered it. They set up a bloody-handed tyranny, and that was the end of the Land of the Wise."

I pondered. "And how is this supposed to cheer me?"

"I'm not such a liar as to promise you that telling the truth is always rewarded in this world. Still and all, it matters to tell it."

It was morning before I got to sleep, and we lugged ourselves out for mass. I looked around for the Wanderer, but missed him. Deacon Ketil assisted the bishop, who was nodding at the slow points.

As we walked back to the hall, King Olaf came up beside Erling, and I heard him say, "I could not sleep last night. I thought about my kingship, and what it means to follow Christ. I will not force you to be a jarl. We will work together, and make a kingdom we can both live in."

"I treasure this gift more than any you've given me," Erling answered, "save only your sister's hand. You'll not regret it."

Then we went in to breakfast. The bishop was blessing the food when Deacon Ketil rushed in and shouted, "Nobody eat!"

"What means this?" the bishop called.

"Dark treachery!" said the deacon. "Demons and witchcraft in the king's own house!"

"Explain yourself!"

"The Wanderer! The tale-teller from last night! Has anyone seen him this morning?"

We all looked around and asked our neighbors, and no one had seen him.

"Come with me to the kitchen house, and hear what I've learned."

Olaf and Bishop Sigurd rose and went out. Erling and I were close behind, and all the company followed us.

The deacon led us to the kitchen house, a short distance from the hall, went inside and brought out the chief cook, a well-fed freedman with a black beard.

"What did the Wanderer say to you?" Ketil demanded.

The cook had a glassy look in his eyes, as if he'd been tippling early in the day. Tonelessly he said, "The stranger came in the night, woke me and said, ''Tis passing poor meat you have for the king's table. Take this.' And he gave us a haunch of beef. We boiled it for breakfast."

"So he gave us meat," said the king. "Where's the hurt in that?"

"Much hurt, if it's meat sacrificed to the old gods!"

"What proof have you?"

"A strange wanderer who will not give his name? Clothed in a dark cloak? He had one eye, didn't he?"

"Did he?" asked the king. "I noticed no such thing."

"Had he one eye?" asked the bishop.

"I saw his eyes," said I. "There were two of them, black as midwinter night."

No one heeded me. Some men said one thing, some said another, but the cook, still fish-eyed, said, "I saw him clearly. He had but one."

"Think of all he said!" cried Ketil. "All that music about dying heroically, even a tale of the old gods! Would a messenger of the true God speak thus?"

"I heard nothing un-Christian from him," I tried to say, but no one listened.

"I must think on this," said Olaf.

"Thank God you took no action on his words," said Ketil.

"I did one thing," said Olaf, looking at Erling.

"I know you'll not break your word," Erling answered.

"No, but I will make a demand of you. This I will have in return for my gift. Thangbrand and Ketil will return with you to Sola, and see that all the heathen are baptized. No more delays."

Erling looked at him and saw there was no shifting him.

"Father Aillil," he said without turning to me, "you will take the second ship and go back to Sola now. Give the people fair warning."

"That they may flee us?" asked Ketil.

"If they wish. I owe them that much. No—I owe them more. But this seems the best I can do."

"Enough," said Olaf. "I'm hungry, and I've much to think on."

"He had two eyes," said I. For all the good it did.

CHAPTER XIV

The second ship was a knarr, brought along to convey Olaf's tribute to the storehouses at Agvaldsness. No friend of ships at their best, I especially mislike knarrs, because it was in one such that Maeve and I were taken from Ireland. Which is unjust I suppose, since the knarr is at bottom a merchant's ship. But I don't reproach myself much over injustices to seacraft.

The crew was made up mostly of men I didn't know well, new to the household since Erling had become a king's man. In fact the only friend (if that's the right word) I had on board was Astrid Trygvesdatter, who'd come along for no reason other than her whim.

I was sick of course. We had to wait at the mouth of the Kormt Sound for a favorable wind, and the one we got was only favorable in that it wasn't actually against us. The clouds hung low, sculpted in strange scallop shapes that put me, let alone the sailors with any weather sense, in nettle shirts. Our trip involved a great deal of tacking and some rowing.

"Who was the Wanderer?" Astrid asked me, standing by me in the stern, wrapped in a sable cloak.

"I can't say exactly, but I'll stake my head he came from God, whatever the bishop thinks."

"A saint? An angel?"

"Perhaps. Perhaps more."

"You don't mean . . ."

"I dare not say. But whoever he is, to call him Odin is a great wrong, as great as that of the men who called the Beloved Beelzebub. I fear for your brother, and for the bishop. They did not know the day of their visitation."

Tacking is a frustrating exercise at best, but when the weather bears down on you, bringing the cobwebby cloud-roof lower and lower, boiling like a kettle, it tightens the muscles of your back so you're stiff afterwards, if you're lucky enough to have an afterwards to be stiff in.

I stood near the steersman, a man named Haakon, and he kept muttering to himself. Sometimes I could make out what he said, though he kept it down, knowing that it's unlucky to share your fears with a shipmate. "Too dark," I heard him say. "Too dark too quickly. It's playing with us, this wind. Letting us make enough way to hope, then pushing us back . . . It's holding us here for the storm, like a goat tethered for sacrifice."

The east wind smacked us in the face without warning, a ship-murdering wind; a wind to peel the hair off your head; and suddenly all was black, and there was sideways rain and lightning and thunder that rattled the planks, as I helped the hands loosen the backstay and drop the ripping sail, taking the skin off my hands. I jumped down in the hold, knee-deep, and helped pass up the everlasting leather bailing buckets.

I was too frightened even to be weary.

We ran westward, into the night and the open sea.

"Men have survived worse blows," I told myself. "At least we're headed west. With luck we can go far without running onto anything."

But luck had been niggling on this trip so far.

There's little to do in a blow like that, if you're not steering or bailing. So when I stumbled and fell facedown in the bilge and couldn't get up again, strong hands pulled me out and passed me to somebody who laid me out on the deck with a sleeping bag over me, and I suppose somebody else took my place. I slept the kind of sleep you sleep in a fever, or after someone has snapped your jaw shut for you with his knuckles. I woke only when someone shook me.

"Look, Father!" cried the man. "We're saved!"

The first thing I saw was golden light that painted us on all sides, leaving no shadows in any direction. I pulled myself up where I could see over the rail.

The whole world was shining and motionless, like a frozen winter landscape, but sun-colored. The ship had seized up on a starboard pitch, so that the rail on that side, where I stood, was on the downslope. The waves were still. The wind and the clouds had stiffened and set like potter's clay.

And there on the sea, in a wreath of light brighter than the rest, stood the figure of a man at least twenty feet tall. It was shaped like a man, but thin, as if stretched. The hair and beard were golden, the ankle-length robe blinding white, girdled in yet more gold. The face was pale and sad, with great blue eyes under downward-arching brows.

The long man beckoned with his right arm. "Come to me, come to me, weary seamen," he said, in a voice high and melodious.

"It is the Lord," said the captain, a seaman named Thorbjorn. "We must go to Him."

"No!" I cried.

"What do you mean?" asked Thorbjorn.

"It is not the Lord."

"It looks like the Lord. It looks just like a crucifix I saw in England once."

"The Lord is not an Englishman."

"Surely He can appear any way He likes," said Astrid Trygvesdatter, who'd slid down beside me.

I supposed that was true, but didn't want to argue it.

"I know Him when I see Him," I said, pulling my rank (quite unfairly) as priest. "That's not He."

Unfortunately everyone knew my reputation. "You've been wrong before," said Thorbjorn.

"Satan appears as an angel of light," said I. "This is too much what we'd expect. He never comes in the way we expect."

"Do not listen to the priest," came the singing voice of the golden man. "I came once before, and was not received, and great was the guilt of the men who turned me away. Bring not such guilt on yourselves."

"I'm coming!" cried one man, and he clambered over the side and began to run over the serried waves.

Others followed quickly. I put my hand on Astrid's arm and said, "Don't go. Trust me in this."

"I never thought to go," Astrid said coolly. "I've great respect for you, Father. If you say that's not the Lord, I believe you."

"You frighten me, lady," said I, as the golden man's light brightened and the entire crew disappeared into it.

"So here we stand, alone on a ship in a storm," she went on. "I wonder what comes next."

She had nerve, that one. I could have wished she'd been a man, and ruled instead of Olaf.

What came next was that the unnatural light faded, but not into the storm we'd had before. Instead we stood on a deserted ship in a workaday seasonal west wind under a pale winter sky. Grappled to our starboard side was a warship; a hundred berserkers were boarding us. Observing all from a place by the mainmast of the new ship was Eyvind Kellda, and Baug Kollasson stood at his side.

"We meet again, Astrid and Aillil!" he cried. "You've not disappointed me—I never looked for you to be taken in by that mannikin show, drowning yourselves like those witling sea-rats. So all is well—I've great plans for you. Men, bind this pair, and make sail for Hafrsfjord."

They'd made Sola their own already, and without bloodshed from what I could tell. Astrid and I entered the steading on foot, with our hands bound behind us and ropes about our necks, led by a mounted Eyvind.

"I've a special place for you," he said, getting down from his horse lightly as a boy. All around us were berserkers. I saw few proper Sola-folk, except for thralls. Asa came out of the old hall and stared as us, but said no word.

"Have you marked how often the Old Ones dwell under storehouses, like rats?" Eyvind asked as he tugged at our ropes and led us toward the southeast corner of the steading. "Whatever you call them— elves or fair folk, or good neighbors—I call them anything I like, they've no power against me—they like storehouses and barns. Depending on their dignity, of course, some like treasure stores and some like granaries, and some like animal byres. But the great ones—so great as remain since you've evicted them—they love the treasure. Here at Sola you've a very old treasure house, and the moment I came near it I could feel the power of its guests."

We came then to the old treasure house, built by Ogmund Karisson, heavy-walled and heavy-doored and leaning just a bit on rotten foundations.

"This house isn't even used nowadays," I said.

"That means naught to the Old Ones. They savor

the smell of gold long gone; the odor of silver spent. That you make no use of the house is all to the good, from their point of view."

At Eyvind's word a berserker unlocked the great oak door and led us up the two steps into the building. He himself stood on the threshold and pushed us in. The floorboards groaned beneath us and we could smell their sweet decay. We moved back near the wall.

"Let me go too," said a woman's voice, and I recognized it for Asa's. I looked out and saw her facing Eyvind.

"You're no Christian," said Eyvind. "I can see it in your soul-flame."

"Nevertheless I'd go with Aillil."

"Why should I do you kindness?"

"You do me no kindnesses. Do you think me a fool?"

"Yes, as a matter of fact. But then that's my chief pleasure in life, watching fools. So go and be one, with my blessing."

Asa climbed the steps and came in to stand by me. The floorboards screamed their outrage beneath her added weight.

"And now the key," said Eyvind, and another berserker came up the steps, carrying one of the smaller anvils from the forge. He tossed it in amongst us.

With a crash and a snapping the floor collapsed. We fell and we fell, screaming, into a misty void that seemed to have no bottom.

The next I knew we all stood in a circular room of stone, no more than two men's height across, with three arched doorways in the wall, one for each of us. A silver cresset hanging above gave out a flickering light. I moved to the nearest archway. It was open, but all was blackness beyond, and as I drew near I felt bitter cold. I reached my hand through and pulled it swiftly back, tucking it under my armpit to warm it again. I feared for a moment I'd frozen it solid.

"What place is this?" asked Asa. "Is this Hel?"

"I think not," said I, blowing on my fingers. "If I've learned anything from my dealings with Eyvind, this is but another seeming. Where we really are I cannot say, but 'tis not where we think."

"Supposing that's so," said Eyvind's voice from no direction in particular. *"Granting that all this is happening inside your heads—is not the inside of your heads a place of terror and wonder enough? Who could bear to have revealed the secrets he hides within his skull-walls? Whose courage and faith are strong enough to brave such final shame?"*

"You're forever missing the point, Eyvind," I cried. "'Tis nothing to do with my courage and faith."

"Is it not indeed?" he asked. *"Let us see—"*

A light began to glow through the archway before me, and it shone at last on the figure of a young girl. I gasped. 'Twas my sister Maeve, as she'd been when she was five. She looked up at me with great, weeping blue eyes.

"You broke my dolly, Aillil! 'Tis the only one I have, and you broke it!"

It struck me like a club to the belly, and my legs went all nerveless and dropped me. A childhood cruelty, forgotten till now, but back of a sudden in all its acid and bile. I remembered the feeling of triumph as I'd torn the head off the thing, and how my mother'd beaten me and asked why, and how I'd tried to think of a reason.

"Be a man, priest!" said Astrid sharply. "I'd thought better of you than this! To be struck down by such a common deed—something any real man has done at least once—"

"You don't ken," I said, moaning on my knees. " 'Tis all one, you see—all of it—"

"*Oh she shall see,*" said Eyvind's voice, "*and presently. I should thank you all—all you moral, decent folk—for the power you give me. Without your weakness I should have no strength. Behold your own weakness, Astrid Trygvesdatter.*"

A young man appeared in the archway before her, lean, brown-haired and pale.

"Edgar!" she cried.

"*Sweet Astrid,*" said the wraith. "*Sweet Astrid of the golden hair. Why did you come to England? Why did you enter my life? And having come, why did you deny me?*"

"I did not know," she said, and there was a sob in her voice. "How could I have known? I was a refugee, a penniless guest."

"*You flew into my soul like a golden bird into a hall—coming out of the sunshine and bringing light with you. I never knew joy until I kissed you. You'd have been my wife, and for you I'd have been a hero and made a name to live in songs forever.*"

"You could have. You should have. You were so fine, Edgar—I've never known a man as fine. Or perhaps one."

"*Yet you broke our betrothal.*"

"Olaf broke it, will I, nill I! I'd never have done such were I free! But out of Russia he comes, loaded with silver and furs, and he goes to King Ethelred and says, 'Give me ships and gold and I'll make myself king of Norway, and get Svein Forkbeard the Dane out of your hair.' And he sets me on his lap and says, 'We must make a high marriage for her, if she's to be a king's sister,' and Ethelred says, 'She's already betrothed, but I see what you mean. I'll buy off the family.' "

"*You could have run with me, golden Astrid. I came to you and begged it. We'd have taken ship for Ireland, or France, or Sarras, or the Isles of the West. It would have made a deed and a song, and we'd have never been forgotten.*"

"They'd have found us and killed you. The world is a pond to Northmen. We have kin and friends everywhere."

"Better to have died thus than as I did."

Astrid brought up a despairing sigh.

"I went on a raid to Wales. I was killed in our first fight there."

"They told me this. I wept for you, my Edgar, and prayed for your soul through many nights."

"Do you know how I died, my sweet, lovely Astrid?"

"An arrowshot—"

"I went to a place in the fight where no man could go and live. I went willingly, almost without thinking to. I went because life was more cruel than death. I went because I could not live without my pearl."

Astrid fell to her knees, head against the stone wall, and purged her soul of salt tears.

"I suppose my Thorstein will be next to appear," said Asa. "That is, if Eyvind thinks me worthy of torment."

"More than worthy," said Eyvind's voice. *"But you underrate my wisdom."*

Within the archway a tiny figure appeared—a babe, less than a year old, naked and weeping and waving arms and legs like a turtle on its back.

"My Thora! My sweet, perfect Thora!" Asa cried, rushing into the archway only to be thrust back, shivering and white, with rime on her hair.

"Your child?" I asked.

"My daughter—" her voice caught "—whom we gave to the gods, to be strangled and hung up like a pig carcass!"

I went to her and held her, knowing naught else to do. Even Eyvind seemed to have found nothing more to say on this score, nor needed he.

"Quite a show, Eyvind Kellda," I said. "You've proved that all men are sinners, and worthy of Hell. When did I ever deny it? Or are you pleased with cruelty only for its own sake?"

"*If need be,*" came his voice, and another figure appeared in my archway.

It was a woman—a woman not fat and not thin, neither young nor old, neither fair nor ugly, with pale hair and brown eyes, whose name I did not know, but whom I could never forget.

"*Do you know me, Aillil the priest?*"

"I know you," I said, shuddering. "You're an Englishwoman."

"*You Irish came in your ships and raided our village. You killed our men, all you could, and you raped us women.*"

"I killed no one," said I, as if that somehow justified me. "I was too young to do any real fighting. But I wanted to prove myself man enough . . . in one way or another."

"*So you shamed me, a woman who'd never done you harm; who'd gladly have given you, or anyone, bread and soup to eat and a warm place by the fire, if you'd shown up hungry at her doorstep.*"

I hung my head. "I did that thing," said I. "I hope it gives you comfort to know I saw my own sister raped, and taken off to slavery. You've your revenge, at least."

"*I want no revenge, man of Ireland. I'm not a vengeful soul. You did not know this, nor did you care to know—and that is the benchmark of your sin.*"

I fell then like a spent berserk, and laid on my back looking at the cresset, and the darkness beyond.

You've wondered, perhaps, how I learned English, so that I picked up its cousin, Norse, so quickly?

You've wondered why I could not forgive Ulf?

I could not forgive Ulf because I was Ulf.

A child's cruelty—an adult's rape or murder—a king's massacre—they're all the same thing at bottom. A working out of some need to prove our strength through the weakness of others. It has naught to do with right—that thing we say we want; everything to do with power—that thing we really want.

I wept loud then, and I wept long. I was shamed to weep before women, but my grief came out with its own voice, like a mandrake pulled up.

"'Tis an illusion," I said at last, when my tears were spent. "All a seeming."

"*A seeming in truth,*" said Eyvind's voice. "*For all these things that trouble you so, that have the power to suck your marrow slowly or strike you down at once like a hammer blow—they are all but dreams within your mind. They are stories concocted by old women to scare children into bed. I no longer believe such stories; I no longer carry such a burden of guilt. For I know I am God; that right is whatever I make it. Thus I do not age, and I cannot be hurt, for my only weakness is gone. Understand this, and you too will be free!*"

"If I'm God, why should I listen to you?" I asked, breathing hard.

"*Perhaps I'm your creation, brought up by your deepest self to teach you what you need to know.*"

We sat silent for a while, the three of us, wrestling each with our own devils.

At last Astrid said, "I heard a learned clerk once, who told the words of an old-time wise man. It went like this—'I know more than he; for neither of us knows everything, but he thinks he knows everything, while I know that I do not. Therefore I know one more thing than he.'"

"Yes," said Asa. "Eyvind thinks he's wise because he's forgotten his own foolishness—like a man who boasts that he's outgrown the need for food, because he's cut out his stomach."

God bless the women. When they're good they're better than us. We men fight and strive and buy and sell and build and tear down, and do all the things that get written on parchment in chronicles, only so the women can carry on the real work of the world, which we'll never fully know.

There was a change in the light then; the color went from yellow to white; we looked up and there above us was the white bear I'd seen before, shedding light down into our dungeon as a tree sheds leaves in autumn.

"Climb up to me," said the bear.

"My lord, we've no ladder," said I.

"Climb the scarlet cord."

And I looked, and there was a thick, scarlet cord, made of some soft, tough stuff like silk, hanging down from the top where the bear waited, in easy reach.

"He'll eat us, surely," said Asa.

"I can't say he won't," I answered. "But if that's his will, I think 'tis better to go and be eaten than not."

"Yes, we must obey," said Astrid, and she set her hand on the cord. "I'll go up first."

We watched her climb. She went easily.

"I cannot," said Asa, putting her hand on my arm.

"You must. I'm certain there's no other way."

"'Tis different for you. You look at the heavens, and you see love behind them. I do not see that."

"You're a brave woman," I said. "Be brave in this. Believe that God exists, and is a rewarder of those who seek Him."

"That He exists I've no doubt. But I think he's as likely to be a destroyer of those who seek Him. I spent my own child on that belief. I cannot climb, Aillil. Will you stay with me?"

"How can I? I'm called."

"I can't come with you."

"Yes, you can. If you can't trust God's bear, trust me. You trust me, don't you? There are things I know—places I've been. If you care for me, can't you trust me?"

She looked up. "Are you well, Lady Astrid?" she called.

"I'm perfectly well. The bear's gone, if that's what's troubling you. I wish you'd both come and not leave me alone up here. I keep having to hide myself from the berserkers."

Asa took a deep breath and grasped the cord. She walked her way up steadily, feet braced on the wall. She was much stronger than she looked.

I came up after. It seemed a marvelously easy climb—almost as if I were being reeled in. But when I rested at it I made no progress.

We emerged through the rotten floorboards into the storehouse. It was no brighter up there than down below, which was all to the good for people who wanted to keep out of sight. We tried not to move around too much, as the boards creaked, and we kept well back from the open door, as Eyvind's wild men came past from time to time. I looked back down into the hole and saw only dirt and wood trash.

"We're little better off now than before," whispered Astrid. "Do you think we can get away to some friendly farm with all these stink-men about?"

"Berserkers aren't known for discipline," I said. "I expect they'll all drink themselves to sleep ere long. But I wonder—I wonder if the bear didn't bring us out for something bigger than an escape."

"What's happened to Eyvind?" asked Asa. "He was everywhere one moment, now he doesn't seem to know what we're doing."

"I think the bear scared him off. In his world, the bear must not exist, so he dare not face it."

"That may be true," she replied. "Or perhaps the bear was another trick of his. How can you be sure?"

"I can't be sure I'm right," I said. "A man who never questions himself becomes an Eyvind Kellda in the end. But I can be sure of the One I know. I can be sure that I've met Him, and that He's spoken to me. Knowledge is thinking and feeling—both, not one or the other."

"Thinking and feeling have naught to do with one another. One is Odin, the other Thor."

"The Word became flesh, Asa. That's how we can know God."

"Flesh is all words and thoughts. Spirit is all feelings and dreams. They don't walk together, Aillil. I know. I've tried. Hasn't everyone?"

"We must go to Somme," said Astrid suddenly.

"What?" I asked.

"Olaf and Erling were following shortly. How soon depends on the winds they get. And we don't know how long we were in the pit, do we? It could have been days for all we can tell. If we can be at Somme when they come, we can warn them that Eyvind and the berserkers hold Sola."

"Eyvind must have men at Somme, too," I said.

"Still, there are bound to be fewer there. And we must try to warn our people."

"It makes sense," said Asa. "When things grow quieter, we must go."

I said to Astrid, "Asa doesn't know why they come."

Astrid said nothing.

"The king is coming, with the bishop and the priests, to baptize every soul here. Every soul. By Thangbrand's means."

"And Erling cannot stop him?"

"He had to agree. But he sent me to warn you all. For all the good it did."

She said, "Still, we must go. Perhaps Olaf will change his thinking if I help you warn him."

"I wouldn't count on it."

"All men honor friendship and service."

"Olaf, yes, I think so. But Thangbrand, and the bishop as he's becoming—they think that to be swayed by friendship is disloyalty to God."

"How can you believe something that makes men act so shamefully?"

"The higher a thing is, the it smells when rotten. A bad man is worse than a bad rat."

"Well, we must go, whatever happens."

"You could run now. Astrid and I can warn them."

"Hmm—I can run into the arms of the king, or into the arms of the berserkers. I might as well stay with you two."

We waited a little longer, and things continued quiet. We made our way carefully between the buildings and over the meadow wall, then around and northward, down the hill and onto the path to Somme. The wind blew cold and we pulled our cloaks tight around us.

"The balefire," I said.

"What?" asked Astrid.

"We should light the balefire."

"One of Erling's fires?"

"No. The king's fire. At Tjora."

"That's only for attacks that touch the safety of the land."

"They're lying in wait for the king. Back in Ireland, we call that an attack on the land."

"You're right of course."

We skirted Somme. It was nearing dawn when we reached Tjora, footsore and tired, not to mention hungry. We crept up the hill and peered at the two men who guarded it, crouched around a small campfire. We'd circled them and come from downwind, and the smell alone was enough to tell us they were berserkers.

We moved back a bit and thought out our strategy. Astrid moved around to the upwind side, which was where they were turned in any case. "Friends, have you anything to eat?" she asked, playing the part of a beautiful woman in distress (and very well). When she could see us moving up from our side she feigned a swoon, and the two berserkers scrambled forward to help her (and likely to use their hands a bit). As they bent down to her, Asa and I ran up and smashed them over their heads with stones. Of course braining men with stones is no exact art—one of them required three or four blows—we may have killed him—I never cared to learn. I took a faggot from the campfire and set fire to the twigs and dried heather piled around the base of the great cone of tarred rails, set upright and stacked against one another. It took a few minutes because of the damp, but the wood caught at last and went up in a blaze and a cloud of black, choking smoke. We moved away quickly then, in case some more of Eyvind's men were about. I thought they'd have trouble dousing it soon even if they were, but I didn't want to be around.

Before we went we pillaged the guards' food bag. We got some cheese and bread, which we wolfed down with more pleasure than we'd gotten from the Jul feast.

"Someone will see the fire," said Astrid, blowing on her fingers to warm them. "One way or another, Olaf will know there's trouble. And all the way up the coast they'll be be raising levies."

CHAPTER XV

Feeling somewhat stronger, we made our way down to the harbor at Tananger. As we'd expected, a scout ship from Olaf came in shortly and took us aboard. We sailed to White Island, halfway back to Kormt, where our ships had come. We boarded *Fishhawk* and waited with Erling another full day for more ships to gather, herded in by the ranging boats sent out in all directions by the king.

At last we had above twenty ships, and a force we judged sufficient to handle any number of berserkers. One by one the long vessels hoisted sail to catch the west wind, and we coasted southeast to Hafrsfjord. There was no hiding our landing, using oar power to bring each ship to one of the three jetties and debark its force. Evening fell before we were all ashore. Olaf's and Erling's bodyguards put up at Somme; the others at other farms. We saw no berserkers about but knew they were watching. We set a guard for the night and planned for battle on the morrow.

I wouldn't be fighting (surely not in the presence of the bishop), but I lay long awake. When I slept at last I dreamed I sat in Erling's hall, on the bench, playing *hnefatafl* with the Wanderer. No one was about but we two.

I had the king and the defenders' pieces; he had the attackers all round. I moved one of my men.

The Wanderer reached across and shifted my man back where it had been.

"Bad move," he said.

It galled me, but I trusted him, so I made another move.

Again he pushed my piece back. "No. You can do better."

I ground my teeth and made a third move.

He inclined his head, sighed and said, "All right. That will have to do."

The game went on that way. My anger swelled like a carbuncle. At last I made a move I thought specially good, and when he undid it I could not stopper my mouth.

"Will you let me play my own game?" I cried. "Perhaps I won't win—no doubt you're cleverer than I—but at least 'twill be *my* loss!"

The Wanderer leaned back and smiled. "Well said, Aillil. A game's no good without the risk of losing."

"Is there supposed to be a lesson here somewhere?"

"You wonder why the innocent suffer—why life is so cruel. 'Tis because the game is real, and no one forces good moves on you. Our choices bear fruit—for ourselves and others. The fruit is real, not a seeming. Otherwise our lives would have no worth. Life is the true Baldur-game."

I arched my back and rubbed it. "There's sense in that," I said. "But it's awfully hard on the small and the weak. 'Tis one thing for Erling to play at the Baldur-game in full armor. 'Tis another to set a child or an old woman out, all unprotected and by no choice of their own."

"That's why Erling was put here, and Olaf and you and every other strong one. To protect the weak."

"Very nice, of course. Except that the strong as often as not are the danger, not the protection."

The Wanderer gazed in my eyes. "There is a way that seemeth right to a man, but the end thereof is death. Men will not believe that their chosen ways are lemmings' paths. The only way to show them otherwise is to let their works flower and bear their fruit. Thus the Baldur-game. All will be made right in the end—though not in any way you'd guess—but before that, men must be permitted to move as they will on the board, and see what it gets them. No one will be able to say they were denied their trial."

I dressed myself in the dark and waited until the men began to stir. When Erling woke I went to him and said, "I must speak to the king."

Erling pulled on his shirt and said, "Why not? Things can scarcely get worse."

When Olaf emerged from his box-bed, Erling and I went to him and Erling said, "Father Aillil wishes a word."

Olaf was pulling on a padded jacket, to go under his brynje. "What will you, priest?" he asked.

"Perhaps you've considered this already," I said, "but a word in your ear can do no harm."

"Say on."

"You're fighting no natural enemy here. This is Eyvind Kellda. With Eyvind, all is seemings and tricks. With him, the great thing is not to believe what you see. The numbers of his force will be other than what they seem—more or less, but certainly other. You may see warlocks, or werewolves, or giants and dragons for all I know. Believe nothing."

Olaf stood and thought a moment. "Makes tactics difficult," he said.

"I can't advise you there. But I can pray for you, with the bishop and other priests."

"I've never despised prayer as a shield, Father," said the king.

The bishop came in and said mass right there in the hall, and we ate breakfast after. Then there was a great jingling sound, like a thousand thousand exceedingly small bells, as those men rich enough to own brynjes pulled them over their heads.

We priests took the lead as we processed out into the yard, into a pale-skyed, cold morning with a crust of snow underfoot. Olaf chose a nearby hill as a gathering place, and we marched there. A horn sounded to assemble everyone, and in about a half an hour the whole host was mustered.

I stood with the churchmen a little apart. "Well, did you warn off all your precious heathen?" Thangbrand asked me.

"I got no chance."

"Then the Lord hath delivered our enemies into our hands."

"Perhaps," said the bishop. "But look up there."

We turned to follow his pointing finger, toward the higher ground of Sola, and along the horizon from one side to another we saw berserkers, armed and straining like leashed dogs, howling and biting the rims of their shields in eagerness. There were hundreds of them, a living wall of iron and teeth.

"There can't be that many berserkers in all the world," said the bishop.

The king's voice recalled us. Olaf had found a large rock to stand on, and his booming voice carried well in the crisp air.

"We will stand in this place and let them come to us," he cried.

Aslak Askelsson, Erling's cousin, objected. "Why would they come to us when they hold the high ground?" he asked.

Olaf bristled at the question, but answered, "Because they are berserkers. Even Eyvind can't hold them forever."

"But the number of them! Berserkers are always most deadly in the first attack, and even Harald Finehair at Hafrsfjord had not so many berserkers as this!"

"I've reason to believe there are not so many as we think. Eyvind Kellda does all by tricks."

"And you're willing to bet your army on this?"

"It seems to me as sensible as attacking that force uphill. Possess your minds in patience, men, and trust your king."

So we waited.

We waited through the morning, and watched the sun move from the mountains on our left and overhead. Women from the nearby farms brought ale to refresh us. New ships with men sailed in and joined us, but I could feel the impatience growing, and many of the newly arrived lords gathered around Aslak, grumbling.

"Men from More," said Thangbrand to the bishop. "There could be trouble."

"What's this about More?" I asked.

"They've close ties to the Trondelag," said Thangbrand.

"So?"

"Why do you think Olaf celebrated Christmas at Agvaldsness this year? When he's always feasted at Nidaros before?"

"I thought he fancied a change."

Thangbrand laughed. "Things are boiling in the Trondelag. They welcomed Olaf like a good herring-year at first, but the heathens are strong there, and they've no stomach for his ways. Olaf wanted to cement his alliance to Erling in case things come to sword-points."

"Then why did he bully Erling so?"

Thangbrand shrugged. "'Tis the only way Olaf knows. He rules by strength. 'Tis as good as any other."

The day waned; the sun sank into the gray sea; the wind stiffened and we all went back to our sleeping places. Spirits drooped; there was grumbling and the skalds found a poor audience. The king drank more than usual (even for him) and went to bed early. The talk trailed off, low but surly, and we rolled up on the benches in our sleeping bags. I found it hard to sleep but managed at last, whelmed with bone-weariness and care.

I felt older than Ossian when the morning stirrings woke me. We heard mass again, but before breakfast Aslak and several of the other lords presented themselves before Olaf's high seat.

"We are leaving," said Aslak.

Olaf called for ale and swallowed a beakerful before replying.

"You were ever a skulking pup, Aslak," he said. "I always looked for treachery from you."

"I am a Norseman!" Aslak spit back, slapping his thigh. "I'm not one of your Slav thralls! I have rights! You spent your life in foreign lands, and you've no inkling what it means to be a king in Norway! Perhaps you could have been a Norse king had you been willing to learn, but you only bark orders like an overseer. You never listen! A king in Norway must listen!"

"You Norse know nothing of kingship. But I will teach you."

"You'll not live that long, Olaf Trygvesson."

"Is that a threat?"

"A prophecy. You pay heed to soothsayers. Perhaps you'd have listened to your lords if we'd torn up crows and brought you the bones to look at." Aslak turned and stalked out, and several other great men went with him. They put to sea while we ate our breakfast.

The Ghost of the God-Tree

We were a smaller force who assembled on the same hill that second morning. Again Olaf stood on his rock and harangued the troops. He was a good shouter, but I thought his heart wasn't wholly in it. The cheers from the men were tamer than the day before.

Meanwhile, the army of Eyvind Kellda, ranged on the heights, looked even larger.

And so we stood through another day. The berserkers shouted insults and obscene songs. They dropped their trousers and showed their bare arses. Our men grumbled, but Olaf held them back. A rain came that turned to snow, and we went back inside.

We ate little and drank much that night. Nobody was in a mood for songs.

And there was evening and there was morning, a second day.

The third day dawned with snow falling, but it thinned as the light rose, and we went out to our place again. Olaf gave no speech. We just stood and watched the berserkers caper. I could have sworn there were yet more of them.

Then at last, as the sun began its short drop into night, they began to advance.

"See!" cried Olaf. "They come! Now we'll have the high ground!"

But high ground seemed little comfort as we watched the gray mass of them approach through the snow. They could surround us easily and attack from all sides. I told myself over and over it must be a seeming—there were never so many berserkers alive at once. But what did I know about such things?

They sang as they came. Not one united song, of course—you'd never get berserkers to sing together—but the hundred songs they sang all at once shared a rhythm; and the discord of their noise was maddening in my ears, like the yammering of a thousand savage beasts that knew not pity.

The bishop called us churchmen away to a hillside some distance off, to watch and pray. I went reluctantly, looking often over my shoulder at Erling and his men. The king's army seemed to me like a band of children, out playing army, suddenly set upon by Assyrians. *The loneliest place in the world*, I thought.

The bishop started us a hymn, and I sang and prayed, my hands clamped together as around an axe haft.

The berserkers did not surround our force, as we'd expected. They came straight on in a mass, screaming, counting on the bone-splintering crash of their onrush. The king, seeing this, ordered his men to unlock the circular shield wall they'd made, and spread the wings out. The flankmen had barely found their new places when Eyvind's mob was on them.

I cannot tell you to this day how they stood the shock. Perhaps our prayers had something to do with it. It was a near thing for a while, but the madmen fell back at last a short distance.

They'd taken their toll though. Half the shields in Olaf's wall were smashed; men from the rear ranks were moving up everywhere to replace comrades being dragged back for tending or burying later. Steam rose all along the line as hot blood melted through the snow-carpet.

The berserk army turned and reformed itself. They were bloodied but not much winded. I could not see how the king's men could withstand them again.

Then something like a mist rose from the earth, and when it thinned—in the silver of the moonrise—we could see that, in fact, there were but a few over a hundred berserkers, less than the king's army, even without the defectors.

"Look there!" cried Olaf. "They are few! It's as I said—only a seeming!"

Then we heard the howling.

The wolves came from our rear, in full voice and at a dead run. The men on the flanks were hard put to turn themselves quickly enough to meet them, and not as well set as they'd have liked when the blow struck.

At the same moment the berserkers hit the front. There was no question of standing or fleeing—the king's army was being smashed between two hammers.

I swear I saw blood spurting two men high, and severed heads and arms flying skyward in the moonlight.

I'd never heard such screaming. Mad berserker screams; wolf howls from Hell; the angry, raging cries of men making their last stands and meaning to sell their lives dearly. 'Twas terrible. 'Twas wonderful. 'Twas very, very lonely.

Then came a new cry. A fresh, human cry. A cry that sounded, to my ears, somehow Irish; and I was not wrong, for it was the men of Lemming's new company of freedmen. Each man had an axe and a shield, and wore a leather war-shirt and a leather helmet (they could afford no better). But they came on with the rage of men fighting for their manhood; they had a thing to prove that night.

They were wonderful.

They saved Olaf and his men.

And they died each last one of them; all but Lemming.

CHAPTER XVI

It looked for a time as if Lemming might be lost too. He came away with a new set of scars for his collection—one on the face and another in the chest muscles, and one that might have bled his life out in the upper left leg. He was a full two weeks in bed—a very long time for him.

"Freedmen. Thralls with arms. And we owe our lives to them," said Bergthor to me in the hall that night. "Damned awkward place to put a man in. But a debt's a debt. It must be paid somehow."

We found Eystein and the guard bound in one of the byres. The only great harm that had been done at Sola was to the women, especially the thralls. The berserkers had used them as you'd expect. None of them actually died though, which is the best I can say about it.

Meanwhile the king nailed up the skins of a hundred shape-changers on the walls of the buildings, and built a mound of severed berserker heads near the boathouses at Somme (Astrid firmly refused to let him pile them in the steading). At their top he sat Baug Kollasson's head (Hoskuld Kollasson was not seen again in those parts). Among the many dead Eyvind Kellda was not found, which surprised no one. Olaf then sent out messengers to call a Thing.

We didn't hold it at Klepp. Olaf wanted to stay near his wounded, so he moved into our new hall and we used the Thing-meadow at Sola. Every free man was to assemble there, to swear that he'd been baptized or to receive baptism, on pain of ... well, pain. There weren't in fact many heathens left in Jaeder by then— we were one of the best-christened places in the kingdom, even before I came. But the heathens were about—many of them refugees like Asa, Ulf and Arnor. Such people might run—perhaps to Sweden— or they could face Olaf, to defy or submit.

I met with Erling in the church and said, "You cannot permit Olaf to do what he plans here."

"I gave my word," said Erling.

"Some things are worse than oath-breaking. King Herod vowed to give Salome whatever she asked; but when she asked for the head of John the Baptist, he should have said no and settled for the lesser sin."

"There's more than one way to cross a king," said Erling.

"What do you mean?"

"This is Norway. The king still rules by leave of the lords, and the lords still need the support of the bonders to hold their high seats. Let Olaf have his say at the Thing. He'll find it takes more than big words to break our traditions and undercut our rights."

That night I had another of my dreams. I thought I stood on a vast, frozen plain, white snow all around, where no horizon could be seen for the mist. A looming white shape, hardly discernible at first, heaved itself out of the cloudscape and came to me. It was the great white bear I'd seen before, with the blue eyes of a man.

In his mouth he carried two gray stone tablets, the

size of fishheads to him, but about an arm long to me. He came near (I knew better than to run, though my knees knocked together) and dropped them at my feet.

"These are the Law," he said to me, in a voice like the ocean. He gave the tablets a cuff with one paw and they marvelously whirled, stood, and came to rest standing face-to-face, heads leaning one against the other.

"Look through them," he said. "Look at me."

"You mean, between the tablets?" I asked.

"Yes."

I walked around to the other side, got down on my hands and knees and peered back through the triangle space framed by the leaning stones.

I saw the bear, but he was not the same. He'd been frightening before, but only because of his size and his—what should I call it?—his bearishness.

But this bear was a nightmare. His white fur shone bright as the sun, and just as hard to gaze on. His eyes shot red flames. His teeth were long as swords, and sharper. He reared on his hinders and slashed the air with iron claws, and the air itself seemed to scream in pain.

I was certain he must slay me and I screamed in death-horror. Yet I had no thought of running. Something within me seemed to accept that I was the bear's lawful prey, and that he could do nothing to me I'd not earned.

I rocked back on my heels and covered my eyes, where the image of the awful creature remained etched as by lightning.

"What did you see, man of Ireland?" the bear asked, and I opened my eyes and looked up to see him as he'd been before, and so I was comforted.

"'Twas you," said I. "Yet 'twas not the same. You were great and beautiful and terrible. I feared you and I loved you."

"You saw Me as I am," said the bear. "Yet you did not see Me whole. You saw only My hinder parts. Something greater remains to be seen. Now let Me show you a more excellent way to look."

He reached a paw up to his face and set the claws about his right eye. To my horror he gouged his own eye out, roaring in pain as he did so, and letting loose a gout of blood that stained his bright fur down to his feet and made a steaming pool there in the snow.

He held the eye out to me, like a blue gem. "Look again, but gaze through this."

I took it from him. 'Twas big as a kettle to me, warm and rock-hard and unworldly lovely.

I went back around, set it on the snow in front of the tablets, then hunkered down and looked again.

This time I saw a man who looked much like the Wanderer, holding children on his lap and laughing with them, while twelve scowling bearded men looked on.

"Do you know what you see now?" asked the bear.

"I think so," said I. "What does it mean?"

"It means that you must look through the Law with My eye. Too often men look through the Law alone, even to look at Me, but that way lies confusion and wickedness.

"There was a time before I gave My eye to men, when they had only the Law to see through, and they did right to follow what light they had. But cases are altered now, and a terrible judgment awaits those who will not use the light they've been offered. Remember this, son of Ireland."

And so I awoke.

The Thing began on a Thursday, as they all do, with the usual formalities that filled up the first day so that the real business didn't begin till the next morning.

Olaf took his place on another large rock (Heaven knows there are plenty of them in Jaeder) and addressed the assembly.

"If you travel the world, as I have," said Olaf, "you see many wonders. In the southern lands there are buildings—often churches—big enough to hold ten or twenty of our great halls. These buildings are made of stone and do not rot away like our wooden ones. Their roofs are tall enough to fit two of our temples underneath. And they have windows covered over in glass, not cows' afterbirth. To stand in such a building is to feel as small as a louse, and to wonder at the marvels that men can create when guided by the wisdom of God.

"To stand in such a building and be a Norseman is to know shame. I've stood in such places and feared that someone would know me for a Norseman, for we Norse raise no such buildings. We've no stonecutters like theirs. We've no painters like theirs. We've no musicians or thinkers or artisans or physicians or teachers like theirs. No, all we can do is rob those buildings, and steal the things that they have made. We are feared in the wide world, yes. But we are also despised as savages.

"I am Olaf, son of Trygve Olafsson. I am king of Norway. The holy Scriptures tell us that kings are appointed by God. I have been appointed to take away the shame of this land. That is my calling. For this I was born. For this I kept alive through kidnapping and slavery and a hundred battles. For this I am here today.

"You have heard, no doubt, that a few of my followers have turned their backs on me. You have heard that I am no longer welcome in Nidaros. So it is. I have made wrong steps as king, I will admit it. But no more.

"For too long I have been lax in following the will of God. I have permitted His enemies to live at peace in certain places. I shall do so no more. I stand before you to declare that there will be no more refuge for heathens within my realm. I demand an oath from all of you. Those who cannot swear to their christening must be baptized, or they will be put to the sword—men, women, children. This is my word. This is the king's law."

A shouting arose from the crowd, a chorus of angry words.

Helge of Klepp went forward, led by his brother, Gunnar of Hauge, a tall man much younger than he. He struck the earth twice with his staff and called for quiet.

"Olaf Trygvesson," he said, "pardon the outburst. Finish your speech, O King."

"My speech is finished," said Olaf, frowning.

"Strange. I missed the part where you ask for our advice and counsel."

Olaf crossed his arms. "Advice and counsel come not into it. I have spoken. Your hersir has agreed. It is for you to obey."

Helge shook his gray head. "'Tis terrible to be old," he said. "Your hearing dwindles; your mind plays tricks on you. I actually thought I heard you say you were above the law. I thought I heard you say you had no need of counsel from your fellow Christians. Since I know you to be a man of God, my old ears must be going the way of my eyes."

Olaf said, "Don't play at riddles with me, grandfather. The Scriptures say that the king is God's minister."

"Yes, but they do not say he can do no wrong. In fact they tell us of many kings—even good kings— who went far wrong, and were rebuked by God's prophets. Good kings should listen to those who love them enough to speak them true."

"Aye, of course! To defy me is to love me. If you slapped my face it would be more loving still. And to slay me or drive me out of the land would be the greatest love of all."

" 'Tis a perilous place to be, where you think only your will is right, and only those who flatter you are your friends."

"Speak truth, Rogalander! The fact is you westlanders have lived without true kings from time unknown. You have stiff necks and will not bow. You do not know how Christians live, and you think you can have your own kind of Christianity, different from that of civilized men. That Irish priest probably filled your head with such stuff."

"Yes, he taught us to do justice, to love mercy, to walk humbly before God. Treasonous, heretical things."

"Heresy is for the bishop to judge," said Olaf. "Bishop Sigurd! Come and teach these people!"

If he expected the grandeur of the bishop to overawe the crowd, Olaf was disappointed. Sigurd's mitre was on crooked, and he had some trouble getting up on the rock. Two of Olaf's men had to help him, and he looked unsteady when he was up.

"The Word of the Lord . . . " said the bishop, in a faltering voice; then he seemed to lose his train of thought.

"The Word of the Lord . . . " he repeated. He dropped his crosier and someone handed it back up to him.

"The Word of the Lord is wrath!" We all turned. Deacon Ketil had mounted another rock, and glared at us with the eyes of a plague angel.

"WHO DO YOU THINK YOU ARE, ROGALANDERS?" he roared.

It was so sudden and unexpected that no one made a reply. His voice was deep, thunderous, not what you'd have expected from him.

"You are barbarians!" the deacon thundered. "You are ignorant; you are backward; your speech and your table manners are uncouth! You are like children who think they can do all that their parents may, but in fact can only make messes and break things!

"You presume to counsel your king! Why would the king need your counsel? You cannot think! You do not know how to think! You have a king, and a bishop, to think for you! Your duty is to obey!"

"That is not the way of Norsemen!" cried Helge. "It is not the way of the gospel either! That way is all about power, and not Christ's way!"

"Christ's way is God's way!" shouted the deacon. "And God's way is the way of power! He is the God who smote Egypt! He is the God who smote the Canaanites! He is the God who sends fire from Heaven and a voice that no man could bear to hear!" He raised an arm and pointed skyward.

My heart stopped. The clouds were rolling in—not just from the west, as you'd have expected, but *from every direction at once*. As water swirls as it pours out a hole in a bucket, so gray-black clouds swirled above us, converging in an angry center over the Thingstead.

A voice made of thunder, a voice that shook the earth and knocked us off our feet rumbled, *"OBEY!"* and blue lightning struck the earth in our midst, deafening us and leaving a smell of burnt air behind.

The next thing I heard was someone crying, "Forgive us!"

Actually it was more than someone—it was nearly everyone. Their faces were on the ground for the most part. I saw only a few standing, or sitting, up: Deacon Ketil, Bishop Sigurd (knocked from his rock but leaning against it), Erling, Helge and the king.

I got up on my hands and knees and crawled to the bishop. He looked dazed. "This is wrong!" I cried, shaking him. *"Don't think?* That's heresy, and you know it!"

He looked at me with wide eyes, the pupils so large

that the gray could barely be seen. "The power—" he said. "The power of God—"

"Strong may be wrong! You know this! You've said it yourself, the devil can deceive us!"

He shook his head. "The power... the power..."

"Slay the heathen! Slay the heathen that we share not their fate!" The cry rose from the assembly. Who knows who said it first? Deacon Ketil, likely enough. I could see the unchristened moving apart, gathering together, raising swords and axes to defend themselves and their families.

The choice I made then took but a moment, and must have looked easy. 'Twas anything but that. In a moment I weighed the life I'd come to know, and life itself, against my troth to One whose face I'd seen but a time or two in my life. The choice was very, very hard, yet wonderfully simple.

It had, in fact, already been made, in a thousand small choices that had shaped the new course of my life. It's a falsehood to think you can practice cowardice daily, then be brave when it comes to the pinch. You do what you are—what you've let yourself become. 'Tis as simple as that, and if you think it isn't you're either a scoundrel or you've lived your life in an herb garden.

"Sanctuary!" I screamed. *"There is sanctuary in God's Church!"*

I leaped and hopped my way through the crowd, still mostly on hands and knees, and made it to the church. I put my hand on the brass ring of the door and shouted, "I cry sanctuary for all who would save their lives! Come in and take protection!"

And they came. They came at a run—most of them.

Some did not come. They looked, with yearning in their eyes, but their fear was too great. For them the church was a magic place, a haunt of spirits, a thing to fear. Even to save their lives they would not cross its threshold. They defended themselves, but could not breast the numbers set against them, driven mad by rage and fear.

Asa was one of them.

Our eyes met across the distance. I tried to shout, "I'll wed you!" but the clamor had grown too loud. While she stared at me, two men of Olaf's army seized her. I saw a bright blade raised in the air, and I screamed in horror—

And then the blade fell, loosely, spinning. The man who had lifted it fell. His companion dropped in the next moment.

And there was Ulf the Idiot, an axe in his hand, doing the simple, right thing—defending his own. Other men set on him, men of Olaf's and Erling's both, but Asa was free, and she ran.

She ran in the direction of the god-tree.

I could do nothing for her. But for the man-prey who streamed into my church, I could do my best. I closed the door after them, in the faces of the armed men who pursued them, and raised Ulf's crucifix.

"In the name of Christ, hold!" I cried, my throat ragged.

The warriors stopped, at least for a moment. Killing a priest was a tall step, even in their madness.

Thangbrand pushed his way through the press of them, a sword in his hand, and said, "Stand aside, Aillil!"

"Not for any man!"

"Then you are self-condemned, and must die."

"This is a good place to die."

"Go to Hell in your sin then!" he roared, and came at me. I stood on the spot, quaking in body but strangely at peace. It's a good feeling to come to the end of your string and know you've done better than you'd expected.

What it is, in fact, is a gift.

And then a bright figure moved between me and Thangbrand. For a moment I thought it was an angel.

It was Astrid Trygvesdatter, in her best robe of ermine.

"Come through me first, Saxon, if you'd kill my priest," she said.

Then Erling was beside her, and Ragnhild, and it was over.

I went among the wounded to the place where ugly Ulf lay. His head was sticky with blood; his shirt was bloody too. He was sweating and he shivered.

He looked up at me and said, "No need for the porridge-test with me. I'm finished."

"You've your wits back," said I.

He nodded, coughed and grimaced. "I've all my senses again, just when I could use to be rid of some."

"Do you know me, Ulf?"

"Aye. You're Father Aillil, who wouldn't christen me."

"We go back further than that, you and I."

He squinted at me. "Do we? I've no recollection."

I spoke through clenched teeth. "No doubt you took many thralls, murdered many innocents, and raped many girls."

His eyes fluttered closed a moment. "'Tis true," he said weakly. "Even among us Norse I was hardly a man of honor. I did these things to someone of yours?"

"To me as well."

He shook his head, slowly. "I see the world as if I stood in a doorway, with my nose pressed up against the frame, looking along the wall. With one eye I see inside, with the other out. Sometimes I can't believe I was ever the Viking Ulf; the next I can't believe I was ever the Christian."

"I've seen both. 'Tis true."

"Do you judge me truly a Christian, Father? Is my

christening worthy in Heaven's eyes? With my old eye I still look for Thor, but I see only Christ!"

I looked away from him, across the yard, where wounds were a-binding and bodies being dragged off. "I know not," said I. "You've never made full confession, but how could you have?"

"I can now."

"I'll get one of Olaf's priests . . . " I started to step away.

"Nay, Father! It must be you! I've wronged you— I must have your pardon!"

"'Tis enough that you ask it. God will accept that for your part. As for my part, I know not if I've pardon to give you."

"Father, take pity! Have you never done an unforgivable deed?"

My heart stopped for a long moment.

"I—" I could not get the words out. I tried again, my voice harsh as sleet. "I. Forgive. You."

I looked at Ulf and he lay with his eyes closed. I thought him dead.

But he opened them again and said, "'Tis a passing hard thing, is it not, this forgiving?"

"Hard as dying," said I.

"More than that, I think. It *is* dying, of a sort. How strange. When I believed in Thor, I dreamed of a warrior's death. Now I get my wish, not from Thor, but from the White Christ. He gives us all things richly—even that.

"I think there's a warrior's death of one sort or another for each who takes the cross and follows Him to the murder-place. Not only for men either, but for women, children, thralls."

Then he fell to coughing, and I gave him last rites. He died near morning, in great pain.

CHAPTER XVII

Asa's body was not among those taken up that evening. I can only suppose she climbed the tree and, as the Wanderer had told us, could not come back.

The matter between Olaf and Erling stood yet unsettled. When the mob was cowed, Olaf came and they faced one another, poised like fighting cocks in a pit. It might have come to battle except for the next surprise.

"*A sign from God!*" came the cry, and it was the voice of Deacon Ketil once again. "Make way! Make way!"

The crowd parted, and the deacon came on. He held Freydis Sotisdatter by the hand.

"No!" I cried. "Have pity, Your Majesty! She's but a child! She cannot help having visions!"

"I do not take your meaning," said Ketil. "I intend no harm to this child. She is a seer. She has a message for the king."

Olaf addressed Freydis. "Is this true, daughter?" he asked.

I turned to the bishop. "You can't permit this!" I said. "The girl needs to be weaned off heathenry, not confirmed in it."

"Perhaps she truly has the gift of prophecy..." he said vaguely.

"No. She does not. She's the daughter of a witch and a smith. She's told me herself she has no faith in Christ. This puts her soul, and the whole kingdom, in peril."

"But Deacon Ketil is a prophet, you see. I cannot gainsay the words of God through him."

"Has this Yorker put a bit in your mouth? You're the bishop! Who's in charge here?"

"I'm not sure anymore..." he said, and I knew I'd lost him. He wandered off in no particular direction.

I looked to find Erling, but things were already in motion.

They'd set Freydis up on Ketil's rock, where she sat much as her mother had when she'd perched on the platform at the great summer sacrifice, the last night of her life.

I could not help myself. After all I'd been through this day, I could not let the smallest one go without one last grab. I ran to her and said, "Freydis, don't do this. I swear to you there are better things in the world than vengeance. Give yourself a chance to learn them."

"Take this man away," she said, and two of Olaf's men grabbed my arms and pulled me off into the crowd. I slumped and stood where they left me. I too had a vision of the future, and I could see no way undoomed.

"This is the year," said Freydis.

"This is the year of the hundred hundreds—the year of the M. The M stands for *Miles*—the warrior."

I shuddered. Where had this child learned Latin? The other priests murmured to one another.

"In the final year of the age, when the Highest One of All stands at the threshold, every servant must work his utmost to be prepared; to have his apportioned work done. The priests and monks must fast and pray with all their strength. The common people must be diligent at mass, and in good works and obedience. And men of war must unsheath their swords, make them sharp and bear them against the heathen, bringing them to baptism by gentle means or hard."

Olaf kneeled, holding his sword like a crucifix. "This is my year," he said. "For this year I was born."

"Yes, Olaf Trygvesson," said Freydis. "For this year you were born. This is the year you will see your Lord. This is the year you will account to Him for the talents entrusted to you."

"Where shall I go?" he cried. "Whom shall I fight?"

"Go to Wendland. Make a pact with Burisleif. Other kings will join you as you cut a swath through the lands of the heathen and turn them to the truth. You will march all the way to Jerusalem and present your trophies to the Highest One when He descends in glory upon the Mount of Olives. It will be a Holy War."

"Holy War!" Olaf shouted, rising and lifting his sword to the sky.

"HOLY WAR!" shouted every warrior, and they joined him in his salute.

In that hinged moment, when all we'd built in Norway began to sag and splinter about us, all things seemed (to me) to halt in place for a few breaths. God's sky rolled up like a fine blue cloak, discovering something the color of molten bronze behind it, too huge to see.

CHAPTER XVIII

The winter that begat the Year of Our Lord 1000 was an itchy one for us at Sola. The king spent much of it just at our shoulder, across the water at Agvaldsness. His reach cramped by the loss of the Trondelag, he paid greater attention to us. In the same way the bishop and his counselors paid more attention to me. I felt like a fat man on thin ice. The baptism issue was settled, of course—all who lived were either Christians (in name at least) or in hiding. Except for Lemming, who had been in bed through the whole thing, and had for some reason been let alone.

On the other hand it was a profitable winter. As promised, Leif Eriksson sent a Greenland knarr, and Erling had walrus ivory and white bearskins, and even a white falcon or two, to sell at his new market—the word spread quickly, and Stavanger began to be known, even that first year, as a rival to Kaupang—or even Hedeby in some respects. Thorbjorg Lambisdatter was there, but Erling kept downwind of her. He and Astrid seemed better friends since the Thing, though I thought they were not yet lovers.

Olaf took blessed voyages up near Stad, where he kept ships patrolling, collecting passage tolls and effectively blocking trade meant for the Tronders. Several Trond ships were seized; a few fights were fought. There was profit in it, and it seemed to ease Olaf's spleen.

"I've begged Erling not to go with Olaf to Wendland," Astrid told me, walking with her spindle in the yard one mild, sunny winter afternoon. "He says things are bitter enough between the two of them, without him giving another offense. And of course he's right. Olaf chafes over those turncoats in the north."

"I suppose you've tried to talk Olaf over."

"Of course I've tried. Mad as he may be, my brother cannot say his sister hasn't striven to set him right. It does no good. He thinks he has a mission. Anyone who opposes it is a tool of Satan."

"Deacon Ketil might as well be bishop. Sigurd does nothing but pray and do penances."

"I think he blames himself for being too kindhearted, and so failing the king. Saints and angels! There are a hundred heresies and a thousand disputed points in the faith, and no doubt they all matter. But I'd think we could at least agree that it's right to love our neighbors."

I stopped in my tracks. "I've thought the same every day since I came to Norway. I believed I was the only one."

"We're fellow laborers, you and I," she said, smiling. "God sent us here to watch over Erling."

I looked her in the eye as I answered. "You sound almost reconciled to your marriage, and to this place."

She answered as plainly as I'd spoken. "I've long been reconciled to my marriage," she said. "No woman could ask for a better husband than Erling, were she Empress of Constantinople. And Sola is become a seat of power in Norway. But there are other . . . things to which I am not reconciled."

"You're very like your brother, you know," I said.

"What cause have I given you for insults?"

" 'Tis no insult. Olaf is a great man. He's taken a wrong turn, but he's a true king. At his best, I love him like Ireland."

Astrid turned away. "Let us speak of love," she said. "Did you love your heathen woman—what was her name—Asa?"

"Am I so easy to read?"

"You keep wandering out to Big Melhaug, the place where the god-tree's ghost used to be."

" 'Tis gone forever. And so is she."

"You'd have wed her then?"

"I think I might have, God help me. 'Twould have been unfitting for a priest, of course."

"Priests marry. Some even keep lemans. But you're Irish, aren't you? No warmth in the night for the holy men of Eire. You live on dew and air, and you've no need to sneeze or spit."

"I think I might have bent at last. Especially to save her life, had it come to that. She said she'd be christened to wed me."

"That was a great gift."

I choked back something in my throat. "A very great gift," I said. "But she's gone. 'Tis true, you see. God wills that priests should live alone."

"Withal you seem to do rather well for a celibate."

A foreigner came to Stavanger one rainy day that winter, off a knarr out of Kaupang.

I thought, *There's a foreigner,* the moment before I knew him by the stitching on his cloak as an Irishman.

Saint Bridget! I thought. *Have I come to think of the sons of Eire as an outland breed? Am I no longer Irish? If not, what am I? God knows I'm no Norseman.*

The moment he saw my crucifix and tonsure he made a line for me.

"A priest!" he cried. "Thank the saints! I heard there was an Irish priest at Stavanger, and I prayed 'twas true! 'Tis harrowing to walk through a market full of Norseman, calling out offers to pay for translation and hoping they don't just rob me—not that I'll not make a contribution to the church, Father."

"Let's get under a roof, my son, and listen to your tale in the dry."

We went to the hall where Erling kept open house, got ourselves something to drink, sat on the bench apart from the rest, and faced each other across the table.

"My name is Cullan Mal Munnu," he said. He had the look of a once-fleshy man who'd missed a lot of meals. His skin sagged and the wrinkles had sunk inward to make great valleys in the flesh under his jaw. He was pale and blue-eyed and his gray hair thin, and his hand shook, making little wavelets in the ale in his beaker.

"I am a man of Cashel. I'd hate to have it known among these foreigners, but I've a bit of the good stuff—land and cattle and slaves.

"My wife died a year since. On her last bed, she spoke of a thing we'd kept locked in our hearts for a horse's life. She begged me to do one thing for love of her, and I do it now. I may be at it for all the time the Lord pleases to give me this side of the great sleep."

He drank deeply, and swallowed as if he had to remember how.

"We had a daughter, you see. In truth we had many children, but some grew up and some died young and we can tell you where each of them is. But we fostered one of our daughters to a nunnery, and the White Foreigners attacked it and took her away with them.

"We scarcely spoke of her for years, my wife and I. I thought it best so, but perhaps 'twould have been better to bring it out into the light, rather than bury it yet living, so to speak. But I feared to open the wound in my woman's heart.

"At last as she died she begged me to sail out in the world and find our girl. I swore I would.

"I'm so afraid, Father—I'd say this to none but a priest. I know how slaves live. I know how I treat my own—especially the women. As often as not I think 'twould be better to leave her as she is, to never know and never force her to face me with it. Perhaps you think me hard."

"Not at all, my son," said I. "Believe me, I know well how you feel."

"I took one of my slaves with me to translate, a Norse lad, promising to free him when the job was done. But he slipped me in Kaupang. And here I am alone, among these foreign thieves, and I suppose one of these days I'll find my silver missing, and that will be the end of my errand."

"I'd not worry overmuch for that," said I. "Rare is the Norseman who'd simply lift your purse. He'd think that a shameful thing. He'd kill you first, then rob you."

"If I lose my purse I'd as well be dead. I could not free my daughter, should I find her, nor get home either, unless I found a kindly merchant headed for Ireland who'd take me on trust . . . I couldn't do that, though. I vowed a vow. I'll not go home without the lass. If I find her and have naught else to buy her with, I'll see if I can trade my own freedom for hers."

"Never think it. Wherever you may be in the north, if you need help, speak the name of Erling Skjalgsson, and word will come here. I'll see you helped, if I live."

"My thanks for that, and a blessing on you, Father. But for now I have my purse, and you to change words for me. To whom should we go first, do you think, to ask about a slave girl named Deirdre?"

My heart leaped at the words. Of course Deirdre is a common enough name among Irishwomen...

"This Deirdre, your daughter," I asked, "What color hair had she? What color eyes?"

"She was like her mother, God rest her. Hair like ripe flax, eyes blue as Lough Derg on a fair day."

"I know such a lass, and her name is Deirdre," I said carefully. "She's about twenty years old—she's not certain exactly."

His eyes stared wide, with white all around the blue. "Does she speak of her home?" he asked. "Does she remember places, or names?"

"No. She was taken young, and has but scattered memories."

Tears welled in the eyes. "Please Jesu, it could be her. She's here, a slave in this place?"

"Not a slave, or not anymore. She married a man— a good man and Irish, who was slain, and my lord Erling gave her her freedom, and her babe's, as payment for blood."

"A babe? My grandchild? A boy, is it, or a girl?"

"A girl, and a fair child. Deirdre is to be wed again, I should tell you."

"To another Irishman?"

"No, a Norseman. A man of respect hereabouts, and part Cornish, he tells me, if that softens the blow any."

"Well, we'll see about that. First I must look on this lass. Perhaps 'tis not she after all. I dare not hope too much."

I called for ponies then and there, and we set out in the rain southwest for Sola. Where Eystein was, there would Deirdre be too, and it was Eystein's duty, as always, to look to the defense of Sola, and keep the watches on the coast.

It was evening when we arrived, and I said, " 'Tis suppertime now, and Deirdre will be in the old hall."

"Serving food, I suppose," said Cullan darkly.

The Ghost of the God-Tree

"Not at all, she'll be sitting with Eystein. They're very devoted, Eystein and Deirdre."

I led him inside, through the entryway and into the dimness and smoke. I took his hand (it trembled like a bride's) and brought him to the place, to the left of Erling's high seat, where Eystein sat. He and Deirdre had their heads together, both holding a single ale-horn, and they laughed.

"Deirdre!" came the voice of my companion.

I turned to look at him, and then back at Deirdre. Looking in those mirrored eyes, there could be no question of the thing at all.

"F-father?" said Deirdre. The white of her eyes had bled out to paint her face.

She fairly leaped over the table and into her father's arms.

There are too few times like that in this world. I think we can get no closer glimpse of Heaven this side of the River than in such reunions, unless we're great saints indeed. And yet even then we have the world too much with us, as the issue well showed.

Cullan's first misstep was to bid Eystein money. Somehow he'd the idea in his head, and could not alter it, that Eystein was Deirdre's owner; and that a Norseman would sell anything for the right price. You don't talk that way to free men in Norway.

I tried my best to soften it as I translated between them, but there was no way to soften the scorn in Cullan's face, or the insult at the heart of his offer.

If Deirdre and I hadn't stepped between them, the tale might have ended there and then, with an Irish funeral.

Cullan then turned to Deirdre. "My daughter," he said, in Irish that Eystein could not follow, "it wrings my heart to know you've lived your years a despised slave among these heathen. You were not born for such. We've a fine farm at home, and horses and cattle and swine and slaves. I've dresses of fine linen and wool for you, and jewelry of silver and gold and amber. At home you'll not be ordered about by unbelievers—you will give orders, and they will be obeyed. And you will have the honor and love of kinfolk who care for you. Turn your back on this pigsty, and this dark-faced barbarian, and come with me back to your own people."

Deirdre covered her face with her hands and fell to her knees, sobbing.

Cullan's face softened. "Perhaps I say too much, sweeting. I've had a picture in my head all these years of you living as a slave. 'Tis strange to me to find you otherwise, and I find the idea harder to hold than water in one hand.

"You must have time to think about all this. 'Tis hard to change all your life in a day. Take the time you need. I'll go nowhere without you."

He reached out a tender, shaking hand to touch her hair, the long hair of a free woman.

"No need to wait," said Deirdre, with a hiccup in her voice.

"What do mean?" asked Cullan.

"I cannot go with you, Father."

"Surely these years cannot have driven you mad? Is she mad, Father?" he asked, turning to me.

"Let her speak," said I.

"What would you do with a daughter who lost her virginity very young?" she asked, still on her knees, looking up, her face wet, smoke ash making streaks under her eyes.

"I—I'd have the rapist killed and I'd find a good nunnery for the girl."

"That girl is I, Father. And the man who raped me is long dead. There'd be no honor and home life for me, Papa. Only the nunnery, and for one who has no call to it, that might as well be slavery."

"But you'd be with your people at least!"

"Eystein is my people—and my child, and the children I shall bear him hereafter. I'd be a shamed outsider in Cashel, Father. Here I'll be the wife of Erling's chief warden, and if I lack honor as a freedwoman, I'd at least have his love, which is no small thing. Such love I'd never find in Ireland."

"I came far for you, my daughter!"

"And the saints bless you for it, Father, and Mother for sending you! 'Tis more than gold to me to know you'd do so much for my sake.

"But life is what it is, not what we'd wish it to be. The life that was taken from me slipped past my reach long since. I've found another now. I'll not break my word to Eystein and turn my back on it."

Cullan shook his head, as if he had water in his ears. "Very sudden this is," he said. "I must give you time to think."

"Time I thank you for, that we may know each other and that you may know your grandchild. But for the rest there can be no question.

"I love Eystein, Father. I love him even more than I loved my Patrick, and I thought there'd never been such love since the Age of Heroes. You've no coin in your purse to outbid love, Papa."

And it was as she said.

CHAPTER XIX

It was a great fleet that assembled in Hafrsfjord for the Wendland adventure in the spring. Ships gathered from all the west, for Olaf yet had friends. Among them was Einar Eindridisson, just a boy then—blond and pink-skinned and rather overpretty; showing no sign of the great belly that would give him a nickname one day. He was but seventeen then, and I wouldn't mention him except for the role he came to play later in our lives. He flirted with Thorliv a bit, but naught came of it.

The fact was, he wasn't up to Erling's standards for a brother-in-law. Hardly anyone in our company was. Most of our force were next thing to exiles—younger sons with nothing to lose and Vikings with a taste for risks and high profits.

But that didn't stop Erling from making alliances. He'd thought over Sigrid's offer to wed Sigurd the hostage, and quickly decided in-laws in the north would be useful. So before embarking we celebrated their wedding at Sola. 'Twas a fine business, with feasting in both halls and brawling and rich gifts for small and great. But the honeymoon was short, for Sigurd would come along to Wendland.

It was in fact a double wedding. We played host as well to the union of Olaf and Astrid's sister Ingebjorg to Jarl Ragnvald of Gotland in Sweden. Afterwards they sailed back to Ragnvald's lands on a Christianizing mission. I thought Ragnvald and his ships might have stayed to join our expedition, but kept the thought to myself. Olaf had always treated Ingebjorg more as a pampered daughter than a sister, and I think he may have been eager to get her out of harm's way in case he should pass from the landscape. Thyri had borne him a son that winter, but the child died after a few days.

This Wendland voyage wasn't a king's venture. It was a desperate, double-or-nothing gamble by a prince whose high seat was rotting beneath him. Who would defend Olaf's interests with so many of his followers out of the land, you ask? Nobody. If Olaf failed in the Baltic, he would never return.

We trooped down to the jetty all together on the last morning, the crews of *Fishhawk* and Olaf's *Long Serpent*. I slipped on the gangplank while boarding (not for the first or last time) and fell between the ship and the jetty in the very moment when she was bobbing out from her mooring. The next moment she'd jerked the end of her tether and was coming back to crush me. I've seen men come out of such vises limp and boneless as jellyfish.

Suddenly the ship checked, and I looked up to see Olaf Trygvesson stretched between jetty and gunwale, holding the great hulk of the thing off with his own tremendous strength. Others joined him quickly, and strong hands pulled me safely up and set me aboard. I cried my thanks to the king, thinking again what a great man he was at his best.

'Twas a grand site to see all those ships—great longships and smaller longships, even lesser craft manned by musters from small farming districts still loyal to Olaf, working their way by braced sail- and oar-power out of Hafrsfjord, then shifting their sails to catch the north-northeast wind that would take us south along the North Way. We in *Fishhawk* were up in the van, sailing just aft of Olaf's *Long Serpent*. They called her the biggest longship ever built, and I could well believe it. I myself thought her a work of overweening pride, and frankly we had to reef our sail to keep from outrunning her. But she was a remarkable piece of work, and I've never seen better carving and paintwork on a vessel (I understand the artisan who did that work had an Irish grandfather).

Our fair beginning did not last. We waited two full weeks at Lindesness for a decent wind for the Baltic. The weather turned dirty; we spent days and nights huddled under our woolen awning tents; and you don't know me yet if you haven't guessed I was sicker than a pregnant bride.

But we got a less-than-hateful wind at last and turned our noses eastward. The skies persisted overcast, but we sailed near enough shore to navigate by landmarks, so we made our slow way, tacking as often as not.

We took the Oresund entrance to the Baltic, the same way Erling had come out on my first voyage with him. The Oresund is not a nice way to go—the currents fight you (and jostle the ship underneath more than I care for), and the road is infested with Vikings, though we'd no fear of them as long as we stayed together. I believe a few of the smaller craft that straggled were lost to pirates, but you expect that sort of thing.

We could have taken the Big or Little Belts, but we'd have had to pay tolls to Svein of Denmark if he'd let us through at all, which wouldn't have been likely.

The placid Baltic is something of a relief after the

The Ghost of the God-Tree

North Sea, and I was grateful for it, though the winds continued fitful and often contrary. I couldn't help expecting to see my sister Maeve somewhere, for it was on Gotland Island I'd seen her last; but of course she could be anywhere in God's world by now.

I stood at the rail one day when the wind was good and we were making some progress, and Erling came up beside me.

"Have you noticed aught uncanny about this voyage?" he asked me.

"No. Nothing at all. The weather stinks, but no more than custom."

"It seems to me that's in itself uncanny."

I thought about it. "You mean we've seen no sign of Eyvind Kellda or his witchery."

"Just so."

I rubbed my chin. "A roaring sort of silence, that."

"So it seems to me."

"What are we doing here?"

Erling lowered his voice so I could barely hear him above the sound of water and the creak of rigging. "I know why I'm here. I'm here because Olaf is my brother-in-law and my king, and it's now he needs a kinsman as never before. But why are you here? Not for your love of sailing, I'll warrant."

"I'm here because I don't wish to be here. I follow the Beloved, and he takes the hard, narrow, dangerous road always."

I did not tell him the further reason—I could not under the seal of the confessional. Astrid had asked me to go and keep an eye on him.

"I'm glad of your company, Father. I expect I'll thank God for your presence in the end, as I have before."

Erling went away then, and I prayed for him, and the king, and the lot of us.

At last we reached our goal—the coast of Wendland. The Norsemen gathered at the rail and discussed the landscape in loud, excited tones. It was the kind of country that always delights Norsemen—flat as old beer, whether in forests or fields.

A Norseman's idea of heaven is flat country as far as he can see. Give him a few acres of even, stone-free earth, and he thinks himself Holy Roman Emperor.

Look at what happened in England. Alfred granted the Danes the Danelaw. They settled down to plow and plant and make little squareheads, and before you knew it they were the dullest folk in England (which is saying a great deal).

Olaf's emissaries had arranged a meeting with Burisleif at Jomne, on Wollin Island. This was the home of the renowned Jomsvikings, whose head was a famous Dane called Jarl Sigvald, and a place where Viking and Slav rubbed shoulders as a matter of course.

Jomne is set on a ridge of high ground between a mireland and a riverbank. Local pilots took us through reedy shallows to the piers. Jarl Sigvald met us there—a tall, paunchy yellow-headed man with pink cheeks and bright eyes and a remarkably ugly nose—long and crooked and swollen red. To my credit I took an instant dislike to him. He seemed to me one of those smiling, open-faced scoundrels who'd knife you in the back for your shoelaces. Perhaps I just misliked his face and his clothing. He was dressed as the perfect East Viking, in fur hat and yellow silk shirt and wide, bloused breeches above soft leather boots, jangling with jewelry everywhere. He also sported many tattoos. He reminded me of slave traders I'd seen in Visby when I'd been merchandise. I'd been inclined against East Vikings ever since.

He led us through the streets of the town, all laid out in perfectly square blocks with a precision I found oppressive. In contrast to the orderly design, the buildings themselves wanted paint and showed rot at the foundations. Jomne looked badly fallen from a high discipline.

The reason was not far to seek. All around were armed men, the famous Jomsvikings who'd made themselves legends in the world and come near conquering Norway at Hjorungavaag in Jarl Haakon's time. Their courage in facing the headsman's axe, and the pardon that spared them following Vagn Buesson's act of heroism, was still sung in every hall from Greenland to Constantinople.

Could these men we saw be the same Jomsvikings? Fat for the most part, filthy, weighed down with baubles, stumbling with drink—and old. The brotherhood that had once drawn bold youths from all the north was now, it seemed, a place for old men to hole up and drink to their past deeds until they drank themselves to death.

Old Bergthor, who walked near me, said, "All these Slavs are thralls!"

Steinulf said, "No, the custom is different here than in Norway. Slav men wear their hair short, or they shave it altogether."

Bergthor humphed. "Well, I call it unmanly."

They brought us to a lofty old hall with a shingle roof in need of work, where we were met by a smiling young man dressed in Slav style (his head was shaved, all but a braid hanging down on one side). He directed a woman to bring Olaf a welcoming ale-horn.

"I thank you, sir," said Olaf after the speech that followed, "but where is King Burisleif? I knew him in my Russian days, and you are not he."

"Very true," said the young man. "I am Mistislav, duke and cousin to King Boleslav." (That was how he said the name.) "My royal cousin begs your pardon that he cannot be here to greet you in person, but he is much occupied with urgent matters for the moment. He has a meeting with the Emperor Henry this year to prepare for. But he promises to make haste to join you before many days. Until that time, accept his hospitality. If you lack anything, he will hold me answerable, so do not hesitate to make your needs known."

Then began a time. We went into the hall, freshly painted within, the floor strewn with fir boughs, the walls hung with ancient rusting shields and banners—trophies of the Jomsvikings in their glory days. Burisleif (or Boleslav) had not stinted on his duties as a host. There was plenty of food—much of it strange, but tasty and plentiful. And the ale and mead never stopped, and the serving wenches were not shy. All in all, it put one in mind of the old Norsemen's Valhalla.

And once that thought entered my head, it would not go away. My thirst dried up and my hunger withered, and when I lay on my back with the whole sodden company in the night, listening to the couples panting in the shadows, I turned it over and over in my mind.

At last I went to the bishop, who'd found himself a hermitage of sorts, a half-ruined fisherman's shed near the quay. I came one morning, without eating breakfast, and found him on his knees facing the sun through the unhinged door.

He looked at me with those dying-man's eyes of his. He was thin as a shadow, and his hair clean white. His tonsure needed renewing and his cheeks shaving, things I'd never known him to neglect before.

"Father, this thing is not of God," said I.

"Go back to the hall, Aillil my son. Go back and enjoy the good things of this world. Lie with a woman. Perhaps it will make you less a prig."

"Begging your pardon, Father, but that's rare counsel from a priest who starves himself and lies alone."

"I've a penance to make."

"And who's set this penance on you? Who is your confessor, Father? Or have you laid it on yourself, set adrift without a polestar on the sea of your own pride?"

"I have failed my king! Had I been harder, less easy-handed with the heathen, his throne might have been established forever."

"The men who turned on Olaf were mostly Christians already," said I. " 'Tis not about the Faith—nor the forswearings in the north, nor this errand of ours. 'Tis about how Christians will live together in the land. We can build on rock or on sand, my lord, and I fear our house is falling."

"Aillil of Ireland. Always so sure of God's ways. 'Tis simple, when you're priest of one church, to see the world all black and white. You do not see the greater matters, the good of all the land."

"Is this not what faith is—to obey when obedience makes no sense to you? If a man tries to save his life in all his choices, he loses his soul—so says the Word. Why should it be different for kingdoms? Is this what it means to be a king, and a bishop—to be a coward and choose the broad way that leads to destruction?"

There was a movement in the shadows, and Deacon Ketil of York stepped into the light. "You ask who is the bishop's confessor," said he. "I have that honor. It is for me to tell him his sins, and to decide his penances."

"Who are you?" I asked. "Are you man or are you devil?"

He looked at me fair with those gray eyes, and for one moment I thought I knew him from some other place, some other time. But I could not name him. I shivered.

"You bring great men to destruction," said I.

"Kings are made for glory, not for long life," said he.

"That's a noble saying," I answered, "but as pagan as horsemeat pie. I've one from the Scripture—'He who would be greatest of all, let him be least of all and servant of all.' "

"Do you speak thus to your bishop?"

"No. I speak thus to you. What learning have you, Brother Ketil? What skill in God's arts brought you to this power you wield? Recite for me the Athanasian Creed if you can."

"Enough, Aillil," said the bishop. "Go back to the feast. Sit by your lord. Leave great matters to your betters."

The bishop's word is the bishop's word. I went from there, sick at heart, and for once drank with a mind set on the waking slumber, the gray and purple land of forgetting. I woke next morning with a hundred razor-sharp needles driven red-hot into my skull, so that whichever way I leaned my brain pressed on their points. I drank to ease the pain, and so it went for many days.

"How many days has it been?" came the cry one morning. I think 'twas morning, but 'twas nearing noon, and we all lay, as had become our custom, in our piss and vomit in the straw on the benches, trying to raise the courage to sit up and face the drudgery of another day of pleasure.

"How many days has it been?" Olaf shouted again, sending red-hot coals down our ears to sizzle behind our eyes. "We came to do God's work, and all we do is feast! The summer passes—the Lord returns any day, and we've not made war for Him!" He reached a long arm from his high seat and grabbed a thrall by the shirt, lifting him bodily onto the bench. "Bring Mist—Misty—bring that fellow from Burisleif, the one who greeted us here. I want to speak to him."

Olaf refreshed himself with his morning draught (no drink seemed to affect him until well along in the night), and shortly the young Wend came in the door, looking fresh and bird-hued as always. He asked how he could be of service.

"Where's Burisleif?" Olaf asked, unsmiling. "I've lost count of the days, and still he tarries."

Mistislav smiled and stretched his hands out. "What can I tell my lord?" he said. "King Boleslav has many matters to attend to, as so great a man as you can easily understand. His heart is sick that he is forced, against his will, to neglect his brother Olaf, but he assures me that he is doing his utmost to come to you as soon as humanly possible."

"Perhaps I've not made myself clear," Olaf returned. "We are here on a mission from God. We have been sent to prepare the way for the return of our Lord; to cut a swathe from the Baltic to Jerusalem, converting Slav and Arab and Syrian and Jew, and so meet Him with worthy prizes when He sets His foot down on the Mount of Olives!"

"And a glorious plan it is; well worthy of so noble a king, as I have heard my lord say many times. But men must build up their strength before such ambitious tasks, and it is my lord's wish that you accept his bounty and make yourselves strong before he joins you in your march."

Olaf stood crookedly, leaning with one hand on the high seat's arm. "Do you know what I believe?" he asked. "I believe your lord Burisleif has no mind to join my march. I think he thinks my army a danger to his lands and his plans, and he's keeping us here under his eye, hoping we'll lose heart with waiting and go home."

"Your Majesty, I assure—"

"I knew men like you in Novgorod, and I knew them in England. The king keeps you at his hand to tell lies in his name, and if the lie be caught he can say he knew naught of it. I may be nothing more than a sea king today, and a drunken one at that, but I'm not a total fool."

"King Olaf is great and wise, famed throughout—"

"Get this man out of here before I hang him up

on the wall with the armor. Sigurd! Erling! Bjorn! Ulf! Come to me. We must plan our campaign on our own, if we're to get no help from Burisleif. And you, Sigvald!"

Jarl Sigvald the Jomsviking stood and said, "Aye, my lord!" His nose was even redder than usual.

"Are you with us or not?" Olaf asked him. "Are you here to help me in my mission, or to be a spy and toady for Burisleif?"

"When I hear the king speak of this great adventure, my heart skips in my chest, and I feel myself a young man again. I've three ships which I am honored to place in your service, and young Jomsvikings to man them. Not true Norsemen, I'll grant, these recruits—mostly Slavs or half-bloods, but brave and handy, and eager to make their names as fighting men."

"Then join us here by the high seat, and we shall make our plans. Men! Drink no more ale than you need to kill your hangovers, and get some food in your bellies. Today we drill with weapons. We've been idle too long."

The men rose, groaning quietly, and I don't think many marked the quiet call of Queen Thyri from the women's bench—"But what about my Wendish lands?"

To say Olaf and his captains planned a campaign is perhaps to hang a long name on a short pup. As a former officer of Valdemar the Russian, Olaf must have had some sense of the distances and obstacles involved, but he spoke of turning westward and subduing the Liutzians across the river (his first step) as if it were a summer stream crossing. The balance of his strategy was to move ever southward, stealing horses, living off plunder, and baptizing all and sundry as he went. The newly baptized would, of course, joyfully join his army, and so we would grow as we went, like a snowball rolling downhill, and sweep all before us.

We pressed pilots into service, boarded our ships and crossed the Odra river, going some ways south, on a Monday in July. It was but a short crossing, hardly time enough for me to get sick, and as we disembarked I went with Erling to the quay, where Olaf listened as Jarl Sigvald argued loudly with the Norse captains.

" 'Tis madness!" said Red Ulf, Olaf's burly forecastleman. "To burn our fleet would be like dumping silver into the sea, and there's no need for it!"

"But think what a gesture it would make!" cried Sigvald. "Men would watch the smoke rise, and they'd ask, 'What does this mean?' and the answer would be, 'This is Olaf Trygvesson of Norway, burning his ships in the Odra to show that he has vowed to fight his way to Jerusalem, and means to finish the march or die, like Lot never turning back.' "

"It sounds well," said Olaf, scratching his beard, "and since the Lord is returning I suppose we'll not need the ships again...."

"My lord," said Erling. "I think this march is gesture enough. 'Twould be a sin to burn the *Long Serpent* without cause."

Olaf turned and gazed at his gilded longship. "Perhaps 'tis weakness in me," he said, "but I love a good ship better than a fine statement. Let the seahorses live for now."

I could see Erling relax then. He'd have done much to defend *Fishhawk*, and he was glad it hadn't come to that. But it made an ill beginning to an ill adventure.

I don't know what I expected. I suppose I'd some idea that warfare in God's name would be different from the common kind. Perhaps I expected our swords to turn into flower garlands whose fragrance would turn wicked hearts to virtue.

The Liutzians are a warlike folk, and oddly enough that worked to Olaf's advantage. He sent out scouts the next morning across the grassy, rolling country to find a likely target, and the men returned that evening to say that there was a fortress not far off being attacked by an army.

We made our own attack at sunrise the next day, just as the Slavs broke through the fortress gates. I watched our assault from a high place, with the bishop and Deacon Ketil and Thangbrand and that sainted crew. Loud were our prayers and we were wet with holy water and fragrant with incense as the bishop said a mass for victory, but my thoughts were undevotional. The fortress was a round wooden stockade with a dry moat about it. All the Liutzians, foes a moment before, fled inside. They made a good defense from the walls, doing real murder with their arrows, but they had no proper gate. Our men dashed forward and picked up the attackers' battering ram. They lifted it, warded by other men upholding a roof of shields, and plowed through the defenders at the breach like a spear through a deer's belly.

I heard the screams of women and children. I heard the cries of brave men in gut-agony. I saw the fortress and all the houses set afire, and livestock and bound captives led out into the open. We went down to them and they were made to kneel as the bishop preached a sermon, translated by Jarl Sigvald.

If we expected the people to quickly embrace the Faith following our blazing show of Christian zeal, we were disappointed. The people knelt, weeping or groaning or just sullen, and none showed any sign of repentance and faith (I wondered how well Sigvald translated the bishop's words, but I'd no way of knowing).

After a moment of awkward quiet, Deacon Ketil stepped forward and whispered in the bishop's ear.

The bishop raised his voice again. "Make it clear!" he shouted. "Make it clear that if they are not baptized now, they will be put to the sword—men, women and children!"

Jarl Sigvald shouted something.

The people only looked at one another.

"This is the last offer!" cried the bishop. "Choose now! Choose you this day! Baptism or the sword! This is the will of God, and of King Olaf of Norway!"

More blank looks. I thought then and think now, if Sigvald had translated cleanly they'd have at least shown some fear. Instead they only looked fuddled.

Then someone—I think it was Sigvald, or perhaps Ketil, roared, *"In the name of Heaven!"*

This was the signal set earlier—the signal to carry out holy justice.

I could not help myself. I left the company of priests and ran to the two nearest children I could see, and I covered them with my body.

I waited for the butchery to begin, for the screams and the sounds of steel cleaving flesh and bone. I prayed God to set Himself between Olaf and these people, by some miracle.

And the miracle came. Instead of hacking and screams I heard voices raised in anger, and all in the Norse tongue. I looked cautiously up.

I saw Erling Skjalgsson and his men ranged to face the king's army, blocking its advance. Olaf was roaring at Erling. "Why do you bar our way?" he demanded.

"I did not come to Wendland for such work. If I wanted to butcher something, I'd stay home and kill sheep."

"It is God's will!" Olaf called.

"No, it is not!" I screamed, rushing forward through the people and thrusting myself between the armies, shouting so I sprayed the king's face with my spittle. "This is the bloody will of Hell! This is such work as Odin would do—no! Odin's followers would kill their foemen and sell the living for silver, but they'd never butcher a whole town in the names of their demon-gods!"

"This is a day of victory for the Lord," shouted Olaf, "and triumph for a Christian king, and you blaspheme it! I've borne with you long enough, Irish hedge-priest! Sigurd, take this person away and put him to the sword!"

"You're no Christian king!" I shouted back. "You're a Viking from crown to footsoles! Baptizing a devil only makes him twice the devil he was before!"

Two Sigurds stepped forward, unsure, I suppose, which of them the king wanted. One was Sigurd Eriksson of Opprostad, looking unhappy about the whole business. The other was Bishop Sigurd, who was not properly a man for the king to order about, but he'd taken up thralls' ways.

The bishop approached me with his arms spread wide, his crosier in one hand. "Aillil. Erling," he said. "Surely you can see that these are matters too great for lone men's consciences. The Lord Jehovah, the Lord Sabaoth of the great armies—"

"Is the Lord Jesus Christ," said I. "I cannot answer for what was done in olden times. But I know what the Lord Christ requires."

The bishop gulped once or twice, as if struggling for air, and Deacon Ketil came to his side.

"Arrogant puppy!" the deacon shouted. His mouth gaped wide and his eyes were red. "You think God has spoken only to you—that your way alone is right!

"Do you not see that this is a spiritual battle? All these people, this town, this world are only a shadow, covering the true reality of the spirit world! If you care so much for these heathens, you may baptize them before we slay them, and so their souls—the only real part of them—will be saved and enjoy eternal bliss! Is it not you who says so often that Christ is found in the place of pain? Their pain will be short and fleeting, their happiness eternal! Repent, and learn the true charity of Heaven!"

"Heresy!" I shouted back. "Damned, Manichaen heresy! Bishop Sigurd—I appeal to you! Is it not heresy to say that the world of matter is an illusion? If that were so, then our Lord's birth, death and resurrection in the flesh were all illusions! I may be no theologian, but even I know this!"

The bishop gulped some more and looked back and forth between us a moment. He deemed Ketil a prophet and feared to defy him, but the Faith is the Faith, and he was not a man to deny it.

"Aillil has a point, my son," he said to Ketil. "Surely you don't mean—"

"You quench the Spirit with this quibbling!" cried Ketil. "The written word kills! The Spirit gives life! We must not be bound by outgrown laws! This is a new millennium, and God is moving in a new way! All who cling to their footling rules will be left behind while the Elect march on to meet the Bridegroom at His return!

"The day of thought is past! Now is the time for feeling and action! I speak in the name of the Lord— listen to your hearts! Your hearts will always tell you what is right! Listen now, men of the north! Listen to what your hearts say!"

And suddenly a silence fell—a weird, expectant silence, like a house swept and garnished, awaiting some tenant who could be named only in whispers.

And a whisper came—a humming in my head that sounded like the voice of Freydis Sotisdatter, hardly noticed at first but rising and pounding so loudly at last in my temples that I thought my skull would split. I did not guess that every other man heard the same, until their chanting grew loud enough to overcow the inner voice—and they chanted just the thing I was hearing.

"Words are a poison, deadly and flawed;
Feelings a strong ale, brewed up by God.

Old things are broken; scrap for the fire;
New things a promise; sating desire.
Bodies are night-dreams, gone with the morn;
Spirits are godheads, ever-reborn."

I shivered to hear it—a song unlearned, sung in perfect unison by two thousand men. I shivered even more when I realized I too sang.

We sang it louder a second time, and louder still a third. The men drew their swords and axes and began to beat on their shields in cadence. I had no weapon, but found myself clapping my hands with them. Images rose in my mind—images of old hurts unhealed, old slights and insults unavenged; somehow it seemed very clear that all these things were the fruit of heathendom, and heathendom must be plucked from the earth like a thistle.

Yet all the while some part of me watched this rising with alarm. 'Twas not right. 'Twas not what I thought or believed. Yet did I have the strength of mind to breast such a storm-surf of passion?

Out of habit I reached for Enda's crucifix. As I touched the one that was there, I remembered that Enda's was gone, and this was only crackbrain-Ulf's.

Yet my mind came clear that very moment. I remembered who I was, and I remembered what I was about.

I must speak to the bishop, I thought, and I began to move to him where he stood, a little back and to one side of Ketil. Ketil stood with arms raised and face turned to Heaven, his entire body thrilling.

I suppose I was the only one who saw Bishop Sigurd raise his crosier and brain Ketil with it.

As Ketil fell, the head-song ceased. The army went silent. Once again the birds sang, once again the insects chirped; once again the fearful wails of our prisoners could be heard.

Bishop Sigurd looked at me as if to say, *I beg your*

pardon. "'Twas heresy, just as you said," he told me. "A pity. A great pity. And now I am become a manslayer."

"I'm not certain of that," said I, looking at Ketil's whitening face, yet turned skyward as he lay in an ever-broadening pool of blood, one eye opened and the other shut. "You thought the Wanderer at Agvaldsness was Odin. He was not. But Ketil—I think Ketil might have been. Odin was ever a raiser of madness."

"Perhaps. If not Odin, some other demon, I suppose. A great loss. He was a most excellent clerk."

"*Roast you, Erling Skjalgsson!*" The voice roared and turned us. It was King Olaf.

"I did not deceive you," said Erling. "Spare your anger for those who led you on miry paths."

"I wagered my all on a single roll of the dice!" cried Olaf. "I'd rather have died on my quest than be shown up a dupe and shamed before what remains of my kingdom! Better to follow a lie to a brave man's death than be left with nothing!"

"Come back with me to Sola," said Erling. "We'll rebuild the kingdom from there. Together we can do it, and make it stronger than before."

"Get out of my sight! Tell my bitch sister she's gotten her wish—I've been shamed and made to kneel in the dust! That will please her! I'll make my own plans for the days to come, and they'll not include you, betrayer!"

He turned and spoke to his commanders, and before long his army was trooping back in the direction of their ships, to row for Jomne. Sigurd Eriksson risked one last, troubled look behind him as he went. I saw Lemming, a head above the other men, looking back at us, while Freydis tugged at his hand to bring him after the king. He stopped and looked back and away, then scooped Freydis up and brought her back to us. It was the firmest I'd ever seen him be with her.

Bishop Sigurd stood a long while watching the army go, then turned to follow them, using his crosier like a staff.

"Stay, Father!" I cried to him. "Olaf will blame you as well! Come back to Sola with us!"

The bishop smiled crookedly, like a man elf-shot. "I am his bishop and confessor," he said. "He needs me now as never before. In time he'll come to his senses, and then he'll need me yet more—if I am alive on that day."

And so he followed his flock.

We set about unbinding the captives and setting them free, then retired to our own vessels with a willing Liutzian pilot to take us away.

CHAPTER XX

We oared up the river and out into the Baltic, catching ere long a usable wind and westing. It was coming onto autumn. The geese made slow arrowheads over us, honking at the injustice of it all.

I'd never seen Erling so fretted. His gaze turned again and again back to the Wendish shore. I spent much time at his side, saying naught.

That first day he hammered the rail with his fist and said, "I must go back. I owe it to my king to try and turn him."

"'Twill do no good," said I.

"Yet I must. 'Tis Olaf. What will we do without Olaf? We nearly had it built, Father—a new Norway with Christian laws and Norsemen's rights as well. I fear there'll never be such a chance again."

He paused a moment, then said, softly so no one else could hear, "He called me betrayer. Could it be thus I'll be remembered when I die? As a man who turned his back on his lord in his hour of need?"

"Never," said I. "Not you."

Just then the lookout up on the sail-yard shouted, "A ship!"

We turned to see it approach. 'Twas a black ship with a wolf's-head at the stem and a blood-red sail. The moment I saw it, a chill trickled down my backbone.

"She comes on at full sail, from downwind!" said Erling. "It's not possible!"

The wolf-ship made an elegant arc, circling us widdershins, sail bellied out all the way; never once tacking. It cut us out of our fleet as a wolf cuts a fawn from a herd of deer, and our other ships did not—or could not—defend us.

"No one can have the wind at all points," said Erling.

"One can," said I.

I'd caught sight of a pale face, staring at us over the ship's rail. It smiled a wide, death's-head smile.

Eyvind Kellda. Eyvind Kellda alone in an uncrewed ship, driven by a wind of his own making.

"We must follow him," said Erling.

"No!" said I.

He turned to me with a question in his eyes.

"He *wants* us to follow him!" I answered. "Isn't that plain? He dangles himself as bait in our faces. What else can he mean but to lure us into some trap?"

"Or away from Olaf!" Erling cried, slapping his thigh. "Of course! Olaf must be in danger, and Eyvind would prevent me returning to aid him! Steersman!" he roared. "Come about! Turn her now!"

"That'll take us straight into the wind!" the steersman answered.

"Then we'll row for the Odra! Down sail! Smartly now! We've no time to lose!"

The crewmen loosed the backstay and dropped the sail, furling it with practiced hands, swinging the yard around and stowing it in its crutches. Our other ships saw the action and did the same. To no avail.

The more the steersmen brought our ships around,

the harder blew the wind out of the east, shouldering us in Eyvind's wake in spite of ourselves, heeling us over on the broadside before we finally came about. I'm a little sketchy on the details, as I was trying to throw up over the side without being pitched overboard.

"Out oars!" Erling shouted. "Row us back to Wendland, lads!"

The first shift sprang to the trees and seized their oars, ran them out through the holes and began their song, pulling with all their might, muscles straining, faces red.

It did no good. We drifted yet westward, along with our sister ships, less swift than we.

Our second shift of rowers joined the others on the sea chests, adding their strength to the pulling force.

Oars snapped. Rowers got scourged by the lashing pine slivers. But even then we made no headway. We blew ever westward, in train with that black-and-red hell-ship.

"Ship your oars, men," Erling called at last. "There's no good in it."

So we sailed day and night after Eyvind, like hounds after a bitch in heat—out through the Oresund, past the Kattegat, into the open sea.

Only then did our following wind slacken and turn northerly, and we lost our headway. Eyvind's black ship pulled away from us, heading north along the coast, fanned by its own pet breeze.

"We can go back to Olaf now," said Erling.

"We can. 'Twill do no good," said I.

"How do you know?"

"Whatever was doing is done, else Eyvind would not have left us. He's finished his business; now he's making his escape—once more. Do evildoers in Norway never die like honest men? Soti had to be killed twice, and now Eyvind needs killing a third time."

"That's our task, isn't it?" said Erling.

"Kill Eyvind a third time?"

"As many times as it takes. It needs must be done. No one's safe with him about. With Olaf . . . gone, I must do what I can to defend the land." He took one last, hungry look eastward, then told the helmsman, "Make north. Follow the red sail."

In the days that followed Eyvind danced just out of reach. It galled Erling, who'd never before seen the ship he couldn't run down. We hoped to catch Eyvind at Lindesness, where the currents and shifting winds can stall sailors for days or weeks, but Eyvind shot past the point like a home-bound pigeon, and we followed as easily, though without closing the distance between us. Up past Agder we sailed, and along Jaeder, passing by Opprostad and nearing Hafrsfjord.

And it was there that Eyvind's ship vanished. 'Twas there one moment and gone the next, like mist in the morning. Erling climbed the mast to scan the sea himself, cursing like a heathen, then slid down with his teeth showing.

"I do not like being made game of," he said. "I do not like it at all. Soon or late, God will put that man in my hands, and I'll not let him slip then."

'Twas drawing to evening, and we saw no course but to go home. We downed sail and rowed for the mouth of the Hafrsfjord.

As we neared and the sun sank, we saw a light burning on the northmost point of the southern jaw of the harbor mouth.

As we sailed past a voice called, "Erling Skjalgsson! I must speak with you!"

We all knew the voice, for we'd heard it many times speaking the law at the Things. 'Twas Helge of Klepp, a blind man far from home, alone and carrying a torch for which he had no use in the world.

❖   ❖   ❖

"The torch was for you to see me by, not the other way round," said Helge as we sat with him on the rocks an hour or so later. We'd entered the fjord and anchored, and Erling and I, Steinulf, Lemming and some others had rowed ashore in a small boat while the rest of the fleet moved in and anchored about us. Lemming gathered some dry wood and moss and made a fire to warm us.

"I had my brother Gunnar bring me here and leave me alone. He didn't like it, but I was in no danger. I'll be in danger later, but why should our kindred lose him along with me?"

"What's this danger?" asked Erling. "You put a shock to us, Helge, showing up like a balefire this way."

"You cannot face Eyvind Kellda without danger," Helge answered.

"Too late. We've lost him. He cloaked himself in darkness and stole away to his friends, the trolls. He's gone and we cannot follow."

"*You* cannot. 'Tis another matter with me."

"You?"

"I've lost the use of my body's eyes. But the eyes of my soul are clear, and God has granted me to see a few of the hidden things. It happened just a few days since, as I knelt in prayer, that I began to see Eyvind Kellda. I know where he is, and I see where he goes."

I asked, "Are you sure this is not some seeming Eyvind has stewed up himself? 'Twould be like him."

"The things I've seen of Eyvind in my soul are not things he'd show of his own will. For instance, what vessel does he seem to you to sail in?"

"A great black wolf-ship, with a red sail," said Erling.

"'Tis no such thing. 'Tis a four-oared fishing boat, with a ragged gray sail. He makes it move at breathless speed, but all the rest is show."

"And he has no guess that you see this?" asked Steinulf.

"This is the everlasting weakness of Evil," said Helge. "We know what he knows; he cannot know what we know. The Light shines in the darkness, and the darkness has not yet comprehended it.

"I doubt not he'll know soon enough he's being followed. But there's no harm in that. He cannot escape the blind man's eyes."

"So we can put back out to sea with the fleet straightaway," said Erling, smacking a palm with a fist. "I expect day or night means naught to you."

"Leave the fleet. Send the levies home. There's nothing we could do with them that we cannot do with *Fishhawk*'s crew alone."

Erling scratched his chin. "I can't just cut them loose. I need to feast them and make gifts. Else men will say that there's no profit in sailing with Erling."

"Send them to Sola then, and have Astrid feast them till you return. You won't be long, however our errand goes. And let's wait for morning ere we sail."

"Is it clearer for you in the light?" Erling asked.

"No, but I'm old and weary. I'd like to sleep before the hunt."

Erling sent men to pass the word from ship to ship, and the twilight swallowed their forms as they sailed south, leaving only the cries of the bosuns and the creaking of the rigging, fading as they went. Lemming went with them, taking his Freydis home.

We set up a tent where we were, and the crew spread an awning and slept in their sleeping bags on *Fishhawk*.

"The end of the world," said Erling in the darkness, when the others were snoring and only he and I awake. Perhaps he thought me asleep too. "This is indeed the year when the world ends for me. The Age of the Viking is gone, as all men know. The world we would have made together in its place, Olaf and I, shall never come."

CHAPTER XXI

Come morning we rowed out of the harbor and northward to Tungeness, where we caught a northwest wind to take us southeastward, between the mainland and Bokn Island. We were heading straight for Stavanger as a matter of fact, but that wasn't our goal. Ours wasn't a very good wind—'twas light and prone to fades and shifts, but we made slow progress, rowing when needed. Erling paced the stern like a hound in a pen.

"Peace, young man," said Helge, leaning over the side as if enjoying the view. "Eyvind does not yet guess we follow him. When he does know, 'twill be too late for him."

"He's slipped death more than once ere now," Erling answered. "Why should this time be different?"

"He's never before dealt with one who saw him as he is." And Helge turned back to his sightless seeing.

At Helge's bidding we turned due east to enter the Aamoyfjord (which isn't a proper fjord at all but a passage between two islands), then passed between Hidle and Heng Islands, and my mouth watered at the sight of our landing place at Tau. There were boathouses there, and a pier to which we made fast.

As we disembarked, Helge said, "The shudder of our feet on fast land gives Eyvind the alarm. He knows we are here."

Erling said, "Then surely we must leave you behind, Helge, and make speed."

Helge answered, "He does not yet know I see him. He thinks you come by chance. Therefore he trusts his cloak of darkness and makes no haste. But let us go speedily by all means."

It was about midday when we started up a well-trodden, steep cattle path into the mountains. We could not see their upper slopes for the mist.

"We'll not climb far unless this fog burns off," said Erling.

"Just come with me, my lord," said Helge. "Think of me as a local pilot on an unknown coast. 'Tis my job to know where to take you, and your job to let me do mine."

Erling had no answer to that. So we trudged uphill. I wasn't as fit as the warriors, and would have fallen behind except that we all had to match our pace to Helge's. Someone had cut him a staff; he leaned on it as he climbed steadily, neither quickly nor slowly, showing no special weariness.

We passed out of the sun into the moon-white, limbo-like country of the clouds. The air grew chill on our sweaty backs, and all sounds muffled.

"You have the helm, pilot," said Erling. "If any man loses sight of the rest, sing out! We don't want anyone pitching off the mountain."

We climbed in column, and the further we climbed the colder and quieter it grew. Soon I wished I'd brought my cloak, and I noticed that some tree branches bore traces of rime—for which it was too early in the year and too low on the mountain.

"I've hunted in these parts many a time," said

Steinulf. "But if I lost myself now I'd have no inkling where to go, other than downhill."

"Hush!" said Erling.

"Why?"

Erling paused before he answered. "I don't know."

But no one spoke again for a time in any case. I felt—and I think all felt the same—that something or other was best not disturbed.

We labored uphill. We shivered. We could see our breath, and the back of the man in front of us, and a few trees near the path edge, and little else. For the rest we might have been in Hy Braseal, for all we could tell.

And then it seemed to me that the mist faded, for the light grew brighter and I could make out more.

All I saw was trees, mountainside trees that grow slantwise to the earth out of piety for the sun, but they were remarkable trees. They were mostly oaks, crooked and black and wind-wrenched, bending their knobbly limbs like old men with lumbago. In fact, the more I looked, the more they resembled crooked old men. I could swear one of them had a face, and eyes—in fact more than one of them had something like a face—an angry face. I could see an angry face on every one if I let my mind dwell on it. . . .

It was when one of them moved that I began to scream.

I did not scream alone.

Most of our party, hardened bullyboys all, took to their heels and vanished downhill to dissolve from our hearing in shouts and clatterings and crashings.

But the bodyguard, the sworn men, God bless them, knew their calling. They formed a circle around Erling, overlapping their shields to protect him. The shield-fort, I was pleased to note, also took in Helge and me. I think these men were no less frightened than the others, but they had sworn their oaths. Irishmen could have done no better.

"Be easy!" cried a voice, and I realized that Helge had been shouting, unheard, for some time. I felt his hand on my shoulder. He was going about the circle, touching each man and speaking in his ear to calm him.

"Be easy!" he repeated. "These are but shadows. 'Tis Eyvind's work—look! They seem to come ahead, but they never close with us. They can do you no harm if you keep your wits!"

Our shouting quieted as we saw that he spoke truth. The trees appeared to move in, dragging their trains of root, reaching out wizened arms to grasp us, but it was only a show. They walked and walked, and got no nearer. The moment I knew this, the seeming ended and the mist crowded in again.

"Eyvind falls prey to his own gullings," said Eyvind. "He thinks all creatures have spirits, and thinks he can rouse them. We know better, and so we are untouched."

"Except for losing most of our company," panted Steinulf.

" 'Not by might, nor but power, but by My Spirit,' " said Helge. "What I mean to do tonight I could do alone, but I bring you all as witnesses."

"A shock like that is itself a wound," said I. "I'm not sure I can suffer many of its like and live."

"You of all men should have no fear for that. You carry a talisman to help you see aright."

"What?"

"That crucifix that hangs about your neck."

"But this isn't Enda's cross. 'Tis Ulf the Viking's. There's no power in it!"

"Nor was there power in the other, except to remind you what is true. For that purpose this one will work as well as the other."

I bristled at that—it seemed a slight to poor Enda, but I hadn't the face to argue the matter.

Helge set out again, his staff tapping on the stones,

and we followed, our heartbeats slowing by stages. He led us unerringly, finding the fords or bridges where we crossed running water, and the causeways where our path leveled and passed through mires.

It seemed the evening must be coming at last, for the mist thickened. I began to wonder if we'd be marching into the night, when human forms appeared—of a sudden—before us.

They emerged, one after another, out of the mist. There, again, was the Englishwoman I'd raped. There were my father and mother and my brother Diarmaid, who had died under the Vikings' axes, and Maeve of course. There was Steinbjorg my woman, holding our baby, whom I'd not protected, and Halla, who had died in the bed of a man she did not love.

All of them stared at me and stretched their arms out and cried, *"Aillil! If only you'd been a better man— a better son or brother or husband or father—or Christian at least—we'd have been spared our fates."*

Ah Lord! How cruel to give us power to choose, and to let our choices bear fruit so heavy and venom-ripe! We are not wise enough to live in your world! We're like parents plucking our children from a burning house—if we take one, another will be lost, and to choose one over another at all is to sin against love. 'Tis a game without rules, played blindfolded on a log bridging a chasm, and all the moves are losing moves. The game itself is punishment enough— what need of Hell?

Then I felt once again that hand—the palsied hand of an old man—on my shoulder, and I came to myself and saw Helge staring me in the face. I could hear weeping and cursing all about me, and knew that every man was seeing a like vision.

"Father!" Helge cried. "You must give these men absolution!"

"Absolution!" I wept. "How can I give what I myself cannot receive?"

"Have you no faith at all? Don't you see this is but another trick of Eyvind's?"

"Even the devil can speak truth now and again," said I. "I've done what I should not, and left undone what I should—"

"The crucifix, man!" Helge grasped my hand and dragged it up towards my breast. "Have you forgotten what the crucifix means?"

The moment I touched the thing, my head began to clear like clouds at noonday. I knew that I forgave Ulf, who'd carved it, and how could I do such a thing except in the strength of a greater mercy? The Lord Christ had endured much evil from men, and yet suffered to the utmost for their good; if sin was a mountain as big as the world, yet His death-cry had rooted it up and cast it into the sea.

"These men haven't confessed to me—" I said, shaking my head to clear it.

"Yet general shrift is often given before battle. Believe me, Father—this is a battle to put Hafrsfjord in the shade."

So I went about to each man, pushed him down on his knees if he wasn't kneeling already, and spoke the words of absolution loudly in his ear. 'Twas like blindfolding skittish horses. One by one they went quiet, and at last all were still. Only then did I look about and see that my ghosts were gone. Now it was deepest dark on the mountainside, and we felt rather than saw the mist.

"I'd fear this night, if I'd not just seen what I fear yet more," said Erling (I wondered what visions he'd seen). "Lead on, Helge, we follow."

Each man hooked his hand in the belt of the man ahead, and I grasped Helge's belt, and we toiled snakewise up the path. We stumbled and stubbed our feet on rocks. All things were upended, for now all of us were blind and only Helge saw, and we could do naught but trust him.

Ask me not how long we trudged, stumbling and cursing, until we came suddenly on a rock wall, lighted faintly by a glowing that spread from twin caves, set side by side before us.

A different scene appeared in each of the caves. In the cave to the right there seemed to be a wide, white desert, sand on sand in wavy drifts under a brazen sky, such as traveled men say you find in Eastland. My tongue parched just looking at it.

Through the entrance to the cave on the left we saw a lush, green valley, watered by a rushing stream, shaded by trees that bore bright-colored, outland fruits. Graceful beasts bounded through thick-carpeted meadows, and birds hued like butterflies flew overhead.

"'Tis a riddle," said Erling, looking back and forth between them. "No doubt one way leads to our goal; the other over some cliff or the like. Which way do you judge we should go, Helge?"

For a reply, Helge vanished before our eyes.

We stood thunderstruck all together a moment.

"Helge!" cried Erling. "Helge! Where are you?"

"Can he have been a seeming all this time?" asked Steinulf. "Has Eyvind been leading us through him?"

"I think not," said I. "I touched him; I'd swear he was real. My guess is that he must have pushed ahead of us, and Eyvind put a seeming in his place. Or perhaps he's here yet, and Eyvind has stopped our eyes and ears to him."

I clutched my crucifix and looked about, but it threw no light on the puzzle.

"Naught to do then but riddle it out ourselves," said Erling. "Were I Eyvind, I suppose I'd go the unpleasant way, hoping that we'd choose the easy one."

"Perhaps . . ." said I.

"But then that seems overeasy. Eyvind is cleverer than that. So perhaps he chose the pleasant way, to confound us."

"I think we must remember what Eyvind believes," said I. "Each of the earlier seemings grew out of his faith. He believes in spirits everywhere, so we saw walking trees. He believes all sin is punished, in this life or another, so he tormented us with guilt. Now here I see him looking at the world. To him all the pleasures of the flesh—food and drink, for instance—are illusions. So he would reject them and choose the way of the desert where he is nearer the nothingness he worships."

"Then 'tis your counsel to go the desert way?" asked Erling.

"Well—" I said, not wanting the burden of this choice.

"My counsel would be to go the pleasant way nonetheless," said Erling at last.

"I don't follow," said I.

"To hunt a beast you must think like the beast, but you must remain a man the while. If you became wholly like the beast you might be a great hunter, but you'd be a werebeast, not a man hunting.

"While we hunt Eyvind we must know how he thinks, but we must not think as he does. We know that the world, and its delights, are not an illusion, because our Lord became a man in this world, and if His deeds in the body were but seemings, then our salvation is a seeming. Therefore we must declare what we believe before God and Eyvind and all Watchers and Holy Ones, by choosing the door of the flesh, in which we rejoice and suffer, and walk in the steps of the Beloved."

"A noble thought," said Steinulf. "But will it bear our weight if we step out into thin air?"

"If I must fall," Erling answered, "let me fall from the height of a noble thought. This time I go first."

And before we could protest he strode forward, spear in hand, and entered the leftward cave. He vanished from our sight in a moment.

"Well, that's done it. Hey for the warrior's road," said Steinulf, and he followed. One by one the bodyguard passed into the illusion, until I stood alone.

I took a deep breath, muttered a prayer, and passed through the gate of Paradise.

CHAPTER XXII

We'd chosen the right way. Erling and the bullyboys waited on the far side.

We all stood on our path again. The trees were sparse here, and we'd outclimbed the mist, so that the moon and stars gave a little light. Light came too from great clouds of moonglow—a brighter new Milky Way—a spiral of cold fire that stretched in every direction, from horizon to horizon—silver tinged with red and gold. There was a sound too—a brazen clanging like hammer blows on a metal sheet, far, far above.

"What kept you?" asked Helge, who stood awaiting us. I poked him to assure myself he was real, and he gave me a whack with his staff.

"The northern lights," said Erling, looking up at the sky. "Not common this far south. 'Tis no ordinary night."

"That it's not," said Helge.

"Which way now?" Erling asked. "Do we follow the path?"

"I expect so. I cannot tell. My Sight is gone, for you need it no more. But bring me with you nonetheless. I must be there for the kill."

"We'd scarce leave you here," said Erling. "Father, you take his hand. We'll see where our path takes us now."

"I know where it goes," said Steinulf. "Now I have some light, I know it like my hand. This path leads to the High Seat."

All the men murmured at that.

"The High Seat is a great cliff overhanging the Lysefjord," said Helge to me before I'd asked. " 'Tis a place of endings and ancient power, where no man goes by night except to make the direst sacrifices. 'Tis just such a spot as Eyvind would seek out."

"Come, men!" cried Erling. "You've been through three tests tonight, and played the man in each. Think you God will forget us now?"

I'll give them this—they were men, those twenty-four, well worth their baubles and their breakfasts. They straightened their backs, lifted their heads, and set off in Erling's and Steinulf's tracks, the shifting silver light gleaming on their helms and spearheads. Helge and I followed, rushing to keep pace.

The track led yet upward, steeply for a time but then at a gentler angle. Our way was easier, and we felt a second strength.

"There he is!" Erling cried. I did not see Eyvind myself from where I was, but the bullyboys did, and our march became a run. Though we tried to stay with them, Helge stumbled often, and he and I fell back and back.

We knew they'd cornered him by the sound of shouting. I near carried Helge in my eagerness, avid and fearful at once, wondering how steel or prayers could be of use in a fight such as this.

We came suddenly to a precipice where the rock fell off sharply above the fjord. We had crossed the mountain. We turned right, for we were now north of our goal, and followed a pathway that had only empty night for a wall on our shield-side in many places. At last we came to a great, open platform of rock, bounded on our left by the featureless dark of open air. Erling and his bullyboys stood in a half-circle near the edge, and within that ring, raised high, I saw the white head of Eyvind Kellda.

I drew Helge near, and Eyvind laughed to see us.

"Is there not a word in your holy book about the blind leading the blind?" he shouted. "Indeed, that prophecy is fulfilled today in our sight!"

"This blind man saw well enough to track you," said I.

"Only when I leave a trail a blind man can follow," Eyvind answered. "Think you I sought to stop you? I was luring you on, dangling your hero-fancies before you, so you'd not turn back and miss my snare!"

"A glib answer from a cornered fox," said Erling. "Will you surrender now, Eyvind, or be slain on this spot?"

"'Tis I who could demand your surrender, Erling Skjalgsson! But I am not merciful. I will cast you all down from here, and break your bodies on the rocks below!"

"Enough then!" Erling cried. "Cast at him, lads!"

And twenty-five spears, gleaming in the blue light, arched up and out toward Eyvind Kellda. Most hit their mark, for these were trained men, but all passed along as through air, and Eyvind stood unmarked while the spears sailed on and out of sight, to splash in the fjord below, too far away to hear.

Eyvind's brass laughter burst forth like a nest of sacrifice-fed rats from a burning temple. As we watched he grew taller in our sight, and he rose like the moon, floating up and out, to hang in midair beyond the precipice. His eyes flamed like red stars, and his face and body glowed like a part of the northern lights hanging curtain-wise behind him.

"DO YOU KNOW WHO I AM?" he roared.

"You are a liar," said Erling Skjalgsson, stepping forward and drawing his sword. "I call you a liar before men, and I will prove it with steel.

"'Tis a strange thing, when you think of it. We've seen you send great seemings to frighten us, but you've not used this power of which you boast to strike at your enemies. So I put you to the proof—show me that you are a warrior. Show yourself a grandson of Harald Finehair."

Eyvind made a noise like the hosts of Midian and stretched his hand toward Erling. "See then my power, son of Skjalg!" he roared.

And Erling flared and burned to ashes in a moment, before our eyes.

My heart fell in on itself.

"DO YOU KNOW WHO I AM?" came the shout again. "I am Eyvind Kellda, master of the dream you call this world! I am Eyvind Kellda, maker and breaker of Law! I am Eyvind Kellda, more than a hundred winters old, and I shall live as long again if I like! I am Eyvind Kellda, who has died and died again! I die for sport! I die for refreshment! I die to fool the gullible into thinking I am out of their hair! Life and death, good and evil, body and spirit—they are mine to command!

"I shall slay you now, Christian men! I shall slay you as I slew your lord, in a moment, all but the blind man! Him I leave to tell the story, that men may know my deeds! Pray to your god, Christians, for all the good it will do—for I send you now to your next life-rings, where you shall be reborn as beasts, every one of you, because you refused the light that I offered you!"

He threw his head back then, and I watched motionless, except for my trembling. I feared in my heart what cry he would make, or what song he would sing, next.

"Strange," said a quiet voice beside me.

I looked at Helge. Something changed as I heard his voice. A blessed doubt entered my mind.

Helge made the sign of the cross on his breast and elbowed me, and I thought to touch Ulf's crucifix. My holy doubt flowered within me.

Every head had turned to us. Beyond the cliff Eyvind's red eyes blazed, but he did nothing to stop Helge speaking. And wasn't that an odd thing?

"Strange," said Helge, "that you'd spare me of all this company—I who sets you at least account, and who cannot tell men how you looked or what wonders you made to appear."

Eyvind scowled and showed his teeth—long and very white, sharp as if filed to a point. He gaped his mouth to cry again, but was stopped once more by Helge.

"Especially when—and I know you know this, Eyvind—I do not see you as these men do. I see you in your true shape, and a pitiable one it is. It comes to my mind that of all men you are most miserable, having entered Hell before your mortal life was done."

"LIES!" roared Eyvind, and his voice echoed back from the mountainsides across the fjord. "You tell lies, man of delusion, and draw these men further astray!"

"I see what is. There is such a thing as truth, Eyvind, whether you'll have it so or no. The world is not what you wish it to be; it exists and must be lived in on its own terms. We men are not what we wish to be; we must repent and be reborn, or carry our evil with us into the everlasting world. You learned the power of dreams, Eyvind. You learned how much can be done by frightening or flattering men, and snaring them in their fears and doubts. But 'tis finished now. 'Tis time for you to return to God the life He gave you, and account to Him for its waste."

" 'Tis done, is it?" cried Eyvind. "What think you of this?"

And before our eyes he was changed to a dragon, red and gold, flapping great green wings that filled the sky from north to south, and pouring smoke from his nostrils, rearing back his head to spout fire.

"Enough!" cried Helge. "In the name of the living God, Eyvind Kellda, drop these veils and show us your nakedness!"

And in a moment the dragon was gone, and where it had hovered we saw nothing.

Only on the very edge of the cliff there stood a withered old man, hairless and covered with scars, pouring blood from the wounds of twenty spears standing in his body. He shrieked and turned from us in shame, like a virgin caught undressed, and the weight of the spears overtipped him. He waved his arms in a pitiful attempt to keep his balance. By him we saw Erling Skjalgsson, unharmed. Erling reached his bare hand out and gave him a single push.

We heard his body strike on the rocks below, and heard the spears clatter as the whole bundle bounced and rolled. Then there was nothing but the sky-lights and the sky-song.

So died Eyvind Kellda, son of kings.

CHAPTER XXIII

We spent the night on the High Seat, talking over the marvels we'd seen. Someone brought out flint and steel and built a fire, and we sat in a circle around it while the lights danced overhead.

"He had real power," said Helge, holding his hands out to the warmth. "He was a warlock born of warlocks, and a great soul even among them. But his power deceived him. Because he could control some things, he came to believe he could control everything, and confused himself with God. Strange to say, his very madness increased his power, for it gave him leave to take risks no sane trickster would dare. And if he failed to do a thing, he simply sent a seeming to make men think he'd succeeded. He came to believe these seemings himself, having persuaded himself that fancies are as real as flesh."

"He carried so many wounds all these years?" Steinulf asked. "His suffering must have been terrible."

"He'd learned to bend his mind so that he did not feel pain—which is dangerous in itself, for it is by pain that sane men learn. The wounds were terrible, and they healed but slowly in his ancient body, but he'd enough magic to keep himself alive. By the end he barely remembered what he truly was. The greatest danger of hypocrisy comes the day one is a hypocrite no more, when one truly believes one's own tales. Such men are probably beyond redemption, though that is not for me to say."

"Olaf will be glad of this, when he returns," said Erling.

There was little night left, and ere long the sun began to unblanket the mountain heights and stripe the walls of the fjord, so that I saw at last how high in the world we stood, and shivered. We stretched our limbs and made our way down the mountain to sail back to Sola. Nothing of interest happened on the way.

It was late summer, and there was hay to make and harvests to get in. The road south got finished as far as Sigurd Eriksson's lands, and more thralls earned their freedom.

And every day Erling climbed atop the home-field fence and surveyed the sea to the south, looking for Olaf. If he lived, surely he'd have seen his folly and headed home . . .

But the *Long Serpent* never appeared.

At last there came a single ship, whose sail Erling knew. She rode low in the water and made her way sluggishly, as if overloaded with men above and taking on water below.

We watched as she hove to and made for the entrance to Hafrsfjord, and Erling called out the thralls to prepare a feast. He sent Eystein and some of the bodyguard with horses to greet the visitors. He quivered like a hound as he stood watching them dock and disembark, a hand shading his eyes.

I saw his shoulders sag as he recognized the leader of the crew. It wasn't the man he expected. 'Twas young Einar Eindridisson, riding slouched, no longer the boy.

Erling greeted him in the yard. "I expected your father," he said as he took Einar's hand.

"Yes, 'tis his ship. I sailed with the Long Serpent. But Jarl Erik let me have this one and sail it home with whatever crew I could put together."

Erling stood stock still at those words.

"Jarl Erik?" he asked. "Jarl Haakon's son?"

"Yes, of course. Do you mean you've not heard?"

"Nothing. Not even a rumor. What of the king? Tell me—what of Olaf?"

"I thought you'd know by now," said Einar, his blue eyes wide. "Olaf is dead, at the bottom of the sea!"

We went through the civilities of the drinking and feasting in the old hall, but quickly and with no pleasure. We were awaiting the moment when Einar would tell his story.

I can see him still, old eyes in a young face, sitting in the guest's seat across from Erling's, a silver horn in his hand, sipping from it often, as if for more than refreshment.

"Olaf was furious after you left him. He sat in the hall in Jomne and drank steadily all day, until he fell into a stupor and slept.

"He spoke much with Jarl Sigvald, trying to make a new strategy for his march to Jerusalem. The bishop he would not speak to at all.

"The next morning Olaf made up his mind. We found him awake at breakfast time, and he told us we would be sailing for England. He was certain King Ethelred would give him ships and men for a voyage to Jerusalem. Instead of fighting our way across Europe, we would attack the Musselmen in Eastland, and baptize them, offering them to the Lord as our tribute when He returned.

"And so we set sail with our fleet, our ships plus

those of the Jomsvikings under Sigvald. There was a rumor about that King Svein and the Danish fleet were out seeking us—they could hardly have missed the news of our voyage—and Sigvald promised he had a hidden way to bring us through the islands to the Belts.

"What we did not know was that the son of a whore was in Svein's pay.

"He led the way into a sound—somebody called it Svold—and suddenly his ships were gone and there was Svein's fleet, along with Jarl Erik Haakonson and King Olaf of Sweden. There they were, and there we were, and we stood outnumbered three to one. There was no parleying, no bid for surrender. We went to arms without delay.

"We lashed our ships together. The *Long Serpent* was far longer than any of the rest of the fleet, of course, and Olaf insisted that she be fixed with her stern flush with the other ships, so that she stuck far out in front. 'Twas suicide. 'Twas murder too—murder of all his faithful men on the foredeck. Whatever was driving Olaf was leading him to forget his duty to his followers, his very kingship. Every man of us aboard the *Serpent* was angry, though most said nothing. Ulf the Red, up in the forecastle, spoke his mind though, and Olaf nearly put an arrow through him.

"King Svein's ships met us breast to breast while Olaf's of Sweden's and Erik's ships began picking off the ships at the outer wings of our formation, one by one. It was only a matter of time of course. Svein's ships made little headway against us, because the *Serpent*'s sides were so high it gave us an advantage, higher ground so to speak. Our men shot down into their decks and killed them from above, as if spearing fish. But the other ships had less advantage; and on the flanks it was plain slaughter, especially on our right, where Erik attacked. He had much of his own to get back, did Erik.

"He left his ship behind and simply fought from

ship to ship, clearing each and going on to the next. Our defense became his bridge to Olaf and revenge.

"I didn't see this all at the time—we've put it together from the stories of the survivors I sailed home with. But we all knew the chief thing. We were being sacrificed to Olaf's death-dream. I was standing near him, shooting arrows, when my bow snapped. The thing was hot as a gridiron. Olaf said to me, 'What did I hear breaking?' and I answered, 'Norway, from your hand, O King!' I think he nearly struck me down then, but instead he handed me his own bow. I tried it, but it broke too, so I fought with my sword thereafter.

"'Twas Erik's force that boarded us at last. They cleared the forecastle and worked their way back. I got struck down and left for dead and did not see the end, but I'm told that Olaf and Kolbjorn the marshal jumped overboard together to escape capture. Kolbjorn the Danes fished out of the sea alive, but Olaf was seen no more. Some say he may have swum free, but I'd seen him go earlier to a chest in the hold to get fresh swords for the men. There was blood running down his arm, leaving a track wherever he went. A wound like that, in salt water, and a heavy brynje on his back—I think he lies in Aegir's hall like a lost anchor."

"And you got quarter?" Erling asked.

"Everyone got quarter at the end," said Einar, "on the condition we took Svein as our king and Erik as his jarl, as in Jarl Haakon's day. We are under Denmark again now, and to speak truth it matters little to me, after what Olaf did to us. Call me betrayer if you will, but I look for better from a king. I certainly looked for better from Olaf.

"Be prepared, Erling Skjalgsson. Svein has given Erik rule of the west from Trondheim south to Lindesness. Make the best terms you can with him, but terms you'll have to make."

Erling spoke no word, but rose from his seat. All of us tensed our limbs, ready for some act of rage. But Erling merely turned and walked down the hearth-way to the entrance room, and passed out from among us.

I followed, drawing my cloak about me, wondering what Erling felt. Was he angry at Olaf? Angry at Einar? Angry at himself? Would he do himself harm? Would he take a boat and sail to Greenland? I was prepared for anything.

Night was falling. I followed him down to the seashore, his thinking place and mine. He walked with head bowed, then sat on a large rock, staring out over the sea towards the last red stain of the setting sun.

When Erling was troubled, his usual course was action—to run or to fight, or to throw stones or ride an unbroken horse. This quiet sitting troubled me more than madness would.

It seemed sin to intrude on his meditation, but I feared for Erling, so I gathered my courage and walked straight to him.

He was weeping. He wept in great, shuddering sobs, like a child, and the sunset shone in his tears.

"My king!" he cried. "Olaf, my king! You went alone to the Loneliest Place, and I was not by you! How could you do this to me? How can I forgive you? How can you forgive me?"

I knew nothing to say, and my words would not have helped in any case. I laid my hands on his head and prayed for him.

We remained thus for some time, until there was only moonlight, and little of that. I heard the approaching footsteps but did not know whose they were until the face of Astrid was near enough to touch. She had come alone.

She placed an arm around Erling's shoulders and said, "Come with me, husband. 'Tis time we went to our bed."

EPILOGUE

So passed the year of the warrior. Summer became autumn, and autumn winter, but the Lord Christ did not return and the world did not end.

Yet it was a real time of tying off for us. Erling had lost his king. He would never find another like him; as long as he lived after, he resisted the thought of a Norwegian king and put no trust in such. Under Danish or Norse rule, Erling was his own sovereign, and all titles mere word-games. But that's a story—or several—for another day.

We had Erik, and Svein of Denmark, as overlords now, at least before the world, but that cut no fish in Jaeder. Erling kept his defenses strong (this included the Company of Freedmen), and one eye open, and the jarl gave him wide berth.

The old man came to us that winter, on a trading knarr from Sweden long delayed by strong north winds and sleet. A fair, crisp day had finally dawned, and his ship made fast along one of the new piers at Stavanger. It was still a small place, this cluster of sheds and booths along the shore of the narrow

The Ghost of the God-Tree

harbor under low hills, but it was profitable and growing—a good place to seek grain and Greenland wares—and Erling even talked of a church for it. I was out enjoying the sunlight when the traveler came walking up to me.

I didn't know him at first. A tall but bent man, he wore ordinary clothes, a little shabby, and his hair was white as snow. He seemed to be bald on top, and then I recognized his tonsure.

"Bishop Sigurd!" I cried.

He smiled, and I saw why I hadn't known him. 'Twas his eyes. He'd had those sick, sunken, puffy eyes all the time I'd known him. Now they were healthy, the eyes of a man at peace.

"Not Bishop Sigurd," he said to me. "Just Father Sigurd now. Like a thrall at the end of the day I've laid down my basket of dung."

I brought him directly to the hall Erling had built for his winter sojourns in the town. We found him and Astrid in private talk, as one often did these days, and they rose with delight to greet their visitor. Erling called for bread and cheese and ale, and bade Sigurd sit on the bench to his right. He and Astrid sat again—sharing the high seat as was their wont.

Sigurd ate and drank sparingly, like a man grown accustomed to fasting, and told his tale.

"Olaf put Queen Thyri on one of the smaller ships and sent it away before the battle began. I was with her, so I was not in the battle, though we saw it all.

"It went as you've heard—Jarl Erik cleared ship after ship and made himself a path to the *Long Serpent*, where he overran the crew. Olaf's men fought well enough, and Olaf himself did great deeds, but I thought they fought as doomed men, and their hearts were not in it. The whole adventure had been a disappointment, and that kills the spirit of even the best fighters.

"So at last we saw men leaping overboard, fleeing

capture, and we saw two men in red shirts leap off either side of the *Serpent*'s stern all at once. We knew them for Olaf and Kolbjorn, for they were dressed much the same that day. You know the rest. Kolbjorn was taken. Olaf was not seen again."

"Was it—would you call it suicide?" I asked.

"I cannot say. He was badly wounded, I'm told, and he wore a heavy brynje under his shirt—well you know the one. Almost knee-length. Hard to shed when you're sinking, and with a bad wound . . . I can't say. But I don't think of him as self-slain."

" 'Twasn't about suicide," said Erling.

"How so?" I asked.

"As long as Olaf lived, his bodyguard—his sworn men—were bound to stand with him, and to spend their lives to protect his.

"By leaping overboard he freed them from their troth. They could then flee themselves, or ask quarter of Erik."

"Olaf . . . " said Astrid. "We grew up far separated, and then he sailed in like a kidnapper to steal me from the life I knew, and we had those few years together when we fought near every time we spoke. Sometimes I think I hardly knew him. Other times I think we were closer than twins."

"If you had been a man you'd have been Olaf," said Erling.

"There you go abusing me again," said Astrid. But she smiled.

"I've a thing for you, Princess," said Father Sigurd. He reached into his shirt and drew out a leather pouch. With stiff fingers he drew it open (its creases showing that it had been tight closed a long time), and he shook a golden ring out into his hand.

"Olaf gave me this before the battle and bade me carry it to you and Erling. He said it ought to stay in the family, and that it was his token that he wished to die at peace with you."

"I know it well," said Astrid, as Erling passed it to her. "'Twas an heirloom from our father, who had it from his father. Olaf left no son. Their legacy shall pass down in the line of Skjalg now."

Sigurd turned to me. "There was a message for you too, Father Aillil."

"For me?"

"Olaf said to tell you that he'd sought the wrong ring. He said you'd understand."

"Well, I don't," said Astrid. "'Tis the right ring. I know it well."

"Not that ring," said I. "The magic ring atop the enchanted mountain. He remembered that, did he? One never knows."

Since that day the story has gotten around (garbled as you'd expect) that Olaf sent a ring to Astrid and Erling as a sign that he yet lived after the battle. Some looked for his return the rest of their lives. Some said he'd gone on a pilgrimage to Jerusalem, or become a monk in some lonely place.

Olaf a monk? There's an unlikely thought.

Of course I've seen unlikelier things happen.

AFTERWORD

Thanks are due to a number of people for help with this book. Mari Anne Næsheim Hall of the Rogaland Historie- og Ættesogelag provided copious material and put me in touch with other knowledgeable people. Torvald Sande also shared the benefit of his expertise. My cousin Tina Andreassen and her friend Stian, who climbed the Preikestolen as my surrogates, deserve much thanks.

Special thanks go out to Torgrim Titlestad of the Stavanger Høgskol, author of *Konge Mellom Jarler* and *Kampen For Nordvegen*. Mr. Titlestad's assistance is especially praiseworthy as his philosophic view of the Viking Age is considerably different from mine. But we share an admiration for Erling Skjalgsson, and we don't disagree on everything. I have made considerable, if selective, use of his insights. He also brought to my attention old stories about Erling and his family of which I had been ignorant. I have done my best to harmonize them with the events of my first volume.

All historical, sociological, geographical, meteorological, orthographic or other errors in the present book are mine and mine alone. That goes doubly for any discernable opinions you may find littering the stage.

—Lars Walker
Minneapolis, Minnesota

LiST OF MAiN CHARACtERS
(with approximate pronunciations)

Churchmen:
The Abbot: Aillil's former abbot from Ireland.
Aillil *(AHL-ill)* The narrator of this book. An imposter priest from Ireland.
Ketil *(KAY-teel)* A deacon from York, England.
Moling: A wandering monk from Ireland.
Sigurd *(SEE-goord)* King Olaf's bishop.
Thangbrand *(TAWNG-brawnd)* One of Olaf's priests.

Descendants of Harald Finehair:
Astrid Trygvesdatter *(AHSS-treed TRIGG-vehs-dahter)* Sister to Olaf.
Eyvind Kellda Ragnvaldsson *(EYE-veend KELL-da RAWNG-vald-sun)* An exiled king's son. A warlock.
Ingebjorg Trygvesdatter *(EENG-eh-byoorg TRIGG-vehs-dah-ter)* Sister to Olaf.
Olaf Trygvesson *(OOH-loff TRIGG-veh-sun)* A famous Viking, heir to the traditional kingship of Norway.

Descendants of Horda-Kari (not from Sola):
Askel Olmodsson *(AHSS-kell AHL-mode-sun)* Son of Olmod the Old.
Aslak Askelsson *(AHSS-lakk AHSS-kel-sun)* Son of Askel Olmodsson.

Olmod Karisson (OLE-*mode* KAHR-*eh-sun*) (the Old). Patriarch of the extended family.

Descendants of Viking-Kari (Kinsmen to Olaf Trygvesson):

Aki Eriksson (*AHK-ee* AIR-*eek-sun*) Brother to Sigurd of Opprostad.

Jostein Eriksson (*YOO-stine* AIR-*eek-sun*) Brother to Sigurd of Opprostad.

Sigurd Eriksson (*SEE-goord* AIR-*eek-sun*) Hersir at Opprostad, south along the Jaeder coast.

Thorkel Eriksson (*TOOR-kell* AIR-*eek-sun*) Brother to Sigurd of Opprostad.

Hladir-folk:

Erik Haakonsson (*AIR-eek* HOE-*konn-sun*) Son of Jarl Haakon.

Jarl Haakon (*Yarl* HOE-*konn*) Jarl (earl) of Hladir, overlord of Norway.

Kark (*Kark*) Thrall to Jarl Haakon.

Hostages:

Sigurd Thorisson (*SEE-goord* TOOR-*eh-sun*)

Thorir Thorisson *TORE-eer* TOOR-*eh-sun*)

Klepp-folk:

Gunnar (*GOO-nahr*) Brother to Helge of Klepp.

Helge (*HELL-ghee*) An old, blind lord.

Refugees:

Arnor Ulfsson: (*AHR-nohr* OOLF-*sun*) A young man, son of Ulf.

Asa (*AH-suh*) Widow of Thorstein

Thorstein (*TOOR-stine*) Died in escape.

Ulf (*OOLF*) Father to Arnor, brother to Thorstein.

Sola-folk:

Bergthor (*BAIRG-toor*) An old warrior.

Erling Skjalgsson (*AIR-ling SHAHLG-sun*) son of Thoralf Skjalg and hersir at Sola.

Eystein (*EYE-stine*) A warrior. Erling's chief of defence after the death of Hrorek.

Freydis (*FRAY-dees*) Daughter of Soti and Ulvig.

Gunnlaug (*GUHN-lowg*) A free woman married to a warrior.

Halla Asmundsdatter (*HALL-ah AHZ-munds-dah-ter*) Erling Skjalgsson's leman (concubine).

Hrorek: (*HROO-rekk*) Erling's chief of defence.

Halvard Thorfinsson (*HALL-vard TOOR-finn-sun*) A young warrior.

Lemming: A thrall (slave) to Soti and Ulvig.

Ragna (*RAHG-nah*) Erling's mother.

Sigrid Skjalgsdatter (*SEE-greed SHAHLGS-dah-ter*) Erling's younger sister.

Soti (*SOE-tee*) A blacksmith and magician.

Steinulf (*STINE-oolf*) Ragna's brother; chief of the bodyguard.

Thorkel: (*TOOR-kell*) A young warrior of Erling's, born in the Norse city of Dublin.

Thorolf Skjalg (*TOOR-olf Shahlg*) Erling's father. The name means, "Thorolf the Squinter."

Thorliv Skjalgsdatter (*TOOR-leev SHAHLGS-dah-ter*) Erling's sister.

Ulvig (*OOL-veeg*) Soti's wife; a witch.

The sons of Kolli:

Baug Kollasson (*BOWG KOLE-eh-sun*) A berserker.

Hoskuld Kollasson (*HOAS-koold KOLE-eh-sun*) A weakling.

Thralls:

Caedwy: An old thrall from Britain; Aillil's house-thrall.

Ciaran: Founder of the Freedman's Company of warriors.

Copar: Turlough's wife.

Deirdre: Wife to Patrick.
Enda: A young male slave.
Gunn: A female slave from Kormt island.
Patrick: Husband to Deirdre.
Steinbjorg: A female slave of Soti's; Aillil's concubine.
Turlough: A cynical man.

Miscellaneous:
Arinbjorn Thorsteinsson (*AHR-en-byoorn TOOR-stine-sun*) A hersir from the Sogn region.
Brusi Arnfinsson (*BROO-see AHRN-fin-sun*) A hersir from the More region. Erling hanged his son.
Burisleif: Boleslav I (the Brave), king of Poland.
Cullan Mal Munnu: An Irishman, father of Deirdre.
Einar Endridisson (*EYE-nar Ein-DREE-deh-sun*) A young warrior of good family from the north.
Leif Eriksson (*LIFE AY-reek-sun*) Son of the colonizer of Greenland. Discoverer of America.
Mistislav: A nobleman of Poland.
Sigvald (*SEEG-vahld*) a jarl; leader of the famous Jomsvikings.
Thorarin Hranisson (*TOOR-AH-reen HRAWN-eh-sun*) Neighbor to the Kollissons.
Thorbjorg Lambisdatter (*TOOR-byoorg LAHMB-ehs-dah-ter*) A young widow and a merchant.
Thyri: (*TEER-ee*) Sister to King Svein Forkbeard of Denmark. Bride to Olaf Trygvesson.
The Wanderer: A man of mystery.

(The pronunciations above are approximate only, and reflect modern Norwegian speech. If you pronounce "Erik" the way you always have [I do it myself], nobody will accuse you before the king.)

—lw

ELIZABETH MOON
THE DEED OF PAKSENARRION

"She's a damn fine writer. The Deed of Paksenarrion is fascinating. I'd use her book for research if I ever need a woman warrior. I know how they train now. We need more like this."
—**Anne McCaffrey**

By the Compton Crook Award winning author of the Best First Novel of the Year

Sheepfarmer's Daughter ♦ 65416-0 ♦ $5.99 _____

Divided Allegiance ♦ 69786-2 ♦ $6.99 _____

Oath of Gold ♦ 69798-6 ♦ $6.99 _____

or get all three volumes in one special trade edition:
The Deed of Paksenarrion ♦ 72104-6 ♦ $18.00 _____

The Legacy of Gird ♦ 87747-X ♦ $15.00 _____
Sequel to *The Deed of Paksenarrion* trilogy, now in a combo trade edition containing *Surrender None* & *Liar's Oath*.

If not available through your local bookstore send this coupon and a check or money order for the cover price(s) + $1.50 s/h to Baen Books, Dept. BA, P.O. Box 1403, Riverdale, NY 10471. Delivery can take up to eight weeks.

NAME: _____

ADDRESS: _____

_____

I have enclosed a check or money order in the amount of $ _____

DORANNA DURGIN's Fantasy

"Doranna Durgin envelops her appealing characters with a rare, shimmering aura of mystic legend."
—*Romantic Times*

"Durgin has a remarkable gift for inventing unusual characters doing incredible things." —*Booklist*

Changespell   87765-8 $5.99 ☐
"Durgin tells this deeply insightful and touching tale with a deft clarity. Her eye for detail will delight and astonish you …"
—*Hypatia's Hoard*

Barrenlands   87872-7 $5.99 ☐
"Ms. Durgin knows full well the value of pacing as she exquisitely choreographs action and character development into a pleasing whole." —*Romantic Times*

Wolf Justice   87891-3 $5.99 ☐
"Wolf Justice will delight fans … Well-rounded and widely appealing, this one comes highly recommended." —*Hypatia's Hoard*

Wolverine's Daughter   57847-2 $6.99 ☐
"Move over, Xena! The adventures of Kelyn the Wolverine's daughter are a pure joy to read. …" —*A.C. Crispin*

If not available through your local bookstore send this coupon and a check or money order for the cover price(s) + $1.50 s/h to Baen Books, Dept. BA, P.O. Box 1403, Riverdale, NY 10471. Delivery can take up to eight weeks.

NAME: _____

ADDRESS: _____

_____

I have enclosed a check or money order in the amount of $ _____

PRAISE FOR
LOIS MCMASTER BUJOLD

What the critics say:

The Warrior's Apprentice: "Now here's a fun romp through the spaceways—not so much a space opera as space ballet.... it has all the 'right stuff.' A lot of thought and thoughtfulness stand behind the all-too-human characters. Enjoy this one, and look forward to the next." —Dean Lambe, *SF Reviews*

"The pace is breathless, the characterization thoughtful and emotionally powerful, and the author's narrative technique and command of language compelling. Highly recommended."
—*Booklist*

Brothers in Arms: "...she gives it a genuine depth of character, while reveling in the wild turnings of her tale.... Bujold is as audacious as her favorite hero, and as brilliantly (if sneakily) successful." —*Locus*

"Miles Vorkosigan is such a great character that I'll read anything Lois wants to write about him.... a book to re-read on cold rainy days." —Robert Coulson, *Comic Buyer's Guide*

Borders of Infinity: "Bujold's series hero Miles Vorkosigan may be a lord by birth and an admiral by rank, but a bone disease that has left him hobbled and in frequent pain has sensitized him to the suffering of outcasts in his very hierarchical era.... Playing off Miles's reserve and cleverness, Bujold draws outrageous and outlandish foils to color her high-minded adventures." —*Publishers Weekly*

Falling Free: "In *Falling Free* Lois McMaster Bujold has written her fourth straight superb novel.... How to break down a talent like Bujold's into analyzable components? Best not to try. Best to say: 'Read, or you will be missing something extraordinary.'" —Roland Green, *Chicago Sun-Times*

The Vor Game: "The chronicles of Miles Vorkosigan are far too witty to be literary junk food, but they rouse the kind of craving that makes popcorn magically vanish during a double feature." —Faren Miller, *Locus*

MORE PRAISE FOR LOIS MCMASTER BUJOLD

What the readers say:

"My copy of *Shards of Honor* is falling apart I've reread it so often.... I'll read whatever you write. You've certainly proved yourself a grand storyteller."
—Lisa Kolbe, Colorado Springs, CO

"I experience the stories of Miles Vorkosigan as almost viscerally uplifting.... But certainly, even the weightiest theme would have less impact than a cinder on snow were it not for a rousing good story, and good story-telling with it. This is the second thing I want to thank you for.... I suppose if you boiled down all I've said to its simplest expression, it would be that I immensely enjoy and admire your work. I submit that, as literature, your work raises the overall level of the science fiction genre, and spiritually, your work cannot avoid positively influencing all who read it."
—Glen Stonebraker, Gaithersburg, MD

" 'The Mountains of Mourning' [in *Borders of Infinity*] was one of the best-crafted, and simply best, works I'd ever read. When I finished it, I immediately turned back to the beginning and read it again, and I can't remember the last time I did that."
—Betsy Bizot, Lisle, IL

"I can only hope that you will continue to write, so that I can continue to read (and of course buy) your books, for they make me laugh and cry and think . . . rare indeed."
—Steven Knott, Major, USAF

What Do You Say?

Cordelia's Honor (trade)	87749-6 ♦ $15.00	☐
The Warrior's Apprentice	72066-X ♦ $5.99	☐
The Vor Game	72014-7 ♦ $6.99	☐
Young Miles (trade)	87782-8 ♦ $15.00	☐
Cetaganda (hardcover)	87701-1 ♦ $21.00	☐
Cetaganda (paperback)	87744-5 ♦ $6.99	☐
Ethan of Athos	65604-X ♦ $5.99	☐
Borders of Infinity	72093-7 ♦ $5.99	☐
Brothers in Arms	69799-4 ♦ $5.99	☐
Mirror Dance	87646-5 ♦ $6.99	☐
Memory	87845-X ♦ $6.99	☐
Komarr (hardcover)	87877-8 ♦ $22.00	☐
Komarr (paperback)	57808-1 ♦ $6.99	☐
A Civil Campaign (hardcover)	57827-8 ♦ $24.00	☐
Falling Free	57812-X ♦ $6.99	☐
The Spirit Ring (paperback)	72188-7 ♦ $5.99	☐

LOIS MCMASTER BUJOLD

Only from Baen Books

visit our website at www.baen.com

If not available at your local bookstore, send this coupon and a check or money order for the cover price(s) + $1.50 s/h to Baen Books, Dept. BA, P.O. Box 1403, Riverdale, NY 10471. Delivery can take up to 8 weeks.

NAME: _____

ADDRESS: _____

_____

I have enclosed a check or money order in the amount of $ _____

Robert A. HEINLEIN

"Robert A. Heinlein wears imagination as though it were his private suit of clothes. What makes his work so rich is that he combines his lively, creative sense with an approach that is at once literate, informed, and exciting."
—*New York Times*

A collection of Robert A. Heinlein's best-loved titles are now available in superbly packaged Baen editions. Collect them all.

MENACE FROM EARTH	57802-2 ◆ $6.99	☐
SIXTH COLUMN	57826-X ◆ $5.99	☐
REVOLT IN 2100 & METHUSELAH'S CHILDREN	57780-8 ◆ $6.99	☐
THE GREEN HILLS OF EARTH	57853-7 ◆ $6.99	☐
THE MAN WHO SOLD THE MOON	57863-4 ◆ $5.99	☐
ASSIGNMENT IN ETERNITY	57865-0 ◆ $6.99	☐
FARNHAM'S FREEHOLD	72206-9 ◆ $6.99	☐
GLORY ROAD	87704-6 ◆ $6.99	☐
PODKAYNE OF MARS	87671-6 ◆ $5.99	☐
TAKE BACK YOUR GOVERNMENT *FIRST EDITION!*	72157-7 ◆ $5.99	☐

Available at your local bookstore. If not, fill out this coupon and send a check or money order for the cover price + $1.50 s/h to Baen Books, Dept. BA, P.O. Box 1403, Riverdale, NY 10471. Delivery can take up to 8 weeks.

Name: ───────────────────────────

Address: ─────────────────────────

──────────────────────────────

I have enclosed a check or money order in the amount of $ ─────